WEAVE
THE
WORLDS

SHATTERED STORIES · 1

WEAVE THE WORLDS

NORAH CASE

STORYSONG
PRESS, LLC

Copyright © 2026 by Norah Case

All rights reserved.

Scripture quotations are from the ESV® Bible (The Holy Bible, English Standard Version®), © 2001 by Crossway, a publishing ministry of Good News Publishers. ESV Text Edition: 2025. The ESV text may not be quoted in any publication made available to the public by a Creative Commons license. The ESV may not be translated in whole or in part into any other language. Used by permission. All rights reserved.

No part of this publication may be reproduced, distributed, or transmitted in any form or by any means, including photocopying, recording, or other electronic or mechanical methods, without the prior written permission of the publisher, except as permitted by U.S. copyright law. For permission requests, contact Storysong Press, LLC. Generative AI training usage of this work is prohibited.

The story, all names, characters, and incidents portrayed in this production are fictitious. No identification with actual persons (living or deceased), places, buildings, and products is intended or should be inferred.

Cover design & typesetting by Benita Thompson

ISBN:
979-8-9940187-0-5 *Ebook*
979-8-9940187-1-2 *Paperback*
979-8-9940187-2-9 *Hardcover*

First Edition: 2026

For Isabel
Without your encouragement, this story may have never reached the world.
Thanks for everything.

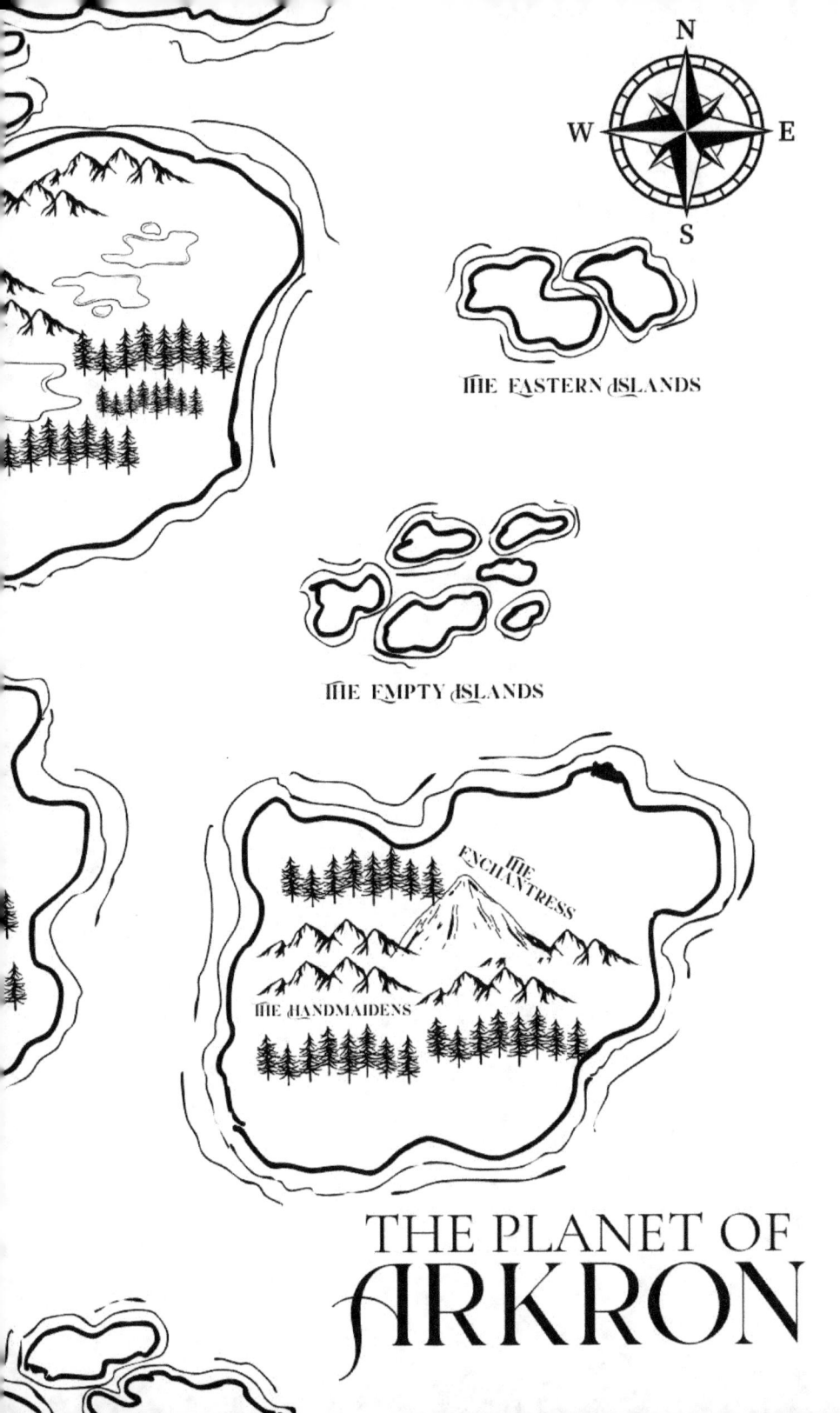

1

THE PENTHOUSE WAS a wreck, but this time Harper had done nothing to cause it.

Heart thudding in her ears, she stepped down from the entryway and surveyed the debris strewn across the common room. The furniture had been overturned, and the cushions gutted of their stuffing. The plants she had tended so lovingly lay strewn across the laminate flooring, their pots shattered. Jagged furrows had been carved in the drywall, as if a monstrous claw had slashed it open. Carbon fiber insulation leaked from the gashes like entrails. Even several of the windows were cracked, fracturing the neon cityscape beyond.

Harper knelt to pick up a semi-intact pot and furiously tried to sweep some of its dirt back into it. Her hands shook. Moons, her whole *body* shook. *You shouldn't feel this upset,* she told herself, tipping the pot back to shake the dirt into the bottom. *This isn't home. This isn't Arkron.*

But it was the home she had here on Mantalor, the unofficial center of trade and diplomacy in the Exlenna solar system. This was the planet where Princess Harper Evensong had made her appearance in the public eye for the first time. She had tried to make the penthouse a haven from the political pressures on this strange world, and all her efforts had come to nothing.

That was what she got for trying to meld who she was and who she had been, she thought ruefully, picking up a fallen leaf and adding it to the pot.

"*By the twin moons.*" Harper's aunt and mentor, Lady Kova, uttered a rare curse as she strode into the common room after her charge. She held her skirt up, unwilling to let it drag through the mess that littered the entryway behind her and the floor before her. "It appears that we've finally overstayed our welcome in Consortium territory." She let go of her skirt, searching for the tablet in her pocket. "This changes everything. If the Consortium is now brazen enough to attack our embassy, I fear that their next step will be harming you. It's time to get you off world." She freed the device and powered it on. The blue sheen cast her hawkish features into ghoulish shadows, and she twisted about, searching for their guards.

Harper remained crouching, trying to straighten the sorry plant. It keeled over between her fingers, its stem frayed. "I suppose our refusal of their proposal today finally pushed them over the edge." She rose, still clutching the plant, and faced her aunt.

Lady Kova turned back to her, frowning. At first Harper thought she was going to rebuff her for her words, but the woman only said, "Set that down. You're tampering with evidence and you're getting dirt on your dress." She brushed past Harper. "Moons! Have two years taught you nothing?"

On the contrary. These last two years on Mantalor had taught her many things, though Harper suspected that none of them would please Lady Kova. A conditioned apology rose to her lips. "I'm sorry, Aunt Kova."

Lady Kova huffed. "It is my duty to train you in galactic politics so that when it is time for you to assume Arkron's throne, you do not present yourself as a backwater hooligan." She brushed aside the mess with her shoe. As Arkron's representative to the Consortium—the coalition of planets that ruled most of the Exlenna—it was Lady Kova's task to oversee Arkron's galactic relations. Harper knew that this strenuous duty was made no easier by having her sixteen-year-old niece underfoot.

"Yes, Aunt Kova." She sighed. This was a speech she heard daily. Lady Kova believed the reminder needed to be applied as regularly as toothpaste to teeth, to prevent the rot of discontent from spreading over her young niece. Unfortunately this recital had only led to it fading into the background, like most regular chores did. Harper acknowledged her words and promptly forgot them. She set the plant on the kitchen island, supporting its drooping stem with a finger. Perhaps she could brace it with a pencil and some string...

"It is also my job to oversee your safety," Lady Kova added, bustling past her towards their bedchambers. "Gather what you can. We must depart quickly." Her clipped footsteps echoed down the empty hallway. Their guards had cleared the apartment while Harper had gathered up the damaged plant and stood outside, giving them privacy. For the first time all day, Harper felt as though she could take a breath without fear of being chided for how the air whistled through her nose.

She refocused her attention on the plant in front of her. Simply propping it up wouldn't do. The stem was too frayed. Instead, she clasped its wounded stalk between her hands. She shut her eyes, dipping into the suppressed well of power inside of her.

"Once," she murmured, "there was a broken stem, and though it was bowed and split, it was not to remain that way forever."

Her palms began to warm, and the stem shimmered faintly. "Its story was not yet told," Harper continued, leaning up against the quartz-topped island to steady herself. The familiar rush of weariness pulsed out from her chest and down her arms as the weaving sucked her strength. Harper pressed on with it. She wanted to fix this. She had to fix this. Everything else in her royal life was spinning out of control; she needed a moment to be someone other than a princess. If only for a few seconds. "It would reform," she whispered, "a testament to the coming Healing..."

The living story seeped from her palms and into the broken fibers. The plant hardened beneath her touch and lifted itself upright. Harper opened her eyes, smiling at her work—

"*Harper.*" Lady Kova's sharp voice shook her out of the moment. Throwing a small suitcase onto the counter, she stalked over to Harper and swept the plant back onto the floor. There was an unpleasant *crack* as the pot hit the hardwood. Eyes aflame, Lady Kova thrust her face into Harper's. "Need I remind you that we are on the cusp of a galactic crisis? And that displays like this not only put *you* at risk but also all of Arkron?"

The storyweaver inside of her shriveled back, while the princess she was training to be stepped forward, holding Lady Kova's eye. "You're right. I'm sorry." The storyweaver surged upward again, making Harper look down. "It's just . . . it was broken and I wanted to fix it."

Lady Kova caught her chin and forced her to look up. "You," she said, "are Princess Harper Evensong, the heir of House Evensong and the planet of Arkron. It is through your throne that you will fix things, not through this very dangerous, very uncouth power."

"It's called storyweaving," Harper whispered, still ensnared by the girl she had been. "I'm just . . . weaving a new story for it."

Lady Kova released her. "If you must indulge yourself, do it on paper. Not in reality." She turned away. "You have two minutes to gather what you want."

"Will we go home?" Harper pressed, rubbing her chin, as if the motion could scrub away her inability to do as she was told. Moons, why was it so hard to jam her feet into her aunt's footsteps? To walk a carefully lined path? Power thrummed in her fingertips again, protesting the idea. If she were to be a perfect princess, why had she been born with such a whirlwind of stories and creation inside of her? Harper dropped her hands to her sides, squeezing them into fists to keep the magic contained.

"I am uncertain," Lady Kova replied. "We may still have a chance to salvage our position in the eyes of the Consortium—but we must get to safety first."

Deciding that it would probably be in her best interests to obey, Harper skittered down the hallway. It was in a similar condition as the common room, with the paintings torn from the walls and light sconces shattered. Harper suspected that the mess had mostly been a means of intimidation—a signal that if she and Lady Kova had been there, they too would find themselves in a similar condition as the wrecked furniture and decorations. But perhaps the Consortium had been looking for something too, some shred of anything that would give them reason to invade Arkron. In that case, the biggest cause they might find was Harper herself. She squeezed her hands into fists as she ducked into her room, willing the power to *go away*.

Harper's room was generally a disaster, so she had difficulty determining if it had been ransacked as well or if the detritus on the floor was a part of her regular mess. She kicked through the clothing on the floor, stuffing a few articles into a bag, and then stumbled over to her desk, where she swept a battered notebook into the pocket of her dress. The dog-eared and rumpled pages were where she hid away the things that tried to spawn from within her. If a weaving was chained down by the ink, it couldn't escape into physicality. So she stuffed them away between the pages and did her best to forget.

But it wasn't as easy when Harper the storyweaver was very much alive within her, swinging back and forth between anger at being locked away in a mental cage and shame toward her own existence. Harper slung the bag over her shoulder and moved towards the door—but a gleam of a light on the wall made her freeze like a lightfoot caught in a hovericle's headlights. Stooping low, she slunk back over to the window and peered behind the curtain.

In the alleyway below, a line of hunched figures hustled near the rear of the building in single file. At first Harper thought they were Arkronen soldiers—but no, Arkronen soldiers didn't wear helmets like that. The lights of the apartment next to them made the blasters in their hands gleam. The model was different from what her guards carried.

Consortium guardsmen. They're coming for us. Harper spun towards the door. Halfway there, she stumbled to a stop and wheeled back to her desk. She snatched up a stray pen and, clutching it in her hand, ran back out to Lady Kova.

Lady Kova was conversing with the captain of their guard, tapping her foot impatiently. She frowned at Harper's wild arrival, but Captain Yarrowriver smothered a smile. Normally Harper would have tried to goad him into breaking his schooled demeanor—it was a game they often played, much to Lady Kova's chagrin. But there was no time for it now. "There are Consortium troops in the alleyway," Harper gasped. "Coming this way."

Captain Yarrowriver snapped into action, activating his comm. "All men, be advised that we have more intruders inbound." He turned back to them. "Our hovericle is on the street beyond, my lady," he said. "It would be best if we proceeded now."

Lady Kova lifted her skirts once more. "Lead the way, Captain."

At his signal, four other soldiers stepped into the room and took up positions on either side of Harper and Lady Kova, placing them in a protective box. As they moved out, Harper peered between them for a last look at the ruined room, wishing it a silent farewell.

They filed down the embassy's steps in a silent line. All the lights were off, and Harper's eyes took the darkness and reformed it into savage creatures that watched their every moment. It wasn't until they reached the embassy's entry that they encountered trouble.

Two of the Arkronen soldiers were sprawled facedown on the ground. Crimson blood pooled across the tiled floor, obscuring its mosaics. A gasp tore out of Harper, and she tried to squeeze between the guards to get to them. They couldn't be left like that; someone had to bless their ending.

One of her guards caught her shoulder and pressed her back. "You must remain between us, Highness," he said. "For your safety."

"Bother safety," she muttered under her breath. How dare the Consortium come into their quiet oasis of Arkronen culture, murdering and destroying? Her palms warmed again, and she clenched her hands. If she wasn't trying to hold onto this blasted royal mold, she would be out there confronting those intruders. Stories would blast from her fingertips until all of this was fixed.

Her eyes strayed back to the fallen men. Well. As fixed as it could be. She couldn't restore souls. Only the Creator had that power.

Abruptly Captain Yarrowriver stopped and raised his fist. The scanner in his hand was blinking, warning that they were no longer alone. The guards clustered tighter around Harper and Lady Kova, raising their blasters.

Six masked guardsmen emerged out of the darkness of the hallway. Their armored suits made them look like beetles, with ebony plating covering their bodies and their faces covered with rounded masks. One bearing the blue stripes of a sergeant on his helmet addressed them, "Lady Evensong and Princess Evensong, you are under arrest for defamation against the Exlenna Consortium."

"Defamation?" Harper muttered. How was it defamation if they had politely said *no thank you* to having their world snatched up by a greedy empire?

Lady Kova replied in a cold voice, "There are treaties protecting the rights of independent planets. We have violated none of them."

The fancy blasters clicked in warning. "Raise your hands," the sergeant ordered, lifting his weapon. His fellows followed suit.

The Arkronen soldiers tensed. They formed a wall and backed from the Consortium operatives, urging the ladies towards the door. Peeking between the elbows and shoulders, Harper bared her teeth at the black-plated men, daring them to come closer.

Lady Kova grabbed her elbow, forcing her to follow as she stepped out of the building. The walkway to the street was lined with another squad of Arkronen soldiers.

Time oozed as Harper and Lady Kova edged through their guards. An armored hovericle waited on the street just beyond the front gate. Captain Yarrowriver brought up the rear behind them, blaster swinging from the house to the Consortium guardsmen lurking in the garden. The stillness of the standoff made Harper uneasy; it was as if she stood before a great storm, watching it swirl closer and closer but not yet feeling the wind and rain.

Then the crack of a firing blaster shattered the standoff. One of their guards toppled down the front steps, blood trickling from his forehead.

The garden erupted into motion. Lady Kova crouched and shuffled to the gate while energy bullets whizzed overhead. Around them, Arkronens fell. Their outdated weaponry was no match for the Consortium's latest tech. Harper knelt beside a decorative tree and freed her pen, prepared to retaliate.

Lady Kova grabbed her arm, squeezing it. "Don't make this worse," she hissed, and dragged her to the gate. Captain Yarrowriver followed, firing at the Consortium guardsmen, but his motions were flagging. He was wounded, Harper realized in alarm. Blood seeped onto his uniform from his shoulder, and he was limping.

"Captain," she began, reaching for him, but Lady Kova pulled her back. The action spared Harper from the captain's fate: His head snapped backwards as another charge found it. He slumped onto the tiled walkway, eyes gazing into eternity.

"*No!*" Harper tried to lunge for him. This couldn't be real. He couldn't be dead; she *knew* him. He had come to Mantalor at the same time as her, to serve Lady Kova. He liked chocolate-covered pretzels, and he had a daughter back on Arkron who was fifteen, only a year younger than Harper. She had known his story, and now . . . now it had ended before her eyes.

What was left of the Arkronen soldiers closed in around Harper and Lady Kova, herding them to the hovericle. "You must go," one of them shouted, firing into the Consortium guardsmen. "We'll hold them off. You're too valuable to be captured."

Lady Kova threw open the door of the hovericle and tossed Harper inside. She scrambled in after and slammed the door, catching her skirts in it. The driver took off, speeding down the neon-bathed streets.

Still clutching her pen, Harper crawled into a seat, gasping.

Contrary to her usually controlled movements, Lady Kova's hands shook as she pulled out her comm. "Driver," she called, "take us to the far-southeast transport station."

Harper tried to loosen her fingers from around the pen, but they refused to budge. "That's the opposite end of Mantalor city from the port," she mumbled. In her mind, the energy bullet collided with Captain Yarrowriver's head again and again. She gripped her pen, trying to imagine a different ending. If she had reacted fast enough, could she have woven a shield to protect him?

"Indeed," Lady Kova agreed. "But there is one more person we must collect—for his safety and ours."

Of course. Pickett, Harper's elder brother, who enjoyed an uncomplicated life as a scholar. He was probably holed up in his mentor's office, watching the Net as he polished his High General's boots. *He* never had to worry about being ambushed by alternate personalities or Consortium guardsmen.

Harper squeezed her eyes shut, imagining herself lunging at Captain Yarrowriver. Tackling him so that the bullet went over his head. Or grabbing his arm and dragging him out of the way. *It's too late.* Tears smarted in her eyes. *His story ended. I can't revise it.*

She sucked in a steadying breath, twisting the pen through her fingers, but found she was still trembling. Being a princess had gotten a good man and his squad killed. If she had leaned fully into her storyweaver self, would still that have happened? The question nagged her as the hovericle rumbled beneath her, speeding further into Mantalor City.

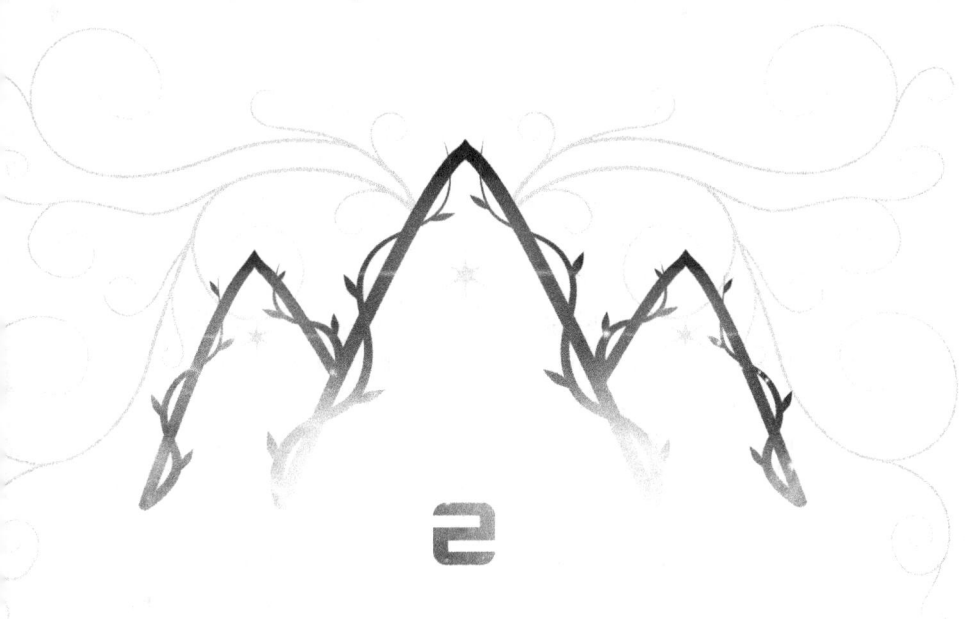

2

Pickett Evensong watched as his life began to burn. Sitting at his desk in the High General's study, he flipped through the Networld newsfeeds, a headache blooming in his temples. After years of cajoling and outright threatening to join them *or else*, the Consortium had issued an ultimatum to the three planets not under its rule: *Join us or face invasion.*

Predictably the three planets—Bagoon, Inerys, and his own Arkron—had declined. The Consortium had been after them for decades once it became clear that separation from their empire had permitted them to recover from the ravages of the Great War. Free to focus on their own people and lands, the independent worlds had been able to implement measures that prevented their resources from being overtaxed. The Consortium's hungry eyes had watched Arkron's forests and prairies regenerate, Bagoon's vast caves clear of smoke, and Inerys's oceans return to their vibrant state. They had leered like a starving man waiting for a plum to ripen, and now it was harvesttime.

Pickett powered off his tablet and laid it face down on the desk to rub his temples. He was surprised that comms weren't already rolling in from his mother, Queen Anrameta, and Lady Kova, ordering him back to Arkron.

He didn't want to go.

The door to the study opened and he leapt to his feet, glad to be shaken out of his thoughts. "High General," he said, bowing. "I trust your business was attended to quickly, then?"

High General Rosemary Vasken of the Neherum swept off her cloak and passed it to him. "Indeed. I presume you've been watching the newsfeeds?"

"Yes, High General." He moved to hang up her cloak, taking heed that its folds did not knock the various bottles of clear and multicolored elixirs from the nearby shelf. He didn't need *that* to happen again. Vasken had a hard enough time convincing the healers in the Passer division to share their store of herbs and solutions for her experiments. It wouldn't do to make her look clumsy. Thankfully, he whipped the cloth up onto the hook without an incident. He returned to the High General's side and began pouring her tea. "Do you think these developments will impact the Neherum?"

Vasken pushed her customary braid off her shoulder as she settled into her desk chair. She rotated to the large window behind her desk. Outside, the Neherum's large campus, Anaya, gleamed from the dozens of lanterns lit against the darkening evening. "I believe it may," she said. "The coming upheaval will be a crucible for our order. However, I am confident that we will emerge stronger than before." She accepted her teacup from him. "Did you finish transcribing those reports I left you? Or did you watch the newsfeeds the whole time?"

The tips of Pickett's ears tingled as an embarrassed flush swept over him. "I finished half of the reports," he replied, crossing to his desk to retrieve them. "Forgive my distraction—my homeworld, as I'm certain you're aware, is one of the dissenters."

Vasken raised an amused eyebrow as she accepted the sheaf of paper from him. The expression stretched the scar on her face, which ran from the corner of her left eye to her jaw, in almost a comical way. To Pickett, it looked like a pencil line drawn down her face. "I did note that," she remarked. "I suppose your family will be recalling you soon? Pity. You are an invaluable help to me."

He bowed again, feeling the warmth of her words within him. Vasken was sparing with her praise, only making it known when she truly meant it. "Thank you, High General. My position as your assistant among the Neherum is a great honor to me."

"I'm aware," she said, removing her sword from her belt. She leaned it up against her desk, where speckles of crimson on the blade below the crossguard caught the lamplight and shone black.

She caught him looking and gestured to the weapon. "If you would, please make an appointment with the smiths to have it cleaned."

"Of course," he said, picking up his tablet once more. "Were you forced to use it today?"

"Unfortunately, yes." The note of excitement in her voice was counter to her words. High General Vasken was renowned for her skill with the sword, and in their current tech age, the opportunities to use it were growing few and far between. "It was the Outcast conclave that overran our research outpost near Bagoon. Leave something unattended for two minutes, and those filthy vultures think they can claim it." She shifted her braid again, tugging idly on the graying strands amongst the crimson locks. Even well into midlife, the general indicators of age—silver hair, lines on her face—only served to enhance her commanding appearance. "Remind me during our next sparring session to teach you the *kata* I used to win. I believe it would be beneficial to your technique."

He smiled. One day, he hoped he would have the same prominence to take other journeymen under his wing and train them as she did him. Perhaps it would be as the next High General, when she retired. Until then, he vowed to make the most of every lesson from her. "I will. Thank you, High General." He powered on his device, prepared to send a comm to the smithy when a new message appeared on the screen, preventing him from accessing any other utilities.

It was from Lady Kova. He lowered the device.

Vasken was watching him, hands folded before her. "Your family needs you, I presume?"

"Yes," he said.

She dipped her head. "Perhaps that session will have to wait."

"I'm very sorry, High General. I'm more than willing to take any remote work you need finished with me."

She waved away his words. "Your first duty is to your family." The heavy note in her voice caused Pickett to cringe. He was bound to his family, yes, but he had also made vows to the Neherum and to the High General. And frankly, satisfying those duties was more fulfilling than doing the ones for House Evensong. On Arkron, he was an extra, the eldest child, not in line for the throne since he was male. At Anaya, he was important. *Needed.*

He took his time packing his bag, making sure to include the reports he hadn't finished. When he was done, he bowed a final, third time to General Vasken.

She regarded him with her usual tight expression. "Farewell, Pickett. I sincerely hope that we may return to our usual arrangement soon."

"As do I, High General. I won't deny that I would rather stay with you and the Neherum."

She tipped her head, a smile loosening her lips. "Indeed? You are welcome, if you would prefer to remain. I am happy to make the necessary excuses to your mother."

The knot that had been tightening in his chest loosened. He *could* stay. He didn't *have* to join Harper and Lady Kova. He belonged here. With the Neherum. And the High General.

And yet . . . it was rare that House Evensong bothered him. They respected his status here. If they were calling upon him . . . then it must be serious.

He had to go. It would be wrong to stay. "Thank you, High General, but I must go."

She dipped her head. "Very well. Safe travels, then."

"Thank you." He took his leave before he could change his mind.

Anaya was quiet as he made his way through the halls and across the courtyards; most of the scholars were either studying in their dorms or sparring in the dojos. Dinner had ended long ago, but as he passed the entrance to the dining hall, he noticed Neherum still gathered around the tables inside.

There were three long ones, one for each of the order's divisions of study: Accipiter—the warriors; Ibis—the researchers; and Passer—the healers. Crossing a courtyard, he passed a cluster of Neherum from Ibis, who were arguing about a passage from a textbook, then a couple from the Accipiter division, who were laughing and wiping the sweat from their brows after a sparring session. As he passed, all of them nodded at him, paying respect to the High General's journeyman—and, perhaps, the Prince of Arkron. Though in Anaya's university setting, that title had little meaning. The normalcy of the evening weighed on Pickett; to his fellows, nothing was wrong. Their world remained unbothered, while his showed fissures. He tried not to be resentful about it.

He swept into the west wing of the castle, where the dorms were situated. Unfortunately for him, leaving Anaya wasn't as simple as getting on the transit. He wasn't the only member of House Evensong within the Neherum's ranks, and it was his duty to collect the others in the event of an emergency.

Regrettably, those "others" had the tendency to make themselves difficult to collect. Striding into the rectangular courtyard separating the dorms from the other parts of the castle, Pickett noticed a group of Fledglings—students at the basic level of instruction who hadn't been sorted into a division yet—gathered by the fountain at the far end. He was far enough away that he couldn't hear their conversation, but an unmistakable voice cut across to him: "*You take that back!*"

Pickett groaned and jogged towards the group, already knowing what he was going to find.

Fayen Longracer stood with his back to the fountain, shielding a young girl behind him. She was pulling on his cloak, trying to drag him away from the group. As she did so, the hood of her cloak slid backwards, revealing her luminous yellow eyes and the cat ears poking from her nest of curly brown hair. Her appearance made something inside Pickett flinch. Evaly had been a Hybri for three years now, but he was still getting used to her odd appearance.

A muscular boy stood between the group of Fledglings and Fayen, slapping a dull training sword against his palm. "I won't, Longracer," he taunted. He jutted his chin towards Evaly. "She's a freak, and she knows it. See? She's trying to run away."

"It's not her fault," Fayen snarled, surging forward. The jerk caused Evaly to fall to her hands and knees with a soft cry. Fayen paused, glancing back at her, and his distraction was all the other boy needed. He lunged at Fayen, swinging the sword at his head.

Pickett hurried forward, thrusting the watching Fledglings aside to break up the fight. Fayen, however, was faster. He reacted swiftly, ducking under the incoming blade. Pickett opened his mouth to warn Fayen not to draw his sword—the boy had only recently earned it, and drawing it on another student over an insult was a fasttrack to expulsion. But Fayen wasn't reaching for his sword—he grabbed the other boy's wrist and forced his sword arm downward. In another motion, he hooked his ankle around one of the boy's and jerked him to one knee.

"Apologize," Fayen hissed into his face.

In reply, the boy punched him in the jaw with his free hand. Fayen's head snapped back, his green eyes going wide. Evaly cried out, trying to pick herself up, and Pickett reached for them both, trying to catch the backs of their tunics to separate them.

Instinctively Fayen reacted by kicking the other boy in the chest. His breath escaped him in a whoosh as he fell backwards, and

Fayen caught the sword as it flew from his grasp. He leveled it at the boy's throat. "Try to mess with my sister again, and I won't use a training sword."

"That's enough," Pickett said, grabbing the hilt of the sword and prying it from Fayen's grasp. It wasn't easy; the boy's grip was strong. "We're going. Evaly, come." He grabbed Fayen's arm and dragged him towards the portico that lined the sides of the courtyard. Over his shoulder, he shouted at the Fledglings, "Your headmistress and the High General *will* be hearing about this!"

"Let go of me," Fayen growled, trying to twist away from Pickett's grip. "Why are you hauling *me* to Vasken? I didn't start it!"

"I'm not hauling you to Vasken," Pickett replied, releasing him. "But honestly, Fayen, can't you learn to turn the other cheek?"

"Not if they're threatening Evaly." Fayen turned back, reaching back for the girl as she emerged into the portico. She moved slowly, as if she were a moth trying to pull itself from a chrysalis.

"They weren't threatening me," Evaly said, finally catching up to them. She frowned, reaching up to touch the red mark on Fayen's jaw. He would have a nasty bruise there by morning. "They were just shooting words. I've been through worse."

"It was only words today," Fayen said darkly. "It might not always be like that." His hands tightened into fists but relaxed to allow Evaly to slip her hand into one of his. He eyed Pickett through his unkempt, brown hair. "It's been a few days. What errand from the High General brings you across our path?"

"Don't be disrespectful," Pickett warned. "And I'm not here on an errand for her. Lady Kova commed me—apparently diplomatic relations between Arkron and the Consortium have taken a turn for the worse. We're leaving now."

"What, it's not safe to be with the Neherum?" Fayen demanded, dropping his hand to the hilt of his sword. Evaly shied closer to him, eyeing the dark alcoves that lined the walkway. "What does your High General think of all this?"

"The High General does not have an opinion," Pickett replied. "The Neherum will be neutral as they have always been. We are dedicated to study, remember?"

Fayen shrugged. "Sure. So how'd she take your resignation?"

Silent Star Sea, Pickett cursed silently. Fayen might not be his little brother—he was the son of Queen Anrameta's chief lady-in-waiting and thereby a ward of House Evensong—but he was just as aggravating as one. "I didn't *resign*," he corrected, directing them to the gatehouse with a jerk of his head. "This is just a . . . hiatus. I'm sure the conflict will blow over."

"What if it doesn't?" Evaly's cat ears were splayed to the side, signaling her unease, and she huddled closer to Fayen. Though she had only become a member of House Evensong four years ago, Pickett found he had a hard time remembering what it had been like before Evaly joined them. In fact, it was hard to picture Fayen *without* Evaly peering around him.

"It will. Don't worry," Fayen said, gripping the hilt of his sword. When Evaly's silence betrayed her discontent with the answer, Fayen shot a look at Pickett. "It will, don't *you* think, Pickett?"

"I hope so," he replied, glancing back at the castle as they exited the guardhouse and made for the transport platform. Anaya's lights twinkled cheerfully in the dusk, like some sort of magical haven from a children's story. "But with the Consortium, there could be any number of outcomes."

"I wish I were still in the dojos," Evaly said. "Training like on a regular night."

Pickett sighed, peering regretfully over his shoulder at the main building again. "Me too." This time, his eyes found what he was looking for: the window of the High General's office. Vasken's silhouette was black against the window as she watched him depart.

On Mantalor, the Star Sea overhead was concealed by a ruddy glow in the atmosphere. It was as if the tangled sprawl of buildings and streets that made up Mantalor City couldn't bear the thought of something so beautiful gazing down on its squalor and so did its best to hide it. On the fringes of the city, though, the blanket of light pollution thinned enough for the most brilliant stars to pierce the shroud.

Standing outside of their hovericle, Harper sucked in a lungful of the heavy night air and raised her hands towards the sky, marking the distance between the visible stars with her fingers. Her mother had taught her how to mark the position of the planets based on the finger length between the stars in the sky. She was trying to locate Arkron, but it was too far to the west, beneath the blanket of light.

She dropped her hand, thoughts turning back to Captain Yarrowriver. She prayed that the Creator had carried his soul gently to the Most High. He had saved them. And she hadn't been able to save him in return.

She sucked in another ragged breath and slumped against the hovericle. Anger coursed through her, as blistering as starship fuel. She twirled the pen through her fingers, feeling her power connect with the tip. A pen wasn't necessary to make a weaving, but it was a helpful conduit. What if she wove something right now to get them offworld, to make sure Captain Yarrowriver's sacrifice hadn't been in vain? But she'd never tested her limits that far before—her weavings had been confined to small things, like healing the plant. Based on the weariness she felt after something like that, she suspected a large weaving would knock her flat. Using her power came with a price.

She had tried to research what that entailed; once, storyweavers had been common on Arkron. And yet that had been in a past Age. After the Great War that had heralded their current era, much of the books—and people—who could have explained it to her were lost.

Perhaps it was a good thing. She needed to focus on who she was supposed to be: Princess Harper Evensong. She tucked the pen away and crossed her arms, squeezing her hands into fists to dispel the thrumming in her fingertips. *You could make this so much more dangerous for everyone if the Exlenna learns what you are.* If the Consortium found out that Arkron harbored more than regenerating land, they would tear the planet apart searching for other empowered storyweavers like her. They could force them to create weavings that would make their empire unstoppable. Every act of resistance would be met with retribution so severe that there would be no recovering from it.

Inside the hovericle, Lady Kova looked up from her feverish work on her tablet. Harper waited for the order to come back inside, but it never came. Lady Kova merely gazed at her for a moment and then went back to work. Despite her strictness, she *did* seem to know when Harper had been pushed over the edge.

A new star gleamed in the east, brighter and more vibrant than those overhead. Harper rapped on the hovericle's window. "Transport's almost here."

The star grew brighter as it raced towards them, revealing itself to be the nose of a worm-shaped train hovering above its magnetic track. It slowed as it drew level with the dim platform where their hovericle waited.

Only three people stepped off. Relief pulsed through Harper at the sight of them; even though they resided on the same planet, it had been months since she had seen Pickett, or Fayen and Evaly. She peeled herself from the side of the vehicle, preparing to charge towards them. After the awful events of the night, she wanted them close, to know that they were all right.

Lady Kova, climbing out of the hovericle, stilled her with a sharp word. "Wait. We must use our safe words."

A few steps away, Pickett stopped Fayen and Evaly and gave a curt nod. "Locked," he said.

Harper nodded, touching the book-shaped locket that hung around her neck. Pickett was one of the few people who knew that it was stuck fast, unable to open.

Evaly spoke up next. "Hazelwood."

"Your medicine," Harper identified. "That keeps you from . . . er . . ."

Evaly smiled wearily and rested her head against Fayen's arm. "That keeps me from ripping apart at the seams."

Beside her, Fayen popped his knuckles. Harper grinned, sensing that her friend was preparing for a performance. Fayen was not one to waste a second in the spotlight. "I present thee with two of them, my noble lady," he said, sweeping into a comical bow. "*The Conquesta* and fish traps."

The safe words weren't needed here; Fayen's flare for the dramatic was impossible to replicate. Harper snatched Fayen's hand and dropped into a curtsey. "Only one so dear to me could name my fondest memories!" she said, matching his theatric tone. "The day we concussed my brother with a book and the day I nearly drowned to catch more fish than you."

"Out of all the buffoonery you two get up to, why does the one involving *me* have to be your safe word?" Pickett muttered.

Lady Kova's face had tightened at Harper's lapse in maturity, and she replied, "Never fear, Pickett. You need to form new ones now that these have been used. And perhaps this time they will be more . . . judicious."

"We'll work on it during the flight home," Harper promised, trying to salvage some vestiges of grace. A man had died tonight for her. Now was not the time to be fooling about. She released Fayen's hand to wrap her arms around Pickett. As usual, he stiffened, clamping his arms to his sides before he loosened and patted her on the back. She tipped her head back to frown up into his face. "You're a terrible hugger—I just escaped from a possible arrest-execution attempt, and all you do is pat me on the back?"

Though his brow furrowed at her words, he rolled his eyes. They were the same hazel hue as hers; really, if he was a bit shorter, the two Evensong siblings might have been mistaken for twins. They had the same auburn hair and pale complexion, as well as sharp jaw. However, Pickett did not share the spray of freckles that Harper bore across her face and shoulders; he had done the sensible thing and spent most of his childhood with his nose in a book instead of running about in the sun. "Fine," he huffed, and gave her half-hearted squeeze. "Does that appease you?"

"Not entirely, but I'll bother you about it later."

Lady Kova's tablet pinged, and she withdrew it from her skirt. "Our transport has been arranged," she announced. "It's in the city's northeast port. If we want to make it in time, we must depart." She climbed back into the hovericle, pushing the door open wider so the rest of them could follow.

"What exactly happened tonight?" Fayen asked, scrambling in after Harper. He dropped into the seat beside her, jostling them both. Evaly climbed in next to him, her face pinched. Perhaps her Hybri was acting up today, Harper thought with a pang. She had often dreamed of healing the girl, but Evaly's case was complex—Harper wasn't certain what a weaving would do to her. Furthermore, Evaly was somewhat renowned in the medical circles on Mantalor... how would they explain it if she was suddenly cured? It could cause more harm than good for the both of them.

"Yes," Pickett echoed, "what happened?" He settled in the leather seat across from them and crossed his legs as if he were in a conference meeting. Harper resisted the urge to roll her eyes. If he kept up this pompous behavior, she was going to have to wrestle it out of him. Not that a princess wrestled, of course. It wasn't ladylike. She noticed that he had taken out his tablet to take notes—ever the Neherum. The order was dedicated to studying the Exlenna and preserving the parts of history that might be lost in their advancing age. Sometimes Harper thought Pickett took it a little *too* far; she hated feeling like a case study.

The hovericle took off with a bump, speeding back into the city. Overhead, the city light leeched away the night sky.

"It was ransacked," Harper said. "We think they were looking for something that would give them cause to invade. Either that, or they were hoping to kidnap us for ransom." She looked at Lady Kova, waiting for her to add more, but her aunt merely nodded and went back to her tablet. Harper suspected she was still trying to salvage the situation.

Pickett frowned, stroking his chin. "Where is Captain Yarrowriver? I'm surprised you don't have a bigger detail." He gestured to their driver who hunkered behind the controls. For all they knew, he was the only surviving member of his squad.

"Captain Yarrowriver is dead," Harper said softly.

Pickett blinked, his controlled features crumbling for a moment. "Oh. I see."

"Were you hurt?" Fayen asked.

"No," Harper said. "Thanks to him."

They fell into an uneasy silence as the hovericle raced along. Every person they breezed by on the street felt like a threat to Harper. Any one of those cloaked figures could be working for the Consortium, looking for them . . .

"I wish I'd been there," Fayen muttered. "I could take on a whole squad of Consortium guardsmen. They wouldn't have stood a chance."

Pickett snorted. "And I could eat a whole stack of frycakes."

Fayen smacked his fist into his palm, grinning. "Is that a challenge, Mister Assistant to the High General?"

"No, it was not," Pickett said, and buried himself in his tablet again.

"I wish you *had* been there," Harper said, turning to Fayen. For the first time, she noticed the bruise blossoming on his jaw. Apparently he had been playing the role of fierce protector again. It was one he'd borne since childhood; she could recall dozens of occasions where he'd insisted upon playing the knight defending the castle. "It would have made for a fine story."

He grinned. "Maybe you could weave it anyway. You know, an unempowered story in your notebook. For inspiration's sake." He bumped his fist against hers. "I'll be there next time. I promise."

They soared into the port only a few strikes before midnight. Compared to the massive spaceport in the center of Mantalor City, this one reminded Harper of the tiny collections of hangars that stored the drones Arkronen farmers used to treat their crops. The siding on the buildings was crumbling off, and many of the lights that marked the starship docks were burnt out. Puddles reflected the cityscape, making it seem as though they might fall into a different realm if they strayed off the walkway. Silhouettes of dockhands moved between the ships like fiends in a nightmare. It was far different from their first arrival on Mantalor, where they'd been received on a bright tarmac bedecked with streamers and other representatives waiting to greet them.

"This feels . . . safe," Harper remarked, leaning past Fayen to get a closer look.

"Perhaps not," Lady Kova said, "but it is less busy than the main port. We should be able to leave unmolested."

Harper noticed Pickett and Fayen exchange looks. They might get away unhindered, yes, but if they were attacked, there would be no one to hear their screams for help.

The hovericle stopped. Cautiously, they got out. The docks appeared quiet, save for a few workers tending to the ships.

Lady Kova consulted her tablet and then fluttered a hand towards a battered freighter drooping beside two others in similar states of disrepair. The ramps on all three ships were lowered, and workers moved in and out between them, stacking crates and dragging pallets aboard. "That would be ours, I believe."

"Are we even certain it's seaworthy?" Pickett demanded, striding towards the ships. "All of these ships look like they're a few loose bolts away from being scrap."

"Well, it *was* supposed to be unobtrusive," Lady Kova replied. "Come; I'd very much like to get aboard and properly tidied."

Harper made to follow her but paused when she noticed Evaly, who stood frozen against the side of the hovericle. "What is it?" she asked, stepping back to her. Fayen dropped back as well, frowning.

"There are more people coming this way," the girl replied. Her cat ears flicked backwards, towards the entrance of the port.

Harper glanced at the dockhands and found that they were gone. Oh, that was definitely not a good sign.

Fayen grasped the hilt of his sword. "If we hurry, we can get on board before they get here."

Evaly was shaking her head frantically, resisting their attempt to haul her towards the ship. "We need cover!"

"The ship will be our cover," Harper said, trying to peer around the hovericle. "How close are they?"

Evaly's nostrils flared as her Hybri senses tried to assess their surroundings. Then she grabbed Harper's shoulder and yanked her down. The sound of blasterfire shattered the night. Flat on the ground, Harper raised her head to see Pickett and Lady Kova sheltering behind several crates near the ships.

"We have to get over to them," Harper hissed. Overhead, blue energy charges streaked through the air like comets.

"We have no cover," Fayen shot back, eyeing the deadly shower as he ripped out his sword.

Harper rolled onto her side, her skirt growing heavy as it absorbed a puddle. Blast. The last thing she needed was to be weighed down by her clothes. The pen in her pocket pressed against her thigh, begging to be drawn like Fayen's sword. "I could *make* some cover," she rasped, wrestling it from the folds of her dress.

Fayen glanced at her. His eyes shone for a moment and then dimmed. "That probably wouldn't be smart, though."

No. It wouldn't. Revealing herself would only make this situation worse, even if it saved them now. She propped herself up on one knee and peered into the cabin of the hovericle. Perhaps their driver could drive slowly down the dock, closer to the ship and serve as a rolling shield.

This was not to be. The man was slumped over the controls, which were painted crimson with his blood. Moons. He was gone now too. Harper swallowed the scream that rose in her throat and made to duck again, but before she did so, she studied their assailants. They were advancing from the entrance, their blasters flashing as they fired. Yes, there was that telltale, beetle-like armor. The Consortium had found them again. She crouched next to Evaly, clenching her jaw. Was it possible to be furious and frightened at the same time? Her heart felt as if it was going to rip itself out of her chest and explode.

Evaly was looking towards Pickett and Lady Kova's hiding spot, her brow furrowed. "What's Pickett up to?"

Harper snapped her attention to him. Pickett was emerging from behind his crate, sword in hand. "What in the Silent Star Sea is he doing?" she demanded, half-rising.

Fayen rose slowly, grinning. "He's going to distract them. And I'm going to help." He charged into the open, sword swinging.

Harper pulled out her pen. To the Deeps with caution. She wasn't going to stand by and let Pickett *and* Fayen die for her.

But Pickett and Fayen didn't need her help. They came level with each other and began a *kata* that was so rapid that they became a blur of motion. Their bodies and weapons danced in a complex pattern that sent the energy bullets ricocheting in a different direction. Stars. Harper had forgotten how strong the moonsteel of Neherum blades was. If a swordsman was fast enough, they could deflect the charges with it.

And Pickett and Fayen were moving very, very fast. "Pickett's been training with the High General," Evaly murmured as they stood, prepared to run. "And Fayen spends all his time in the dojo, trying to one-up him."

It was clear to Harper that Fayen would soon surpass Pickett in skill. He was a blur of motion, his sword a nothing-streak in the air. With one hand, he seized one of the crates beneath the foremost transport and hurled it into the no-man's land between them, still deflecting the charges with his sword.

Harper and Evaly tore away from the hovericle and sprinted towards it. Charges whizzed around them; Harper could feel the heat as they tore holes in her sleeves and skirt, narrowly missing her arms and legs. They dove behind the crate, waiting for a lull in the firestorm. Fayen surged past them, leaping onto the crate to draw fire. "*Go!*" he roared.

Harper grabbed Evaly's hand and dragged her backwards. Which ship had Lady Kova pointed out? Wasn't it the middle one? Her knees banged into its ramp and she scrambled onto it, pulling Evaly up with her. They rolled into the ship's hold, knocking into the crates stacked there.

Pickett leapt in after them, sword clutched tightly. "To the cockpit," he ordered, "and strap yourself in."

"But what about Fayen?" Harper demanded, struggling to her feet. The ship rumbled furiously beneath her, putting her off balance, and she heard the telltale hiss of the ramp beginning to retract.

"He's coming!" Pickett said, twisting back to track Fayen's progress. "Get up there!" There was a dangerous note in his voice.

Harper stumbled through the ship's hold; it was stuffed with further storage crates and other supplies. A ladder led up to the cockpit, and she shimmied up it, even though her limbs felt like water. Evaly followed, wheezing. The moment Harper tumbled onto the loft, she felt engines shift beneath her. The ship's hum became a roar as its thrusters lifted it from the dock.

Harper found her feet and looked around. The cockpit was empty. "Didn't Lady Kova hire a pilot?"

Steadying herself on one of the chairs, Evaly leaned towards the controls. "Apparently not. It's automated."

Pickett's voice rang up from below. "Is Lady Kova up there?"

"No . . . Isn't she with you?" Harper called back.

Nothing. Harper felt her heart plunge into her stomach and then fall beyond it. "Did we leave her?"

Evaly stumbled back to the ladder. "Fayen! Is Fayen aboard?"

More silence. Then Pickett's face appeared at the top of the platform. His expression was grim, his forehead wrinkled with worry. "Lady Kova was running for the ship . . . but perhaps she ran for the one *next* to this one. *Silent Star Sea*."

"What about Fayen?" Evaly demanded, her voice climbing to a shriek.

Pickett turned to her, running a hand through his hair. "I thought he was behind me. He must have run for the ship Lady Kova was on."

Evaly's chest heaved, panic sprawled all over her face. Harper caught her shoulders and pushed her into one of the seats. "It's okay," she said, trying to soothe her. "He's probably with Lady Kova."

Evaly nodded, still gasping for breath. Harper pulled her into an embrace, holding her in the same way that she had seen Fayen hold her, trying to soothe her.

Pickett sank into the pilot's chair and probed the controls. "It's locked on a trajectory," he said. "But I can't see where to . . ."

"So we have no idea if *we're* on the wrong ship or if Lady Kova and Fayen are," Harper replied, squeezing Evaly tighter. She looked at Pickett over the top of Evaly's head. "I could—"

"No," he snapped. "Don't even suggest it. We're in enough trouble as it is, and I don't need you spawning magic portals or some other crazy thing. You have to control yourself, *do you understand?*"

Weaver Harper's anger licked at her insides, but Princess Harper pushed her down and nodded obediently. She hugged Evaly close as the ship lurched again. The rumble of the engine became a piercing whine as the hyperdrive revved and the stars before them stretched into the yawning white-blue of hyperspace, swallowing them whole.

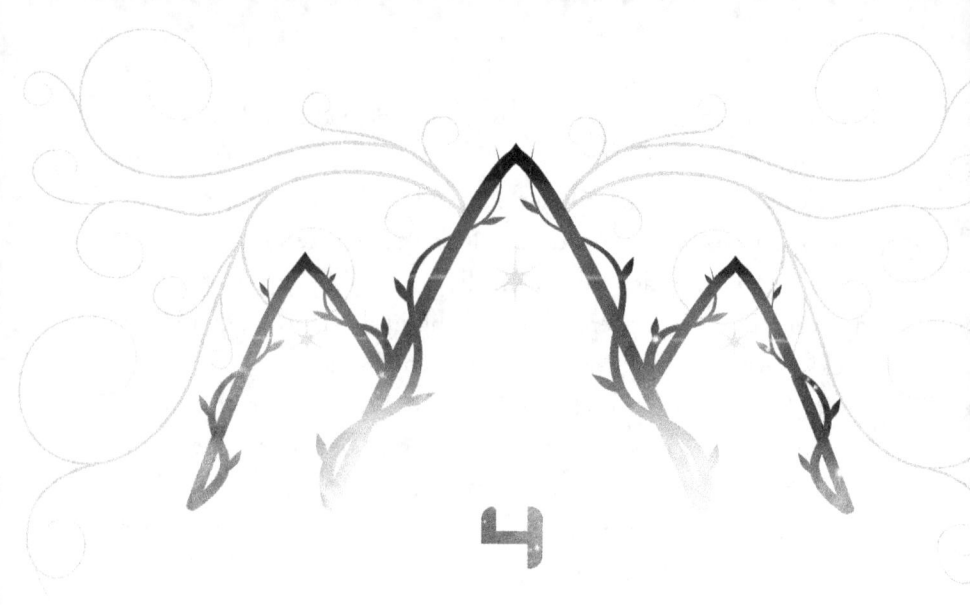

4

The rumble of the freighter magnified the constant ache in Evaly's bones. Just when she was certain she had accepted the pain, a new burst caused a limb to jerk or her stomach to lurch. For her own safety, she sat on the floor in the corner of the cockpit, her back resting against the wall.

Her Hybri senses twitched every which way, picking up the murmur of Harper and Pickett's voices, the growl of the engines, and the hiss of the pressurization system. The ship reeked of grease and fuel, and a sickly, fruity smell wafted from the ripped and faded cockpit seats, suggesting that the last occupant had been smoking a steamstick. She drew herself into a ball, pressing her hands over her human ears and flattening her cat ears against her head to try and block out some of the noise.

There had been a time when blasting off wouldn't have caused such pain. She had been a normal little girl, with a normal family—a family that was dead now . . . She pressed harder on her ears, trying to drown out the noise within, pushing away thoughts of her past and the creature that lived inside of her. She was a different Evaly now. With a new family. A family that was being fractured before her very eyes.

Her chest tightened as she thought about Fayen. What if he hadn't made it onto Lady Kova's ship? What if he was lying on that dark dock, lifeless?

No. No, no, no. She shoved the image from her mind. He would be okay. He had to be okay, because if he wasn't, she wouldn't be. Without him, she was weak. Helpless. Orphaned.

Her senses alerted her to Harper's nearing presence before the girl squatted next to her on the dull steel floor. "Hey," she said. "Did you bring your meds with you?"

Evaly forced herself to uncover her ears, though she remained scrunched in the corner. She fumbled with the little bag she kept tied beneath her cloak, pawing through the detritus inside to find the containers of medicine that kept her functional. She spilled them out onto the floor. Under the flickering lights, the colored jars and containers of herbs, oils, and medicines cast a haunting kaleidoscope of colors on the metal. The effect was like light streaming through stained glass windows in a palace, but in a far more sinister way. Harper caught up the jar of oil used to calm Evaly's knotted muscles. "Where does it hurt the worst?"

"The back of my neck," Evaly replied. "And my shoulders."

Harper poured the oil onto her palms, not seeming to care that some of it dribbled onto her fine skirt, and set to work. Evaly gasped faintly as she dug at the knots, massaging them out. Normally Fayen did this for her; after several years of practice, he had learned a cadence that got the oil into her but didn't leave her with bruises afterwards. During their occasional visits to the Arkron embassy, Harper had also learned how to administer her treatments—and her massages came with an added side of storytelling, which made the experience more enjoyable. However, she was unintentionally rougher. Evaly's Hybri could feel the surge of power beneath her fingertips and reached out to meet it.

"I wish I could get rid of it," Evaly mumbled.

Harper's hands paused for a moment and then began rubbing again. "I know how you feel."

"I hate not feeling whole anymore." Evaly arched her back as another spike of pain shot down her spine. "I know it's supposed to be a symbiotic relationship. The Hybri and me, coexisting. But I wasn't born like Hybris are supposed to be; I was made." She looked down at her hands, watching them tremble as the creature raged inside of her. The child she had been on Hylon would have been terrified of her. Perhaps her first family would have found her revolting as well. Hylon was steeped in traditions and ancient codes; if she'd been turned into a Hybri there, she might have found herself Outcasted. She shuddered at the thought.

"I'm sorry," Harper murmured. "Maybe it won't always be this way."

Evaly would have laughed if it hadn't hurt so much to do so. Harper's work was helping, but there was still an ache that spread throughout her. This time, though, she recognized it as worry, not her condition. Worry for Fayen. Worry for Lady Kova—as unpleasant as she found the woman at times—perhaps jettisoning off alone. Worry for herself and her friends, blasting towards a destination they didn't know. And worry for her new home among the Arkronens, threatened by the Consortium.

She looked at Pickett, who was perched on the edge of the pilot's seat. Stuffing leaked from one side of it, and looking around, Evaly realized that the cockpit was in a similar state of disrepair. The ceiling lacked plating, exposing the ship's wiring. The walls and floor had dents in them, and the control board wobbled dangerously with the engine's rumble. Pickett had propped his tablet on the controls and steadied it with one hand while he feverishly tapped on it with the other.

"Do we know where we're going yet?" Evaly ventured.

"No," he said. "I'm trying to get into the system . . . but this ship is literally a shell. It's going somewhere, controlled by someone on the other side. I just can't figure out where—but I've been able to track our progress with the star-charts, and . . . well . . . " He trailed off, rubbing the back of his neck.

Harper got to her feet and began plucking at the book-shaped locket she always wore. "We're not aimed for Arkron."

"No," he said. "If we were, the trajectory would have shortened by now. We're headed beyond Arkron . . . beyond any of the planets."

Evaly felt the ache of anxiety surge inside of her. "You mean it's taking us to the *Fringe*?"

Pickett nodded.

Evaly let her head fall back against the wall. "Oh," was all she could whisper. The Fringe was the outer edges of the Exlenna, a strip of empty sea that yawned out into eternity. It was dotted with the occasional spaceport and inhabited by the Outcasts, the nomad vagabonds who lived on ancient starcruisers. Evaly glanced back up at Pickett. "Remember last year, when that group from Ibis went out to study an Outcast crew?"

"The High General still has Accipiters looking for their bodies," he replied grimly.

"Well . . . maybe this transport is going to one of the research stations out there," Harper offered, getting to her feet.

"Perhaps," Pickett said, though Evaly saw the way his hand tightened on the hilt of his sword. "We can hope. But we need to prepare." His eyes skated over her and he turned away, already knowing that she was not the place to look for support.

Evaly huddled into herself again, the familiar sting of shame coursing through her veins.

"I can help," Harper said.

Pickett shook his head and returned to his tablet. "It would be unwise, Harper."

She huffed. "Why? Outcasts aren't politicians! They're not going to try to manipulate Arkron because I grow a tree with some ink!"

"No," he agreed, "but you would likely fetch a high price in their slave market if they discovered your abilities."

Harper's mouth had been open, but at that, she closed it and lowered her head. "Right."

"Fayen would have been a good resource," Pickett muttered. "It's unfortunate that he ended up with Lady Kova."

Evaly gathered her cloak around herself again as a chill swept through her. "We *hope* he ended up with Lady Kova."

"He's strong," Pickett said, hammering away on his tablet. "Wherever he is, he'll be fine."

Harper made a humming sound. "He'll need that strength if he's alone with Lady Kova."

Pickett eyed her, but Evaly allowed a small smile to reshape her frown.

A chime from the ship's controls drew their attention. Pickett leaned forward to study it and then sat back, jaw tight. "We're nearing our destination. We'd best get ready."

Even though her limbs were trembling, Evaly pulled herself to her feet. There would be no Fayen to support her this time. She would have to carry herself. She didn't know if she had the strength for it, but she would try. She had to stay alive to get back to him.

At thirteen, she'd already lost one family. She didn't intend to lose another.

It was the pain that dragged Fayen back to consciousness. He jolted upright and instantly regretted it. Agony ripped through his side, and he cursed, pressing a hand against it. It came away bloody; the initial cauterization of the energy charge was peeling off, and blood seeped through his shirt.

As he had made to leap aboard the ship after Pickett, a charge had taken him in the side. *I should have kept going. I should have jumped aboard anyway.* The sudden burn had dropped him to his knees, and that was all the guardsmen had needed to surround and stun him. *Embarrassing.* It was only an energy charge! He was used to being whacked around in the dojo—that was part of being a good swordsman, after all. You had to learn how to push through the pain.

And yet this had been entirely different. It was like a white-hot drill was lodged beneath his ribs, burning every time he took a breath.

I just have to get used to it. He tipped his head back and tried to regulate his breathing. *Accept that it is there and push past it.* Though they had taken his sword, they hadn't chained him up; he was certain he could finagle his way out of this cell. If only his side would stop throbbing. *Evaly lives with pain like this every day,* he chided himself. *Because of you.*

The thought forced him to his feet. He limped over to the cell door and peered out of the tiny window near its top. It afforded a dismal view: gray walls, low-cut carpet. No guards, at least that he could see. It didn't *look* like a prison—the design reminded him of an office complex. Maybe this was just a temporary place they were holding him in.

He turned and accessed the rest of the room. White cinder walls. A bunk with a thin mattress, covered in a rubber sheet. High windows on the wall across from the door.

Hand clamped over his wound, Fayen dragged himself to stand beneath the windows, craning his neck to look up at them. Could he find a way to climb up to it? Maybe he could break the glass . . .

Tentatively he raised his arms over his head to see how far his fingertips were from the ledge. Pain ripped down his side, and he felt his wound widen. Cursing, he dropped his arms and tried to stanch the flow leaking from it. It was too bad they'd taken his cloak; it would have made a better impromptu bandage.

The door clattered open. He spun about as a medic stepped into the room. The man's eyes widened. "You're on your feet? They said you were injured . . . " He trailed off, catching sight of the bloody stain. He set his bag down on the bunk. "You are, then. Don't worry, I'm here to patch you—"

Fayen bolted past him out the door. He squeezed out just before it shut, startling the guardsman on the other side. "What the Deeps?" he cursed, charging after Fayen. "Didn't you take a charge to the side . . . ?"

Fayen sidestepped his outstretched hands and sprinted down the hall. Desperation made the ache from his wounds fade until it was merely a faint pulse in the background. He would get out of here. Get out and find Evaly. He had made a promise to her, and he intended to uphold it, come Deeps or starless skies.

The accident wouldn't have happened if it hadn't been for him. She wouldn't have been exposed to the Hybri that had thrown her body into chaos . . . she wouldn't have to spend her every waking moment in pain as they wrestled for dominance. He was the strength for her weakness.

He swung around a corner, startling another pair of guardsmen. Beyond them, a glass door was haloed in brilliant sunlight. A keycard console blinked beside it, but it was still a way out. A crazed laugh tore out of Fayen, and he staggered towards it, raising his arms in front of himself. In his combat class at Anaya, he had been taught that hitting a carded door just beside the terminal was occasionally enough to disrupt its signal to the entrance and force it to open. If you could ram it hard enough, of course. Fayen tucked his head down and threw his whole body at the area.

The result was the same as a songbird slamming against a picture window. Instead of going *through* the door like he had intended, he bounced off and landed flat on his back. This knocked the wind out of him, and the pain came roaring back.

Up. Get up. He staggered to his feet, and spun about.

Three guardsmen pointed blasters at him. Behind them, the healer hovered anxiously, fidgeting with his glasses. Fayen snarled at them, noting that each had a keycard dangling from their belts.

He chose his target and lunged towards him.

Their blasters rang again. Fayen kept low, trying to avoid the stun charges, but two of them caught him anyway. Darkness sprawled across his vision, but he shook his head as he grappled the guardsman, trying to snatch his keycard.

More stunners struck him. He slumped to his knees, clutching the keycard, and turned to crawl back to the door.

The next shots found his head and chest, and he crumpled over, his passage to freedom squeezed between his bloody fingers.

"That's definitely an Outcast ship," Harper muttered, planting both hands on the transport's controls so that she could lean into the viewport. Her breath fogged the glass, and she had to scrub away the vapor to see again.

Drifting closer to them over the waves of the Star Sea was a massive starcruiser. Harper judged it to be about the length of a small town and nearly as deep—if, say, a small town were violently uprooted from the topography in one solid slab and lifted vertically into the air. It could have leveled an entire district of Mantalor City by landing.

Fading letters on its stern identified it as *The Star's Ransom*, accompanied by an insignia that looked faintly like the wings of a songbird. Below that was the Outcast symbol, a vivid *O* glyph. In contrast to the name and the ship's personal symbol, this was obviously freshly painted. The Consortium required large Outcast ships to be clearly marked; crews that failed to follow the law were incarcerated and forced into labor. That had been one of the pieces of

Consortium legislation that Lady Kova *had* supported. "It's like marking the place where a bee's nest is," she had said. "That way we can leave each other alone."

"Get back," Pickett said, grabbing Harper by the back of her dress and hauling her away from the viewport.

"Oh, come on," she retorted, slipping back around him to watch once more. "Their scanners have probably already picked us up. We're in a supply ship. I doubt they'll shoot us down."

"You don't know that," he argued, catching her arm and pulling her back around. His gaze slid down to her gown, and he frowned. "Do you have anything you could change into?"

Harper looked down at the garment. Even with the stains at the hem of her skirt from their misadventures and the splotches of oil from tending Evaly, it marked her as highborn. She saw where Pickett was going with his question. "Yes, I packed some other clothes. I'll go change." She swept up her bag and climbed down to the hold—stepping on her skirt several times as she did so.

In the hold, she began wrestling with the dress. The bodice was fitted to her, and usually Lady Kova unfastened the buttons for her at the end of the day. They refused to come loose for Harper. With a soft growl, she yanked at the fabric. Several of the buttons obligingly slipped through their holes, but others tore free with a *pop!* and launched into the recesses of the hold.

"What was that?" Pickett called from above.

"Just me," Harper replied, clutching the fabric of her bodice together and feeling her cheeks flame at her imprudence. Oh, Lady Kova would have a fit.

But she wasn't here.

Lady Kova wasn't here.

The reality of it struck her for the first time. Yes, Pickett was still here to chide Harper in her absence, but somehow he felt like less of a presence than their aunt. He cared about propriety, yes, but perhaps on a different level than Lady Kova. He wouldn't sit on the throne someday. His dreams lay with the Neherum and his honored High General.

Harper was *free*.

Guilt instantly flooded her. She had no idea if Lady Kova was safe, and here she was celebrating her absence. "I am Princess Harper Evensong, the heir to House Evensong," she whispered, trying to catch herself before she spiraled too far into the wondrous possibilities. "And one day, I will take the throne."

Yes, one day she would take the throne. But it would not be *this* day.

As she struggled out of her dress, her power thrummed in her palms. For a change, she did not try to suppress it. She closed her eyes, imagining the feeling in her fingertips exploding across her skin into hundreds of tiny supernovas.

"Uh . . . Harper, you're glowing."

Harper's eyes flew open at the sound of Evaly's voice, and she looked down at her hands. They were the same as they always were, dappled with freckles. She turned towards Evaly, frowning as she lifted her arm to examine her elbow, hoping to find some light there. She had no such luck.

Evaly clung to the ladder, face amused. "It's gone now. But your skin . . . it looked like you were full of stars. *Glittering*."

Saying that she *felt* as though she was made out of stars would probably only confirm her insanity. But Evaly only smiled. "You're amazing."

No, she wasn't, Princess Harper protested. She was a troublesome, foolish creature. Nonetheless, the words made her almost as warm as her power had. "Thanks, Evaly."

"You should probably finish changing, though. If Pickett comes down and finds you lolling about..."

"Right, right." Harper riffled through her bag and pulled out a long-sleeved lace-up shirt and a pair of trousers.

She pulled them on and then stepped back into her shoes. These were low-cut boots; for all of her nattering about presentation, Lady Kova believed in sensible footwear. She finished lacing them just as Pickett slid down the ladder. He didn't use the rungs.

Sure, Mr. Journeyman-Assistant-to-the-High-General could slide down the ladder, but she had to step ladylike on each one and nearly break her leg tripping over her skirt.

"We're being pulled into the main hangar now," Pickett said. "Normally a ship like this would probably dock at a lower hanger, but I'm guessing that once they realized we were aboard, they changed the trajectory so they could properly . . . greet us."

"So we're going to have a welcoming party," Harper replied, picking up her dress and wadding it into a tight bundle. "How nice of them."

"I'm not certain that being greeted with blasters pointed at my head is very 'nice.' Stash that dress somewhere. They'll go through our bags, and that'll be a giveaway."

She looked around and then scrambled over to one of the crates in the far back and pried it open. It was full of what appeared to be bandages; she pushed them aside and shoved her dress down into the depths of the crate, then yanked the lid back over it. Her locket clattered against the side of the box as she did so, and she gripped it in one hand, afraid of it catching and breaking off. It had been a consolation gift from her mother before her move to Mantalor, and she was loath to lose it. Once the crate was secure, she stuffed the necklace down her shirt, where it bounced against her heart.

The transport landed with a bump that set them all off balance. "We're here," Evaly said, wrapping her cloak around herself.

"Well, how do I look?" Harper asked Pickett. "Messy enough to be a refugee?"

He pressed his lips together. "Almost. Can you rat up your hair a bit?"

"With pleasure." She began undoing the braids woven into her hair, ripping her fingers through the weaves so that they had a tangled, half-undone look.

"We're new to the Fringe," Pickett said, turning to face the ramp. "We were Outcasted because of our criminal records, and we're looking for work."

Evaly swiveled amused eyes at him. "Criminal records?"

"*You* can be Outcasted because your people are afraid of you, then."

"That's probably what would have happened to me if my accident had happened while I was still on Hylon," Evaly remarked.

"Good thing you're Arkronen now, then," Harper said, moving to stand next to her. "There used to be Hybri enclaves everywhere." *At least . . . until the Great War, anyway.* No part of Arkron had emerged unscathed after it.

With a hiss, the ramp began to lower. Stale, gaseous air washed over them, carrying the heavy odor of starship exhaust. Pickett straightened his shoulders and marched down the ramp. Harper and Evaly fell in behind him, keeping in a close huddle. Outside, the hangar was a cavernous room painted in mostly gray hues. Small starfighters hung in racks overhead, and behind them was a huge, translucent barrier—an air veil that allowed the room to remain pressurized while giving the ships easy passage into the Star Sea.

They were greeted by a ring of Outcasts encircling the bottom of their ramp. Each one leveled a blaster at them. They all wore the same uniform: a dark blue jumpsuit with a songbird insignia on the breast. The crispness of the outfits surprised Harper; she had always pictured Outcasts as a grimy bunch, dressed in rags or stained clothing. While these uniforms were certainly worn, they were clean and pressed.

Pickett raised his hands in a nonthreatening gesture. "Please," he said meekly, "we mean no harm."

The blasters didn't lower.

"We're refugees," Pickett tried again. "Recently Outcasted. Looking for shelter in exchange for work."

Still there was no movement. The Outcasts kept them pinned, like hunters watching a lightfoot for the perfect time to strike.

Harper frowned. Letting the Outcasts keep her group waiting would only put them in charge of the situation. It was important to play their roles of destitute refugees convincingly, but eventually they'd have to think up a way to escape. And to do that, *they* would need to take the situation in hand.

She stepped out from behind Pickett and put her hands on her hips. "Are you going to tell us what to do or just make us stand here so you can gawk at us?"

She marched down the ramp, avoiding Pickett's arm, which tried to stop her. She stopped in front of the centermost Outcast and thrust her chin forward. "We would like to speak to your superior or whoever is in charge of processing the refugees."

The woman continued to stare ahead as if she hadn't heard Harper's demand. The tip of her blaster lifted slightly, signaling that Harper should step back.

Jaw set, Harper tapped its barrel with a finger. "We are *not* going to stand around forever. Take us to your commander!"

The woman took a step back. Harper dropped her hand, pleased that they were finally getting somewhere.

Then the blaster cracked. The report echoed around the hangar.

Harper wasn't sure if it was the woman who had fired or one of the other Outcasts—all she knew was that she'd been struck squarely in the chest. She staggered backwards, landing on the ramp. She'd been shot. She'd been *shot!* She was surprised by the blackness welling in her vision. Was this shock? She felt herself fall backwards, her head connecting with the ramp so hard that her ears rang. Intermingled with the noise was Evaly's cry of protest, followed by a curse from Pickett. His face swam in her vision. She felt his hand feel her chest and then heard him say distantly, *"It's only a stunner. Silent Star Sea, Harper . . ."*

Then the ship spiraled away, and she plunged into blackness.

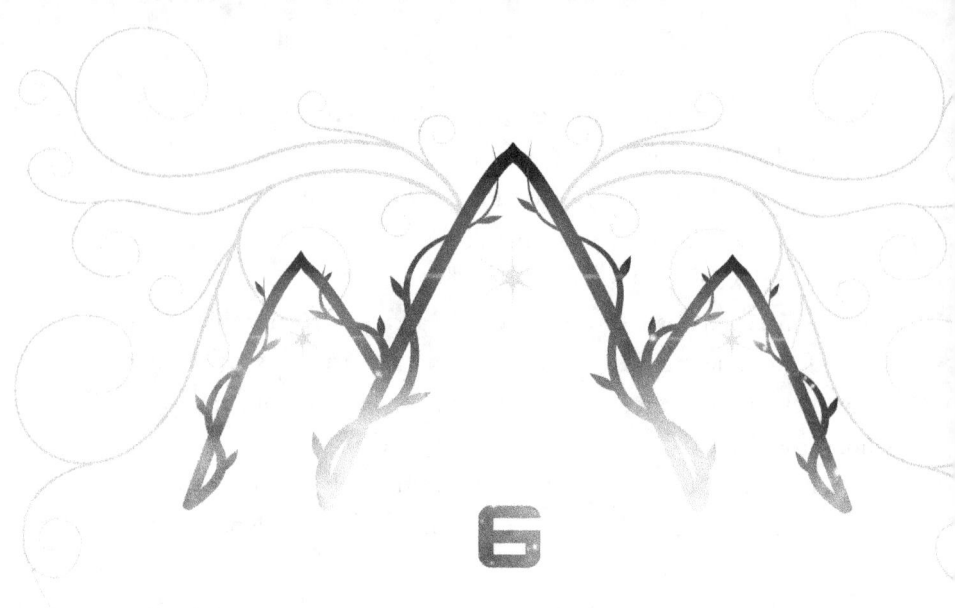

6

Harper would be fine. Pickett was certain. His horror gave way to annoyance as he turned her over, checking for other injuries. She'd have a sore chest and a bump on her head, but otherwise, she'd live. Which was good, because when she woke up, he was going to give her a tongue lashing so severe she was going to wish she was still unconscious.

Looking up, he saw that the Outcasts were parting to make way for a new figure, who had just stepped off the steps from a deck overhead. "Looks like the commander's here," Evaly murmured, kneeling next to him.

"It would appear so," he muttered, and rose to his feet to meet the mistress of the ship. The Outcasts saluted when she stopped at the foot of the ramp, and she gestured for them to stand at ease. Pickett bowed. "Ma'am, we are at your service. I apologize for my sister's behavior."

The commander tipped her head to the side, assessing him. At least, he thought she was assessing him. She wore a smooth mask over her face; it had narrow eyeholes, which were painted to look like wings were blossoming from the corners of her eyes. A curtain of straight, black hair framed the mask, and she reached out with a gleaming prosthetic hand to push it aside. She wore a long-sleeved tunic and trousers, accompanied by leather boots. It wasn't an extravagant uniform, perhaps, but her air made up for her lack of decorum.

She stalked up the ramp to them. Pickett took a step backwards, but she caught up to him. Her flesh hand reached for him and caught his star-tree necklace.

Blast. He had donned a scarf in an attempt to hide it but must not have arranged it well enough to completely obscure it. If he had been wise, he would have taken it off . . . but removing it felt like a violation of his vows to the High General. Even here, masquerading as an Outcast, he was still her journeyman.

The commander spoke at last. "Neherum." He was surprised by how clear her voice was, despite the mask. "It seems that you have already blown your cover."

"On the contrary," he replied, "there was no cover in the first place. I was a Neherum, true, but was recently expelled from the order. The necklace is merely a token from the life I used to lead."

She released the necklace, and her head dipped slightly. "Was the sword a token also?"

Right. Reluctantly, he unbelted it and held it out to her. "Yes. One I hope will be of use to your enterprise, should you agree to shelter us."

She accepted the weapon and passed it off to her crew. "You must have done something quite terrible to be removed from their respected order."

"It was," Evaly piped up. "He was caught makin' out with the High General's daughter."

Pickett whipped towards Evaly, indignation and horror sweeping through him. The High General didn't have a daughter—he knew she had once been married, but her husband was dead, and they had apparently never produced any children. And if she did have a daughter, he wouldn't dream of such a horrendous offense! How had she come up with that? Did Fayen truly joke so much about his "adoration" of the High General?

The commander wasn't paying attention to him, however. The mask had shifted to Evaly, and her metal hand reached out and caught her chin, forcing her to look up so that her yellow eyes gleamed. She held her there, silent for a moment as she looked at the girl and then said, "Your Hybri is a cat, I presume?"

Evaly held steady, though Pickett saw a shudder run through her at the metallic touch. "Yes."

"How large?"

"I don't know. I've never transformed."

"How old are you?" the commander asked, releasing her.

"Thirteen," Evaly replied.

"And you're with him?" she asked, gesturing to Pickett.

"We met on the transport," Evaly replied. "I am Outcasted because of my Hybri."

The commander laced her hands behind her back and stepped away from them. "You will find that we have no such prejudices here." Her head tipped down to Harper, who lay on her side at Pickett's feet. "Brash, isn't she?"

"You don't know the half of it." Pickett sighed. At least that was a truth he didn't have to fabricate. "To be fair, your troops did keep us waiting."

"That is standard procedure here," she replied. "I find that being forced to wait at gunpoint often reveals a lot about a person."

Well. She did make an interesting point. "And yet," Pickett said, "your troops carry stunners instead of blasters. You don't shoot to kill."

"We don't believe in waste in the Fringe," she answered, and turned away from him. "They appear clear enough," she announced to her soldiers. "Search them."

The troops converged around them, splitting into groups to attend to each of them. Pickett tried to keep an eye on the girls, afraid for their safety. Despite the rather formal reception, these people were still, at their core, Outcasts.

After a thorough pat down, the woman who had stunned Harper announced, "Their persons are clean!"

"Search their bags," the commander ordered, sounding almost bored.

The soldiers herded the three of them—with Pickett supporting Harper—to the bottom of the ramp while they rifled through their things. The commander stood in front of them, hands still clasped behind her back. From her stance, Pickett began to wonder if she was missing a leg as well; her figure seemed to list slightly to the side. "What are your names?" she asked.

Evaly glanced at Pickett, seeking guidance. He drew in a breath, prepared to offer fake names. The High General had taught him to keep several memorized for situations like these; that way, he could offer them quickly and avoid arousing suspicion for a delayed response.

But before the words could come out of his mouth, Harper grasped his shirt. She was regaining consciousness, blinking groggily up at him. "Pickett," she mumbled. "My head . . . "

Silent Star Sea. If he tried to give a fake name now, the commander would know he was lying. They would have to take this risk and hope that they'd be off the ship before anyone realized who they were. He gave a curt nod to Evaly and looked back to the commander. "Pickett," he said. He prodded Harper in the side. "This is my sister, Harper."

"And I'm Evaly," the girl added.

The commander's chin tilted up. Pickett frowned, noting the motion. Had his risk been foolish? Had he just given them away? "Do you have surnames?" the commander asked.

"I thought the Fringe was a place of new beginnings," Pickett said. "Do our surnames matter?"

"You will find that the Fringe is rarely like the stories the planet-siders tell about it," she said. "No, I suppose they don't matter—for now. I will warn you, though, that no matter how far you try to run from who you are, it will always find you."

"A statement that is both ominous and comforting," Pickett agreed. He really wished Harper would wake fully; his arm was beginning to ache from supporting her.

The soldiers returned with their bags and tossed them at their feet. "Nothing dangerous, Commander," one of them reported. "Just the regulars."

One of the knots of anxiety inside of Pickett tightened as he remembered Harper's dress. He would have to find a way to completely dispose of it later, before the ship was unloaded. If he couldn't avoid using their real names, at least he could hide that bit of evidence.

"Good." The commander beckoned them off the ramp and into the hangar proper. "Follow me then."

For the first time, Pickett took a good look around. The hangar was a cavernous room, as long and as wide as two city blocks. Racks overhead stored small starfighters, while larger transports docked on the floor. Behind them rippled the large air veil that he had seen earlier, which allowed ships to come and go while maintaining pressure in the hangar itself. There was evidence of wear and tear—the walls and floor were dented and scratched, and some of the lights flickered ominously. Even so, it was apparent that things were orderly and maintained to the best of their abilities.

It was so counter to what he had been raised to think about Outcasts.

The commander noticed his marveling, for she remarked, almost casually, "Expected a sacrifice or some other evil thing to be taking place in the middle of the room, didn't you?"

"Something like that," he admitted. "You don't have the most savory of reputations planetside."

She snorted. "I'm aware. You're lucky that transport was contracted to us. The other enterprises wouldn't have been so friendly."

"Stunning my sister was friendly?"

"She asked for it."

Well, Harper *had*. The commander showed them down a hallway to a small room lined with benches. "Wait here. Someone will bring food, and you'll be assigned quarters. We'll discuss assignments tomorrow." She turned to go, once again combing her hair away from the front of her mask.

"Thank you," Pickett said, depositing Harper onto a bench. "And . . . may I ask *your* name, Commander?"

She hesitated in the doorway. Perhaps she feared that he really was an informant, and so was trying to settle on an alias. Or she was just uncertain.

Finally she said, "Just call me Commander."

It appeared that she liked to be as cloistered with her name as she did her face. "As you wish, Commander," he replied.

She nodded curtly and swept out of the room. As soon as she was gone, Evaly sank down on one of the benches and laid down on her side. "How is Fayen going to find us in the Fringe?"

Pickett sighed. He had been expecting the question from her, but finding Fayen was going to be the least of their worries now. The boy was strong and clever. Pickett was certain that he would find his way to Arkron and they would reunite there. "We're among the Outcasts —and even though these seem like *good* Outcasts, we have to be careful." He gestured to Harper. "Arkron rests on her shoulders. We have to make sure she gets out of here alive."

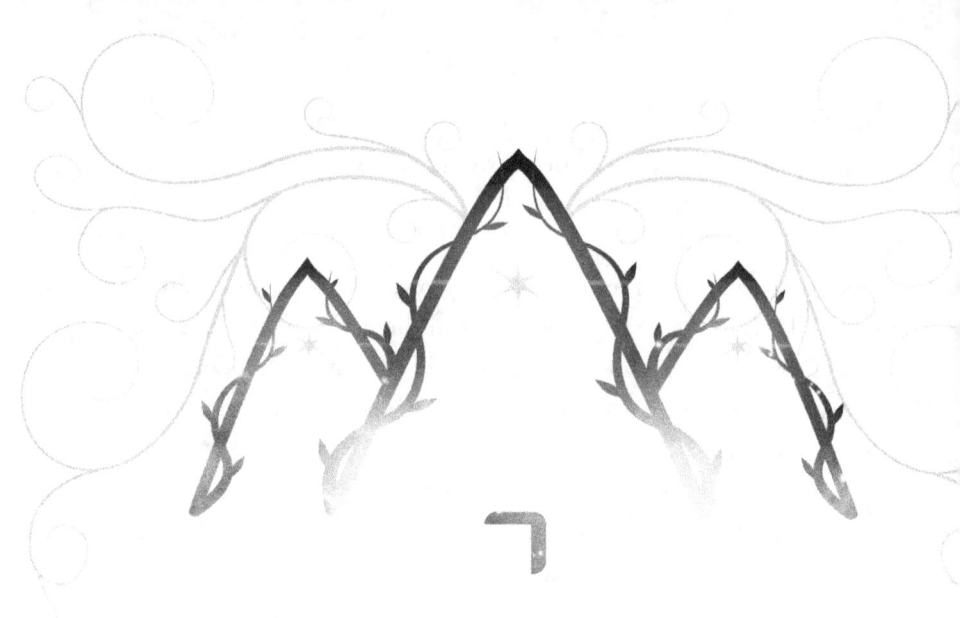

7

"Remind me not to get stunned again," Harper mumbled, squinting at the faint outline of Pickett hovering above her. He was haloed by flickering, overhead lights that made her eyes ache. Her body felt like it was made of water and her thoughts were merely floating on the surface of it. Moons. Getting stunned was *not* fun.

"I'll do my best," he said, drawing back. "But given your nature, I have a feeling that you will continue to find trouble no matter how many admonishments I give you."

She tried to prop herself up on an elbow, but it gave out beneath her and she ended up on her back once more. Stars. Her limbs ached, and whatever hard surface she was lying on was doing nothing to soothe them. "I was trying to help," she grumbled, squinting at him. "Trying to be a forceful leader like you all want me to be."

"I had it under control," he replied. She heard the rustle of clothes as he sat down somewhere near her. "Part of being a good leader is knowing when to delegate tasks, Harper."

She flung a tipsy finger at him. At least, what she *thought* was his general direction. The room was bathed in a whitish sheen. Blast. "I didn't delegate the task to you," she countered. "You just put yourself in charge!"

His hands found her arms and pinned her against whatever it was that she lay on. "Yes, because it's my job right now to protect you," he said, irritated. "And while we're here, you *will* listen to me, do you understand? These people can't know who we are or what it really is that we're running from."

His face was coming into sharper focus, and she could see that his expression was serious. "All right," she whispered. "I will." *At least, I'll try.*

Pickett stared into her face a moment longer and then released her. Harper tried again to sit up and found that her limbs were beginning to obey. Finally she got a good look at the room: It was a boxlike space, with benches set against each of the walls. She was laid out on one of them; across from her, Evaly sat on another, eating something that smelled spicy from a dented bowl.

When she saw Harper was up, she raised her fork in salutation. "Hungry?"

She was, Harper realized. Her last meal had been at Mantalor's parliament building, just before they'd learned of Arkron's condemnation for its refusal to join the coalition. With the attack on the penthouse, their escape, their accidental abandonment of Lady Kova and Fayen, and finally their arrival in the Fringe, she hadn't thought much about her stomach. "Yes," she admitted.

Evaly slid off her bench and carried another bowl to her. It proved to be full of a pungent, orange curry over noodles. Harper gratefully accepted it, but before she thrust her fork into it, she held it towards Pickett. "May I eat, or do you have to clear it for poison first?"

He frowned at her, sensing the note of sarcasm in her voice. "Evaly detected nothing unusual."

"I'm pretty sure it's fine," the girl said. "The spice makes it hard to be certain, but I don't taste anything funny."

"We both ate it, and we're not dead yet," Pickett grunted. "Just eat."

Grateful, Harper coiled the noodles around a fork and scarfed them down. After a few mouthfuls, she waggled her fork at Pickett. "So . . . they're feeding us, and we don't appear to be chained up. I presume we're not prisoners, then?"

"Right," he agreed. "They've bought our story."

Harper fished around in the curry for more noodles. "So. Where do we go from here? We have to get back to Arkron. Or find a way to contact home."

"Evaly and I were discussing that before you awoke," Pickett said, rising to pace between Evaly and Harper's bench. "The fastest way out would be to steal a ship. However, that would also be the most dangerous. We could be caught before we are even out of the hangar, or they could destroy us the moment we fly out."

"Could we buy a ship?" Harper asked.

"We could, but being in possession of so many orbs would make us suspicious."

"So," Evaly said, draining her bowl and setting it aside, "we're aiming for communication instead." She started to wipe her mouth on her sleeve but then winced and dropped her arm as a spasm made it quiver.

"We're going to try and connect to the ship's long-range comms to contact home and request a pickup," Pickett explained.

Harper drank her curry, cringing at the spiciness. "Okay. We can't just use our comms now that we're aboard?"

"No," Pickett said. "Our personal comms aren't designed for sea-to-planet communications. We have to use a device from this ship with a more powerful transmitter."

"Great, so we need to steal a tablet or something."

"Right," Pickett said. "Which is something *I* will handle."

Harper set her bowl down and ran her tongue over her lips. Her mouth felt so hot she wondered if she could breathe fire if she tried really, really hard. Arkron's cuisine listed more on the sweet side of the food spectrum. "Then what am I supposed to do?"

"Play along," he said. "Act like a refugee. Do the tasks they give you—assuming they're not dangerous."

Well, that could be fun. Acting like an Outcast . . . it would be a nice deviation from the tightrope of highborness she walked on Mantalor. Her power thrummed inside of her, already beginning to weave a new story for herself. Harper. Outcast, secret storyweaver. Hesitant to use her powers in the open but pouring them out at night for the benefit of the destitute of the Fringe . . .

Pickett snapped his fingers under her nose, dragging her back into the present. "That look worries me."

Harper looked up at him, unable to hide a smile. "It shouldn't. I'll be good. I promise."

He frowned, disbelieving. Before she had to endure another lecture, however, the door to their room slid aside and an Outcast bounded into the room. She was short; even Evaly was half a head taller than her. Her skin was dark, like that of the people from the planet Joane, and her eyes were a luminous, icy blue, gleaming like stars in her face. Her hair was braided in dozens and dozens of plaits, which faded to cyan tips down her back. They were interspersed with decorative metal wraps. She smiled at them, hugging a tablet to her chest. "I'm Captain Ziah, second to the Commander and in charge of settling sparrows—refugees—like yourself!" she announced.

Pickett stepped forward. "I was under the impression that the Commander herself would be coming back to retrieve us."

Captain Ziah laughed. "Oh, the Commander would like to, but she's the *commander*, after all. She can only be in so many places at once. That's what I'm here for." She opened up her tablet, balancing it on one hand. "I'll issue you IDs and assign you quarters and tasks." She stepped aside to allow another person into the room. He was a medic, Harper guessed by the crimson patch on the shoulder of his jumpsuit. "Before we get to that," Captain Ziah said, "Tuck here is going to make sure that you're not bringing any viruses aboard. Because if you are, that'll mean a detour to the quarantines."

"Understandable," Pickett said. "We'll submit to a physical."

The exams only took a few minutes each, with the medic listening to their breathing, then checking ears and mouth for any sign of infection. It was rather comical to watch him start when he realized Evaly had four ears for him to check instead of just two. Harper clutched the edge of the bench for hers, trying not to think about all the exams Lady Kova had put her through upon her arrival to Mantalor. She was stringent about Harper's health, ensuring that the future queen was in perfect condition. It was a nice change to have a healer turn away with a shrug and say "She's fine," instead of lecturing her on the contents of her shampoo or the kind of toothbrush she used.

It was going to be so, so nice without Lady Kova for a little while, even though her absence worried Harper.

"They're all in good health," the medic announced to Captain Ziah, shouldering his medical bag. "Better than most newbies. They're fine to release."

"Excellent!" Captain Ziah pulled three metal wristbands from her pocket and passed them out. "Here are your IDs. Let me show you around your new home!" She opened the door, inviting them out.

Harper sprang up, shaking Pickett's hand off her shoulder, and followed.

"You'll likely spend most of your time on Level Three or Level Four," Ziah said, leading them to a set of lifts, a short walk down a barren hallway from the waiting room. "It is where the quarters and many of the occupations you'll likely work in are situated."

Level Three was a cavernous room built around a circle cut in the floor. Out of it rose a towering canopy of trees from the level below. Spreading out from the center to where they stood at the lifts was ring upon ring of shops and apartments reaching for the ceiling far above. This was a large screen, programmed to reflect a real sky.

It was as if someone had picked up a little village and transposed it into the heart of the ship. Harper clasped her hands, hugging them to her chest. "Oh, it's amazing!"

"Let me show you to your quarters," Ziah said, beckoning them down the steps from the lifts. "Then we'll discuss occupations."

Harper barely heard her. She was quickly losing herself in their surroundings. There were people everywhere, sweeping leaves from the trees off the front of their shops, loitering in doorways to talk, or walking in groups with shopping baskets. Despite their rugged appearance, they were fascinatingly normal, and Harper wanted to know their stories. Each and every one of them.

That was perhaps the thing that confused her most about being Princess Harper Evensong. Lady Kova—and, by extension, her mother—was training her to be a servant of Arkron. But they often neglected to point out that Arkron was made up of people and their stories. As a princess, she was sheltered from the very people she was supposed to rule. Perhaps if she was permitted to be among them as she was with these people, the trials she suffered under Lady Kova would seem worth it.

"What do you do with the bodies of those who pass here?" Pickett asked, craning his neck to look up at the leafy canopy. "I assume you have no land for burial?"

"Indeed. They are cremated," Captain Ziah replied, "and, depending on their wishes, their ashes are either returned to the Star Sea or pressurized into a stone that is added to our Hall of Memory."

"They're not used as fertilizer for the trees?" Pickett asked.

Harper and Evaly turned to look at him, both speechless. How could he treat something like death so callously?

Pickett shrugged. "Ashes are a good way to keep soil healthy, and organic matter is even better . . ."

"*Pickett!*" Harper hissed. "Show some *respect.*"

"It was a valid question."

Evaly folded her arms. "Does that mean when Harper kills you we should stick *you* in the garden?"

"Might as well put my body to good use. I'm not going to need it anymore."

"Erm . . . right." Captain Ziah looked amused. "I'll make a note of that on your records. We're nearly there." She led them up to one of the apartment spires, the metal wraps in her braids clattering cheerfully together. She stopped beside a spiral staircase and patted it enthusiastically. "This is where you'll be! Fourth floor . . . " She trailed off as a figure emerged from around the steps. "Commander?"

Harper's breath caught at the sight of the woman, and she couldn't tell if she was awestruck or afraid. It was like seeing a story come to life; the very air around her seemed to hush in her presence. She towered over Ziah—she was nearly taller than Pickett, and her masked face tilted downward to look at them. Her hands had been laced behind her back, but when she released them, Harper saw the gleam of prosthetic fingers on her left hand. Oh, this woman had stories. So many of them.

"Commander?" Ziah repeated. "Is something the matter?"

Harper sensed Pickett stiffen beside her. A knot of anxiety tightened within her. Had they been found out already? Had they found her dress, or some other clue? Her hand found Evaly's, prepared to pull the girl after her if they needed to flee. But flee where? Suddenly, the ship no longer seemed like a wonderland—it could become a prison very quickly.

"Nothing is wrong, Captain," the commander replied. "I merely wanted to oversee this group's assignments myself." The mask over her face made it impossible to tell who she was looking at. She rested her metal hand on the railing of the spiral staircase, gripping it gently as if she were anticipating something.

"Of course," Captain Ziah said, still frowning. "I was going to place them in the general probation sectors, but if you had other wishes . . . " She stepped back, inclining her head.

The commander fluttered her flesh hand at them. "Where are you skilled?"

"Administration and communication," Pickett replied instantly. "I studied both with the Neherum . . . "

The commander's mask tipped towards him for a moment and then twisted back to Ziah. "Thinks he's big for his boots. Sanitation."

Pickett began to bluster, but the commander ignored him, turning to Harper. "And you?"

She swallowed hard. Political skills would be of little use here, and, obviously, trying to finagle herself into a higher position would only earn her the lowest. "I am willing to work wherever you need hands, my lady," she said, lowering her head. "However, I do have an affinity for storytelling." Weaver Harper swelled within her, eager for the chance to gorge herself on so many stories. "And some record-keeping skills," she added.

The commander's mask considered her for a moment, and then she said, "You can assist our records team, then."

Excitement erupted inside of Harper. "Thank you," she said, resisting the urge to bounce on the balls of her feet. "I won't let you down, Commander—"

But the woman had already moved on to Evaly. The girl had sunken into her cloak, and Harper could sense her swaying. She'd been overtaxed. Perhaps the commander saw this, for her voice softened. "Are you well, child?"

Evaly sucked in a ragged breath, pulling herself upright. "Yes, Commander. I have no particular area I'm skilled in. I am at your disposal."

"You're only a child. We have a school for those your age."

"No, thank you," Evaly said quickly. "Please, Commander, I would much rather wash dishes or some other chore."

"Perhaps she could help me . . . ?" Harper began, but the commander raised a hand. She fell silent, biting her tongue. Moons, would she be foolish even here? She'd gained a perfect position for a storyweaver; it would be terrible to lose it because she couldn't hold her tongue.

The commander addressed Evaly once more. "Do you have any training with your Hybri?"

"No, Commander."

"In that case, I would like you in the dojo to learn how to use it."

Evaly's lips parted in shock. "I . . . I can't! I don't know—"

"Those are my orders." The commander turned to Ziah. "There are more supply ships due in a few days. I need to make arrangements for them." She looked back at the trio, the empty eyes of her mask boring into them. "Welcome to the *Ransom*. See that you don't disrupt our peace." With long, limping strides, she disappeared between the buildings.

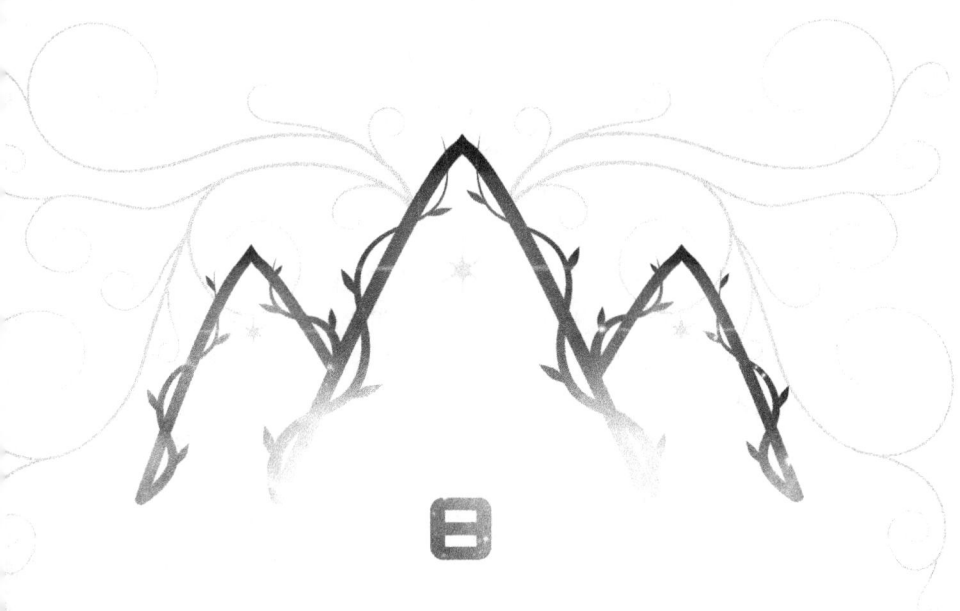

Fayen tried to rub his eyes, but resistance on his wrists wouldn't let him. Groaning, he peeled open his eyes and looked down at his hands. Binders were clasped around his wrists, and these were attached to chains that trailed off the side of the bunk. He grunted and sat up. His bloody shirt had been replaced with a thin hospital smock; from the faint draft blowing against his back, he guessed that it was one that fastened with ties.

He raised his hands experimentally. There was more leeway on his leash than he expected. It was probably just to keep him from bolting out of the room again. It would be a pain for them to have to come in to unfasten him every time he needed the toilet.

He lifted his smock. A bandage was wrapped around his wound. Well, it made sense that they'd want to keep him alive. He rolled off the bunk and stood up, trying to shake the cobwebs from his mind.

This was a new room. It was mostly the same, with a bunk and white walls, but this time there were no windows to the outside. Pity. The door, though, was a white-blue ray field. Well, this was going to be tricky to get out of.

As he was examining this new barrier, two guardsmen appeared in front of it. A young man stood between them, dressed in a white jumpsuit. He appeared to be around Pickett's age—perhaps a little older—with tousled raven hair, blue lips, and violet eyes. *Inerysian*, Fayen thought. The young man also wore a pair of glasses, which he was trying fruitlessly to resettle on his face by scrunching his nose.

"They've brought me to warn you," he began, "that these two will stun you if you try to run out again."

Fayen crossed his arms, ignoring how it made his side twinge. "What if I try anyway?"

One of the guardsmen shoved the young man's sleeve up, revealing ugly welts. They looked fresh.

"Then they beat you," he replied, grim.

They beat you if they can catch you, Fayen thought. But he pressed his lips together and nodded. Obviously they were planning to take him *somewhere* if they had dragged a fellow prisoner up to give him a warning. He would let them think he was compliant—and then he would be *gone*.

One of the guardsmen tapped a control on his bracer. The binders around Fayen's wrists fell away with a soft hum. The translucent shield came next. He took a step forward, holding his hands crossed in front of him obligingly. One guardsman stepped forward, reaching for him, but Fayen pounced. He used his crossed arms to shove into the man, knocking him backwards.

"No!" the other prisoner cried after him. "Oh no . . ."

He burst into the center of a stark room. It was mostly bare, save for the windows overhead, letting in shafts of light. In the center of the room was a cluster of small tables, which sat empty. A pair of double doors stood adjacent to his cell. He flew for them, wrestling with the handles. The guardsmen must have come in this way, and if he could just get the door open—

The handle remained stubbornly stuck. A hand clamped down on his shoulder and dragged him back, then threw him against the wall. One of the guardsmen loomed over him. Fayen could see his own reflection in the bug-like eye-shields of the mask. His face was flushed, but his jaw was clenched.

The guardsman clutched an electrified baton in his free hand. "You were warned," he snarled, and brought it down against Fayen's stomach. He gasped but bit back the cry of pain. He wouldn't give them the satisfaction. Still, his body curled instinctively around the injury. The guardsman kicked him over and rained down blows on his back. Without the protection of a complete shirt, his bare skin took the brunt of the assault.

Fayen bit his lip so hard he tasted blood. *Don't make a sound. Don't let them see you break.* It would end eventually; they had treated his previous wound, which meant that they didn't want him dead. At least, not yet.

Finally the blows stopped. The guardsman stepped back, panting.

Fayen raised his head, blinking stars from his eyes, and offered a faint smile.

The guardsman punched him in the jaw, right where he had taken the earlier hit from his classmate. The enhanced gauntlets the guardsmen wore meant that the blow was much more savage. Fayen felt his head connect with the metal wall, spirals of color erupting before his eyes. He heard the sharp tones of the guardsmen and then something thudding shut, rattling the wall beside him.

Footsteps hurried towards him, and he opened his eyes to find the Inerysian crouching beside him. "I told you not to run!"

"That wasn't a stunner," he grunted, pushing himself into a sitting position.

He sat back on his heels, shaking his head. "No. I suppose they wanted to teach you a lesson." He caught Fayen's chin, forcing him to look up so that he could see his jaw. "This needs ice. Give me your shirt."

"What?"

He waggled his fingers impatiently. "I need something to wrap the ice in. They'll give you a jumpsuit soon, don't worry."

"I don't need help," Fayen said, climbing to his feet. "It's not that bad." The motion caused his back to scream in pain; the world tilted around him, and the next thing he knew, he was slumped on the other prisoner's shoulder, trying to blink the stars from his eyes.

"Right," he said, rolling his eyes. "Come on . . . " He dragged him to one of the circular tables in the center of the room and plopped him into a chair. He pulled off Fayen's smock and carried it over to a water dispenser fixed in the wall. After bullying a few ice cubes from it, he wrapped them in a corner of the smock and carried it back to Fayen. "Keep it on your jaw. It would be a pity for it to swell so much that you're not able to insult the guardsmen the next time they come. I'm Colten, by the way."

"Fayen," he replied. "Did the Consortium kidnap you too?"

He nodded, settling into the chair beside him. "It's obviously politically motivated. My grandmother is the Grand Chieftess of the Gathered Islands. With me as a bargaining tool . . . " He lowered his eyes, face worried.

Reluctantly Fayen pressed the ice to his jaw. He didn't *want* to need help. He was stronger than this. He'd trained himself to be for Evaly. Silent Star Sea. He had to get back to her. She had to be so frightened out there alone—and who was helping her with her medicines? Surely Harper would remember, but her thoughts were so often full of political problems and stories clamoring for her attention. Would Pickett remember? *She's my responsibility. She's only thirteen. She shouldn't have to bear the weight of her sickness alone.*

The coolness of the ice did soothe the ache. "Unfortunately for the Consortium, I'm just the son of a lady-in-waiting. I'm not worth too much."

"They might disagree," Colten said, reaching out to adjust the position of the ice on his face.

He grunted, eyeing the windows overhead. How thick was the glass? Were there alarms wired on the outside of it? Was there a way he could get up to them? "Well, if they do, I'm not going to be here to see it."

9

THOUGHTS OF HER royal self faded into a pinprick inside of Harper as she sat on the steps of their quarters. It was high enough that she could gaze over the majority of the rooftops, but low enough that Pickett wasn't worried about getting trapped should they need to make a quick exit. On the walkways below, the hum of conversation hovered in the air like the whine of cicadas in the summer on Arkron. Overhead, the "sky" was fading into a ruddy red. There was no makeshift sun. Perhaps the commander thought that the sight of it would only remind people that they were trapped here, unable to breathe fresh air or feel real grass beneath their feet.

A day had passed since their arrival on the *Ransom*. They had spent it in orientation; Harper had hoped that they would jump straight into their vocations, but Captain Ziah had ordered a more thorough tour for them.

Pickett had been pleased. "It's good to get a lay of the ship," he insisted over dinner. "In case we can't steal a tablet and request a pickup, we may need to consider alternate methods of getting home."

Harper flexed her fingers and opened her palm. She began twisting the fingers of her other hand atop it as she started to pull the tale into Being. It would be easier to do this with a pen, but Pickett had commandeered hers. She wasn't certain if it had been a way to keep her in check or if he had genuinely needed it for something.

No matter. Storyweavers had functioned without pens for Ages. A pale mist appeared between her hands as she whispered to herself, "*Once, there was a land without a sun, moon, or stars . . . When it was day, light bled into the sky, and when it was night, it bled out. The people of the world accepted it as fact, except for one little girl. She was determined to find the source of their light. So she set off on a journey, chasing the light as it seeped from the sky at night . . .* " The mist began to solidify as she selected a shard of the story and poured a bit of herself into it, making it real. Her chest throbbed, sending weariness pulsing through her. A small, glowing ball of a light fell into her hand. A sun, from the story.

A hand dropped onto her shoulder. Harper snipped off the weaving and fisted her fingers over the ball, hiding it. "Pickett, I—"

Evaly sat down beside her, shifting her cloak so that it draped around her like the folds of a magnificent gown. "Should you be doing that out in the open?" There was no reprimand in her voice, just an honest question. Her tone was a welcome relief from Pickett's admonishments. Evaly understood better than anyone what it was to have *something* inside of her fighting for control.

Harper sighed, squeezing the miniature sun in her hand. "No. It's not safe. But it just . . . slipped out. I don't have to be the princess here. I can be the storyweaver." She tilted her head towards the darkening screen. "This place is intoxicating. *So many stories. So many ideas I could draw from.*"

Evaly rested a hand on her knee. "I can feel it when you shift between them."

"You can?"

"Yes," Evaly said, blinking owlishly at the walkway below as a particularly rowdy bunch of Outcasts swaggered by. "I can't tell if it's a smell or something else . . . I don't understand my Hybri. But there's a difference. Like opening one book and smelling the pages, and then opening another and smelling a slightly different scent. Do you know what I mean?"

"I do," Harper said, rolling the glowing sun around in her hand. She wasn't certain how to explain that there were two Harpers living inside her body. Demure Princess Harper, who obeyed every order and squeezed herself into the tight garb of royalty, and Weaver Harper, who had perpetually messy hair and wasn't afraid to raise her voice. "When I was little, they somehow coexisted," she remarked. "But when I had to start my training on Mantalor . . . when I had to become the future queen . . . it's like a fissure opened, and then became a chasm. I don't know how much longer I can keep leaping between them." She squeezed the little ball again, and it shattered. "Sooner or later, I'm going to have to pick one or the other. I know the right choice will be being a princess . . . But I must have story-weaving powers for a reason, otherwise the Creator wouldn't have empowered me."

Evaly's feline ears pricked towards the glittering splinters, which dissolved into mist, then lay back against her head. "The ways of the Creator are a mystery." She pulled her cloak tighter around herself. "I wish you could use your power to get us back to Arkron. To Fayen."

"Me too," Harper said, drumming her fingers on her leg. "I mean . . . theoretically, I could do something . . . "

"Harper, Evaly." Pickett appeared in the doorway. "Come inside." His expression told Harper that he had overheard their conversation, and a flash of annoyance rippled through her. How long had he been eavesdropping?

Evaly sighed, then mimicked Pickett's stern expression. "We'd better do as he says." Together, they entered the small apartment. It consisted of a common room, a bunkroom, and a narrow washroom. The walls were bare, save for a few scribbles and stains from the previous occupant. "I'm going to bed," Evaly said, turning towards the bunkroom. "I have to report to the dojo tomorrow." She shuddered, her ears going flat against her head. "Sound night."

"Tomorrow is one more day closer to Fayen," Harper reminded her.

Evaly's ears did perk at that. "Yeah," she said, offering a wan smile over her shoulder. Then she disappeared into the bunkroom.

Harper found herself wishing the promise brought her comfort too. Of course she wanted Fayen back. Regaining him meant going home, however. And she wasn't sure she was ready to do that. She missed Arkron desperately, but it was the Arkron of her childhood she yearned for. The Arkron that was wind and water and bark under her fingernails and stories beneath river stones. That Arkron had been lost the day she'd jettisoned off to Mantalor.

"I hope I didn't overhear you plotting to weave something." Seated at the small table in the common room, Pickett arched an eyebrow at her. Papers were littered across the table, and he was feverishly working away at them, making notes and scribbling out paragraphs.

"No." Harper walked over to him and peered at the pages. They were all embossed in the corner with the spreading star-tree of the Neherum. "You brought work with you?"

"Did you think I was just going to loaf around the whole time?" he demanded, signing his name on one of the reports and turning it over to work on the next one.

She sat down beside him. "I'm surprised the word *loafing* is in your vocabulary, because you don't know how to do it. But . . . work for the High General? How did you even sneak those in?"

"There are special pockets in my bag," he grunted. "It's not like I can go out and steal a tablet right now. So I might as well get these done." He set the pen down. "I've been thinking; the Commander mentioned that there were more supply ships coming in a few days. If we can't steal a tablet, getting on one of those might be our next best option to getting out of here."

Harper shrugged, glad that the ships weren't due for another few days. She wasn't ready to leave just yet.

Pickett picked up the pen again, glancing at her. "Did you want something?"

"Do I have to want something to sit with you?" she asked.

"Well . . . I suppose not." Her presence seemed to make him uncomfortable. Hesitantly, she lowered her head onto his shoulder. They had been close as children. Before he had gone to Mantalor to train with the Neherum. It was tradition within House Evensong for the firstborn, if male, to study with the order. It gave them valuable administrative and defense skills that became useful when they became the advisor-bodyguard of their younger sister, who would rule.

But that tradition had driven a wedge between them. Pickett flinched at her touch. He seemed like a stranger now, another guard assigned to her by Lady Kova. "Maybe I just wanted to be an annoying little sister," she said, lifting her head again.

He huffed. "Well congratulations, then, you've accomplished that very quickly. I'm busy. Don't you need to do a skincare routine or something? Lady Kova would be furious if I let you undo all her hard work."

Harper traced a finger over her freckled cheeks. "I liked the way I was before. I know I was . . . feral . . . but I was a *part* of Arkron. I had her skin beneath my fingernails and her breath in my lungs, and now . . . I'm Princess Harper. Poised and perfect and *not* a part of Arkron."

Pickett shuffled his papers. "It's just because you've been gone for so long. I'm sure you'll feel differently once we're home."

She looked down at her hands. Her fingernails were manicured to perfect ovals and painted with a clear polish to make them shine. She turned them over, feeling her power thrum in her palms. "Will I?"

He shrugged. "You're probably just maturing as a leader. Feeling separated from your people is a part of it because you *are* separate from them. You can't lead a planet from a cottage or a shop in Jana. You have to be out in the eye of the Exlenna, representing them."

"But that doesn't seem *right*."

He bent over his work again. "No, it probably doesn't. There'll always be a disconnect. That's just how monarchies are. Once you accept that, you can better reach the people who can then reach the people below them, and so on, until everyone has their needs met." He sounded as though he were quoting from a textbook—which, Pickett being Pickett, he probably was. "It's a power structure," he continued, "and, when maintained in a healthy way, leads to a smoothly running queendom."

She stared at the back of his head, trying to fit her brain around that. It made sense, yes . . . but at the same time, wasn't it more impactful if she wasn't afraid to meet their people at their level?

Her power hummed again, and she pressed her hands against her chest, unconsciously trying to quiet it as Princess Harper lapped at his words. Her gift made her such a danger to herself and Arkron. Why? Why had the Creator made her like this, with the constant tension?

Pickett looked back at her again. "Did all of that just go over your head?"

"No," she whispered. "It's just intimidating me. I wish you had been the firstborn daughter. You're good at this kind of thing, and I'm . . . just . . . me. I wasn't made for these things."

Pickett sighed and straightened. He took his time stacking up his papers, quoting the *Accords of Arkron* as he did so: "'And Arkron's ruler shall be a woman, the firstborn daughter of the queen, because she was created first to be a mother, and a mother's calling is to protect and nurture her children. So Arkron's queen shall protect and nurture this world as if it were her own child.'" He tucked his reports away and turned towards her. "You were the firstborn daughter of House Evensong. Therefore, you *were* made for this."

She clenched her jaw, willing the tears welling in her eyes not to spill over. His voice was so unconcerned. To him, it was a simple matter. And perhaps it should be to her, but no matter how much she wrestled with it, it refused to shrink into something she could tidily pack away in the back of her mind.

Pickett made a frustrated sound in his throat. "Are you upset?"

"No."

"That was the most unconvincing *no* I've ever heard, and the High General has been training me in interrogation." He rubbed the back of his neck in frustration. "What do you *really* want?"

"I told you," she said, crossing her arms and getting to her feet. "To be an annoying little sister. Not your princess or your future queen. But I see that those things are inseparable to you. Good night, Pickett." And she slipped into the bunkroom, leaving him alone at the table.

10

THE *RANSOM'S* RUMBLE amplified the ache in Evaly's bones. It kept her awake all through the night, like the thrum of someone's too-loud speaker, and in the morning it echoed hollowly through her stomach, making her too nauseated to eat. She missed Anaya's tranquil halls and quiet rooms—and most of all, Fayen's steady presence beside her.

Especially now that she had to face the monster living within her.

The *Ransom's* dojo was dismal compared to the ones she was used to at Anaya. It was a large room, outfitted with mats—many of which were leaking stuffing—and other dilapidated equipment. There were no windows, and many of the overhead lights were burnt out. It was eerily dark in contrast to Anaya's pristine rooms. The windows there were covered in rice paper because the instructors believed that they were a distraction. However, they still let the daylight in. And the mats were always clean and properly arranged.

It's unfair to compare that to this, Evaly told herself, drawing her cloak tighter around her shoulders. *This is all they have.*

She was alone in the room. Perhaps the commander had ordered it set aside for her training. But how was she supposed to train? She'd spent the last three years suppressing her Hybri. And now she was supposed to just... let it out?

The door to the dojo banged open, and Captain Ziah bustled into the room. "Ah, good! You're already here."

"Are you training me?" Evaly asked, staring at her dubiously.

"Yep!" Ziah unzipped her jacket and removed her shoes, leaving her in nothing but a pair of leggings and an athletic shirt. "You can leave your things on the bench."

Evaly obeyed, slowly removing her cloak and shoes and arranging them beside Ziah's things. "What do you know about Hybris?"

The woman winked. "More than you probably expect." Then she vanished, her form flickering away.

Evaly shied backwards, eyes searching the air for some hint as to where the woman had gone. Perhaps she was hallucinating. She had before, right after the Hybri had entered her...

There was a light tap on her shoulder, and Ziah reappeared beside her. "I'm a Hybri too."

"I wouldn't have known," Evaly said, trying to soothe herself by hugging herself tightly. "You don't have any external characteristics."

"Most Hybri don't." Ziah strolled onto the mat before them, stretching. "You should warm up," she said, rolling her shoulders. She sank into a low *kata*, breathing deeply as she moved through the motions.

I'm not most Hybri, Evaly thought. "I'd rather not wear myself out before we even start," she replied.

Ziah cocked an eyebrow at her. "You've truly had *no* training."

"I've had some swordsmanship training."

Ziah straightened and shook out her arms. "That's not the same thing." Her eyes flicked towards something over Evaly's shoulder. Evaly glanced behind her as her ears picked up the sound of the door sliding open and closed. Her eyes met the commander's faceless mask. The woman sat down on the bench beside their things, silently watching. Evaly's skin prickled. She knew this was a test of sorts—the question was, would she purposefully fail it, or would she strive to learn something? Which would be more dangerous? She wished Fayen were here. He would know what she should do.

Perhaps he would have her stall. Evaly stepped onto the mat and cocked her head towards the commander. "Does she always wear a mask?"

"The Commander does what she thinks is best," Ziah replied, sweeping into another stretch, "and follows the recommendation of the ship."

Evaly planted her feet on the mat, feeling the ship vibrate up her legs and into her core. "Is the *Ransom* alive?"

Captain Ziah grinned. "Of course it's alive. How else would it have lasted so long in the Star Sea? She is our mother. A good, kind lady that shelters us. And Ja—the Commander is her mouthpiece."

Evaly noted the slip-up. It also seemed unusual for Ziah to speak of her commander so formally. Which, perhaps, was to be expected; if she was second-in-command, she was likely more intimately acquainted with her. Still. Something rubbed Evaly the wrong way, a sense that something wasn't right. Or perhaps not even that. She didn't sense any danger . . . more like there was something she wasn't being told.

Before she could try to weasel more information from Ziah, the woman flickered and disappeared. Oh, moons. Evaly had been expecting a lengthy lecture on how to invite the monster inside of her to come out, not a sparring match. She crouched, tracking, listening hard for her footsteps. And then ducked into a roll, avoiding a light kick.

Ziah rematerialized, frowning. "Are you going to transform?"

Evaly straightened and shook her head. "Isn't this enough?"

"Well, it would be easier to train you if I could see your shape. Do you have a shape?"

"I don't know."

Ziah folded her arms. "Have you ever transformed before? Even partially?"

"Look at me! I'm *stuck* in a partial transformation!" She turned away, trying to draw in deep breaths to calm herself and quell the anger twisting inside of her.

Ziah huffed. "Listen, kid. You can sit here and bemoan what happened to you, or you can stand up and learn how to use it. Who knows? Your accident might end up being a blessing you didn't know it had the capacity to be because you were too busy disparaging it. But you're not going to find out unless you *get up and fight for it*. If you want to utilize it effectively, you need to learn how to make peace with it. You are a team. Together, you can be strong."

Strong, like Fayen. Strong, like Ziah and her Hybri. What if she *could* learn to harness the creature inside of her, if only for a short time? Could it help them get home sooner? Back to Fayen? If it could, then perhaps it would be worth the discomfort of trying. She looked back to Ziah and nodded curtly.

The woman smiled. "Good. Usually a fight is the best thing to draw it out, since it forces you to think in the moment." And then she threw a punch at Evaly.

Evaly ducked. *I should have seen that coming.* She could sense that Ziah was restraining herself . . . but at the same time, even a light punch from an adult was going to leave a mark. She tried to reach for her Hybri, which was buried deep inside of her.

It recoiled at her attention and shrank away. *No, I actually need you this time . . . Come on . . .*

She snatched at it as Ziah scored a light hit on her shoulder. The blow made her crumple to the mat. Fresh aches exploded all over her body, but she pushed them away and got back up. *Come on,* she pleaded as her Hybri scrambled away, deeper within her.

"Focus on it," Ziah's voice said from somewhere around her. She was camouflaged again. "Welcome it. It wants to keep you alive. It wants to help you. You are one."

Welcome it? She despised it. It was an invader that her body was trying to reject as if it were a parasite or an illness. But it wasn't; it was a being in and of itself that she was *supposed* to get along with. It took over her senses when it wanted to take in the world, and shrank deep inside of her when she cursed it aloud. Evaly spun around, trying to pin down where Ziah's next punch would fall, all the while urging herself to transform.

The blows found her in the back in sharp succession. She fell face first onto the padding. And this time, her limbs went rigid. Apparently her Hybri had finally decided to make an appearance. It felt like she was being turned inside out. Every nerve was on fire. Her muscles were splitting, her joints popping out of place . . . Someone was screaming, and it took her a moment to realize that it was her own voice.

"Ziah, get a medic." The masked face of the commander appeared above her, hand on Evaly's shoulder. "She's shaking." She leaned closer, pushing Evaly's hair out of her face. "Evaly, can you hear me? It's okay. You're okay."

The cool of her prosthetic against her cheek drew Evaly back into the present. Her Hybri shriveled back inside of her, leaving her listless on the mats. "Can you breathe all right?" the commander asked, draping Evaly's cloak around her, tucking it in like a blanket.

"I'm not supposed to be like this," Evaly whispered. "I wasn't born Hybri. I'm an accident."

The commander's hand tightened on her shoulder. "I have come to learn that there are no such things as accidents."

Evaly squeezed her eyes shut. If that were true, then it had been the Creator's cruelty that had killed her first family and left her crippled like this. "I don't want this," she said. "Why are you making me do this?"

The commander was quiet for a moment. She loosened her grip on Evaly's shoulder, though her hand lingered there, as if she were trying to offer some sort of feeble comfort. Finally, she asked softly,

"Is it impossible to believe that the Creator might have a plan for this? That there might be something good on the other side of this struggle?"

Evaly wanted to shout *yes*; struggle was all she had known for the last three years. There was no other side to it! But she had no strength to do so and curled up in response, her back to the masked commander.

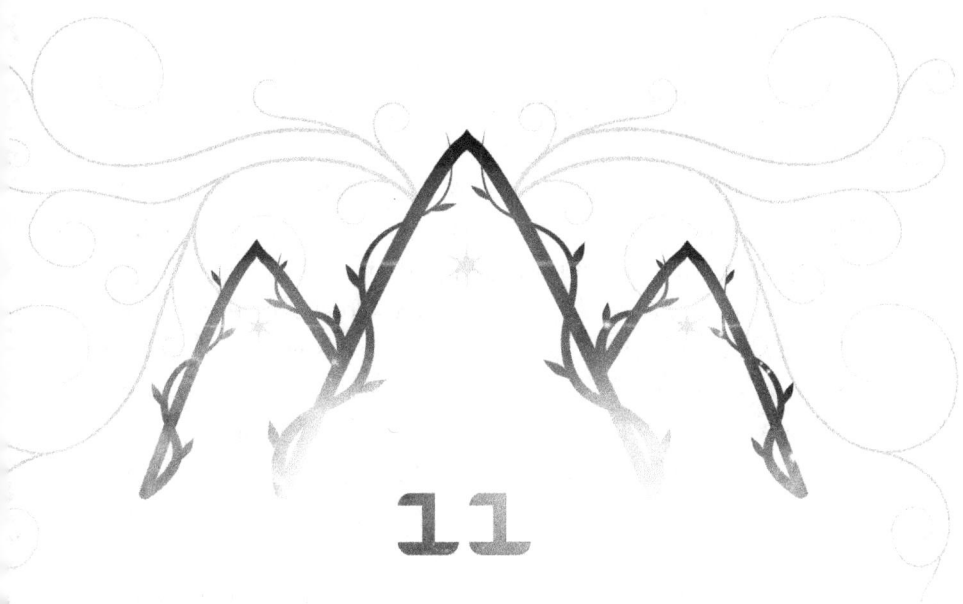

11

The aspect of the *Ransom* that irked Princess Harper the most was the water conservation. Showers were strictly rationed, and she was going on day four without one. Her long mane had grown even wilder, and she had taken to wearing a kerchief over her head to hide its greasy roots. After years of a strict beauty regimen to maintain her appearance, it felt wrong to let herself go to seed like this.

Her rugged appearance only further unleashed Weaver Harper. It was nearing lunch on their third day aboard, and Harper nibbled on her allotted biscuit as she trotted away from the *Ransom's* seeding rooms on Level Four. She'd been sent to interview a gardener about some missing information in his files and now had his story safely tucked into a folder under her arm.

Evaly and Pickett had long since dispersed to their separate tasks—Evaly to the dojo again and Pickett to the work crew he had been assigned. He was still hoping that he would be permitted to work on the bridge. Harper didn't have the heart to tell him that he probably wasn't going to be accepted. They were too new. He was too . . . pompous. The Outcasts—at least the ones on the *Ransom*—were more sensible than half the people in the Consortium. The commander had seen through his hubris straight away.

Her path back to the lifts passed the door to the great conservatory. Each breath on this level was like inhaling through damp linen; it was purposefully humid to help the plants. Through the glass doors, she could see tendrils of green and splotches of vibrant colors. It reminded her of the garden that House Evensong kept in the center of Solstice, their main home in northern Arkron. Her mother, Queen Anrameta, kept flowers from all over the Exlenna within it.

Harper paused. Her superiors in the records room hadn't given her a time to be back. What if she took a quick detour? She stepped up to the glass door and tugged on it.

It was sealed shut, locked. There was a scanner affixed near the handle; she tried swiping her ID bracelet beneath it but to no avail. She was barred from the lush world beyond.

"What are you doing?" A harsh voice made her wheel about. It was an Outcast dressed in a pilot's jumpsuit with armor over top. He held no weapon, but his fingers drifted close to the butt of his holstered blaster. Was he guarding the garden?

Harper jumped away from the door. "My apologies. I was merely curious if the garden was open or not."

"You have to have special clearance to enter," he replied, still watching her with narrowed eyes. "Resources are precious. We can't afford to have people mooching off of it."

Mooching? Harper scowled. She wasn't *that* hungry yet. "How do you get clearance?" she demanded.

"By saying *please*."

The Outcast stiffened to attention and saluted. "Commander!"

Harper turned to see the woman limping towards her. As always, she wore her mask, though today her hair was twisted into a pretty braided crown. Harper offered a salute too, unsure of how to greet the woman. She was technically under the woman's command now . . .

"You don't have to salute," the commander said. "You're not in the military."

Harper dropped her arm, blushing, and began to offer the Arkronen gesture of respect instead. However, she froze halfway through it, remembering with a spike of horror that she wasn't supposed to be using it. *Silent Star Sea, I'm an idiot.* She straightened from the motion, hoping that it had been distorted enough that it wasn't recognizable as Arkronen. The commander's veiled face lingered on her for a moment longer, as if she was regarding her with a raised eyebrow, and then it tilted towards the other Outcast. "Let her in."

"But Commander—"

"I will accompany her." She rested her hand on the door, and it slid aside without the aid of a code or a keycard.

Moons. How had she done that? Harper was too busy drinking in the sweet garden air to contemplate it too long. It was as warm and welcome as the breath of a loved one against her during an embrace. "Why don't you allow people in here?" Harper asked.

"We used to," the commander replied, setting off down one of the angling paths. The room was nearly as large as the Level Three above it, though it bore more of a hexagonal shape. Raised beds contained a variety of vegetables, herbs, and berries. Towards the center of the room, the crops gave way to shrubs, flowers, and the makeshift grove of trees. "It's been a lean year, and unfortunately that usually induces a spree of thieving," the commander explained. "I hope that soon we will be able to reopen it to the entire crew again. Being able to walk under the trees is . . . cathartic, I think."

Harper thought of the sweeping forests back home and nodded. "When I was little, I used to be a great tree climber. My mother called me a little *cubra* because I would go so high and never want to come down. Your problems always seem smaller from the top of a tree."

"Or the bottom, looking up," the commander agreed. "What's a *cubra*?"

Right. They didn't have wildlife in the Fringe. Must less Arkronen wildlife. "Um . . . it's furry," Harper said, trawling through her list of possible descriptions. "With short legs and claws. And a round snout."

"Like a dog?" the commander asked, pointing out a root before Harper could trip over it. In the absence of soil to burrow into, the roots of the trees spread out across the floor under the thin layer of dirt, like a snarl of veins across an old woman's hand.

"Much bigger than a dog," Harper replied. Blast. What was the Common Tone word for it? "It sleeps through the winter and eats berries. And lightfoot meat . . . "

"Sounds like a bear from my homeworld."

"Yes!" Harper cried. "It's like a bear." She tipped her head back to look at the tangle of branches overhead. The railing that encircled the trunks was visible through the leaves. Though this space did its best to mimic a lush glade, it was impossible to escape the artificiality of it. The vegetable beds were too orderly. The tree branches were pruned to keep them from growing into the wall. It reminded her of the manicured parks she had visited in Mantalor City.

I miss Arkron. It was an admission that both Princess and Weaver Harper agreed on. The Fringe was robust with the opportunity to be free of the pressures House Evensong placed on her. Yet no matter how hard she tried to weave herself a new story here, without Arkron and without Princess Harper, it simply wouldn't stick. She had been made for the whispering grasses, dark forests, and jagged peaks of her homeworld. She was like the plants wilting in the flowerbeds; she could grow, but her roots would be weak.

She would have to go home sometime and face who she was supposed to be. *But not this very moment,* Weaver Harper interjected, urging her to take out her notebook and kneel down to capture the patterns in the bark of the tree. Happy to oblige, Harper squatted in front of the trunk and set to scribbling away as fast as her hand would let her, translating the bark into words that she could use later.

It was such a bother that her fingers moved slower than her brain! There was so much she wanted to put down but not enough time to do it, thanks to her blasted humanity.

The commander brushed a few leaves off a large, raised root—there were many of them, serving as makeshift benches, Harper noticed—and sat down. She groaned softly as she did so and rubbed her left thigh. Perhaps her prosthetics caused her pain. "You're from one of the forested planets, then?" she said. "But not Inerys, obviously. You don't have their hair or eyes."

"Erm . . . sort of," Harper replied distractedly. She shook out her hand; her fingers were beginning to cramp from writing so quickly. "There's a pretty balanced topography." She scrambled over several of the roots to get a picture of the tree as a whole. "What about you? Lots of trees where you were from? Or were you born here?"

The commander was silent for a moment. Harper's gaze trailed from the tree to her masked face. It must be nice to be able to hide behind a decorative plate like that, leaving people to guess who was behind it. A stalwart commander? A gentle friend? The stories people told themselves about her seemed to give her a certain power over them.

"I don't like to think about my homeworld," the commander finally said.

So she was a planetsider by birth. "Oh." Harper perched herself on the root across from her, wobbling precariously. "Do you wear that mask because of your injuries or because it helps you maintain your grip on the ship?"

"I . . . What?"

Harper waved her pen at her. "I'm trying to figure out your story, Commander. The mask makes it difficult, but I like a challenge."

"A challenge," the commander repeated. "Have you considered that some people might take offense at their stories being seen as a challenge?"

"I . . ." No, she hadn't. Stories were meant to be shared, weren't they? But . . . what if someone didn't want to share theirs? Were they entitled to their silence?

"Why are you so enamored with stories?" the commander demanded, grabbing Harper's wrist and forcing her hand upward. Her masked face leaned close, inspecting Harper's fingers, then her palm, and her metal finger brushed over it, as if searching for something. "You're a storyweaver, aren't you?" Her grip became painful. "Not just the kind that huddles over a tablet drinking caf and writing sappy novels. You're an *empowered* one. You can bring things to life by telling a story about them, but you need other stories to draw from. Though doing large weavings probably wears you out, right?"

Could she tell that just from touching her? Moons, what was she supposed to say? Princess Harper would deny it. Weaver Harper would embrace it. Harper remained silent as her two halves warred.

"I'm not the only one that wears a mask," the commander finally said, releasing Harper's hand. "It would seem that mine is more secure than yours."

Harper gripped the wrist the commander had just released, rubbing the sore skin. "How did you do that?"

"I can hear things most people can't," the commander replied. "My reasons for wearing the mask are my own. Make up whatever story you want about me. *I* know who I am." She stood suddenly as the Outcast guard from the corridor came crashing through raised beds towards him. "What is it?"

"Commander," he panted, "there's a mob."

"The new supply ship," the commander groaned. She began limping towards the exit. "Come, Weaver. This will be something for you to harvest. Besides. Records is going to want a report for this."

"Why would there be a mob after a supply ship?" Harper asked, scrambling after her. "There wasn't one when we arrived on ours!"

"That's because the pilots you met weren't only there to greet you," the commander grunted. They stepped into the lifts, and the commander stabbed the button to carry them upward. She crossed her arms, arching her neck in agitation. "We grow enough food here that, with proper rationing, we don't starve. But we want for other things—textiles, tools, shoes—things that we can't make in the Fringe. Sometimes the crew gets . . . overexcited."

Overhead, an alarm began to wail.

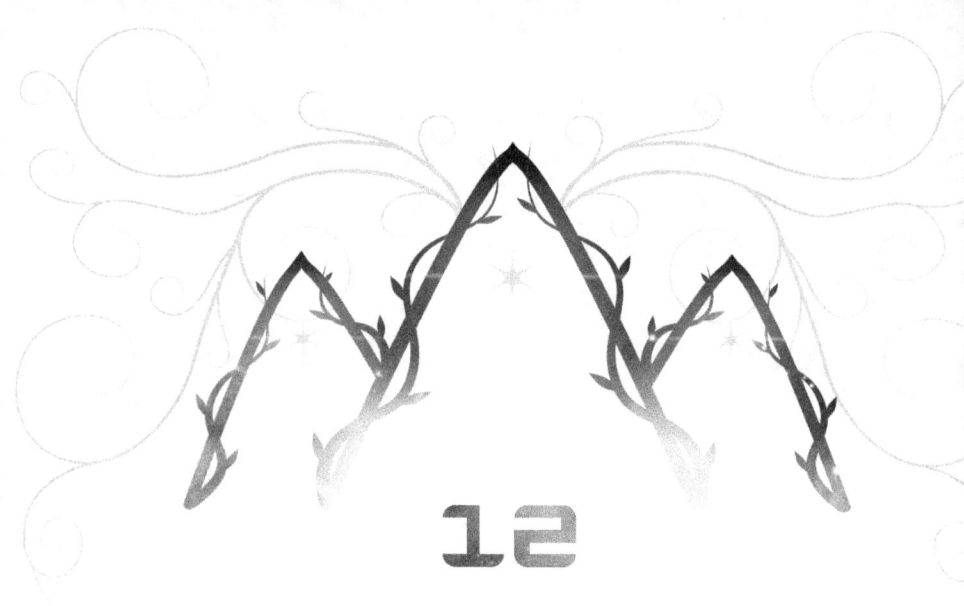

12

Harper hadn't realized just how many people were on the *Ransom* until she and the commander arrived in the hangar. A transport ship—much larger than the one she, Evaly, and Pickett had arrived on—sat in the middle of the room. Outcasts swarmed it from all sides, emerging from rooms and passageways around the hangar. They seemed to be led by three particularly gruff-looking Outcasts, two of which held some of the people at bay while the third tried to pry open the ramp.

Harper immediately lost the commander in the crush. She clambered up onto a stack of crates near the lifts, feeling vaguely anxious about the chaos. She saw no weapons, but there was shouting and scurrying and fists swinging. It reminded her of their escape from the penthouse, and of Captain Yarrowriver, falling over dead in front of her again, and again, and again.

You have a job to do, she told herself, gripping her recording folder. *Come on . . .*

The crate shook as someone scrambled up behind her. She twisted around, prepared to jump away—but it was only Pickett. He reeked of cleaning solution, and his shirt clung to him, drenched with sweat. He poked a finger at the supply ship. "That's our ticket off here."

"Will you actually be able to get this one to go where we want?" Harper demanded. "Isn't it just another shell?"

"It's arrived at its destination, which means the computer won't be locked anymore," Pickett replied. "All we have to do is get into the cockpit."

Harper eyed the swarm of humanity below. "I think that's going to be a lot harder than you anticipate."

"No, it won't," Pickett insisted. "We can just move with the crowd." He was already scrambling off the crate. "This is our chance, Harper."

"What about Evaly? She's down in the dojo."

Pickett's jaw was set as he looked back up at her, eyes grim. "We can't squander our chance to get out of here. We have to get you back to Arkron. Evaly knows this."

Harper recoiled from him. "I'm not leaving her!"

"Harper, I'm not arguing with you!" He reached back up and caught her arm, dragging her after him. She landed awkwardly on the deck, dropping her recording folder. When she stooped to pick it up, Pickett grabbed her shoulder, forcing her to remain upright, looking at him. "As a ruler, you're going to have to make tough calls. We can come back for her."

She knew he was lying. There wouldn't be the time or forces to spare to return to the Fringe once they reached Arkron. They'd be too busy trying to stave off a Consortium invasion. And yet Princess Harper knew that he was right—this was their chance to get back to Arkron, now. Weaver Harper was enraged. How dare he be so willing to leave Evaly behind? She felt her fingers warm, and she squeezed them into fists. What if she did something to get all three of them out of here now? What if . . . ?

A hand landed atop one of her fists, and Harper's breath escaped her in a relieved gasp. Evaly stood beside her, cat ears pinned back against her head, face pinched in discomfort. "Ziah was called up here," she explained, "and I figured we'd be trying to make a run for it."

Pickett nodded curtly. "Glad you could make it. Let's move." He grabbed Harper's hand, and with Evaly holding onto her, they pushed into the mob trying to breach the ship. The Outcasts working to get the ramp open began to succeed; it was lowering slowly with a sickening squeal.

Pickett strode forward purposefully, elbowing stomachs and stepping on feet where need be. Still, his efforts weren't enough; someone crashed into Harper, tearing her from Evaly and Pickett's grasp.

And suddenly she was alone in the crowd, pushing towards the ship. She twisted about, trying to find Pickett and Evaly, but there were so many heads, so many bodies.

I wasn't ready to leave anyway. The treasonous thought danced through her mind, stilling her. No, she wasn't ready to leave. The commander had outed her as a storyweaver and hadn't scolded her for it. This place was freeing. She could breathe here.

But Lady Kova, Fayen, Arkron . . . She squeezed her hands into fists again, trying to make the surge of power *go away*. She stood on tiptoe, trying to find Pickett. She spotted Evaly first; Pickett had hoisted her onto his shoulder. Her yellow eyes latched onto Harper, and she waved furiously. They were nearly to the ship now, and the ramp was almost lowered. Harper reached for them, trying to thread her way through the people.

Then something collided with Harper's stomach. Similarly, the people around her doubled over, hung up on the barrier that had emerged from the floor. Harper gripped the metal railing to steady herself, staring at it. Where had it come from? Was it concealed within the floor until someone flipped a switch?

However it had appeared, it now blocked the Outcasts from the ship. An aisle between the two pens led to the ramp, where the Outcasts working to lower it paused, tools still in hand.

"That is *enough*." The commander stood in the center of the aisle, her masked gaze sweeping across the penned-in Outcasts and the ones trying to break into the ship. Her hands hovered in the air in front of her, as if she were prepared to fight. "Xan!" she addressed the woman who had been working on the ramp. "What is the meaning of this?"

The woman lowered her tools. "We don't feel like we're getting our due, Commander," she replied, voice stiff.

The commander stepped forward. "And why is that?"

The woman tugged on her rumbled shirt, displaying the holes in it. "Look at us! We work to keep this enterprise in good repair and standing, and yet we're still forced to dress and act like paupers!"

The commander lowered her hands. "I understand. But surely you must acknowledge that creating chaos like this is not going to strengthen us!" She was drawing nearer to the woman now, offering one hand to her. "I know it's been a lean year. But you have to trust that I am working on fixing this problem. But to do that, I need you on my side. Will you stand by me?"

The woman stared at her outstretched hand for a moment, face contorted. Around her, her fellows shifted uneasily, exchanging glances. It was clear that she wanted to slap it away, but with so many eyes watching, would she?

She accepted it reluctantly. "Aye, Commander."

"Good." The commander squeezed her shoulder with her other hand. "Now, let's get this ship unloaded so we can use the supplies." She turned back to the mob, swiping her fingers downward. The barriers sank back into the floor. "The ship will be moved to the lower docks. If you're on the unloading crew, congregate there. If you were allotted something from this shipment, go to the quartermaster. You'll have it by this evening." As soon as she finished speaking, the ship hummed to life once more and drifted out of the hangar.

There goes our chance to escape, Harper thought, but found herself relieved. As she turned to find Pickett, she caught sight of the commander's mask, tipped towards her once again.

"Is this place still as wonderful as you thought?" she asked, stepping closer.

"It's more like my home than I expected," Harper replied. "You're a good leader."

The commander lowered her head. "I try to be. But I'm . . . only me." She inhaled. "That'll have to be enough." Her masked face dipped towards Harper's hands. "Is that a good story for you?"

"Yes," Harper whispered. On that, both Princess Harper and Weaver Harper agreed. The commander was everything she was not but wished to be: a good leader, sure of herself. Something Harper was beginning to doubt that she would ever be.

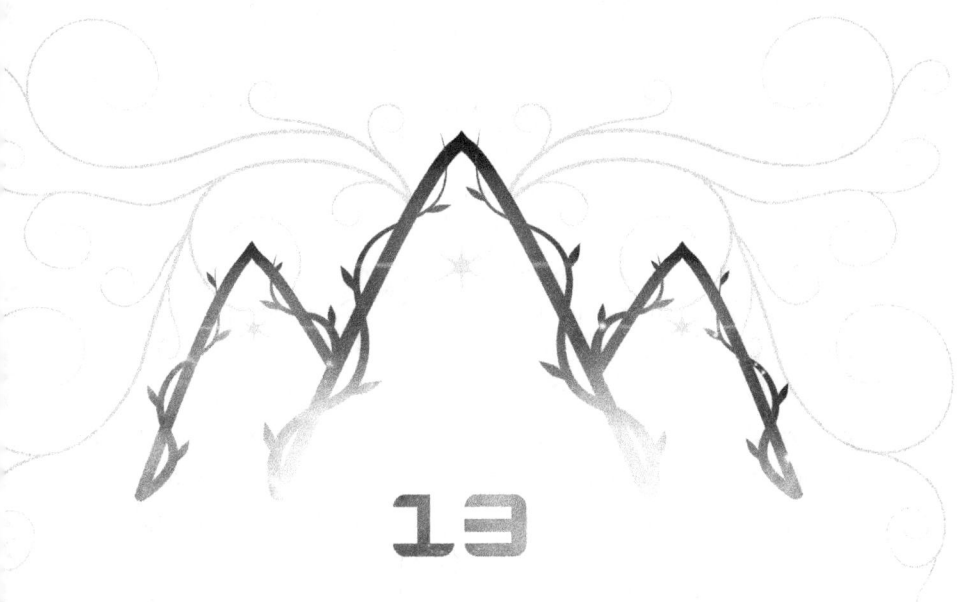

13

INCARCERATION WAS NOT suiting Fayen well.

"Whatever you are doing, it ez disgusting." A Joanen man, seated at one of the tables in the common room, scowled at him. He had arrived the day after Fayen and had spent most of the time in his cell or sitting at the table, complaining about the food. His name was Venden, and he was the son of Joane's Prime. "Are 'ou still planning to stack 'ze 'ables and climb out like a squirrel?"

There was a sneer in his voice, and Fayen bit his tongue to keep from retorting. Yes, he was still thinking about it. He had made the mistake of mentioning it to Colten while within earshot of Venden. He had been met with laughter and threats to report him to the guardsmen. Venden believed that they would be released soon and did not want to stir up further trouble with the Consortium.

"I was thinking about my sister," Fayen said, forcing his fingers away from the bandage around his side. Colten had replaced the wrap with an adhesive patch that itched like he'd rolled through nettles. "How worried she must be." *And how worried I am about her.* Was she taking the supplements she was supposed to? Were her muscles being massaged to stave off the spasms? "She needs special care," he added. He tugged on his hair. *Silent Star Sea. Couldn't I have made it a few more steps to the ship?*

Venden fluttered his hand. "Why be concerned? Surely there are others in your palace that care for her. Or ez Arkron so poor that you do not 'ave servants?"

"Arkron is *not* poor," Fayen retorted, dropping his hands to cross his arms. "That's the whole point of why we're here, isn't it? Our worlds are rich in resources that the Consortium wants to steal."

"Ze Consortium will not be stealing from my world," Venden said. "We will make a deal with them, and we will be compensated. There ez a peaceful solution to this." He lifted one shoulder in a shrug. "Perhaps Arkron ez just too stubborn to see that."

Fayen stopped his pacing to turn to him. "So it's foolish to stand up for your homeworld and its people in the face of a galactic bully?"

Venden shrugged again, this time with both shoulders. "If you want your sister to die, zat is your choice."

Seething, Fayen took a threatening step towards him. "My sister is not going to die. Not as long as I'm breathing."

The man lifted a lazy eyebrow. "Zat might not be for much longer if your world doesn't yield."

With another step, he was in front of Venden and grabbed the neck of his shirt. The Joanen's blue eyes went wide as they landed on Fayen's clenched fist. "I *will* escape from this Deeps-hole," Fayen growled, "and if I have to hurt you to keep you from reporting me, I will."

"Fayen!" Colten emerged from his cell and raced over to him, grabbing his arm. "Let him go."

"No," Fayen growled. "Not until he learns—"

The doors to the room hissed aside, revealing a squad of guardsmen. At their head was a man Fayen was growing to loathe: Captain Keir, the guardsman overseeing the Consortium's political prisoners.

"Longracer," he ground out in his gravelly voice, "release your fellow prisoner." An electro-stick snapped to life in his hand, suggesting that he wouldn't ask twice.

Fayen released Venden, shoving him hard against the table. A moment later, Fayen himself was pinned against the table beside Colten, hands being cinched behind his back.

"Something tells me they're not taking us somewhere for a better dinner," Fayen muttered. Unfortunately, he was overheard by Captain Keir, who kicked him in the back of his knees. Fayen collapsed to one knee, banging his chin on the table. Blood, metallic and hot, filled his mouth from where he'd bitten his tongue. When Captain Keir jerked him back up and around, Fayen spat the mouthful all over his breastplate.

The captain backhanded him across the face. "Insolent boy."

"You started it," Fayen retorted. He grunted as the captain dragged him to the door. "So, are we going on a field trip? Hopefully somewhere with a cliff I can push you off of?"

The quip earned him a blow to the ribs, just above his wound. He was unable to restrain his gasp but remained upright. Glancing over his shoulder, he saw Colten and Venden being led after them. "They're coming too?"

Keir grunted. "Prince Venden is being released. His planet has wisely allied with the Consortium. And for his good behavior, Colten will be allowed to speak with his family directly."

"And what about me?" Fayen demanded.

"We have something special for you." Keir hauled him into a small room, only a few steps down the featureless hallway from the prison. At first Fayen thought it was some sort of torture chamber. There was a window across from the door, behind which he could see technicians working. A narrow node sat in the center of the room, looking like a tall lamp missing its shade. What would it do? Fire a laser through his brain? Electrocute him?

"Your planet is refusing to consider negotiations because they are accusing the Consortium of kidnapping your princess."

"Princess? She didn't make it home? But they were on the ship . . . " Panic was beginning to pulse through him. If Harper hadn't made it home, that meant that Evaly hadn't either. "The Consortium doesn't have them?"

Keir kicked him to his knees again in front of the node. "Do you think I'd be putting up with your insolence if we had a different prisoner? You're going to record a video that will be broadcasted to House Evensong on Arkron."

"Like a ransom note?" Fayen stared at the top of the node. It had a round, black dome on the top, like a beady eye. A recorder. It reflected his face back at him, revealing his magnificent black eye and bruised cheeks. What good would a ransom note do? He knew he was loved in House Evensong, but he was just the son of a lady-in-waiting. He wasn't worth exchanging an entire planet's freedom for.

But to a young, impulsive princess with a rebellious streak and a secret power, he might be. He doubted that the Consortium knew about Harper's storyweaving abilities, but he had no doubt that she wouldn't hesitate to reveal them if given the opportunity to rescue him, if she saw the recording.

I can't do this.

Captain Keir grabbed the scruff of his neck and forced Fayen to look up at the recorder. "Your script will be projected over the window there. Just try to cooperate, will you?" He pressed his blaster against Fayen's side. He guessed it was set to stun, but all the same, it sent a shiver through him.

A light blinked on in the node atop the dome and words appeared behind it, above the window to the tech booth. *House Evensong,* they read, *I come to you with a plea of help . . .* Fayen snorted. A plea for help? That made him sound like a maiden in a tower. His eyes skated over the rest of the message. It was mostly bunk about opening negotiations with the Consortium—he noticed that they didn't mention Harper. Perhaps the Consortium wanted Arkron to think that it had its princess and was keeping her in reserve.

Keir jabbed him in the side again. "Get talking."

Fayen took a deep breath and glared at the recorder. "The Consortium," he said, "is a bunch of smelly layabouts who will never have our world. Keep fighting." Then he surged upward, banging the top of his head into Keir's chin. Stars spun in his vision, but he felt the captain pull away from him, cursing. Fayen lunged for the door, but the captain recovered and grabbed him around the middle, throwing him across the floor. Fayen crashed into the narrow recording node. The pole snapped upon impact, landing atop him.

He sprang to his feet, dragging it up with him. It made an awkward sword, but it would do. He gripped it by the base and swung it towards Keir. Taking a fighting stance strained his aching side, but he held it anyway. He would defeat this man and every guardsman that came into the room after him. He would escape. He wouldn't be a bargaining chip, and he'd be back to Evaly soon . . .

He struck Keir in the side, sweeping him against the wall. Keir grunted, catching the end of the pole and yanking Fayen towards him. Fayen tried to pull it back—for a moment, a fierce tug-of-war ensued. Fayen could hold his own, but his injuries weakened his grip. As Keir rallied for a hard pull, Fayen released the node. Keir staggered back into the wall, finding that he was the only one holding the metal pole now.

With him distracted, Fayen lunged towards the door, slapping the controls with his palm. Did he have time to find Colten? He couldn't leave him here with them, but all the same . . .

His breath burned in his lungs, and his pulse crashed in his ears. He felt lightheaded, but as the door hissed open, he charged.

Straight into a wall of guardsmen. They caught his shoulder and threw him back against the floor. Fayen leapt up to face them once more, hands balled into fists, when movement from the tech booth behind him caught his eye.

A familiar silhouette stood behind the window, watching him. For a moment Fayen thought he was hallucinating—but there could be no mistaking that braid or that scar. It was High General Vasken. What was she doing here, watching him fight?

Seeing that she had his attention, she leaned towards a microphone on the controls before her and spoke. "You never stop fighting, do you, Mr. Longracer?"

Captain Kier's arm snaked around his neck, trapping him. Fayen clawed at the man's bracer, kicking at the guardsmen trying to restrain him from the front. All the while he strained to look behind him to see if she was still watching.

A blow to his stomach made him twist back around, lashing out with as much strength as he could muster. The guardsman fell back, only to be replaced with one of his fellows. Fayen lashed out at him too, kicking and screaming.

No, he never stopped fighting. He couldn't.

14

Pickett was beginning to wonder if the stench of cleaning solution was going to burn his nasal cavities for good. He was an advanced journeyman Neherum, the High General's Personal Assistant, and the Prince of Arkron. And he had spent the last five days on his hands and knees. Scrubbing. Floors. He had recited every platitude about humility that he knew, trying to placate himself, and then quoted the Accords, reminding himself that it was his duty to protect his sister in whatever way he had to.

But as he hobbled into the mess hall with an aching back and sore knees, his hands chapped and raw, his thoughts were black. They had almost made it out yesterday. If Harper hadn't dallied, they might be home on Arkron now. He could be training, or finding some way to serve the High General from home . . .

The chatter within the mess hall made his ears ring, and the childish pictures from the crèche hung on the wall panels made him scowl. He picked up a prepared tray and scanned the bustling room for Harper. It wasn't hard to find her. The Evensong auburn hair shone among the darker heads of the Outcasts. She sat at a table in the middle of the room, pen skating over the page before her.

Pickett swept in and claimed the spot before her, slamming his tray down onto the table.

Harper raised an eyebrow at him. "Hello, Pickett."

He did not return her greeting and started eating instead. Seated next to Harper, Evaly gingerly sniffed in his direction, and then shook her head in a silent *leave him alone*.

Good. He was in no mood to talk.

Harper huffed. "Bad morning?"

"Harper, I've literally spent the last four hours pushing a mop," he snapped. "I really don't want to listen to your nattering today."

She met his gaze, lips pursed.

Evaly set something onto the table and scooted it towards Harper. Her little jar of oil, dangerously low. Her Hybri training was taking a toll on her. She nodded at it, and then at Pickett's hands. And then kept eating.

Harper sighed and uncapped it. "Give 'em here."

"No," he said.

She dipped her fingers in the oil. "So. You would rather let your hands bleed as a testament to your suffering?"

He huffed, but set his fork down and extended his hand. She was right. That was rather pathetic of him. The High General would be ashamed of him if she saw him now. Harper began to rub the oil into the cracks on his hand, clucking in sympathy. "Poor Pickett. You're not used to manual labor, are you?"

"No," he muttered, wincing as the oil met the raw flesh. "It's humiliating."

Harper raised an eyebrow at him. "If the High General had asked you to do it, would you have?"

He scowled at her tone. "Of course. I respect her."

Evaly pushed her bowl away from herself. "And you don't respect the commander? She's treated us fairly."

"Only because she doesn't know who we are," he replied.

Evaly frowned. "I think she would treat us the same if she did. She's kind. She watches my trainings with Captain Ziah."

"She's an *Outcast*," he protested.

"We're Outcasts right now too," Harper mused, finishing with his left hand and moving onto the right, forcing him to juggle his fork around in order to keep eating.

"We're only Outcasts for the time being," Pickett corrected.

Harper didn't reply. She made a show of squinting at his hand, trying to scrub the oil into one of the cracks. He grabbed her hands with his other, forcing them to still. "I'm scheduled to clean the bridge today," he said. "That means I'll have a good chance at getting a tablet. When our escort comes, we're leaving, do you understand me?"

"Yes," she said, trying to pull her hand away.

He held her fast for a moment longer. "You can't dawdle like you did yesterday. We have to get home." What was it that Lady Kova always told her? Something about being a princess and not a storyweaver? He couldn't remember; he had never paid enough attention. So he settled on, "Just remember who you are, all right?"

Harper's face darkened, but he released her and shoved the rest of his food into his mouth. "I have to go. Try to behave yourself." He flexed his fingers, finding that the skin on his hands didn't ache as badly. "Thanks," he added to Evaly, getting to his feet. "Be ready, the both of you. If I can get the message out, there's a good chance that our escort will be here before midnight."

Harper's expression remained dark, and her hand closed around her pen again. Even so, she nodded.

Outside of the mess hall, his crew was assembling once more, gathering their supplies. Pickett hefted his bucket of bottles and brushes and followed them into the hangar, then up the steps to the bridge. It was a high deck suspended partway over the hangar, filled with tech stations, monitors, and holographic maps. In the center of the deck was a wide chair with a triangular back: the commander's seat. It was surrounded by several smaller seats—one for each of the overseers of the *Ransom's* various sections, Pickett assumed.

The commander was there, perched on the edge of her seat as if she were a bird about to take flight. Captain Ziah had drawn one of the smaller chairs up close to her, and they were conferring over a tablet.

Behind the commander's seat was a communications station, with tablets secured in stands upon it. Picket's heart soared at the sight—there. That was their ticket off this miserable hunk of steel. Gripping his bucket, he strode to that section of the bridge. The sanitation crews weren't usually assigned a segment of floor; they picked where they wanted to start and worked towards each other from there.

No one paid him any attention. It was so odd compared to Anaya, where people had parted to make a path for him. It felt *wrong*. He was the High General's journeyman, and the Prince of Arkron . . . this wasn't who he was.

He stopped a short distance away from the communications and knelt, opening his supplies. It would look suspicious if he went straight to the station. No, he'd have to work his way there. He dribbled some of the cleaning solution on the floor and started scrubbing. Once again, the smell burned his nose, and his eyes smarted. But if he could just keep his attention on those tablets and the promise that by this time tomorrow, he'd be sipping chai back home on Arkron . . . he could endure.

"It's not a coincidence that they sent this transmission into the Fringe." The commander's voice broke Pickett's focus. He was straying closer to her throne than he realized. He began to backtrack, scooting towards the communications station once more. "Play it again."

"Aye, Commander," said Captain Ziah.

The sounds of a scuffle, muted by a tablet's speakers, echoed across to Pickett. Then, a familiar voice: *"The Consortium is a bunch of smelly layabouts who will never have our world. Keep fighting."*

Pickett froze, listening as grunts and curses followed the outburst. There was the sound of something shattering, and then a robotic voice said, *"If House Evensong wishes to see its members returned, the Consortium suggests that Arkron meet the Council on the* Void *to reopen negotiations."*

Silent Star Sea. *Fayen.* The Consortium had Fayen. *Members.* Did that mean they had Lady Kova too? And the *Void.* That was the Consortium's flagship. Accipiters often used it as a waystop during their expeditions into the Fringe and other planets.

Pickett sat up, head spinning. Captain Ziah was speaking and, unconsciously, he tipped his head closer to listen.

"The only reason they'd send this out here is if they think there are Evensongs out here," she said. "I've been trying to see if I can get our Networld receivers online to figure out what the Deeps is going on planetside, but we're still blocked. But why would there be royals in the Fringe?"

"Unless they were running from the Consortium," the commander said. Pickett heard a metallic tapping noise, as if she were drumming her fingers on her mask.

Oh, Silent Star Sea. She was piecing it together. He glanced up at the communications. He was so close. All it would take was a single SOS, signed with his name. What would the commander do when she realized who they were? Hand them over? Hold them for ransom to see who would pay the most to get them back? He began scrubbing again, frantic. Scooting closer and closer to the communications.

"There's also the matter of this." The seat creaked faintly as the commander rose. There was the sound of snapping fabric, like sheets on a clothesline rippling in the wind.

Now pressed against the communications station, Pickett risked a glance that way. His heart rose into his throat at the sight of Harper's rumpled dress, dangling from the commander's steel grip. He had tried to go back for it, his first day on the sanitation crew. They had been working near the lower hangars, where the transport ships were stored. He'd been caught before he could slip away, and been forced to spend an extra hour scrubbing baseboards.

"This was in the supply ship that came five days ago."

Ziah was silent. Pickett reached for his bottle of cleaning solution, but his anxious hand knocked it over. It hit the deck with a clatter, rolling away towards the commander's seat.

She lowered the dress at once, whipping her head towards him. He froze, hunched against the console, hand still reaching for the bottle of cleaner. *How undignified.* He straightened. "Commander."

Her mask tilted up. "What are you doing?"

"Cleaning the floor, Commander, it was on the schedule . . . "

"You've barely moved from that spot. I've been listening to you."

He winced. He should have made a better show of keeping his brush moving. Well, he could still salvage the situation, couldn't he? Perhaps a direct approach would be better. "I need to use the comms."

"Are you aware that Outcast transmissions have codes attached to them that are blocked by Consortium firewalls?" she asked, rolling Harper's dress into a bundle and dropping it into her seat. "Even independent planets . . . like, say Arkron . . . block our transmissions. If you're trying to reach someone planetside, you won't be able to."

Arkron. So she knew. He fought to keep his face smooth, but could feel his composure slipping. "That is unfortunate."

"It is," she said, resting an arm on the back of her throne. "Much heartache could be prevented if the planetsiders trusted us enough to let comms through. Now perhaps, Highness, there's a story you'd like to tell us?"

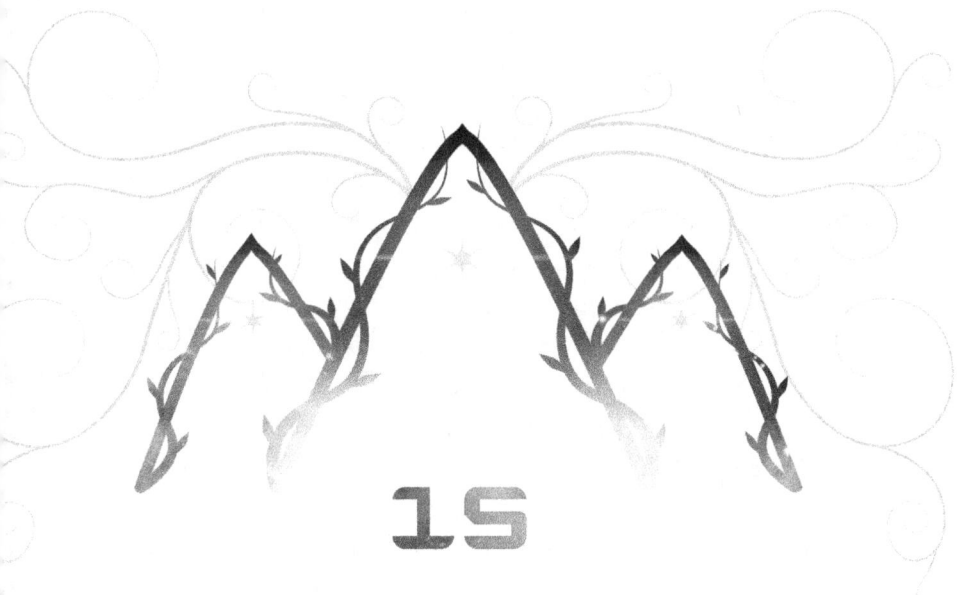

15

"And that's how I ended up on the *Ransom*," Melina said, pressing her hand to her chest and bowing to Harper. "Our good lady has helped me heal in ways I never thought I would."

Harper mirrored her gesture. She presumed it was a movement of respect or gratitude but couldn't match it to any of the ones Lady Kova had made her memorize. It was likely a product of the Fringe's fusion of peoples. It was similar to the Hylonese bow but also tied in the hand movements of many Joanen cultures. Fascinating. She'd have to make a note of it. "Thank you, Melina. The more time I spend on the *Ransom*, the more I learn to hear her." She rested a hand on the table, absorbing the rumble of the ship. Evaly still found it painfully loud, but Harper had come to love how it hung perpetually in the background, like soft music tinkling in the back of a chai shop. The *Ransom* was alive, singing softly over her people and serving as a delicious melting pot of stories for Harper's soul.

Melina rose, gathering her long veil around herself, and made the motion again, her gnarled hands pressed close to her heart. "Thank *you*. There is much healing to be found in sharing one's story."

"Yes, there is," Harper agreed, rising with her. She felt the tingling warmth of rightness slide through her. Being here on the *Ransom*, it was healing for her too. "I'm privileged to listen to them. And your records will be updated with the proper birthplace, of course."

Melina bowed a third and final time and then vanished into the bustle of the market ring. Hugging the papers to herself, Harper made her way to the lifts. She'd only collected the information that she'd been instructed to—the woman's correct birthplace and birth date—but so much more had come out in the process.

Harper sighed, rubbing her fingers over the intercessor glyphs she had drawn on the tops of her hands, trying to smear the ink away. On Arkron, the people painted the glyphs on themselves and their work in an attempt to direct the Creator's attention towards it. And to remind them to pray as often as they saw it. Her hand had started to cramp that morning, and so she had drawn them on to pray for strength.

She had grown up using the intercessors for everything. However, when Lady Kova had brought her to Mantalor, she had discouraged them, claiming that the ink staining her skin ruined her royal image. But Princess Harper was locked away inside of her. And so Weaver Harper drew the intercessors. She still remembered to rub them off afterward. Pickett would throw a fit if he saw her flaunting an Arkronen tradition here. She stepped into the lift, rubbing her inky fingers on her trousers in an effort to clean them.

Pickett. Arkron. Home. Her throat tightened, remembering that they might be in their final hours here. This time, she'd have to go. Even if she tried to find some excuse to stay, her crown would dog her steps. She pressed her papers to her lips and whispered under her breath, "*I am Princess Harper Evensong, and one day, I will rule Arkron.*"

Her stomach twisted in a way that had nothing to do with the lift's lurching stop. She shuffled off with the other passengers, turning to make her way to the records room when a hand grasped her elbow. It belonged to a pilot wearing a faded blue jumpsuit. "The

Commander would like to see you," he said. "You've been summoned to the bridge."

The commander? The bridge? What did the woman want? She had made it clear that she didn't want to share her story, and Harper doubted that she was being reassigned to a different position so soon after starting her current one. Unless . . . but no. She couldn't have guessed who they were so soon, could she? They'd been careful . . .

She swallowed hard, remembering her conversation with the commander in the garden. She hadn't been as careful as she should have been. And the commander had deduced that she was a storyweaver. Was she summoning her to use her powers? Both? Panic made her feel lightheaded. She pulled away from the pilot's grip. "I have to turn in these records." Perhaps she could escape into the bowels of the ship and hide there till help came. Or find a way to steal a ship. But the commander had a special relationship with the *Ransom*. She would know where to find her no matter where she went.

Unless, of course, Harper used her powers. Even though she had leaned into her weavership the last few days, the idea made her uneasy. What *would* she weave? It wasn't that she lacked ideas . . . She didn't know which one would work for this situation.

"The Commander wants you *now*," the pilot said, his hand drifting towards the stunner on his belt. Harper winced, remembering the pulsing ache of the weapon. That was something she had no interest in enduring again.

"I . . . see," she said. There was no running, not now. "Well, it would be wrong to keep her waiting, wouldn't it?" Inhaling raggedly, she strode towards the hangar, leaving him to hurry after her. If she could act like she had a measure of control over the situation, then perhaps she could find a way to reinvent it.

The commander was waiting for her in the sitting area of the bridge. Once again, Harper was struck by her imposing figure. She sat cross-legged on her triangular throne, mask tipped upward as she watched Harper approach. Pickett and Evaly sat together on one of the smaller chairs that ringed the commander's, flanked by two pilots. Pickett met Harper's eye and shook his head, almost wearily.

So their secret was out. Still gripping her record papers, she stopped before the commander and inclined her head. "You wanted to see me?"

"Indeed." The commander pulled a bundle from behind her and shook it out across her lap. Harper winced at the sight of her dress. Lady Kova would be furious at the state of the garment. "I'm afraid that it is time for your act to come to an end, Highness."

Highness. The word grated in Harper's ears. "I see," she said, fighting to keep her voice level. It was time. She had to return to being Princess Harper. *But . . . I don't want to,* she thought bitterly. "If I might ask, how did you know?"

The commander sat back in her seat. "I had my suspicions. The dress was found the day after you arrived. You weren't exactly subtle about your nationality when we spoke a few days after. And then there was this." She activated a holographic node on the arm of her chair. A face appeared, painfully familiar with his green eyes and hair falling over his forehead. Fayen. Bruised and bloody, but still defiant.

Evaly gave a pained cry and struggled to rise, but the pilot pushed her back into her seat.

"The Consortium is a bunch of smelly layabouts who will never have our world. Keep fighting," Fayen said. Then he lunged backwards into the person behind them, ramming his head into their chin. The image dissolved, replaced with the Consortium's four-pointed compass insignia. *"If House Evensong wishes to see its members returned, it suggests that Arkron meet them on the Void to reopen negotiations,"* the recording said and then flickered off, leaving empty air in its place.

"Why would the Consortium beam a transmission like this out into the Fringe?" the commander asked. "Unless they suspected you might be out here." The commander's hands gripped the arms of her chair, though her voice was steady. "You have brought grave danger to my people. If the Consortium finds out that we've been harboring you, they'll crush us!"

"We'll leave," Harper replied swiftly. "Let us borrow a ship, and we'll be gone. We have no interest in bringing trouble to you." Her eyes remained on the space where Fayen's face had been. The Consortium had him. They were holding him. She could *not* allow that.

It looked like their trip home was going to require a detour.

"Of course," the commander said. Her tone shifted, faintly sarcastic now. "I'll give you an Outcast ship that will be blown out of the sky the moment you enter your planet's airspace."

"We don't need it to take us to Arkron," Harper said. "We need to get to the *Void*."

Pickett bolted up, ignoring the pilot trying to pull him back down. "What the Deeps is wrong with you?" he demanded. "The *Void?*"

"Did you not see that they have Fayen?" Harper demanded. "You're just going to leave him in their hands? And what if they have Lady Kova? We can't abandon them!"

"So, naturally, your solution is to hand yourself over to them." He struck his forehead with the heel of his hand. "Do you *ever* think things through?"

"You didn't let me finish!" she retorted. "We're not handing ourselves over; we're taking back what's ours. We get Fayen. And then we can take a ship from there that doesn't have an Outcast code."

"You're insane," Pickett spat.

"Maybe," Harper said, tightening her arms around the records still in her arms. "But we have to try, Pickett. Fayen's House Evensong. And don't your Neherum codes have something to say about standing by your brother?"

Pickett's mouth opened for another protest, but Harper could see that she'd struck a mark. If she couldn't appeal to him as a member of House Evensong, then she could appeal to him as a Neherum. "You've trained together. Studied together. Now he needs you. He needs *us*."

Pickett closed his mouth, but crossed his arms. He muttered something to himself, but added, louder, "Fine."

"Good." She turned back to the commander, who had been watching. Or so Harper had thought. The woman's gaze was tilted towards Evaly. The girl sat hugging her cloak around herself, rocking back and forth. Seeing Fayen in such a state would have been hard for her. "All we need is your help, Commander, this one last time. Just get us to the *Void*, and we'll leave you in peace. And I will do everything in my power to ensure that the Consortium leaves you alone."

The commander's mask tipped back to her. "I hope that you are aware just how hollow that promise is, Highness."

Harper grimaced. She was. If Arkron was facing an invasion of its own, they'd have no forces to spare to protect an Outcast enterprise. And yet it was the best she had to offer. "I know," she said. "But every second we're here gives the Consortium more time to realize that you have us, and target your enterprise." She stepped closer to the throne. "This is such a beautiful place." Her voice broke as she said it, imagining all the things she would never learn about the wondrous *Ransom*. "Don't let it be destroyed because of us."

The commander was silent for a time, though her hands released the arms of her seat. Finally, she nodded to herself and stood. "I'll do better than give you a ship," she said. "I'll escort you to the *Void* myself."

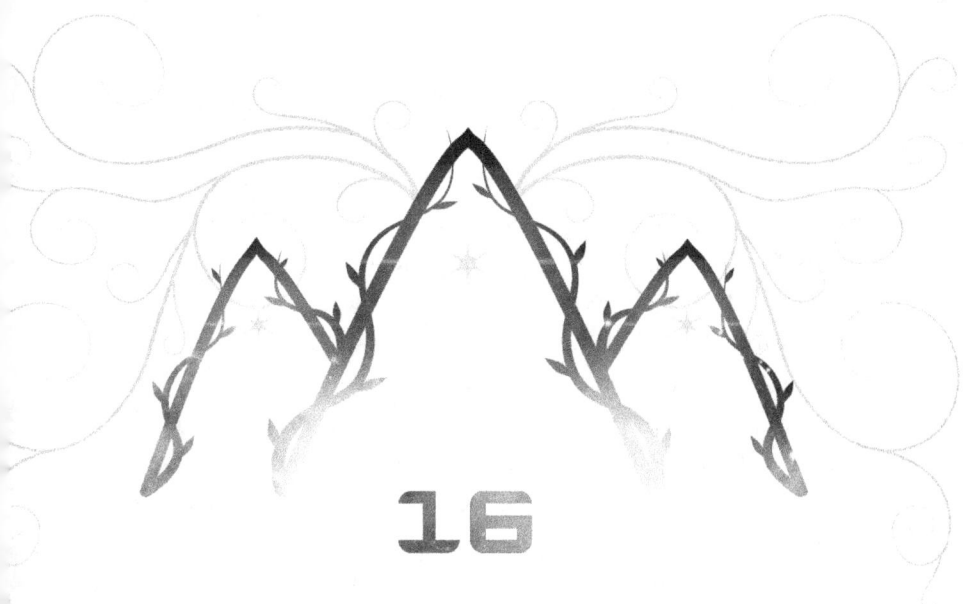

16

Rather than stacking tables and breaking through a bulletproof window for his escape, Fayen—at Colten's urging—chose to lean into his other strength: his gift for overdramatization. It wasn't as fun without Harper to orate with, but he was capable of playing the court jester on his own.

In the days following his brief encounter with the High General, he moped around the prison, lounging against the tables and sprawling over his bunk for hours in an effort to appear sicker than he truly was. Frankly, it wasn't hard to do. His body ached ruthlessly. As he lay on his bunk, watching the light slide across the floor of the common room, he allowed himself to wonder how much more of this he could take.

The sight of the High General simply *watching* him be beaten had rattled something inside of him. She was his leader, and the leader of all the Neherum. She was Pickett's mentor. And she had just stood there and then made fun of him. Was it some sort of test? Perhaps, when all this was over, he would receive journeyman status early. Except, his experience here was making him never want to set foot on a Consortium planet again.

He knew the Neherum had a policy of neutrality towards galactic politics. But the Consortium guardsmen had beaten him—savagely. Wouldn't that have warranted some sort of intervention on her part? Why had she been there in the first place?

His thoughts circled round and round. *I have to get out of here. I have to get back to Evaly. What if I can't?*

Colten appeared in the doorway of his cell, holding another bundle of ice. He looked as haggard as Fayen felt, though Fayen suspected he would take the prize of worst looking. "Hey," the healer said, stepping in when he saw that Fayen was awake. "How do you feel?"

"Like the picture of health," he said, trying to sit up. The motion sent shocks of pain through his core. "I think I could stop a starship with my bare hands if I felt so inclined."

Colten snorted and pushed him back down. Once again, they were the only two prisoners left in the circular room. Venden had been released and was probably sipping some fruity drink back home on Joane. Fayen hoped he choked on it.

Colten probed his stomach, pulling him from his thoughts and eliciting a hiss from him.

"Stop that," Fayen groaned, pushing his hands away. "You're making it hurt more."

"So it does hurt, eh?" He quirked an eyebrow at him. "Mr. Strongman is finally showing some humanity? Let me see."

"It's fine," he protested, gripping the fastenings of his white jumpsuit before Colten could pull it open. "Besides, I wouldn't want you to feel threatened by my muscular physique."

Colten rolled his eyes. "I'm studying to be a healer, Fayen. I've seen it all. Come on." He slapped his hands away and pulled open the jumpsuit.

His sharp intake of breath made Fayen crane his neck to look down. "What?" He knew he was a mess of bruises, and his torso didn't look any worse than the rest of him.

"Did they kick you?" Colten asked, pressing light fingers to his abdomen.

Fayen winced, trying to push him away. "Yeah, they kicked and punched . . . It was a fistfight! But I kicked and punched them too."

Colten pulled his fingers away, replacing them with the bundle of ice still wrapped in Fayen's old smock. "*They* have armor. You have to stop provoking them. I'm worried that you're bleeding internally."

"Well, that'd be a new one," he remarked, tipping his head back and shutting his eyes.

"You're not taking this seriously enough." Colten stuck his face close to Fayen's. His glasses were in danger of slipping from his nose. "These could be life-threatening injuries. You *have* to stop fighting."

Fayen snapped his eyes open, meeting the young healer's gaze. "Never."

"*Fayen.*" Colten tugged on the ends of his untidy hair. "Why? Is it your planet? Your sister?"

Sister. Evaly. He swallowed and forced himself to sit up. "Yes."

"If she's anything like you, then she can hold her own, can't she?" Colten sat down on the edge of his bunk, awaiting an explanation.

Fayen looked away. "No. She can't. She's sick, and it's my fault."

"I'm sure that's not true, even if it often feels like it."

Fayen shook his head and looked down at his hands, which were calloused from holding his sword. "No, it *is* my fault . . . We were paired together for a Fledgling outing with the Neherum. She was ten. I was thirteen. We were touring one of the Catenan research facilities in Mantalor City, and I . . . wandered off. She came with me because we were supposed to stay together."

He clenched his hands into fists, wishing he could go back and strangle some sense his younger self.

"They were studying Hybris there. You know, the shape-shifters. There was this *thing*, floating in a tank, and I went to look at it. I tapped on the glass, and it woke up." He could still remember the thrill of seeing the creature squirm to life, a dark shape on its bed of goo. "And then it just—*jumped*. Right through the glass. I got out of the way, but Evaly—it went straight into her. And her body's been fighting it ever since." He exhaled, forcing his hands to relax. "I promised to protect her. To make up for what I'd done. She was an orphan, and I got my mother to adopt her; as House Evensong, she had better chances at treatment, but none of them have worked. So I have to be strong to be her strength. Because it's my fault that she has to be in pain every day."

"You were a child," Colten said, laying a hand on Fayen's shoulder.

"A stupid, *stupid* child," he corrected. "This is the price that I pay for what I did. I *will* be strong for her. I'll get out of here. I'll get us *both* out of here."

"Don't make promises you can't keep," Colten returned. "You have been strong, so strong. But Fayen, you're only human. You can only take so much." He paused and then added, "Did your sister ever *ask* you to spend your life like this? To fulfill this vow you seem to have pledged to her?"

Fayen stared at him, a retort welling inside his chest. He could take this and more if Evaly had to suffer every day. And asking him to protect her? She never needed to ask. They were family. She was his responsibility. But before he could protest, the door to the common room hissed open and Captain Keir and his squad strode in.

Fayen groaned but quickly refastened his jumpsuit, pushing the ice away. The guardsmen seized him and Colten and marched them out of the room. As before, Fayen lurched against his captors, trying to shake them off.

Colten caught his eye and gave a slight shake of his head. *You can only take so much.* What if he was right? If he died here, he wouldn't be able to keep protecting Evaly. But could he really let himself be turned into a pawn for the Consortium?

"So, are we going back to record another message?" he asked, craning his neck to look at Keir. This time, the man held Colten's bonds, forcing him forward.

The man grunted. "You'll see."

Sure enough, they were pushed into the recording room. A new node had been affixed to the floor, and Fayen strained to see into the tech booth beyond. Had Vasken come to watch again?

The guardsmen pushed him to his knees beside Colten. Why would the Consortium want to record them both? Was the message going to be broadcasted to both Arkron and Inerys?

Colten cursed as Keir grabbed a fistful of his hair and yanked it, pulling his head to the side. There was a glint of metal, and suddenly a knife was pressed against his throat.

"What are you doing?" Fayen demanded, pulling in vain against his captors. His wrestling felt weak. His stomach ached, and all of the other bruises and fractures around his body sang in a chorus of discomfort. *You're only human.* No. He had to be more, for Evaly, for Colten, for Arkron.

"People of Arkron and Inerys," Keir began, ignoring Fayen's question. "Your continual refusal to yield to Consortium negotiations *will* have consequences. Inerys, you have made your choice." He pressed the knife against Colten's throat.

"No!" Fayen shouted, lurching towards Keir. His head banged into the man's arm, sending the knife askew. Pain roared through Fayen's middle at the motion, making him crumple. But Colten was still alive, scrambling away from the captain. His glasses fell off in the tussle, but with his hands behind his back, he couldn't retrieve them. Blood beaded on his neck where the knife had nicked him, but the wound wasn't deep.

"You're a monster," Fayen shouted at Keir, aware that his voice betrayed his powerlessness. "This is *murder.*" The other guardsmen came for him, grabbing his arms and pulling him upright once more.

"Arkron, there is still time," Keir continued, ignoring him. "Agree to negotiations on the *Void*, and Fayen Longracer will be spared the sentence of Colten Vander." Out of view of the camera, he made a motion to his guardsmen. Two of them grasped Colten's upper arms and dragged him towards the door. "Prisoner transfer initiated," one intoned quietly to his comm.

They were taking him away? Would they kill him later after all? He heard the crack of a stunner, and Colten went limp in his captor's arms. His glasses crunched as one of the guardsmen trod on them as they towed him out of the room.

Hanging in his guardsmen's grip, Fayen closed his eyes. And found a final reserve of strength.

A roar tore out of some desperate place in his soul, and he surged to his feet. He tore one arm from the guardsman's grip and seized the knife from Keir, wresting the hilt from his fingers. He sunk it into the shoulder of the other guardsmen holding him, cursing. The man roared and stumbled into his comrade.

"Shut the recorder off!" Keir yelled, spinning towards the techs. "He has the knife—stunners, now!" He reached for his own, only to find it in Fayen's hands.

Fayen fired twice. The guardsman armor was sturdy, meant to deter stunners, but not if they were fired into the visor. At close range, the first shot shattered the bug-like face-plate, and the next knocked the man out. He fell into his fellows while Fayen charged out of the door.

The pain in his body faded to a pinprick as he surged down the hallway, bursting into a sunlit stairwell beyond it. His pulse roared in his ears, nearly drowning out the sound of reinforcements running up the stairs towards him. Frantic, he looked back and forth, scanning the scene for Colten.

There was no sign of him, and Fayen knew he didn't have time to check every room. He shut his eyes for the briefest moment, whispering an apology. He couldn't save Colten, not right now. Stars, why must he be so helpless? Why couldn't he save everyone?

Opening his eyes, he found his way out: a landing just below him. It featured a window within a narrow door, painted to match the wall. It should lead to an emergency staircase on the outside of the building. He sprang down to it. It was locked, but the glass was designed to be breakable for precarious situations. And his certainly fit the description. He swung his shoulder at the glass. It shattered easily, though the shards cut into his arm, leaving spatters of blood on his white jumpsuit.

He didn't use the stairs. He could feel his body burning as he swung over the rail, but it was a distant sensation. Another rooftop loomed below, and he twisted into a roll as he landed on the rocky surface. He came up from it, panting, and scanned his surroundings. There was another building with a flat roof just below this one. He staggered across the roof and swung over the edge. He landed in a crouch and rose again, automatically walking across it to the next jump.

Then a voice made him freeze. "Well done, Mr. Longracer. You've arrived five minutes earlier than I expected you to."

At first, Fayen thought that he had only imagined her voice. Turning, he saw Vasken standing at the edge of the roof behind him, hands clasped behind her back. She was facing Mantalor City's cityscape, which rose above a nearby tree line like the tips of a crown.

She had been waiting for him.

"Pickett didn't speak of you often, but when he did, it was with admiration," she reminded. "He was impressed with your progress in the dojo—as am I."

"Pickett would be ashamed to know he's been serving a Consortium sympathizer," he replied, tightening his hands into fists. Could he fight her? *I don't have a choice.*

"If only everyone was as stubbornly loyal as Pickett," she agreed. "It would make leadership much easier for myself and others." She turned towards him, becoming nothing but a silhouette against the sinking sun. "You are strong and passionate, Longracer. But that combination also blinds you."

He shifted into a defensive pose. "To what?"

"Your weakness." She swept towards him, her cloak billowing behind him.

He leapt to the side. She didn't have her sword out, but her steps followed him. "I don't have any," he snarled, trying to scrape up some of his bravado. He had little left. It had fled along with Colten's limp form as he was pulled from the recording room.

"Is that so?" Her foot came out of nowhere and hooked around his ankle. She upended him with a jerk; he landed on the rough roofing with a grunt. Pain exploded through his sides, his body reminding him that he was not as strong as he needed to be. He rolled away from her before she could pin him with a foot on his chest and stood up, hands raised in front of him defensively.

"Yes," he said, blowing his hair out of his eyes. He allowed his stance to loosen for a moment. Perhaps there was a small chance . . . "But I don't want to use my skills against you. Please, High General. If the Neherum are truly neutral, can't you let me pass?"

She prowled closer, hands behind her back again. "You amuse me, Longracer. We have the same goal, you know."

He tightened his form again. "No, we don't."

"We both want to see peace for the Exlenna. Me for my Neherum, and you for your family. But that is only attained if all of the planets cooperate." Her fist came out of nowhere.

He blocked it with a knifehand, but her other fist found him in the jaw.

Fayen blinked away stars. *That* was an impressive *kata*. He danced away from her and then lashed out in three quick sidekicks. She was wearing leather armor but grunted nonetheless. He had landed a hit on her! If he didn't feel so lightheaded, he would have laughed.

He spun towards her, prepared to kick again, but she caught his foot and twisted it. He hit the roof but used the fall to jump up close to her and punch her other side. "Too bad I don't have my sword," he said. "This would be a lot faster with blades."

"Hmm." Vasken retreated several steps. "You wish to die faster?"

"Oh, no. I don't think you're going to kill me, High General," he said, following. "The Consortium needs me alive. Which means that there's no way for you to win this." He lashed out again, moving into the most complicated *kata* he knew. She replied with one of her own, and they sparred, moving back and forth across the rooftop as the sky darkened overhead.

He barreled into her, trying to drive his shoulder into her chest to push her off the roof.

"Silly boy," she murmured, catching him in a headlock.

He growled and sank to his knees, forcing her to stoop over to maintain her grip on him. He twisted back and forth, succeeding in getting her grip to loosen. He grabbed her leg, trying to yank it out from beneath her, but she kicked him with the other in his already aching ribs. A cry tore out of him, and Fayen rolled away.

This time it was harder to get up. He staggered to his feet, wheezing. When had it become hard to breathe? He could taste blood in his mouth. Was that from his bleeding lips or from inside of him?

Vasken stood haloed against the sunset, hands spread to receive him. "Weary yet?" she asked. "Give the word, and this could be over."

He wiped his bloody nose. When had that happened? He wasn't sure. "I'll do this all night if you want."

She laughed, and he charged again. This time she sidestepped. His momentum would have carried him over the edge of the roof if she hadn't snatched the neck of his jumpsuit, jerking him around so that he hung by it with his back to the ground. He scrabbled for purchase on her arms, but his fingers glanced off the smooth gauntlets she wore over them.

She tightened her grip on his shirt and leaned close, smiling. "You are a vibrant adversary—I'll give you that," she said. "However, you have neglected one important part of being a warrior."

He bared his teeth at her; he had no air left to demand what it was.

Her smile widened. "There are some adversaries that you will always be too weak to face." Then she jabbed something into his neck. A syringe? Was it a sedative?

He grunted, trying to pull his head away, but his movements felt sluggish. Whatever she had given him was working fast. Either that, or his wounds had finally caught up to him.

Vasken dropped the syringe and tossed him over her shoulder. He hung there, as useless as a sack of flour, limbs too leaden to fight. "We have a transport to catch," she said. "You're due on the *Void*, my boy."

Fayen had no strength to protest.

17

Keep fighting. Fayen's words rang within Evaly's head as she made her way to an unobtrusive shuttle docked in one of the *Ransom*'s lower hangars. His bruised face, teeth clenched defiantly, felt imprinted in her mind. How much worse did he look now, after fighting back?

Was he even still alive?

Her Hybri twisted within her, jolting through her veins and then retreating. The week of training had done little good in convincing her to make friends with it. If anything, she was more convinced that they would be forever incompatible.

She stopped, gripping her chest. There was chaos inside and outside of her. The incessant hum of the *Ransom* throbbed in all four of her ears, and her Hybri twisted around and around inside of her, agitated by her anxiety. She couldn't breathe. She was a bomb waiting to explode—she tried to cover her ears but could only cover her human ones. She tried pinning her cat ears against her head, but the vibration of the ship only shook through her core. There was no escape from any of it.

A hand landed on her shoulder. "You all right, kid?" Through her blocked ears, the commander's voice sounded as though it were underwater. "Are you afraid of going?"

"Fayen needs us," she whispered. For what good *she* would do. He was the strong one. But perhaps with Harper and Pickett, they would have a chance at extracting him. If not, she'd rather die with her family than be left alone, like after her birth family had died.

The commander cocked her head towards the shuttle, which Harper and Pickett had already boarded, and then stepped in front of Evaly, blocking her path to the ramp. "You could stay if you wanted," she said. "Continue your training with Ziah." Her hand rested on the lower part of her mask. Was she about to remove it? "You would be welcome here."

Stay on the *Ransom*? With Outcasts? Why did the commander care so much? Was she that interested in Evaly's Hybri? If so, she was no better than the students at Anaya who made fun of her for it. They cared about it, not her. It had stolen her very personhood.

"House Evensong is my family," she said. "They took me in when I had no one."

"What if you did have someone? Here in the Fringe?"

Did the commander mean herself? Evaly shook her head, drawing her cloak around herself. "I lost my first family," she said. "I don't want to lose this one."

"You'd be surprised how often lost things are found in the Fringe," the commander said, releasing her. "But . . . I understand." Her voice had hardened, but Evaly could smell the sadness rolling off of her in dark waves, like heavy thunderclouds before a rainstorm. Evaly watched her limp towards the ship, head cocked in confusion. Why was she so disappointed? The commander had attended all of her trainings, watching quietly from the corner, but she had spoken very little to her. But this wasn't the kind of grief that came from losing a potential asset. Normally that was accompanied with a spicy undertone of anger. This was just heavy, unreleased grief.

Even though it made her dizzy, Evaly hurried to catch up with her. "Will you take off your mask now?" she asked. "It would be nice to see your face just once, before we part."

The commander paused. Then, over her shoulder, she said, "I think it would be best if I didn't. Come. We'd best get you to your brother." She strode up the ramp, past Pickett and Harper, who were already strapped in their seats.

Evaly followed, sitting down beside Harper. The girl sat hunched in her seat, arms wrapped around herself. "Are you ready?" Evaly asked, touching her elbow.

"To leave this place?" Harper gave a soft, bitter laugh. "To go back to being a royal? No."

The shuttle jolted as it lifted off from the dock and dipped into the Star Sea. The *Ransom*'s song faded as they drifted away, then disappeared completely as they jumped into hyperspace. Evaly found that she could take a breath.

Pickett glared at Harper from the seats across from them. "We need a real plan, Harper. And it can't involve your . . . you know." He glanced toward the commander's silhouette in the chair.

"It's all right, Pickett. She knows," Harper said, running her fingers through her hair. Evaly could sense the faint surges of her power thrumming against her fingertips. It was almost like her Hybri, but less painful. Harper looked *exhilarated* when the surges came.

"She . . . what?" Pickett looked at the commander again, his face wrinkled. "She knows?" Evaly could sense the tangle of confusion—and, perhaps, respect?—wafting from him. The commander knew about Harper's storyweaving and hadn't tried to use her?

"Yes," Harper said, then attempted to change the subject. "Plan. I've been to the upper levels of the *Void* before, for conferences and such, and you've been to the lower levels—that's where they'd have spaces for Neherum and other travelers. The detention block is probably on the lower levels. I'll go to the top and create a distraction while you two get Fayen."

She makes it sound so simple. Evaly shook her head. This was the Consortium's flagship. It wouldn't be easy to infiltrate.

"Create a distraction how?" Pickett demanded, narrowing his eyes.

Harper threw up her hands. "I don't know! I'll break a vase or something. Moons, Pickett. I won't use my storyweaving."

"Good," he said, leaning back in his seat. "The last thing we need is the Consortium realizing what you are. They'll nix the 'negotiations' altogether and go after you. And if they think that there are others like you on Arkron, they'll raze the whole planet."

Harper squeezed her hands into fists. Small streamers of light glowed atop her knuckles and then fled back up her arms. "It's like being able to see but being forced to wear a blindfold," she muttered, scowling.

"How will we get off the *Void* once we have Fayen?" Evaly asked, remembering again how battered he had looked. Would he even be able to walk?

"The ship has escape pods," Harper said. "We can meet at those and jettison away."

Pickett pressed the heel of his hand to his forehead. "This is a *terrible* plan."

"Well, you'd better think of something else quick," the commander called over her shoulder. "Because we're here."

So soon? Evaly thought, wincing as the ship rumbled out of hyperspace. She craned her neck to see past the commander, out the viewport. The *Void* was built in a semicircle around the pyramid-shaped center. It looked more like a floating palace than a functional community like the *Ransom*. It was designed to shuttle the Consortium leaders from planet to planet in the utmost luxury, as well as host galas within the Star Sea itself. The exterior was garnished with elaborate façades and huge windows, and at the very top was the glass dome of the stateroom, which was illuminated by a huge chandelier.

"Do you have clearance codes to offer them?" Pickett demanded, looking at the commander again.

The commander didn't reply. Evaly sensed unease drifting from her but also resolution. And, again, that heavy sense of grief. She reached over and flicked the comm on. A voice blared from its speaker: "*Ransom* transport T-seventeen, you are cleared for landing in Hangar Portside, Hangar three-oh-one . . . "

"They're clearing *you?!* What is this?" Pickett tried to leap to his feet, but iron cuffs sprang out of his seat and pinned his upper arms back. Harper and Evaly were similarly pulled captive in their seats.

"I'm sorry," the commander said, masked face set towards the Void. "This was the only way to make sure my people remain safe."

"You sold us out," Harper said, voice bitter. "We trusted you!"

"I know." The commander's voice was heavy. "But this is how it has to be."

The cockpit filled with painfully bright, fluorescent light as the commander guided the ship into the hangar. Evaly squeezed her eyes shut, willing herself to wake up from this bad dream. Was there still time to overpower her and take control of the ship? Pickett might be able to, or Harper, with her abilities. But Pickett had no way out of his restraints, and Harper wasn't supposed to use her power.

That left Evaly with her dysfunctional Hybri. *Welcome it,* Ziah had said. They were supposed to be a team, able to change back and forth at will. Why couldn't that be the case with her Hybri? Why couldn't she just . . . make . . . it . . . work? She reached for the creature inside of her, catching it and dragging it upward. *Please. I need you. I will . . . I will let you be a part of me.*

A bit of the resistance inside of her loosened. She breathed out softly, releasing her hold on the creature. It stayed close to her, not shying away. What if they could meld? What if she could be strong, strong enough to save Fayen and get them off this ship? The Consortium wouldn't expect to be greeted with full Hybri.

Please. I won't fight.

For a moment there was stillness inside of her. Then the creature surged upward. A gasp tore out of her—she was being turned inside out, her body was changing—her hands were becoming paws, fingers, claws. *We're working together!* Evaly realized. *Like we're supposed to!*

For a blissful moment she tasted joy. And then everything crumbled. As quickly as the rush of power had come, it drained from her. Fireworks of pain exploded up and down her limbs and through her core. She slumped against her binders, the world spiraling into fragments of color and sound around her. Her Hybri retreated, writhing into a painful knot inside of her.

Weak. I'm too weak.

The next thing she knew, she was being dragged to her feet by a guardsman. He stank of too-hot plastic. "Be careful with her," the commander said from somewhere nearby. "She's just a child . . ."

Rough hands searched her, snatching her cloak and yanking away her small bag of medicine. Evaly shut her eyes again. It took all of her focus to remain on her feet, and even then the guardsman ended up pulling her along. She couldn't tell where they were going, only that this ship echoed much worse than the *Ransom*, that the lights were too bright, and that her limbs felt like water. She tried, feebly, to pull herself out of the guardsman's grip, but he tightened his hold on her arm. Where were they going? She felt as dazed as a sleepy child pulled from a hovericle. They passed a room filled with guardsmen that surrounded Harper and Pickett, but she was pulled further down a hallway. She caught flashes of the commander's mask behind her—why was the woman following? Why hadn't she run back to precious *Ransom*?

She heard the hum of a ray shield disengaging, and she was pushed to a cold floor. She sat up, blinking—and there he was.

But no, this couldn't be Fayen. Her Fayen was always on his feet, ready to throw a punch at any threat facing them. This Fayen—didn't even look like Fayen. He was unconscious—his face was covered in bruises, and one eye was swollen shut. He wore a bloodstained white jumpsuit, and his chest rose and fell in ragged, heaving breaths.

She crawled to him, placing her hands on his shoulders. "Fayen?"

The sound of her voice didn't rouse him. She patted his cheek. "Fayen, please wake up. We need you. *I* need you."

He remained still, his breath sighing out of his bloody lips. He couldn't save her. Not this time. She picked up one of his hands and held it to her cheek. Her Hybri shifted, sending skitters of pain through her core. She shut her eyes, trying to will it to be still. How she wished she could simply tear her own skin open and pry the accursed thing out!

Heat flared inside of her, as if the creature were infuriated by the idea. Evaly slumped beside Fayen, lowering his hand to rest in her lap. "I'm sorry," she whispered to the Hybri—even though she wasn't certain it was even capable of hearing her. "You didn't ask to get stuck with me. But here we are."

The heat retreated, fading to a faint, pulsing warmth somewhere in her sternum. It didn't hurt.

It didn't hurt.

When had she ever been able to sense the Hybri without pain accompanying it? She had assumed her body would reject the foreign organism for the rest of her life. She had assumed that *she* would reject it for the rest of her life, a hideous twist of her life's story at the hands of an unforgiving Creator.

What would happen if she didn't?

18

THE COLD OF the wall's metal plating seeped through Harper's shirt as she leaned against it, side by side with Pickett. In front of them, a trio of guardsmen stood with their blasters raised, pinning them in place. *They won't kill us now,* she thought, clenching her hands. Her wrists were bound together in front of her, so tight that her skin throbbed.

The *Void's* brig atrium was a sterile place, reminding her of a hospital waiting room. The walls were white, the floors gray, and there was a high desk near the door, where a senior guardsman sat, drafting their prisoner logs. Evaly had already been dragged back to a cell, limp in her captor's grip. Had she suffered another episode with her Hybri?

The commander stood beside the desk, enduring her own pat-down. Her head was lowered, unwilling to look at them. A flush of anger ran through Harper when she glanced at the expressionless mask. She had admired this woman, and she had sold them out to the Consortium. It was clear that she was remorseful, but that hadn't stopped her.

If I were in her shoes, would I have acted any differently? Harper wondered. The commander gave her all for the *Ransom*, even acting against her own desires. She had taken them to the enemy herself rather than risking a single member of her crew. She was like an extension of the ship itself, orchestrating everything for its wellbeing. Would Harper be able to do the same for Arkron? It was what she had been raised for. All of her training was meant to prepare her for the moment that she took the throne. And yet she failed to fit into the royal mold Lady Kova, her mother, and the rest of Arkron needed her to fill. She had wanted to stay on the *Ransom*, and they'd missed their chance to go home. She'd insisted that they rescue Fayen—and now they were prisoners themselves. Bargaining chips.

Why can't I be who I was born to be? She shut her eyes, trying to will Weaver Harper away. She had to be the princess in this moment. Poised and prepared to speak for her world.

But could Princess Harper get them out of this?

The guardsman behind the desk stood, hefting a tablet. "We'll have to confirm their identities before you are free to go," he said, addressing the commander. His fellows pushed her blaster, personal comm, and knife over the desk, and he caught them and thrust them out of sight.

"They are House Evensong. I am not here on a fool's errand," she replied, straightening at once. Her voice rose slightly from its respectful pitch.

"It wouldn't be the first time your kind has tried to hoodwink us. Let's see if it holds up to a DNA test," the guardsman drawled, striding up to Harper and Pickett. A patch on his breastplate identified him as Captain Keir. He grabbed Harper's chin between his fingers, forcing her to look upward. "They *do* match the description."

He dropped her chin and seized her fingers, pressing them against the screen of his tablet. The screen flashed as they were scanned. From his pocket he produced a small, cylindrical device that drew a bead of blood from her finger. This was dropped onto the tablet's scanner. After a moment, it was met with a cheerful chime. "Well, I'll be Deeped," Captain Keir said, turning to the commander. "You were telling the truth."

Behind her mask, the commander snorted softly. Ruefully, Harper rubbed her fingers together, trying to dispel the ache of the sting. There was something primeval about a DNA test; it boiled you down to your biological self, the construct of cells and order of genes that the Creator had selected to combine into the auburn-haired, freckled-faced, gawky Harper Evensong.

A fresh drop of blood formed on her fingertip, and she found herself looking at it almost fondly. It was a scrap of her barest self without the trappings she was forced into.

Captain Keir moved on to Pickett and yanked his Neherum necklace off. Pickett's jaw clenched; it was obvious that he was resisting the urge to snatch it back. It was as dear to him as Harper's locket was to her. "This will be all the confirmation we need from you," the guardsman said. "If it matches a registered Neherum—"

"It will," Pickett said. "I'm the High General's own journeyman."

The captain held up the necklace, letting it dangle lazily from his fingertips. "Indeed?" He gestured to two of his underlings, who grasped Pickett's arms. "You will be interrogated elsewhere, then," he drawled.

Interrogated? They already had proof of who they were; what more could the Consortium want? Were they going to beat him as they had Fayen? Harper's power warmed in her palms. Pickett had forbidden her from using her powers, and she doubted that diplomacy was going to keep them from hurting him.

Pickett met her eyes and mouthed, *Don't.*

Deeping older brothers. She turned her head away as he was led out, feeling more tangled than before.

Captain Keir's attention had returned to the commander. "There was not an alert for a child," he said, waggling his tablet towards the hallway that Evaly had been dragged down.

"She's House Evensong too," the commander said.

He lowered his tablet and said coldly, "If you think you will be paid extra, you are mistaken."

In a strained voice, the commander replied, "She's chosen them, and I do not seek payment. Our agreement was that in exchange for princess and prince, the Consortium would leave the *Star's Ransom* enterprise in peace."

"Indeed?" Captain Keir raised his chin. Two guardsmen closed in on either side of her, pulling her arms behind her back. "I'm afraid the deal has changed, Commander Clarkson."

Commander Clarkson? The name was oddly familiar . . . Clarkson had been Evaly's surname before her adoption into the Longracers. Perhaps the commander was from Hylon too. Harper shook away her curiosity—this wasn't the time for speculation. "That's not fair," she burst out. "She did exactly what you wanted, just to protect her people!"

Captain Keir eyed her. "Not so demure now, are you?" He stepped close, putting his helmeted head near hers. "Let me make something clear right now: The Exlenna belongs to the Consortium, girl. That includes the Outcasts."

Harper met his gaze. "The Consortium does not own Arkron."

His eyes squinted faintly behind the visor, and she had the impression that he was smiling wolfishly. "Not yet." He caught her chin again. "But it will soon. I think you're due for an audience with the Seven, aren't you?"

The Seven. The council of seven galactic leaders that oversaw the Consortium. Harper had stood before them with Lady Kova before but never on her own. Facing them would take every bit of her training. To them, she was the heir to a world they hungered for. A bargaining chip.

Something tightened inside of her, and she jerked her chin out of the captain's hand. She couldn't let them view her that way. That gave them too much control.

Captain Keir's attention shifted back to Commander Clarkson. "Put her with the other two."

The other *two*? Harper's stomach flipped. One was doubtlessly Evaly, and the other—she had assumed—was Fayen. Had Lady Kova made it home, then? Or worse, had she been executed already?

No, we would have heard something. And if she were here, Lady Kova would already be facing the Seven. She would insist they handle things diplomatically. She would see them locked in a cell for who knew how long, forced to ride out the political storm instead of becoming one of its winds.

Harper couldn't handle things like a princess. They were far past that. She squeezed her hands together, a bit of light seeping from between her fingers. She could weave a new story for this situation. The Consortium needed to see that Arkron wasn't to be trifled with. A demure princess couldn't do that with political platitudes.

In that moment, she made a choice. The time for empty words had passed. It was time for *power*. "You will take me to see the Seven," she said. "Now."

"They will summon you when they are ready," Captain Keir replied with a sneer.

"They will see me," she snapped, and poured the might of a thousand words into her voice. *"Now."* The effect was an echoing of her tone, as if a thousand people had risen up and cried the word at once. The binders burst from her wrists, scattering across the floor in shards of metal. Light erupted from her hands, threads of stories spiraling out from within her. Years of pent-up ideas surged within her, all just within reach. And for the first time in her life, she threw open the floodgates.

It felt good. It felt *glorious*. She was Harper Evensong, an empowered storyweaver. She would see that the Consortium left Arkron alone for good.

Captain Keir sprang backwards, hand flying to his blaster. His comrades raised theirs and fired, but at a sweep of her arm, the stunners were deflected. With another sweep, she threw them against the walls and *pushed*, pinning them into the metal.

"What *are* you?" Keir stood alone, his blaster leveled at her. This time the mockery in his voice was gone, replaced with a warble of terror. She aimed her threads at the blaster, crushing it in his hands, and commanded the crumpled metal to reform, wrapping around his ankles and pinning him to the floor. The sea of stories surged within her, opening thousands of possibilities. She used the threads to lift herself off the floor, fist raised towards the ceiling. Towards the stateroom she needed to reach.

"Everything," she replied, and launched herself upward.

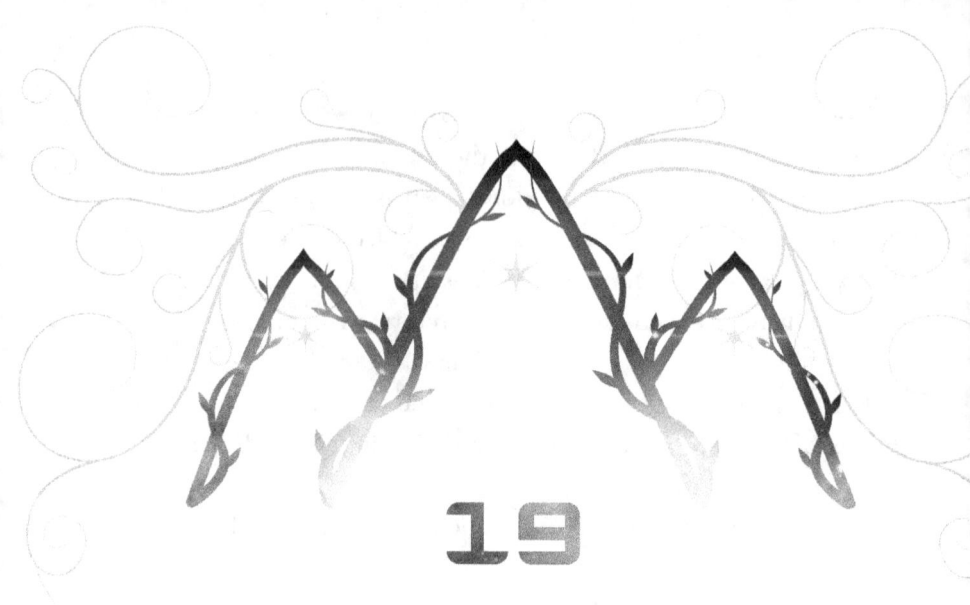

19

The further Pickett's captors marched him from Harper, the tighter the knot of anxiety in his chest became. Leaving her alone in a situation like this would be like stuffing a lit stick of blastpowder in a cardboard box. The sharp tilt of her head and the light behind her eyes as he was led away made him sweat. In childhood, that expression had usually been followed by some form of chaos. He had hoped that her years with Lady Kova had smoothed away her wild edges, but their recent time together had shown him otherwise.

Moons. This *interrogation* had better not take long. He had to get back to Harper before her impulses killed them all.

He was led to an upper level of the ship, where the functionality and the luxury of the *Void* began to intertwine. The steel walkway was giving way to diamond-patterned carpet, and the austere walls now bore the occasional splash of paint. Interesting. This didn't seem like the kind of place to interrogate a prisoner. Pickett wasn't certain whether he should be concerned or comforted by it.

The answer to this came the moment he was shoved into a spacious office. The room was outfitted with a fine, wooden desk and a trio of matching chairs around it. Tasteful paintings hung on the walls, but the fixture that captured Pickett's attention at once was the High General, who stood in front of a large viewport, admiring the Star Sea.

The knots of worry in his chest loosened at once. The sight of her was as relieving as if he had been a lost child in the market and had finally found his mother. "High General!" he cried, stooping into a bow. "It's so good to see you."

She turned about, her face crinkled in concern. "Release him at once," she ordered the guardsmen, "and remove his chains."

"But ma'am," one of them began, "he's a royal prisoner . . . "

The High General gripped the hilt of her sword and started forward. "He is my journeyman," she said. *"Release him."*

The guardsmen exchanged looks and apparently decided that the wrath of their commanding officer would be less painful than the wrath of the High General of the Neherum. They let go of Pickett's arms and then removed his cuffs.

"Leave us," she ordered.

They obeyed, scurrying from the room.

Pickett massaged his wrists; the binders had chafed his work-wearied hands. "High General, I didn't know you had business on the *Void*. It's—it's such a relief to see you."

"Likewise," she said, and grasped his hands. A yelp escaped him; she frowned and held them up. "Look at these," she muttered. "What did they do to you? They've wrecked your grip with these cracks!"

"It's from scrubbing floors, High General," he replied, ducking his head for a moment. He had forgotten that such work could hamper his swordsmanship. She would likely put his training on hold until he had healed. He risked a glance at her face and noted with a start that her lip was split in the corner and that there was a bruise on her cheek. "High General, are you hurt?"

"It is nothing." She released him, dropping her hand to the hilt of her sword. "Battle wounds, Pickett, battle wounds. Victory always comes at a price." Her voice hardened. "Why were you scrubbing floors?"

"That was the duty they gave me on the Outcast ship," he replied, still trying to fathom how she had managed to get hurt. Who had she been fighting? They must have been skilled to be able to score any marks on her. She was the High General. She was practically invincible!

She shook her head. "My apprentice. Scrubbing *floors*."

"It helped me keep up my strength," he offered. "I know it's likely to put me off swordsmanship for the moment, but I assure you my physique did not suffer otherwise."

"Bother the swordsmanship. We'll find a way around it." She took a step back and angled her head to assess him from head to toe, as if she didn't believe him when he said he was unhurt. Like a mother checking to make sure her child's elbow wasn't scraped in addition to their knee.

When he returned home, would his mother do the same? Or would she be more worried about Harper, the heir? He pushed the stinging thought away as the High General spoke again: "I am sorry you were forced to dwell among those barbarians."

Barbarians might be too harsh a term, he thought, remembering Captain Ziah's cheerful reception and the commander's composed leadership. "They are a unique race, High General," he replied. "Their culture would be an interesting study, if we have the resources in the near future; many of our perceptions about the Outcasts were incorrect. I'd be happy to draft a report for you about it."

She waved him off. "Pickett, that is of little importance at the moment."

His ears tingled in embarrassment. Right. His predicament was more pressing. "Would you be able to help us?" he asked earnestly. "You're the High General . . ."

She was already shaking her head. Her braid whipped about, thwacking against her back and chest. "The Neherum have always maintained a stance of neutrality," she said.

He had guessed the answer, but it still hurt. Just once, couldn't she be as loyal to him as he was to her? He thrust the thought aside quickly. Things didn't work like that. She had to do what was best for the Neherum, not her personal feelings. "Of course. Forgive me. I had hoped that your presence here was a sign . . . " He lowered his head. The Neherum were permitted to use the *Void* as a waypoint during their travels. It had been foolish to think that the High General was here to aid in House Evensong's plight with the Consortium. She was likely passing through on her way back to Anaya from an investigation elsewhere in the Exlenna.

She stepped away from him and sat down behind the desk. "I cannot help your sister," she said. "Nor can I help Miss Clarkson or Mr. Longracer."

He looked up. "So Fayen is here. How did you know?"

She laced her hands together. "As High General, there are few things that escape my attention."

He had to sit with that for a moment. She had known Fayen was a prisoner, and hadn't alerted him? Or House Evensong? Or even tried to get him out? It was somewhat disconcerting . . . but then again, intervening might be a breach of the Neherum's neutrality. He didn't have a right to feel hurt, Pickett decided. She was doing what she believed was best for the Neherum.

"However," she continued, "you are a different situation, Pickett. As my journeyman, I could grant you immunity. You are my personal assistant, and a good one at that." She offered him a rare smile.

Fresh warmth flooded through him. *A good assistant.* He was valuable to her. She was willing to bend the rule for him and only him. He was more to her than he was to House Evensong.

And yet . . . "What are the stipulations of this?" he asked.

"You would have to depart with me," she said, and held out his ID necklace. "Without your sister."

✦

Even with her eyes closed and cat ears pinned against her head, Evaly's senses tried to suffocate her with a combination of blood, sweat, and molten stories. At the same time, she paid it no mind—she couldn't. Not when she and her Hybri were so close to unifying. Beyond her cell, she could hear the guardsmen shouting and alarms blaring as they scrambled to go after Harper.

But for a change, the chaos inside of her was lessening. It was almost as if she had reached the eye of the hurricane—the storm still raged around her, but for the moment, she held herself still, face-to-face with the creature inside of her. Her muscles were jolting and spasming, and her Hybri twisted inside of her, trying to decide if it needed to make itself bigger or smaller and failing to do either. She didn't try to push it away or drag it outward. It was just as frightened as she was, trying to make sense of who they were.

What if they weren't that different? What if the commander had been right—what if the Creator had let this melding happen for a reason?

So she crouched beside Fayen, clutching his hand, and accepted the creature inside of her. They shared a skin. Somehow, they'd have to learn how to get along.

Her limbs began to tingle again, but the ache was more akin to growing pains than the deep burning of her usual pain. She inhaled sharply as it spread, pulsing out from her core and down her limbs, to her fingers and toes. She could feel her flesh rippling, starting to transform—panic began to well up within her, but she sucked in ragged breaths, forcing herself to be calm. What would happen when the shifting was over? Would she open her eyes and find herself in a new form?

She never had the chance to find out. Behind her, the ray shield disengaged with a hum. Her Hybri shriveled back into her, and she slumped over Fayen, stunned by the sudden draining.

Someone was tossed into the cell beside them, landing with a bang of metal on metal. The commander climbed shakily to her hands and knees, trying to rise. A guardsman stumbled in after her. His armor was battered, and he appeared to be limping. A tendril of twisted metal clung to his leg like a stubborn piece of greenery.

"You!" he roared, kicking her in the side. She collapsed back down, cursing. "You brought her here to destroy us!"

"I didn't know she was so powerful!" the commander cried, struggling to sit up. The guardsman kicked her squarely in the chest. Evaly winced at the crunching sound. The commander reeled backwards, colliding with the wall. Her hand went to her chest, and Evaly detected a whining noise coming from her. Had the blow injured some cybernetic piece of her?

The guardsman lunged at her, catching her by the throat and dragging her upward. "She's a *monster!* You will pay for this, Outcast." He struck her temple with the butt of his blaster. The commander wheezed as the impact smote the mask from her face.

Evaly gasped as she met the Outcast's eyes for the first time.

Her mind was playing tricks on her. The pressure of their situation was too much, and she was hallucinating. Or the guardsmen had secretly drugged her or something.

Her dead sister's face met hers.

A tangle of scars stretched from the corner of Jael's left eye and down the side of her face, twisting the skin into mottled ridges. Weary circles lay under her eyes. Her skin was paler than Evaly remembered, but her brown eyes were still piercing.

That is, until they rolled back into her head and she slumped backwards, unconscious from the blow. The guardsman cursed and dropped her to the ground. "I'm not finished with you," he growled, sinking his boot into her side for good measure. He spun towards the door, holstering his blaster once more. He paused, his cold eyes skating over Evaly and Fayen. Perhaps his wrath had found a new outlet.

Her first instinct was to cower against Fayen, but she stopped herself. No. She couldn't, not now. She could be more. She *had* to be more.

She met his eyes, glaring at him with all the force she could muster. Perhaps she wasn't strong enough to take him in a fight, but she could tell him that she wasn't afraid.

Their gazes locked for a moment. Then he snorted and climbed out of the cell, reactivating the ray shield behind him.

Jael groaned, her eyes fluttering open. Carefully laying Fayen's hand onto his stomach, Evaly crept over to her. This wasn't a dream, nor some stray fragment of Harper's weaving. This was . . . this was her sister. And all Evaly could think to say was, "You're supposed to be dead."

"Yes," Jael whispered.

Evaly struggled to her feet, trembling. "You died on Hylon of the plague."

"I almost did." She tried to sit up but only collapsed against the wall. Rasping, she added, "And when I crawled out of the house, they branded me unclean and Outcasted me."

"Why didn't you tell me?" Evaly demanded. Inside of her, the Hybri began to roil again. None of this made sense. She had been on the *Ransom* for days. Every day Jael had watched her train, and said nothing. "You're different than you were on Hylon," she said.

Jael's chest was heaving. "We both are," she said.

Yes. They were. Evaly wasn't the spry eight-year-old that had shipped off from Hylon in the name of opportunity. She was a cripple now. A member of House Evensong. A Hybri. And Jael was an Outcast commander, the leader of a rugged community that she clearly loved.

Jael unfastened the top of her coat and peered at her chest. She groaned softly and turned her head away. "Not good."

"What is it?" Hesitant, Evaly peered over the neck of her coat. The shirt beneath was a rumpled blue, but beneath that it looked like shards of metal poked through the fabric.

"My ventilator," Jael whispered. She clenched her metal hand. "I'm more broken on the inside than I am on the outside." She shut her eyes, and for a moment Evaly wondered if she had blacked out again. Then she opened them, meeting Evaly's gaze. "I'm sorry. I don't know how to get you out of here."

Evaly sat back, hunkered between her and Fayen. "That's okay," she said. She dipped into herself again, searching for her Hybri. It met her tentatively, still afraid but softening. She wasn't strong, not yet. But she was changing. Growing. "I think I have an idea."

20

PICKETT'S HAND REACHED for his necklace, which swayed hypnotically from the High General's hand. Just before his fingers connected with the chain, a guardsman burst into the room. "High General!" he said, snapping a salute.

Her attention swept to him, and she scowled. "What is it? I do not appreciate you and your comrades barging into my study without so much as knocking!" She glanced at Pickett and added under her breath, so that only he could hear, "Imbeciles. I would never stand for this shoddy performance at Anaya."

He nodded in agreement. His hand still hovered before him, ready to accept his necklace back. Ready to slip back into the role where he really belonged. It wasn't an abandonment of Harper and House Evensong; on the contrary, being at the High General's side would make him privy to information that could aid in their resistance against the Consortium. If she chose to share, that is. Nonetheless, she valued his help. Therefore, he was confident that she would confide in him.

Just like she confided in you about Fayen? He shook off the thought and reached for his necklace again. But the High General was no longer holding it out; her attention was on the guardsman again. "Well?" she said, dropping her hand to the hilt of her sword.

The guardsman saluted again, somewhat awkwardly. "I was ordered to inform you that Princess Evensong has escaped her confinement and is seeking a confrontation with the Consortium."

Pickett closed his eyes, grimacing.

"And why is this my concern?" Vasken demanded. "Can't you idiots stop her?"

The guardsman stuttered. Pickett didn't blame him; the sight of an empowered storyweaver wasn't something that was easily put into words.

"It's not that simple, High General," he explained with a sigh. "My sister has . . . abilities."

"Abilities," the High General repeated, her brow creasing. "What sort of abilities?"

"The sort that could eject us all overboard if she's not calmed down."

Her eyes widened. "*What?*"

"I know the Neherum are neutral, but it would be best if we helped them . . . eh . . . contain her," he said, sidling towards the door.

She caught his arm to stop him. "I see. In that case, it would be best to diverge yourself from her so that these idiotic thugs the Consortium calls its army do not recapture you." She held out his necklace again.

He took it and slid it over his neck. The familiar weight settled there, and he sighed in relief. "Thank you, High General. I apologize for my sister. Once she is contained, I will stand by your side again." He did his best to smooth his rumpled clothing. If only he had his uniform and armor!

She patted his arm. "Don't worry about your decorum," she said. "Given the circumstances, it can be excused. The pendant is enough."

"Thank you, High General," he said. To the guardsman, he asked, "Where is she?"

"Already in the stateroom. Sir," he added.

"Good." He started out the door but remembered his place and invited the High General out first. She dipped her head as she swept past him, and he measured his steps to match hers.

She glanced at him, a smile playing around her lips. "Your presence at my side may ease the Consortium's wrath upon Her Highness."

"Perhaps," he agreed. "Proof that not all of House Evensong's members are . . . " He trailed off, searching for the right words. "As difficult as her."

She gave a short laugh. "Perhaps you are too harsh on your sister, Pickett. She is, after all, still a child, and prone to immature ways."

He shook his head. "She's trained with our aunt for years. She should understand who she is meant to be." Over his shoulder, he called to the guardsman, who was hurrying behind them, "Are the lifts still operational?"

"As far as I know, sir," he replied, huffing behind his helmet.

They skidded to a halt in the lift atrium. Across from them were the lifts—and barring their way was a massive crater in the floor. The carpet was smoking and the metal was twisted, wires sparking. Peering into it, Pickett saw that it had blasted through several levels below.

The High General's jaw dropped. "She did this? Is she a Hybri?"

"Not exactly," Pickett said, picking the edge of the crater that seemed the most secure and beginning to skirt along it.

The High General followed, flattening herself against the wall beside him. "Pickett, I need to know what we'll be facing."

He made the mistake of looking into the crater again. This time the sight made him queasy. The jagged circle was like a portal to the Deeps. House Evensong had kept Harper's power a secret for years to protect her from either exploitation or assassination. The admonishments he'd heard as a child still rang in his ears—and yet Harper had chosen to reveal herself. He found that he had no qualms about telling the High General. She deserved to know. "An empowered storyweaver," he finally admitted, forcing his head back against the wall to keep his vision level.

"An *empowered storyweaver*?" Her voice was stunned. "They're supposed to be extinct!"

"Arkron is . . . special," he grunted. The ruined plate beneath him shifted, threatening to send him skidding into the hole. He leapt for the other side and tripped over the rug but righted himself before it was too embarrassing.

Meanwhile, the High General had reached the unsteady place. She tried to mirror his acrobatics but undershot the other ledge. She tottered on the edge of it, eyes wide, but he jumped forward and caught her arm, pulling her to safety. "Glad to see my reflexes didn't weaken in the Fringe," he said, offering her a smile.

She straightened her jerkin. "Indeed. I can't even begin to fathom how often you must have had to protect yourself."

A part of him wished he had some sort of horrible thing to recount, but the fact of the matter was, the most horrible thing he had seen was the accumulated grime on the deck plates. "As I said, they would be a fascinating subject of study," he said. "The culture, at least the culture on the *Ransom*—I'm sure every enterprise is different—is much less aggressive than I expected. The commander was . . . intriguing." He jabbed at the lift's controls, trying to summon one.

The High General shifted her braid off her shoulder. "Do not let your curiosity distract them from what they really are," she remarked. "Savages. They think of nothing but orbs."

The commander hadn't turned them in for orbs, though. She had only wanted to see her enterprise safe. He could respect that, couldn't he? She wasn't a savage.

The lift arrived with a cheerful chime, and the door slid open to reveal Evaly, ashen-faced but upright. Sprawled on the lift's floor was Fayen, unconscious, and slumped against the wall beside him was the commander. Maskless, for the first time.

Pickett's jaw dropped at the sight. "Evaly? What is this? How did you get out?" He dropped to examine Fayen, though his gaze slipped back up to the commander. Her face was angular and bearing the markings of a recent fight, though there was something familiar about it. She was hunched over, protecting her torso as if she had been kicked in the ribs. Despite her pinched face and shallow breathing, she dipped her head respectfully. "Highness."

"Pickett," Evaly said, "this is my sister. From Hylon."

"What?" Pickett gripped Fayen's wrist, feeling for his pulse. It was erratic—he was seriously damaged. "You're Jael?" His thoughts stuttered to a halt as his mind began to fit the pieces together. She had taken a special interest in Evaly aboard the *Ransom*. She was from Hylon, evidenced by her appearance. And while there were obvious differences in hair and eye color, their facial shapes were similar. "Didn't you die of the plague?"

She gave a hollow laugh and tipped her head back against the lift's plating. "The girl from Hylon died. But Jael Clarkson is very much alive."

"Why the Deeps didn't you tell us? Why didn't she tell us?" He shot the question at Evaly and gingerly lifted Fayen, searching for any bleeding wounds. His jumpsuit was stained with blood, but Pickett couldn't find the injury that it was from.

The High General stepped into the lift behind him and ordered the door to shut. "This should make for an interesting ride," she remarked. Her expression was one of amusement, as if she were at the theater, watching a drama.

Evaly shook her head. "Not now, Pickett." She steadied herself against the wall, eyes still on Fayen. Frankly he was surprised that she wasn't on the floor with him. Where had this newfound strength come from?

A rasping cough tore out of Jael and she doubled up, a thin trail of blood appearing at the corner of her mouth. Tears mingled with the blood on her face. "We're different now," she whispered. "She's happy with you."

Pickett shook his head, still at a loss. He couldn't understand why she had waited to reveal herself—and why in the Silent Star Sea would she have turned them in if Evaly was her sister? Then again, if he were in her boots . . . if he had built a new life for himself and then was reunited with Harper, who had also become a different person . . . would he do anything differently?

They were already in a similar situation. He had his life with the Neherum, separate from House Evensong. He had just chosen the High General over her. Did he have any room to judge Jael?

Evaly eyed the High General uneasily and knelt beside Pickett. "We need your help," she whispered. "I got them this far, but I don't know what to do from here. They're both so sick, Pickett."

He looked over his shoulder at the High General, seeking guidance. But helping him help the others would break her vow of neutrality. She merely raised an eyebrow at him in silent challenge. She was waiting for him to act, to show where his loyalties truly lay.

Jael began to cough again, harder this time. Pickett winced, glancing back at her, and then mumbled an apology to the High General. Stepping carefully around Fayen, he knelt beside her. "Where does it hurt?" he asked, painfully aware of Vasken's eyes on him.

Jael licked the blood from her lips. "You shouldn't help me."

In response, he pulled her arms away from her chest.

"She was kicked by a guardsman," Evaly said. "Hard. It broke her ventilator."

Ventilator? So her prosthetics aren't her only additions. Pickett eyed the broken wires poking through the Outcast's shirt.

The lift stopped, and the motion knocked him off balance. The High General caught his shoulder, steadying him. "We've arrived. It's time to go."

"Go?" Evaly looked between him and the High General, her cat-ears flicking backwards. "Go where? Pickett, you're not leaving us, are you? You're going to let the Consortium have us?"

"I . . ." he began, searching for the right words, but the High General answered for him.

"Pickett has resumed his position as my assistant. In order to have amnesty, he must remain at my side."

Evaly's eyes narrowed into a glare. The vivid yellow of her irises reminded Pickett of embers. "So you've chosen her over us?"

"It's not like that . . ." Pickett turned to the High General. "We can't leave them. They'll both die without help."

"Longracer has become a pawn of the Consortium," she replied, her hand dropping to the hilt of her sword. "And she is an Outcast. She is none of our concern."

But Fayen's a Neherum too! Unease rippled through him. "Respectfully, High General, I believe that it is . . ." He hesitated, trying to formulate a way to convince her. There had to be a middle ground. Surely he could remain with her but ensure that they survived. "Fayen's one of us! And the Commander may have forced me into manual labor, but she *did* shelter us in the Fringe. For that, I am in her debt. Additionally, the codes require us to render aid to the defenseless."

The doors to the lift hissed open, but the High General stepped between them, preventing them from closing once more. She folded her arms, regarding him somberly. "It seems that we are at an impasse. Interfering with this situation would break our policy of neutrality towards the Consortium."

"But it's wrong to leave her like this," he insisted. "And we were going to stop Harper anyway. Doesn't that count as interfering?"

"There are bystanders here who may be injured if she is not stopped," the woman replied. "But this"—she gestured to Jael, Fayen, and Evaly—"goes too far. I will not force you to come with me. However, if you stay with them, you will be forfeiting the amnesty you have under me in this situation."

He stared at her at a loss. Had he regained his place at her side only to lose it already? Jael gave a wheezing cough behind him. He glanced back to see a fresh trickle of blood leaking down her chin. Her face was deathly white, and her breathing was labored. Her eyes latched onto Evaly, and she rasped, "I . . . love . . . "

Evaly's cat ears splayed sideways as she swiveled between Pickett, Jael, and Fayen's prone form. "Please," she whispered. "Pickett, please."

His pendant weighed heavily around his neck. His instinct told him to go with the High General. It would be better for House Evensong in the long term. But this wasn't right. He couldn't just walk out and leave them like this. He would never forgive himself if Fayen and Jael died here when he could have helped them. Helping them was the right thing to do. Why didn't she see that? What was preventing her from acting by their codes?

He bowed his head. "I'm sorry," he said to the High General. "It appears that we must part again."

He gripped his ID necklace, prepared to remove it, but she motioned for him to keep it on. "It is yours. Perhaps it will remind you of who you are in the coming days. I sincerely hope that the next time we meet, you will be able to resume your duties in full." Then she stepped aside, revealing a squad of guardsmen waiting for them, blasters drawn.

21

THE INTERCESSORS ON Harper's arms gleamed electric blue as she threw open the doors to the stateroom. With her strengthened arms, they flew apart with a bang and toppled from their hinges with a resounding crash. Around her feet, a swirl of story threads twisted, leaving in their wake glittering slivers of light that spiraled through the air like fireflies.

She raised a trembling finger and pointed it at Speaker Archer, who served as the Seven's chairman. He sat at the head of a long table with his fellows—a table arrayed in a lavish meal. Steam rose from platters of food, and seven glass goblets of wine twinkled beneath the crystal chandelier.

The Seven sat frozen, some with forkfuls of food halfway to their mouths. Speaker Archer's goblet was partway to his mouth; some of the crimson liquid had splashed onto the neck of his fine robe when she'd blown down the doors.

"I," she thundered, "am Harper Evensong. And I *demand* you give an answer for your infringement on my world and my House."

Guardsmen emerged from the corners of the room, running to encircle the table.

Harper cast them away, murmuring their story under her breath—*"They were ensnared by the floor, unable to move . . . "* The tiled plating of the floor rose up in the shape of hands, trapping the guardsmen's legs.

With another gesture, she pinned the Seven back into their chairs with a thicket of twisting vines, whispering, *"They were trapped by thorns as cruel as their own plans."*

"What is the meaning of this?" Archer gasped as the vines stopped just shy of his neck.

Harper forced them to rustle higher. "The Consortium," she said, raising her voice, "has committed offenses against Arkron that I can no longer overlook. You attacked myself, my brother, and other members of our household, driving us from Mantalor. You are responsible for the death of the captain of my guard, a good man. You held Fayen Longracer hostage and tortured him in order to manipulate us into coming here. You betrayed an honorable woman when she brought us to you because you see her as a lesser being." She urged the vines higher. "I will *not* allow this to continue."

"Come now, child, we only wanted to negotiate!" On Archer's left, one of the Seven spoke. She was an albino woman with sharp eyes and a haircut that was perfectly level with her chin. Harper recognized her as Empress Lara of Catena, the ruler of the Exlenna's most heavily industrialized world. She strained against her bonds, trying to break free. "There is no need for this magic trick!"

Harper tightened the brush around her, whispering for it to sprout thorns near the woman's neck. The woman yelped in surprise as the barbs snagged her skin.

"You think this is a magic trick?" Harper demanded. "You *will* leave my world in peace, or the Consortium will face my hand. And it is very heavy." She launched herself into the air to hover above them and laughed. The motion made sparks skitter away from her, as if the sound of her voice was the pop of a burning log. "I am justice. A good story is a circle, with an end that balances its beginning." She swept closer to Speaker Archer and swept her hand out, inviting the strands to mesh together. They began to intertwine into a sword. "An attack for an attack. A life for a life. And then I will go in peace, and peace will reign unless you choose to disturb it." She could see herself reflected in Archer's glasses, a distorted devil alight with otherworldly power.

And to her surprise, the sight didn't empower her further. She looked like a monster. A creature come to weave destruction instead of hope.

This . . . this wasn't who she wanted to be.

But it is what you must be! Weaver Harper urged. *It is what they have driven you to!*

Resistance in her story threads made her glance at her hands. The urgency of the power had faded, and the words were struggling to flesh themselves into Being. Her arms felt heavy and her chest burned, as though the glorious molten gold from before was too hot and now scalded her flesh.

No. Don't let them see that you're weakening. She poured all of her attention into the sword, whispering that it was made of unbreakable metal, with an ivy hilt—but the protests from her body continued to mount.

"Harper, stop!"

Pickett's voice broke her focus. She looked over her shoulder and found him standing in the ruined doorway, surrounded by guardsmen. He was holding Fayen, who hung limp in his arms. Beside him, Evaly supported Commander Clarkson, who was coughing. Her mask was gone, revealing a bruised, bloodstained face. Behind, an entire battalion of guardsmen filled the long corridor.

The message was clear: They had brought her friends to try and bargain with her. If she continued her attack, they would be killed.

"Harper, would you stop and *think* for once in your life?" Pickett shouted. "You're wasting your energy trying to play Creator when you could be helping us!"

"I *am* helping you!" she screamed at him, landing atop the table, close to Archer. He shut his eyes, cringing as far away from her as he could. "I'm helping all of Arkron!"

He flinched at her magnified voice but pressed on. "No, you're not! You're going to make this so much worse. *Come down.*"

She looked over her shoulder at him again and saw, for the first time, the fear in his eyes. His face was red with anger, but his eyes, like Archer's, reflected her glowing might with terror. She had frightened the unmovable, unemotional Pickett.

Oh, moons. She wanted to frighten the Consortium, not her brother. The threads in her hand slowed to a crawl. Archer peeked an eye open, obviously surprised that he was still alive. Weaver Harper tried to surge forward again, incensed, but she met a wall. A physical wall of exhaustion and an emotional wall of reluctance. She didn't want this to be what the Exlenna thought of when they heard the name House Evensong. She didn't want fear to linger in Pickett's eyes when he looked at her.

She clenched her jaw but dismissed the sword. It evaporated into tiny stars that spiraled upward before disintegrating. "This isn't over, Speaker," she snarled, and drew away from him. Her gaze found the rest of the Seven, and she flung her arms out. "That goes for all of you. Leave Arkron alone, or we will repeat this day."

She commanded her threads to carry her to Pickett. They obliged. Slowly. More sparks flew into the air, but Harper couldn't tell if it was from her storyweaving or if she was beginning to hallucinate. Like the sword, she dismissed the threads holding her up, and she dropped to the floor, though less gracefully than she would have liked.

The guardsmen behind Pickett and the others raised their blasters, but Harper swept them aside and raised the doors back to their proper place. It took more effort than she expected. Was she only tired? Or was there something wrong with her weavings? "Are you ready to go home?" she asked, surprised by how hoarse her voice was.

"Are you?" Pickett's face had molded to impassiveness, but his eyes were still rounded.

Harper looked back at her work, and rather than feeling a chill of pleasure, she felt a throb of unease. She would rather be going back to the *Ransom*, to keep honing her weavings. Then Fayen coughed, sagging lower in Pickett's arms. Harper lowered her head, admitting defeat. "Yes. Let's go home. To Arkron."

She was aware of the eyes in the room on her as she raised her hands again, summoning every bit of strength she had left. She could take them to a ship, but Jael and Fayen were in serious condition. And there was no point in hiding her gift anymore. The Exlenna knew now. The days of hiding behind the perfectly manicured mask of a princess were over.

A ring of light erupted in front of her, growing wider and wider until it stopped at the size of a mirror. It hissed ominously, and Harper felt the burn in her chest again. A deep sense of urgency pulsed within her, and she stepped into the portal and offered Evaly her hand. "Come on. We need to hurry."

Evaly hesitated for a moment, but accepted her grip. Together they guided Commander Clarkson into the weaving, and Pickett followed, bearing Fayen. Before the ring of light shut behind them, she heard Archer's voice echo across the room: "This will not be forgotten, Princess!"

No, Harper knew it wouldn't.

Harper struck the carpeted ground face first. She lay there for a moment, her heart racing. The power drained out of her limbs, leaving them trembling and weak. Her chest was throbbing, throbbing, throbbing, as if someone had shoved a dagger up to its hilt into her.

She had done it. For better or for worse, Weaver Harper had revealed herself to the Consortium and the rest of the Exlenna.

"Harper?" Pickett's hands landed on her shoulders and he rolled her over. "Are you alive?"

She blinked up at him, taking in the room. A spackled ceiling hung overhead, and looming over her was a large wooden desk. "Did we . . . " She coughed, and then groaned. She had just accomplished a godlike show of power. Shouldn't she be glowing or something? Why did she feel like she'd been hit by a hovericle? "Did we make it?"

He looked up, and then a smile softened his hard expression. "Yeah, I think so. Listen."

It was hard to hear over her thudding heart, Commander Clarkson's rasping breath, and Fayen and Evaly's simultaneous groans. But after a moment, she heard what he had. Birdsong. Sweet and lilting, outside a window overhead. And beyond that, the rush of wind through a myriad of trees.

Home. They were home.

Harper struggled into a sitting position as the door to the study opened. Lady Kova bustled in, holding a cup of chai. She froze when she saw them, and the cup slipped from her fingers. Hot chai spread across the ivory carpet in a brown tide. Lady Kova looked at it, and then at them. Then she did something so undignified that Harper fought the urge to cover her eyes to spare her the shame.

She screamed. And then slumped against the door in a dead faint.

22

"Do you have *any* idea of what you've done?" Lady Kova slammed the door of the common room so viciously that the paintings clattered against the wall.

Harper rose from her seat, pushing her damp hair behind her ears. Knowing that this confrontation was coming, she had bathed and changed into a simple gown and surcoat, hoping that appearing collected would help alleviate her aunt's fury. Clearly there was no such luck. Retorts filled her mouth, but she bit her tongue to stymie them. Back talk would only further infuriate her aunt. Lady Kova's anger was like a firecracker: It burnt white-hot and explosive for a moment, and then fizzled to a smoky haze. The longevity and thickness of that smoke depended on the severity of the offence.

Lady Kova prowled in front of her, weaving a tight circle on the trellis-patterned rug. "I thought I had trained you better than this! You could have lain low and waited for an opportunity to escape from the Outcast ship. You could have found a way to send us a message. You could have cooperated with the Consortium and let us find a way to extract you! *And instead you decided to attack them with your story-weaving!*" She stopped pacing and spun to face Harper, her chest heaving. "Don't you understand how this looks in the eyes of the Exlenna? If they didn't have just cause to attack us before, they do now!"

Harper hugged her sides and did not reply. *Let her burn out. Let her burn out and then try to explain yourself. Then you can go see the others or think of a way to fix this. Or take a nap.*

Moons. I'm so very tired.

The last few hours had been a splotch of color and motion. She had landed them at Solstice, House Evensong's estate in northern Arkron. Harper's childhood home. After making sure Lady Kova hadn't hit her head during her faint, Pickett had immediately set about calling for emergency transport for Fayen and Jael. They had been rushed to the capital city, Jana, where specialists awaited them. In the midst of the medical chaos, Harper had chosen to remain at Solstice. She wasn't ready to face the tensions in the capital. The people would be demanding answers. Arkron's representative council would have words for her. And her mother . . . Harper swallowed hard. What would her mother have to say?

"Consortium ships are already on their way!" Lady Kova said. Her face was flushed, and her hands were balled at her sides. "Do you have anything to say for yourself, Harper?"

Harper drew in a deep breath. The two thin slashes over her heart tightened painfully with the motion. She had discovered them after shucking off her rumpled tunic. As far as she knew, she hadn't been struck with anything, which meant that they had appeared after her outpouring of power. It seemed that instead of only making her chest hurt, large weavings would actually physically wound her. "I stand by what I did. The Consortium needed to be sent a clear message that Arkron will not allow itself to be trifled with."

Lady Kova threw her hands heavenward. "Creator have mercy. What has gotten into you? You are a princess! You are supposed to *think*—to think about how every action has a consequence!" She lowered her hands to wring them. "Oh, child. This isn't who you're supposed to be!"

It was Harper's turn to tighten her fists. "But this is who I am, Aunt Kova."

Lady Kova's jaw tensed. "So I see," she said. "So you are a storyweaver. A rebel. A war-bringer. *Not* the princess you were born to be."

Harper raised her chin defiantly. "I was born with this gift for a reason. Perhaps a weaver is what I am truly meant to be."

Lady Kova stalked across the room and thrust her face close to hers. "You do *not* get to pick and choose who you will be."

Harper held her gaze. "Really? Then who does? You?" Lady Kova wasn't the one weaving her story. She was a part of it, yes, but Harper didn't want her steering *everything*. Not anymore. Not since she'd tasted what it was like to be something else, something less constrained.

Lady Kova reared backwards. Harper braced herself for a slap, even though that was not Lady Kova's usual method of punishment. Perhaps her words had been uncalled for. She should have held her tongue. But moons, she was so tired of doing so. So tired of trying to squeeze herself into Lady Kova's mold.

"Kova. I believe you've said enough."

Lady Kova spun about to face the new voice. Harper's heart plunged into her stomach as she peered around her to see Queen Anrameta in the doorway.

Anrameta released the doorknob, her hand hovering in the air. Unlike Lady Kova's prim gown, she wore a sleeveless shirt and robe, and her hair was combed up into a knot atop her head. A few stray wisps escaped from it, and Harper couldn't believe how many of them were gray.

Then again, it had been two years since she'd seen her mother in the flesh. As always, Anrameta wore her crown: It was a circlet of silver twisted into ivy, and the band rose upward into three triangular frames. Set in the frames were thin plates of sapphire, which gleamed in the late afternoon sunlight.

"I didn't think you'd fly out here," Lady Kova said. Her voice was dry, and Harper detected a note of embarrassment in it. It was improper to be caught quarrelling.

"I believe Lady Longracer has things well in hand in the capital," Anrameta replied. "I would like to speak with my daughter."

Lady Kova stiffly stepped away from Harper, who had the sudden urge to cower behind her. She was used to her aunt's scoldings but had no idea what to expect from Anrameta. The last time they'd been together, she'd been a child. Now, everything was different. She was older, her misdeeds bigger.

"Alone," Anrameta added. Her voice was calm. Her hazel eyes gleamed fiercely.

Lady Kova's lips thinned into a line and she glanced back at Harper. "As you wish. We will continue our discussion later, niece." She swept out of the room, brushing past her sister and shutting the door softly behind her. Even as angry as she was, she didn't go about slamming doors.

Harper hadn't realized that she was holding herself ramrod straight until Lady Kova was gone. As if she were a puppet clipped from its strings, she slumped. Just as quickly, she straightened to give her mother the gesture of respect. If Lady Kova was incensed, she couldn't even begin to fathom what her mother's feelings for her would be. What did she say? Where did she start? She wasn't the same girl that had been sent to train under her aunt on Mantalor. But that had been her mother's goal, right? To make her into a real princess? Her chest tightened in a way that had nothing to do with her wounds.

"Hello, Mother," she finally offered. Should she have said *Mama*? *Mother* seemed more appropriate now, but did Anrameta see it that way?

Anrameta's breath escaped her in a gasp, and suddenly she was across the room and Harper was in her arms. "Oh, my love, my love, I was afraid you'd never come home." Anrameta's lips kissed every inch of Harper's bare skin they could find, and she cupped her face between her hands. "I was afraid, so afraid."

Harper's shoulders stiffened in shock. This wasn't the reunion she had braced herself for, and the defenses she had erected were swiftly undermined by the wave of her mother's love. To Anrameta, she wasn't a princess or a storyweaver or a rebel or a war-bringer. She was just her daughter. Tears pricked her eyes, and before she could stop herself, Harper was weeping too. "Mama. Mama, I'm sorry. I was just trying to help."

Anrameta brushed her tears away and kissed where they had been. "I know, love. I know your heart was good."

Harper rested her head against her mother's chest. She heard the unspoken *but* at the end of her sentence, yet chose to ignore it for now. She looked down at her hands. "I should have helped Fayen and Jael. But by the time we got home . . . I was so tired."

"It's all right. Pickett tells me they are both stable for now." Anrameta caught her hands and squeezed them. "You are not the Creator."

The words gave her pause. No. She wasn't. In the heat of her empowerment, she had felt as though she could be. Then her strength had flagged, and she was reminded of who she was once again: a frail, limited human. It was so *aggravating*.

Anrameta released her to grip her shoulder, steering her towards the balcony affixed to the side of the common room. The doors were propped open, letting in the warm summer breeze. Stepping outside, Harper drank in a lungful of her home's air. Solstice was nestled in a small hollow within the wooded northern mountains. Before them, trees stretched outward in a tapestry of green, ignited by the setting sun. Here and there, the limbs of dead trees jutted upward, a sobering reminder of the planet's history. But they were fast being choked by the life of their fellows. "I know Lady Kova has already imparted the seriousness of your actions," Anrameta said, "but I fear I must bring it up as well."

Harper squeezed her eyes shut. "I know. It was risky. But I had to do something, Mama. I know they were not the methods you or Lady Kova would have liked me to use, but they were effective." She felt her palms warm again and rubbed them on her thighs in an effort to cool them.

"They are effective for *now*," Anrameta corrected. "True, the Consortium isn't on our doorstep yet. But they are coming."

The sorrow in her mother's voice penetrated Harper deeper than Lady Kova's anger had. For the first time in days, the princess pushed the weaver aside and resurfaced. She surveyed the damage and instantly flooded Harper with horror. The potential outcomes of what she had done—besides outcomes of victory—danced through her mind.

If the Consortium decided to retaliate, they could face genocide. Furthermore, Anrameta had spent her life working to mend the fractured relationship between House Evensong and their people and had largely succeeded. But if they realized that she had kept the secret of her daughter's powers from them, it could mean an upsurge in violence, like the period of unrest when Harper's father had been assassinated. And if they knew she was responsible for bringing the Consortium to them . . . they could be facing a full revolution.

"Oh, moons," she whispered as the weight of it settled onto her shoulders. She slumped forward, gripping the railing. "Aunt Kova is right—I didn't think. *I didn't think.*" She pressed her knuckles against her forehead. "That's . . . that's not the kind of leader I should be."

"I know, love." Anrameta wrapped an arm around her shoulder. "What's done is done. We will prepare as best we can and face what will come when it comes. Arkron is gifted at survival."

"It shouldn't have to be."

Anrameta's eyes darkened. "No. But that is her story. The Creator will see it redeemed." She smiled and lifted Harper's chin. "There is one good thing that has come from this already, you know."

Harper tried to match her smile and failed. "Oh?"

"It brought you home."

A sob tightened Harper's throat. "I never wanted to leave," she whispered, and hid her face in her mother's chest. Anrameta pulled her close, and they stood silently in the oncoming twilight as war ignited—not outside on Arkron but within Harper's own heart, as the princess and the storyweaver began their fight for dominance once more.

23

AFTER SEVERAL DAYS of intense healing cycles, the bruises on Fayen's face had begun to fade. However, he remained limp upon his bed, vital signs still fluctuating. Evaly ran a light finger over his jaw, tracing the place where he had taken a punch for her the day they'd left Anaya. His skin was ashen beneath her fingertip, and his breath was barely a sigh.

The stillness of the royal family's private medical ward wrapped around her like a cloak. It was tucked high in a corner of the royal palace called the Cleft. Unlike Mantalor City or the *Ransom*, there wasn't the constant rumble of traffic or engines on Arkron. The capital city of Jana was busy, but the bustle was muted in comparison to where she had been.

And yet there was an edge of unease to the quietness. Arkron's capital city wasn't known for its night life, but the last time she'd visited, there had been some sort of movement: lightfoots bleating, faint music from a tavern. With the threat of the Consortium now looming over them, most people had taken shelter in their homes.

She glanced out the window just beyond Fayen's bed to the dark sky beyond. So far, the Consortium ships hadn't entered their atmosphere. But every so often, a trail of fast-moving stars would race overhead: surveillance satellites. They were scanning the land, eyeing it like a piece of meat and deciding which parts would be the best to carve up first.

Shuddering, Evaly rose from her seat on the edge of Fayen's bed and drew the curtains closed over the window.

"Still here, lass? It's late." Lady Longracer stepped into the room, a healer's satchel over her shoulder. She wore a sleeveless robe over top a shirt and trousers, like most Arkronen women. Her graying brown hair was pinned behind her head, and she shared Fayen's emerald eyes. Dangling from her belt was a corroding star-tree necklace set with purple beads. It was a relic from her days as a Neherum, when she studied healing in the Passer division. "You should rest. We don't need you going down for the count too." She set her bag down on the nightstand and leaned over her son to check his vitals. "Do you need more of the oil for your joints?"

Evaly shook her head, returning to the bedside. "I haven't needed it."

Lady Longracer's brow creased as she looked up from her work. "Haven't needed it?"

"I don't hurt as much as I did." She sat down on the edge of the bed again, taking Fayen's hand. It hung limply between her fingers, almost lifeless. "Something changed on the *Void*. I didn't fully transform . . . but I got stronger somehow. I got us out of the cell by prying up the ceiling panel and smashing the controls behind it. I don't think a *normal* person could do that. And then I dragged both Fayen and Jael out of the cell and into the corridor to the lift." She laughed. "If there had been guardsmen, I don't think I would have made it. But they were all either unconscious or gone, thanks to Harper." She dropped her hand to rub her knee. "I still ache, but it's a different kind of ache. Like . . . like growing pains."

"I see." Lady Longracer drew back, frowning down at her son. For a change, Evaly's ailments were not the center of her attention. "By all accounts, he should be awake! We've repaired the internal damage, but he's still weak." Shaking her head, she pulled his arm flat, exposing his elbow. From her bag she withdrew a blood test kit. Evaly winced at the sight. She was painfully familiar with them. They'd been a daily occurrence for months after her accidental melding with her Hybri.

"Jael is almost awake, though," Lady Longracer added, gently probing against Fayen's skin to find a vein. "You should go to her."

Evaly's gaze flicked to the curtain behind her adoptive mother, which split the room in half. She'd been in the room this whole time, concealed by the curtain. And Evaly hadn't been able to bring herself to sit with her. A part of her had been convinced that she'd simply imagined the face behind the mask. Her sister was dead. The Evaly that had lived with her was dead also, transformed into someone—*something* else. She should be ecstatic that her sister was alive. And yet there was a sense of bitterness. Why had she hidden herself on the *Ransom*? Did Evaly matter to her so little now?

"It's always nice to wake to a friendly face," Lady Longracer reminded her.

"I . . ." Evaly found her Hybri roiling within her, sending tremors up and down her limbs. "I want Fayen." She watched as Lady Longracer pressed a cylinder against Fayen's arm, cringing at the click it made as it sank into Fayen's vein.

"I suspect Fayen is going to be asleep for a little while longer," she replied. "Go to her, Evaly." The tone of her voice made it clear that it wasn't a suggestion.

Swallowing the rest of her complaints, Evaly slipped off of Fayen's bed and walked to the curtain that divided the room, pushing it aside. Like Fayen, Jael was partially propped up by the bed and dressed in a loose gown. Her black hair fell in tangles across the pillows. Her head was tipped sideways, her breathing even. Somehow seeing her softened like this loosened something inside of Evaly. How many times had she woken up to a similar scene? Yet that had been a lifetime ago.

Jael murmured something in her sleep and turned her head, revealing her scars once more. This wasn't her sister, not anymore.

Evaly began to turn back towards Fayen, but Jael's rasping voice made her freeze.

"Stay. Please."

Evaly returned to her. Jael's eyes were half open and glassy. She was still heavily drugged, but she tried to push herself upright on the pillows.

Evaly caught her arm. "You probably shouldn't move."

"I've had worse," Jael whispered, but she did stop struggling, collapsing back against her pillows. Her eyes roamed the room, taking in the tiled floor, high ceiling, and curtain windows. "I'm not on the *Ransom*."

"No. You're on Arkron."

"Does the *Ransom* know?" She tried to sit up again and this time succeeded, though her head drooped as if it weighed too much for her neck.

"I . . . don't know." Evaly hadn't left the medical ward since they'd arrived. "I can ask Pickett to comm them."

"Please do." Jael pressed a hand against her chest, wincing. "How long have I been here?"

"A few days. Almost a week."

Jael's hand rose to her face, as if searching for her mask.

"It got left on the *Void*, I think," Evaly said. "I didn't think to grab it."

"It wouldn't be the first one that I've lost." Jael dropped her hand and sank back against the pillows, exhausted. Her eyes found Evaly. "You got us out of there."

"No, I didn't. Harper did."

"I meant out of the cell," Jael said. "You dragged me and your brother. You got strong."

"I . . ." No, she wasn't strong; neither was her Hybri. But together they were something, something that she was just starting to understand. Did she owe Jael that? She had insisted that she train with her Hybri on the *Ransom*. And yet she was finding it hard to feel anything for this woman, who wore pieces of her sister but was so very different. A relic from a different life that Evaly had thought she'd put behind her. "I figured something out, yes," she finally said.

Jael smiled, a painfully familiar smile that Evaly never thought she'd see again. Shouldn't she feel elated by the sight of it? Why did it make her stomach clench? "That's great news," Jael said, her smile fading. "I'm sorry—about the *Ransom* and the *Void*. I should've told you who I was. I was just . . . torn."

Evaly found herself crossing her arms, trying to hug herself for comfort. "Maybe you shouldn't have. You don't know me anymore. I don't know you. We're not who we were."

Jael's head lowered. "I know. But—if you'll let me—I'd like to get to know you again."

The plea in her voice made something inside of Evaly unravel. She'd heard that tone once before—right before she had been sent to Mantalor. Jael had pleaded with their parents not to send her, or else let her go with Evaly. But her pleas had gone unanswered. The opportunity to join the Neherum had been too good a chance to pass up, and Jael had been needed on Hylon.

"Lass." Behind her, Lady Longracer's voice carried an edge of urgency. "Lass, I think he's waking."

Fayen. Evaly shot a fleeting look at Jael and rushed back to Fayen's bedside.

His eyes were open, blinking blearily around the room, searching for someone. "Mama," he mumbled, latching onto his mother's face. Then his gaze dropped to Evaly beside her, and he gave a shuddering gasp. "Evaly!"

He fought to sit up, to kick off his blankets, trying to tear off the medical equipment attached to him. Lady Longracer caught him and forced him back, pinning him down with practiced hands, making soothing noises. Still, Fayen struggled, trying to reach for Evaly. She grasped his hand again. This time, his fingers wrapped around hers, though his grip was weak. "You're okay," she promised. "I'm okay. We're both okay." *For now,* she couldn't help but add silently.

"Safe?" he rasped. "Are you safe?"

"Yes," Evaly assured him. "We both are."

Lady Longracer smoothed back his hair. "She pulled you out of that Consortium cell herself, lad."

Fayen's feverish eyes grew confused as they darted between his mother and her. "Protect you," he whispered, trying to squeeze her hand. She barely felt the pressure—his struggles were growing weak as unconsciousness tried to claim him again. "*I'll* protect you," he insisted, voice faint.

"I know you will, once you're better." Evaly leaned down to kiss his forehead. When she came back up, he was still again. "What is wrong with him?" she demanded, releasing his limp fingers. Her Hybri rustled uneasily inside of her, and she was forced to brace herself against the side of the bed.

"That's what I'm trying to find out," Lady Longracer said, lifting the small vial of his blood towards the lamp. "I'm going to request a deep analysis of this . . . " She cast a haggard look at her son. "I'm going to be completely gray before he's a man," she muttered. "Can you get him settled again? I want to get this downstairs."

"Of course." Evaly drew the blankets back around Fayen and began reaffixing the medical nodes on his arms that he had knocked loose. It was only then that she remembered Jael—but, looking over her shoulder, she found her asleep once more also. Her face was tipped away from Evaly, its scarred side upward. A painful reminder of all that had changed and all that was changing still, faster than Evaly knew how to comprehend it.

24

PICKETT HAD BEEN ten the last time he'd been in House Evensong's private medical ward. So far, it was the only time he'd been a patient there; Harper and Fayen had pushed him off a large rock at the beach, and he'd needed stitches. He still had the tiny scar on his temple, which he kept hidden by his hair.

He smoothed it down almost unconsciously, trying to ensure it really was hidden as he pushed into the ward. The reek of antiseptic burned his nose, and he sidestepped to allow an apprentice to push a cart of supplies past him.

The atmosphere in the ward was subdued—healers went about their work, heads down, murmuring amongst themselves. Pickett shared their unease. They had been on Arkron for over a week now, with the Consortium looming just beyond their airspace, scanning and watching. It felt as though Arkron were a glass terrarium, and the Consortium and its leaders stood on the outside, tapping the glass as they tried to decide what they would reach in and pluck from it. The knowledge of their ominous presence weighed on Pickett's shoulders like a mound of bricks.

Or maybe that was just Arkron's gravity. Pickett was still reeling from the change of atmosphere; normally a ship's descent was enough to help a person shift from the looser artificial gravity to regular gravity. But he had returned planetside through a blasted *magic portal*.

His sister was so Deeping weird. Even after a week, he still saw her glowing figure imprinted on his retinas when he closed his eyes. Her skin had twisted with light, as if the Star Sea had been infused into her. And she had been flying. Supported by cobalt and golden threads to rain judgment on the Seven. He'd seen her weave before, of course, but it had never been on this scale. He hadn't known that she was capable of doing something like it.

She was dangerous. Powerful. Arkron's goddess guardian.

Further proof that he was just the extra.

And yet Harper had begun to flag towards the end—he had seen the strain in her face and watched the story threads flicker. Did that mean she couldn't be all-powerful for long? Could her power be used *up*? What were the implications of that?

As he strode through the ward, the healers moved around him without a second glance. He huffed, wondering if he should have worn his crown. Would that have made them pay attention to him? Or would they still ignore him, the useless firstborn?

He caught a passing apprentice's arm. "Excuse me," he said, fighting to keep the irritation out of his voice. "I came for an update on Commander Clarkson."

The girl wrinkled her nose. "The Outcast? What about her?"

"She is under the care of the healers here," he said, allowing a hint of warning to seep into his voice.

The girl's face finally registered recognition, and she quickly offered him the gesture of respect. "Right. Of course. Erm . . . "

"She's stable, Pickett." Lady Longracer joined them, pulling off an apron. "I've had her moved to a private room—she needed space to recuperate." She stood on tiptoe to kiss his cheek. "I'm glad you're safe. Why haven't you been here yet?"

"I didn't want to be underfoot, *Amitan*," he said, using the old Arkronen word for "aunt" or "close female family friend who is as good as an aunt."

Her green eyes crinkled at the corners. "Not as happy as you would be to be back at Anaya?"

"Well . . . no," he admitted.

She patted his arm. "Despite the fact that you might feel otherwise, we are glad that you are here with us. As far as Commander Clarkson goes—I expect she will recover, and quickly. She has the most complex body I've ever seen; her surgeon must be a genius—so intricate! Most people have to breathe into a ventilator for it to work, but hers processes the air once it's already inside of her." She shook her head. "I did my best, but I'm a healer, not a mechanic. Despite that, I expect it'll hold her until her primary healer can assess her. She does have one on her ship, I presume?"

"Yes, I'm sure," Pickett said. "I have been in communication with the *Ransom*, as Evaly requested; they've been apprised of her condition. I've come to relay that, if she's able to take visitors."

"She's resting now," Lady Longracer replied, balling up her apron and tossing it into a bin of other soiled linens. "I'll inform her later." She caught his arm and dragged him to a room. "Come, help me check on my other patient. It would be good for him to see you."

He resisted. "Surely Evaly is enough entertainment. Really, *Amitan*, I'm supposed to comm the High General." He had been comming her twice a day ever since their return and had yet to be answered. Still. He hoped that his consistency would earn him her good graces once again.

Lady Longracer frowned. "The High General can wait. Please, Pickett. Fayen . . . " She trailed off, trying fruitlessly to fix several strands of hair that escaped her bun. "Fayen is not going to recover as quickly as we hoped."

"Of course not; he had numerous internal injuries."

She shook her head. "It's not that. Those are healing. There's something else in his bloodstream. A poison."

Poison? Fayen had been poisoned? "Is he dying?" Pickett demanded, even as his brain began to scroll through possible antidotes.

"No. He's just . . . weak. Very weak. It's too early to tell how debilitating it will be."

Well, Fayen wasn't going to be happy about that. "I'll do some research," Pickett offered. "Perhaps there's a homeopathic remedy you haven't considered yet."

She nodded. "I'll share my notes with you. Maybe together we can find something that'll help him. Now please, will you see him? He could use the distraction."

Pickett sighed but dipped his head in affirmation. Lady Longracer smiled and pushed the door open.

Pickett froze when his eyes found Harper perched on the edge of the bed. Fayen sat in an armchair across from her, with Evaly hovering over his shoulder. "I thought you were at Solstice," he said to Harper, shutting the door louder than he meant to. Lady Longracer gave him a scolding look before taking up a tablet to skim the data on it.

Harper closed the book she had been reading aloud and laid it primly in her lap. Her hair was combed into a tidy knot, and she wore a flowing blue gown. It seemed that Lady Kova was trying to tame her wildness again. "I flew in today. I'm addressing the Chamber the day after tomorrow. Assuming we're not invaded before then."

He tried to keep a smirk from curling his lips. Perhaps a confrontation with the Chamber would finally put her in her place. "Did Mother come back too?"

"Yes." Harper patted Fayen's knee and stood up, tucking the book under her arm. It was a massive volume: *The Conquesta*, an epic saga about a man rising from slavery to empowered knighthood and then kingship. Pickett had once been concussed by it when Fayen had dropped it on his head. The tome looked especially big under Harper's arm; without the power running through her veins, she looked smaller.

There were lilac circles under her eyes, and he could see a bandage poking over the neck of her shirt.

"Were you hurt?" he asked, gesturing at it.

"Sort of," she replied, adjusting her grip on the book. "I'm not sure what happened. It appeared after my weavings on the *Void*. It's fine, though. I'll let you have a turn with Fayen." She brushed past him. Unconsciously he stepped out of her way. Harper's lips parted, as if she wanted to say something. But she didn't, and disappeared into the hall.

"Did you come just to stand there and gawk?" Fayen's irritable voice crashed into Pickett's thoughts with the violence of a toddler tripping into a vase. "I'm fine, Mom," he grumbled, trying to push away Lady Longracer's hands as she took his vitals. He gripped the arms of the chair to push himself to his feet. Evaly started from her place behind him with a murmur of protest and moved to help, but he sent her back with a cross look.

Pickett stepped towards him. "Don't. It would be better for you to rest."

Fayen glared at him. With eyes hollow from his illness, he looked like a wretch coming to beg for orbs. "I've been on my Deeping butt for the last week. Don't you get on me too."

"Right." Pickett caught his elbows, trying to study him. The boy felt brittle, and though he straightened, Pickett felt him trembling.

"Will you tell them"—Fayen waved a furious hand at Evaly and his mother—"that if they would let me start training again, I would get better faster? Do you have a training sword I could borrow? Those Deeping Consortium dogs took mine."

"A training sword? Fayen, you're in no condition to do even a basic *kata*."

Behind him, Evaly caught his eye and shook her head in warning. Fayen's expression darkened, and he pulled away from Pickett, trying to stand on his own.

His legs folded beneath him. Lady Longracer and Pickett both caught him and lowered him back into the armchair. Evaly grabbed his arm, holding him in place before he could try to get up again. "Please," she said. "Resting is another way of getting strong, right?"

Fayen set his jaw and refused to reply. Pickett took Harper's former spot on the bed and folded his arms. "Evaly is right. You'll get better faster if you let yourself rest."

"I can't. We're about to be invaded. I have to get up." He met Pickett's gaze. "We need to talk about who we're facing."

"The Consortium, I know," he replied, frowning.

Panic gleamed in Fayen's eyes; Pickett glanced at Lady Longracer, worried.

"No," Fayen said. "Vasken's working with them."

Well, that was all the confirmation he needed. "Fayen, you're really not well," Pickett began, but Fayen cut him off.

"I'm not insane, Pickett! *She pushed me off a roof!*" Fayen half rose from his chair, but Evaly pulled him back down. "She's helping them, working as their enforcer!"

Pickett rose, looming over Fayen's crumpled form. "You're not in your right mind. The Neherum are neutral. She upholds that!" *To the point where she wouldn't help us on the* Void, he added silently. He wasn't sure why the memory still stung. She had only been acting in accordance with the Neherum's traditions. He understood that. And yet she hadn't helped the injured, as the codes dictated. And she hadn't helped him.

"Not in my right mind?" Fayen staggered to his feet again. "I know what I saw, Pickett! She's with them! And if you're not careful, she's going to use you to get Arkron!"

"I've heard enough." Pickett forced Fayen into the armchair with a firm hand on his chest. "I'll comm her and get to the bottom of this."

"She's just going to lie to you!" Fayen shouted.

Pickett ignored him and swept towards the door. The High General was the High General for a reason. She upheld their codes and walked with the upmost honor. And he was her closest assistant. She wouldn't hide something of this scale from him—and she would never attack her own Neherum!

She didn't tell you that Fayen was in custody. He slammed the door to Fayen's room harder than was perhaps necessary. So what if Vasken hadn't? It would have been a violation of her neutrality. She had to do what was best for the Neherum, and if she was caught feeding information to House Evensong, it could draw the Consortium's unwelcome attention. She knew what she was doing, and he trusted her.

But she didn't trust you. And she wouldn't help Jael and Fayen when they were dying in the lift.

He dug into his pocket, wrapping his hand around his personal comm. *Why won't she comm me back?* She had said he was valuable. She wanted him back as her assistant. Here, he was nothing. He hadn't even seen his mother yet—she'd been too busy fawning over Harper at Solstice.

Harper's the heir. It doesn't matter. I don't matter. He stalked down the steps from the medical ward, trying to push away his emotions. He hated coming home. There were too many reminders that he was only second place here. The extra. He couldn't even fathom the disappointment that Arkron must have felt when he was born: a boy, unfit to rule.

He could barely contain a snort, and skipped the last two steps to the landing. As he descended into the main part of the Cleft and then climbed a different staircase to House Evensong's living quarters, he silently wished for the Neherum campus's orderly corridors and clearly labeled rooms. Anaya was orderly and dependable. Everything here on Arkron was so tangled. He knew it was supposed to be an aesthetic choice, but all the same, it annoyed him now that he was used to something different. Something better, perhaps.

He made for his bedroom, longing for a shower and his mattress. That was one perk about being home: He could spend as long as he wanted drowning his sorrows in the hot water, and people assumed he was recuperating from their ordeal. He slunk past the common room, only to be called back to the doorway by the sound of his name.

His heart sank, but he squared his shoulders as he stepped into the room. "Yes, Mother?"

Anrameta sat on the sofa, a pile of papers in her lap. Sitting next to her was Harper's crown, with a polishing cloth draped partially over it. Even partially obscured, the amber and rubies of its three triangular plates gleamed like fire. It made his emerald and bronze circlet seem dull. In fact, he wasn't even certain his crown fit—it had been years since he'd donned it. When he'd left for Mantalor six years ago, he had buried it in his underwear drawer at Solstice.

He tore his eyes away from her diadem and came closer as Anrameta beckoned him in. "Yes?"

"I could use your input," Anrameta said, offering him a warm, disarming smile. "What do you make of this?" She passed him the topmost paper from her stack. On it was a rough sketch of two adjacent lines. They were close to each other but not quite intersecting.

"What is this?" he asked, holding it farther out in front of him as if the distance would give him more insight.

"Those are the marks on your sister's chest," she said. "She thinks they are from her storyweaving."

"It caused physical wounds?"

"That's what she thinks," Anrameta replied. "I am curious what their appearance might mean. They're too fine and clean to be accidental. It's almost like they're markings."

"Hm." Pickett studied the markings for a moment longer and then handed back the page. "You may be right. It's obviously tied to how many weavings she brings into being. I'll visit the archives and see what information I can find." He turned to go, but Anrameta caught his hand.

"You don't have to go this very minute," she said. Her hazel eyes were identical to his and Harper's; no matter how much he tried to garb himself in his other role as a Neherum, all he had to do was look in the mirror to be reminded of his House Evensong heritage.

"I don't mind doing so," he stated, trying to pull away.

Her grip tightened, and she yanked him down into the seat next to her. Moons. He had forgotten that his mother could match him in strength; she had been the one to introduce him to swordplay, after all. "No," she said. "I would rather you be here. With us. It has been so long, so long since we've been a proper family."

He wanted to point out that they would never be a proper family—not with Father dead, Lady Kova too proper to do anything but sit in an armchair and sip chai when they were together, and Harper running around spawning brambles and portals and setting her skin aglow with story magic.

Anrameta draped her other arm around him and then pulled him close to kiss his cheek. "My son. You've been home nearly a week and I've barely seen you. I'm so sorry."

"We were both occupied," he replied offhandedly. "Harper needed your counsel."

Anrameta frowned at him and then seemed to dismiss his tone. "How has your assignment with the High General been?"

His stomach twisted as a combination of pride and distress swept through him. "Excellent, although I'm afraid that recent events have put a strain on it. I look forward to resuming my duties once this is over." Anxiety crept into his voice. "At least, I hope she permits me to. I have denied her twice."

"It is my prayer that it is so," Anrameta said. "And if not, new opportunities will arise, I am certain."

It was his turn to frown. He didn't want another opportunity; he had spent years carving out a place that was truly *his* among the Neherum. "I will find a way back to them."

She pulled him close against her, ignoring his resistance. "Perhaps. But do not fret about it too much." She brushed some of his hair off his forehead, her thumb brushing lightly over his childhood scar. "You always have a place with us here."

Though he let her embrace him again, he found himself struggling to agree.

25

"Are you ready to meet the Chamber, love?" Queen Anrameta slipped into Harper's room, bearing her freshly shined crown. The morning light ignited the three triangular plates in the center of the band, making them look like tongues of flame.

Harper saw its reflection in her vanity mirror and quickly turned away from it. "I'm nearly there." With a subtle hand, she flipped her storyweaving notebook shut. Weaver Harper had spent the morning scheming of ways to escape the impending confrontation with Arkron's royal chamber of representatives and advisors. To keep her stories from leaking into reality, Princess Harper had ensnared them in ink, where they wouldn't be able to cause any problems while she faced the council.

Anrameta's eyes flicked towards the book and then to Harper's black-stained fingertips. Sadness flooded her face, and she set the crown down to catch Harper's offending hands and squeeze them reassuringly, not caring that the ink transferred to her own skin. "No matter what they say today, I want you to know that I am *not* ashamed of you."

Don't cry, Harper told herself as her throat tightened. *Don't cry. It'll smear your makeup.* "Thank you, Mama," she whispered, staring at her crown. It was made in the same style as Anrameta's, with an ivy-themed band and three triangular plates in the front. But instead of silver and sapphires, Harper's was gold and the plates made of amber and rubies. It had been crafted especially for Harper when she was born, the band being resized every so often to ensure it continued to fit her head.

"No matter what they say today, remember who you are." Anrameta released her to pick up the crown again and settle it atop Harper's carefully sculpted halo of braids. Though she herself had remained distant, Lady Kova had sent a troupe of hairdressers up at first light to preen Harper for the morning. After being allowed to rest for so long, her scalp was screaming in protest. Really, her whole body was. She had squeezed back into a red Mantaloren dress, the tight bodice of which was making the markings on her chest burn. Her feet were jammed into delicate flats. Already, she was sweating so badly that she could tell she was in danger of soaking through the underarms of the dress.

"I," Harper began, lowering her head under the weight of the crown, "am Princess Harper Evensong, the heir to Arkron."

"Yes," Anrameta said. "And its protector." She tipped Harper's chin up and carefully wiped some of the makeup off her face with her sleeve. "And you don't have to go looking like a porcelain doll. Honestly, Kova gets carried away sometimes." She smiled. "Just—be who you were made to be, all right?"

And who was that, exactly? The almighty storyweaver or the proper princess? For Anrameta's sake, though, she smiled. "Yes, Mama."

"Good. Now, let's not give your aunt any more cause to despise us." She pulled Harper to her feet and out of her dim bedroom.

To Harper's surprise, an escort awaited them in the hallway. Fayen leaned against the wall with his arms crossed dramatically, head tipped back as he watched them emerge. His skin was still dangerously pale, and Harper guessed that his pose was a veiled attempt to mask his need for support. Nonetheless, the sight of him shook her from her brooding thoughts. Harper waggled a finger at him. "Did you sneak out when Evaly's back was turned?"

Fayen grinned. "Nah. They let me go."

Unconvinced, Anrameta put a hand on her hip. "Really? I distinctly remember your mother telling me that you would need at least another week of bed rest."

Fayen shrugged and peeled himself from the wall to offer both of them his arms. "Of course, of course. What man couldn't do with a little extra rest? Unfortunately, I'm not the lazy type."

Harper snorted, noting the way that his legs trembled. How long had it taken him to get here? She looped her arm through his, steadying him. Anrameta sighed but did likewise with his other. "What about all those homework assignments you showed me were marked *missing* on your school tablet?" Harper demanded.

"That's a different kind of laziness," Fayen said, earnest. "That's being lazy with your mind. I was talking about being lazy with your body. It's two different things, Harper."

"Right . . ."

"You can't have both," Fayen insisted. "I can be incredibly productive with my physique, or I can be incredibly productive with my brain. There aren't enough hours in the day to do both."

His words earned him a scandalized look from a passing maid. Harper elbowed him in the ribs. "You might want to watch your tongue. This isn't Solstice; there are people here that might take your . . . eh . . . maxims to mean alternate things."

He shrugged. "That's their loss, then." With that, he veered their conversation into a different direction. "Did you eat an orange today?"

"Er . . . no?" Harper exchanged a baffled look with her mother.

"You didn't eat an orange?" Fayen's expression was outraged. "Then how . . ." He paused to grunt as they descended a staircase, wincing. Anrameta and Harper waited for him to recover. "I'm fine," Fayen muttered, pulling them to start again. "How will your words be sweet and binding? Here." He produced a fruit from his pocket and pressed it into her hand. "And did you put salt on your head?"

"No . . ."

She ducked before he could fling the handful into her eyes.

"And did you kiss your locket?" he demanded.

"No!"

"Then how are you expecting this to go well?" he cried. "You can't break the honorable tradition, Harper!"

Oh. Right. His "honorable" tradition. A laugh tore out of Harper. "I have forgotten it for many months. Please forgive me, my most honored advisor," she said, patting Fayen's arm.

They had reached the doors to the council chamber. Anrameta unhooked herself from Fayen to look at the pair of them, her brow furrowed. "I'm very confused, my dears."

Fayen wailed, sagging against Harper. "It is the Way of the Orange! Oh, if only everyone followed it, then all rulers would have seasoned words. There would be no more wars or strife, for all would speak wisely!"

"It's a thing we started on Mantalor," Harper admitted, smiling bashfully. "Lady Kova wouldn't let me draw intercessors on myself, so Fayen came up with this instead." She peeled the orange and stuffed a slice into her mouth, and then dusted her head with more of Fayen's salt. Then she yanked her locket out from beneath her bodice, and kissed its cover. "There, are you happy now? My words will be seasoned and measured."

He stuck his nose in the air. "Excellent."

Anrameta shook her head, though a smile turned the corners of her lips. "You amuse me. Thank you, Fayen, for a moment of levity." She faced the chamber's doors, and Harper watched as her entire being shifted from that of her mother to the queen of Arkron. Her stance became firmer, and her eyes hardened. Even her voice had an edge to it. "Wait two minutes and then follow me."

Harper dipped her head. Her crown nearly made her pitch forward, but she hauled herself upright. Anrameta threw open the doors and marched inside. Harper heard the buzz of conversation cease and the rustle of dozens of people rising to her feet. Pride made her chest swell—her mother could command a room just by her presence.

The burn of her weaving marks reminded her that this would never be her. *But I can try. I am Princess Harper Evensong, and one day this world will be mine.*

Locked away inside of her, the storyweaver laughed like a drunken woman.

"Are you going to finish that, or can I eat it?" Thankfully, Fayen's timely interruption pulled her from her thoughts. She gave him the orange. He shoved one of the slices into his mouth, giving himself a stringy, artificial grin. "You're going to do great," he said around it.

"I'm going to try," she replied. "Thanks for coming for us."

He saluted. The tape from his in-vein ports still clung to his hand. "Anything for my princess." He cocked his head, frowning, as Evaly's voice echoed down from the staircase above. "I'd better get going." He flashed another orange-filled grin and limped off down the hall.

Harper turned to face the chamber doors. Out of the corner of her eye, she noticed servants beginning to cluster into the hallway, hoping to eavesdrop the proceedings. Among them was a girl close to Harper's age, dressed in a gray mourning robe. Harper recognized her at once—it was Captain Yarrowriver's daughter. Her throat tightened instantly as her mind replayed his death.

It was murder. The Consortium murdered him. And they'll murder more Arkronens if we let them invade.

I can't let that happen.

It hadn't quite been two minutes, but she shoved into the chamber anyway.

Silence fell at her appearance. Anrameta stood before her throne in the center of the room, bathed in a kaleidoscope of colors from the stained glass windows overhead. She glanced at Harper, lips turned downward at her early appearance. The royal chamber sat in a raised semicircle facing her. There were eight of them in total—Lady Kova, who served as Arkron's galactic representative, and then seven lords and ladies who represented Arkron's seven kingdoms.

"Princess Harper." Lord Leland, chairman of the council, rose to his feet. "You owe us an explanation."

"I have come with one, my lord," Harper replied, striding over to stand before her small throne on Anrameta's right. "The Consortium attacked Lady Kova and me on Mantalor. They killed Captain Yarrowriver—an honorable man—and caused our accidental separation. Pickett, myself, and Evaly Longracer were sheltered by Commander Clarkson of the *Star's Ransom*—"

"Who later turned you over to the Consortium," Lady Hoperiver interjected.

"As I have made abundantly clear to Lady Kova, Commander Clarkson did not do so for personal gain. We were a threat to the peace of her enterprise." Harper laced her arms behind her back, squeezing her hands together to keep angry wisps of weaving from escaping. Moons. They were so much harder to suppress now that she had thrown open the floodgates of her powers. "She is welcome on Arkron as long as she chooses to stay."

"*That* is not a declaration you have the power to make, Highness," Lord Leland said. "Your mother must draft the pass, and we must approve it."

Harper felt her power quiver at his conceding tone. She could show them, if she wanted. Show them the *Ransom*, force them to see why Commander Clarkson had done what she needed to do . . .

But she stopped herself. The Consortium had needed a show of power. The Chamber did not; they needed reassurance. "Forgive me, my lord," she said. "Allow me to continue my story. After we arrived on the *Void* and Pickett was separated from me, I realized that the Consortium needed a firm declaration instead of a soft intonation—"

"And so you proceeded to attack them with your—er—condition," Lord Leland interrupted.

Her condition? When he put it that way, it made it sound as though it was a grievous affliction. To them, perhaps it seemed that way.

Lady Wateryew rose to face her. "This . . . this is power on a level that Arkron has not seen since before the Desolations of the Great War. The people have only heard rumors of what transpired on the *Void*, but it will not be long until they learn the truth. What will happen then? You are dangerous."

Harper was getting somewhat sick of being told that. It wasn't like she was about to *explode*. It took *effort* to pull things into being. "I am only dangerous if I choose to be."

Silence followed her words. Belatedly, she realized how threatening that had sounded. "My actions were in Arkron's best interests," she insisted. "The Consortium has proven that it is willing to take drastic action to claim Arkron. Are you just going to sit by and let them have it?"

"Of course not! But there are diplomatic processes in place that would have allowed us to continue our denial," Lord Leland said. "Negotiations would give us more time, and we could have offered small treaties that would allow them to take a little of what they want without consuming the whole planet! There were peaceful solutions to this."

"Those processes would have left myself, Pickett, and the Longracers in their clutches for months, and as Fayen's treatment proved, they would have used us to force your hand. The Consortium will no longer accept Arkron's denial. They are prepared to take decisive action now."

"Which you have sped up!" He thumped his fist onto his desk. "Must we push back against them so hard? Perhaps if we were given time to foster a relationship with them, their presence could be a boon to us!"

Queen Anrameta stepped up behind Harper, her skirt rippling ominously. "Evidence of the Desolations from the Great War is all around us, Leland. Look out the window at the ocean. You will see that it is not blue but green and murky. Our land is sundered. Our people have only just begun to have adequate food stores again. Joining the Consortium would be akin to stitching the skin over a wound but not repairing the damage within. We will bleed out beneath them, and when we are unable to meet any more of their demands, they will crush us. I will not have a ruined world be the heritage I pass on to my daughter and our people!"

The members of the Chamber exchanged glances. Lady Kova massaged her forehead with the heel of her hand, flipping through some papers with her other. Desperation pulsed through Harper at their silence. Were they truly considering negotiating with the Consortium? Didn't they know they'd be trampled?

They have to see. I have to make them see! But I can't explode like I did on the Void. Hesitantly she ventured, "Lords and Ladies . . . may I have leave to demonstrate what my gift can do?"

Looks of terror crossed several faces. Harper held her hands out, hoping the gesture made her seem unthreatening. However, the ink stains on them probably didn't help. "It will not be as dramatic as my actions on the *Void*. Allow me to tell you a story."

Lady Kova's skirts rustled as she leaned forward. "I do not believe that such a frivolity will be necessary—"

Harper plowed forward before they could stop her. She shook a pen out from her sleeve and cast a misty screen before her, like in one of Mantalor's cinema theaters. Then she began crafting her characters; she couldn't afford to give them form, but a fuzzy silhouette should do. Then she stepped into the center of her self-made stage and spoke. "My tale begins with an old woman in her rocking chair. One day in early spring, she called her two youngest granddaughters to her and asked them to follow her down the lane to two small plots of ground. 'These shall be your gardens, my dears,' she explained. 'I am giving them to you to take care of. Plant flowers, herbs, and berries, and tend to it well. I look forward to seeing them when I return from my journey.'"

Twisting her pen about, Harper made the smoky figures move through the air like puppets. "And with that, she kissed them and departed. The young girls, eager to please, did as their grandmother asked. The ground in their plots was tough and dusty, worn from years of misuse. The work was not easy, but gradually, through the water of their love, the flowers began to bud, and new shoots began to spring forth. There was much rejoicing in the two little plots as new life was brought about." The chamber began to fade away as Harper sank further into the tale. This was for the Chamber, yes, but it was also simply her and the story, dancing through space and time. "One day, a rich lady was riding past in her carriage and spotted the two small gardens—for indeed, they were plots no more. She ordered her driver to stop, and then descended to the ground, where the two girls greeted her respectfully.

"'Little girls,' she said, 'I am going to plant a large garden in the area surrounding your little plots. Would you sell them to me so that they might be part of something grander?'

"One sister agreed readily.

"The other thought carefully for a moment and then refused. 'Grandmother told me to work my plot, and so I will. I fear what other hands will do to it.'" Golden threats pulsed down Harper's arms from her chest. She could feel it burning, as though someone were digging a hot needle into it. *This is too much. I'm using too much, aren't I? But what's my limit? I can't stop.* She tried to pull herself out, to see the Chamber's response, but she was in too deep. The story was all she could see.

"She would not be dissuaded, no matter how many coins the lady offered her and no matter how much her sister tried to reason with her.

"Several weeks later, the lady's garden was sown, and the first sister's plot was absorbed into it. No longer did she have to work it, for the lady's gardeners did it for her. But the gardeners did not come out of love for the garden. They came only for the pay. The land suffered because of their lackluster care; the bushes and trees did not produce, and the flowers withered.

"On the other side of the fence, the second sister worked every day, even through the hottest days of summer. Because of this, her flowers blossomed and her bushes yielded many berries." Harper stifled a gasp as her chest throbbed. The burning needle was fast becoming a knife. Why did it hurt so bad? With the Seven, she had drawn brambles into existence, created a sword, and held herself aloft. Why was this draining her already? Gritting her teeth, she pressed on.

"When the grandmother returned, she was overjoyed with her granddaughter's garden, though the land was still hard and tough. She offered to work in it with her, to make it all the more beautiful. She was deeply saddened by her other granddaughter's garden but did not offer to help unless the girl came to her first. The plot of ground had been her gift to the child; she would not interfere where the child did not want interference. But she grieved as the land that had been her gift to the child became a lifeless wasteland."

As she ended the story, the illusion shattered around her, bursting into golden flakes that faded into nothing. Harper found herself stumbling backwards into Anrameta, dizzy.

Her mother caught her, steadying her. She murmured something in Harper's ear, but she couldn't hear it. The front of her shirt was wet—was that blood? Was her chest bleeding? Oh moons, why must she be so limited?

She looked at the Chamber, trying to gauge their reactions, but few of them were paying any attention to her. A few cast uneasy looks her way, but they all seemed to be looking at their desks or listening to aides that had appeared behind their chairs.

A low whine hummed in the air—at first Harper thought it was merely a result of her weaving, but as her head cleared she realized it was an alarm, pulsing from their personal devices.

"Lord Leland, what is it?" Anrameta demanded, keeping a steadying hand on Harper's shoulder.

He rose, face grim. "Highness, Consortium ships have entered our atmosphere. The invasion has begun."

"No," Harper whispered. They were out of time. She squeezed her hands into fists, trying to draw some power into them. It oozed sluggishly through her veins. What was happening?

"Mobilize our forces to prepare to meet them," Anrameta ordered.

"But the negotiations!" Lord Leland protested.

"Did you not pay attention to anything we've spoken of today?" Anrameta demanded. "This is our world, Leland! Our home! Will you offer it up to these predators on a platter? Authorize this, now."

Silence reigned as the alarms continued to pulse. Harper clenched her hands, trying to summon more stories. If they hadn't believed her tale, would they believe it if she launched herself upward to meet the ships?

Her chest throbbed. Moons. She wasn't sure she could do it.

Then Lady Kova rose, gripping her tablet. "They've been mobilized." Her gaze landed on Harper. It remained as hard as ever, but she said, "We must protect our garden."

26

A SHARP THWACK made Evaly jump. She toppled out of the window seat from where she had been watching Consortium ships take up position over the capital city. The *Void* now hung like a crib mobile far overhead, gleaming in the sunlight. The translucent shield that had been deployed around the palace distorted it further into some nightmarish collage of metal—even more so from her now-awkward position on the ground.

Fayen had smacked his bedspread again with his training sword, creating another *thwack*. "I wish," he grumbled, "that you would let me go to the dojo." He stood on the other side of his bed, trying to crouch into a *kata* position. "I'm getting stronger, I know it—hey, where'd you go? Oh, moons, did you fall?"

She heard him trying to shuffle around the side of the bed, and scrambled to her feet, hands raised. "I'm fine! I just slipped out of the window seat, that's all."

He was halfway around the bed, leaning on the sword like it was a cane. She had to force herself to smile reassuringly. He still looked horrible; his tallow skin and blue-tinged lips reminded her of a corpse. At least his eyes were bright again, though his expression was often dark.

"You should be resting," he said, tapping the tip of the sword on the ground. "You've been through a lot."

"I'm fine," she insisted, sitting down on the edge of the window seat once more. "Really. You're the one we're all worried about for a change."

He scowled and straightened, hefting his sword. "But your Hybri . . . "

It stirred within her, sending skitters of discomfort down her limbs. The sensation didn't last, though, as the creature settled down. "It's fine," she said.

"What do you mean by fine?" he demanded, limping closer. The effort made him pant. She began to offer him a place beside her but stopped. He would only be upset by it.

"On the *Void*," she said. "We made peace."

His eyes widened. "Did you—did you transform?"

"Not completely. Not yet. But together, we were strong." She found herself staring at her hands, unable to look at him. She was afraid of his response, she realized. He had dedicated his life to protecting her, and now . . . was she throwing that back into his face?

Her Hybri began to roil within her, igniting fresh waves of pain through her core. Did it fear him? Did it fear further repression? They had lived in his shadow for so long. But now that wasn't possible.

"That's . . . " Fayen was struggling for words. Evaly glanced up to see him trembling, fighting with every ounce of his effort to remain upright, gripping the weapon. "That's good," he finally said. "I thought . . . you'd be that way forever." His grip on the sword finally failed, and it toppled to the ground with a clatter. He bent to pick it up, but the effort was too much. He lowered himself to the ground, his back resting against the bed. "I thought I'd be your protector forever." There was a note of bitterness in his voice.

She slipped off the window seat to sit across from him. Her body was throbbing, and she forced herself to accept the feeling rather than push it away. Her Hybri was uneasy because she was uneasy. "I still need you," she said. "More than you know, Fayen. But right now, it's okay if you're weak."

His knuckles tightened on the pommel of the sword, and he pulled it into his lap. "No, it's not." He waved a hand towards the window, indicating the shield protecting them and the ships beyond. "The Consortium is *here*, and Pickett doesn't believe me about the High General, and Harper's in trouble, and you . . . " He trailed off for a moment, then finally added, "I'm needed."

She reached out and caught the sword. He tried to pull it back, but she easily wrested it from his grasp. "I know. But please. Take a break. You're going to hurt yourself." She rose, clutching the sword behind her. "I'll give it back in an hour. Only if you rest."

"Where are you going?" he demanded. "We're supposed to shelter in place."

It was true; Lady Longracer had belayed the orders earlier before rushing off to attend the queen. Evaly suspected that they would soon be evacuating Jana, but it was just as dangerous to rush out as it was to stay in. "I'm not going far," she promised. "I'll be back in an hour."

She shut the door before she had to see his miserable face again and sagged against it, clutching the sword to herself as she tried not to cry. Her Hybri twisted within her. Was it worth being strong if it had to bring her brother so low?

And yet if she had melded with the Hybri for a reason, it would be wrong to suppress it again.

Faint strains of song cut through her turmoil like sunbeams through storm clouds. All of her senses swiveled in the direction of the music. Her heart knotted—she knew that voice. Jael. Evaly hadn't spoken to her since the day both she and Fayen had awoken. She hadn't known what to say. But she *did* have an hour she was supposed to be away from Fayen.

And that song—that song was from long ago, awakening blurry memories from when she had been far younger. *I can't keep running from her.* She stepped across the hall and into Jael's room.

Her sister sat on the edge of the bed, her back to her. Unlike Fayen, it was clear that Jael was regaining her strength. Her skin had a warm glow to it, and her hair was bound back in a tidy braid, and someone—likely Lady Longracer—had given her a pair of loose trousers and a sleeveless shirt. With her arms bare, Evaly could see the raised scars lining the area where metal met flesh on her shoulder, almost like stitches trying to hold the artificial limb to her body. Her remaining arm had a dainty, black tattoo coiling around the upper part of it. From what Evaly could tell, it was some kind of flower. Jael was absently rubbing it as she sang, "*Let my wandering feet find their rest, I've traveled 'cross oceans and deserts and fens—*"

"I remember that song," Evaly said, stepping into the room.

Jael twisted about in surprise, then smiled. "Really? You were little while we were still performing. Papa used to open shows with it."

"You sang with him," Evaly continued, circling around the bed to face her.

"Yes. Sometimes I wonder . . . if the plague hadn't come through, would we still be making the circuit every year? Or would they have found a way to Outcast us even then?" She smirked. "Those Hylonese don't like free spirits."

"I don't remember," Evaly replied softly. In contrast to the sharp, painful memories of that last several years, Hylon was merely a jumble of song and color. Their parents had been musicians, traveling through a circuit of villages every year before returning to Port Ruby to teach music during the long winter.

Jael shrugged. "The musical profession is somewhat frowned upon—performing is fine for unwed people, but for a whole family? Uncouth." She shifted, and Evaly realized why she hadn't risen to greet her—her flesh leg was shackled to the bed.

Evaly felt her throat tighten as the Jael of Hylon she had begun to see was replaced with the Jael of the Fringe. She'd loved the Jael of Hylon. She feared the Jael of the Fringe.

"How's your brother?" Jael asked, dropping her hand from her tattoo.

"Frustrating; why'd they tie you up?"

"Well, I'm not exactly *supposed* to be planetside, am I? I'm an Outcast. And I turned you over to the Consortium and all that—I'm surprised they haven't tossed me into a cell already. Or worse." She shifted again, causing the shackle to jingle musically. "It's a good thing that they put it on my right leg, because if it were on my left, I could've just popped my foot off and been as free as a lark. Heh." She rolled her prosthetic foot on its metal ankle.

"Would you have escaped, if you'd had the chance?" Evaly asked, the twisting starting inside of her again. She fumbled behind her for a chair and sank into it, laying the sword across her lap. "Surely you want to get back to the *Ransom*. To your people . . . I did have Pickett comm them. They're permitted into orbit around the moons."

Jael's joviality evaporated. "Thank you. It's a relief to know that they're near. And I . . . don't know." She gnawed on her bottom lip for a moment. Evaly was struck with a fierce memory—Jael, working on homework at their table on Hylon. Chewing her lip as she struggled through arithmetic. Guitars and violas hanging from the walls. The tang of cinnamon in her nose. "I've been asking myself the same question. I need to get back to them. But all the same . . . " She drew in an uneasy breath. Evaly heard the machine in her chest kick to life, processing it. "There must be a reason that the Creator brought us back together. I'd accepted that I'd never see you again, and then . . . then you walked off that ship, and . . . " She pressed her hands over her face. "Silent Star Sea. I'll go to the Deeps before I walk away without trying to find that reason. Even if it is simply a kindness, after . . . everything." She clenched her metal hand gently, then dropped it into her lap, looking exhausted.

They were caught between worlds, Evaly realized, gripping the hilt of the sword. The world of their past, the worlds of their present, and the worlds of their uncertain futures. Were those worlds even compatible? Jael was an Outcast Commander. Evaly was a Hybri, Neherum, and a member of House Evensong. And despite all that, they had landed here, in the same room, together. That couldn't be a mistake, could it? The Creator was a storyweaver, after all, weaving the threads of their lives and worlds together, even if she couldn't understand the direction they were taking.

She was different. Jael was different. Yet they were still the same in some ways, remembering the same songs, sharing the same blood.

Could they meet in the middle and forge a new path? *If you'll let me, I'd like to get to know you again.* Glancing up, she found that Jael was watching her, almost desperately. "Thank you," she said, "for choosing to stay. For me." She rose, hesitant, and then knelt beside the bed and began wrestling with the shackle.

"Should you be doing that?" Jael asked. "I don't want you getting into trouble because of me."

Evaly summoned her Hybri, inviting it into her limbs. It was still uneasy from her turmoil but accepted the challenge. Cupping her hands around the metal, she squeezed, and it shattered beneath her strength. If she could do that without fully transforming, what would she be able to do in her alternate shape? "We'll be evacuating north soon. I don't want you left behind." She stood and then sat down beside Jael. "Those flowers—on your arm. They're from Hylon, aren't they?"

Jael nodded. "I couldn't let it go. Not completely."

"I don't want to either." Though parts of her still protested, she laid a hand on Jael's metal arm. It was surprisingly warm, the metal smooth and worn after years of use. "We're both changed—and still changing. But I'm learning that you're right. We're here together for a reason, whether it was because I needed you to convince me to accept my Hybri on the *Ransom* or for some other reason that we don't know yet. It would be wrong to squander that." She looked down.

"I'm afraid, Jael, that I'll lose you again, and I'm still hurt that you turned us over to the Consortium—even though I know why you did it." She sucked in a ragged breath, feeling her Hybri twist again. She sat with the unease for a moment, then released the air in her lungs. "But I'm willing to try and get to know you again."

"Thank you," Jael whispered. Tears glimmered in her eyes, and she laid her hand over Evaly's, which gripped her arm. It wasn't quite an embrace—it was awkward and different. But Evaly was learning she could accept it like her Hybri and move forward. With Jael by her side.

27

"I NEED TO talk to you."

Pickett's sudden appearance at Harper's elbow made her start, sloshing chai over her wrists. She tore her eyes away from the projection of Arkron and the Consortium ships making their way across the world.

"I'm busy," she hissed, setting her cup down on the small table beside her. She wasn't certain why she had still been holding it; the drink had gone cold long ago. Anrameta's study had become a war room in the hours since her audience with the Chamber. A huge projection of the planet hovered over the rug, tracking the Consortium ships. Anrameta and Lady Kova leaned over the large desk, conferring about troop numbers and movements. Lord Leland stood at another table with several other members of the Chamber, planning evacuation routes.

"Really? Because to me it looks like you're just sitting on your rear, watching."

"I'm staying out of the way," Harper replied, using the hem of her shirt to clean the drink from her wrists. Given the situation, no one had batted an eye when she'd exchanged her gown for more practical attire. "They know what they're doing. I think"—she swallowed hard—"I think I'd just make it worse if I tried to help."

The realization had been creeping up on her all day, as if she were sinking into a muddy mire that was gradually suffocating her. Every time she'd tried to use her powers, it had led to more trouble. Those ships were going to make landfall because of her. This chaos, it was all because of her and her inability to be who she needed to be.

Why would the Creator have made her a storyweaver if all it was going to do was cause harm?

In the projection, the ships continued to blink hypnotically. They hadn't converged over Jana—not yet. They were spreading out over the planet, whether to build bases or deposit troops, Harper wasn't certain. Arkronen ships tried to engage them, but their navy was hopelessly outdated in comparison. The Consortium had access to the best tech in the Exlenna. Arkron was decades behind. Their pilots were out there dying in a fight they would never be able to win.

"I just need a minute." Pickett's voice was impatient. "Come on." His arm came under her elbow, forcing her to her feet, and he ushered her out into the hallway. It was crowded with aides and servants, and he shouldered his way through them, towing Harper along until they reached the seclusion of a nearby sitting room. Pickett fastened the door against prying eyes and turned back to her. "I've been doing some research about storyweavers," he said. "Mother asked me to. But—"

"—You couldn't find much on them," Harper finished for him, crossing her arms. "You think I haven't tried to do my own research? Almost all of the sources were lost during the Great War when the Four Libraries burned."

"Yes, yes, you're right." He powered on his tablet, flipping through his files. "Most of the research was lost, but I was able to piece together something I think you need to know about." He turned his tablet around so that she could see the screen.

She squinted at it. The room was dim, and the screen was so bright she could feel her eyeballs searing. Grimacing, she tapped the screen to bring the image into focus. It appeared to be a rumpled page, torn from a book. It was burned at the edges. On it was an illustration—a human chest. Etched into the skin above where a heart would be were four lines, intersected.

Harper's hand rose to her chest. She had two of those lines now, still fresh and throbbing. "What do you think it means?" she asked, trying to read the curly labels surrounding the picture. They were too smudged for her to decipher.

"As best as I can tell," Pickett explained, "those are the markings that appear when a storyweaver uses up their power."

"I . . . I see." *Uses up.* So it *was* finite. Bringing a weaving to life had always exhausted her, but on the *Void*, she had felt a difference in the threads. They had felt strained, threatening to break. She had felt the same thing during her weaving for the Chamber. "What happens after it's gone?"

Pickett pulled his tablet away, clearly hesitating.

"What?" she pressed, craning her neck to peer at the ugly markings in the drawings.

"These drawings are from cadavers, Harper."

"So? It's not like I would lay there half naked and let someone draw my—" Her eyes widened as realization struck in a chilling wave. Her hands groped for her necklace, squeezing around the locket in an effort to draw some comfort from it. "Oh . . . When you use your power up . . . you die?"

"From what I could piece together . . . yes." Pickett powered down his tablet, leaving them standing in the dusky room.

So all those years of suppressing my stories . . . it wasn't just keeping me proper, she realized, fumbling for a seat before her legs collapsed. *It was keeping me alive.* But now she had revealed herself, letting herself taste the sweetness of doing what she thought she had been made to do. *But why would I have been made to do it if it was going to kill me?*

For surely it would kill her. The Chamber had made it clear that they feared her power, but with the might of the Consortium descending upon them—and their inadequate resources to resist—she might be their only defense. She gave a soft, bitter laugh at the irony. Weaver Harper had wanted to escape the oppression of Princess Harper's responsibilities. Now her abilities might be the only thing that could stop the Consortium.

The wounds on her chest burned afresh. Was this why she had been born a storyweaver? To give herself up as a sacrificial lamb for Arkron? This was her world. It was her task to somehow help it heal, as her mother had and her grandmother before that, along with all the Evensongs descended from the Great War. Shouldn't she feel happy, rather than terrified and bitter?

She pressed her face into her hands. *I'm a monster.*

"Erm . . . are you all right?" Pickett's silhouette hovered near the door, still clutching his tablet.

She laughed. All right? *All right?* Fury blazed within her for a moment. Didn't he know how lucky he was to be the firstborn male? To be unempowered? To not have this awful weight threatening to crush him?

Her chest constricted as a furious shriek rose in her throat, but she swallowed it down, quashing the feeling. This was her burden to bear. She couldn't be angry at him for trying to prepare her.

"I don't know what to do," she whispered. "I feel . . . trapped. But I *shouldn't* feel trapped. This world is my inheritance. My responsibility. It's wrong of me to try and run from it. Especially since I've brought the Consortium down on us." She pulled off her crown, staring at the crimson plates. Even in the dim room, it caught the light and twinkled. It should belong to someone else. Someone worthy to carry on House Evensong's mission of healing Arkron. She wasn't sure that she could ever be that person.

Pickett took a hesitant step towards her, then halted. "Harper, I . . ."

His tablet flashed.

"Is it your High General Vasken?" Harper asked, putting the crown back on her head.

"No," Pickett said, tapping on the screen. "No, something's overriding the device—what in the Silent Star Sea . . . ?" A hologram blossomed out of the tablet's projector.

Harper's breath caught. A goddess of power and destruction hovered in the air before them, suspended on story threads and clutching a glowing sword. It was her, as she had been on the *Void*. In the image, her sword was level with Speaker Archer's neck. Though his face was frozen in a terrified expression, his lips moved, relaying the message: "People of Arkron, behold the secret House Evensong has kept from you. The heir to your throne bears a power like no other—a power she is willing to abuse for her own ends."

Pickett pummeled his device, cursing as he tried to shut it off.

"Rather than protecting you, Arkronens, she used it to perpetrate a vicious attack during our peaceful negotiations in an effort to save her loved ones. She chooses them over you, Arkron."

"But I thought I *was* protecting Arkron," Harper whispered, her throat tightening. "Oh, Silent Star Sea. I was so wrong." Her glittering figure looked monstrous now, a harbinger of destruction rather than creation.

"The Seven's plea to you is this," Archer's voice continued. "Do not resist our arrival. Let us expunge the rot of House Evensong from your midst and usher in a new, prosperous Arkron."

The projection closed, leaving them standing in darkness—until an enormous light blasted through the windows, nearly blinding them. A moment later, a *boom* echoed through Harper's very bones, shaking the paintings from the walls and knocking vases from the sideboards.

"They're bombing us directly," Pickett said, stuffing his tablet away. His voice was calm, but Harper caught the tremor in his hands as he fumbled with his pocket. "C'mon—the shield can only take so much. It's time to go." He hurried out into the hall.

Harper followed on his heels, reeling. The Cleft was within the capital city—the bombs would hurt the buildings around them and the people within them! If they were trying to make a good impression on the Arkronen people, they were off to a terrible start.

Not that I did much better.

The hallway was in chaos. Servants, aides, and Chamber members dashed about, fleeing to the evacuation points or trying to gather their staff. The pandemonium sent faint memories rushing through her—the Cleft had been ablaze like this once before: the night her father had been murdered.

An insurgent group had stormed the Cleft, seeking to assassinate House Evensong. She had been a small child then, but she could still remember the shock of being jerked from her bed by Anrameta. The shouts coming from below had been a harsh anti-lullaby and, still half asleep, she had started to cry. Her mother had hushed her as she ran up the stairs. She remembered the blast of cold wind as they reached the rooftop, and the ship waiting for them there. They had huddled aboard, waiting as long as they could for Lander Evensong. And he had never come.

She still remembered Anrameta's trembling voice trying to tell her a story to quiet her. It had been fragmented by her distraction, and Harper remembered petulantly demanding that "Papa tell it instead." To which her mother had wept. Pickett had been crying too. Come to think of it, that was the last time she had ever seen him do so. Would he weep for her, if she died pouring out the rest of her power?

She found herself frozen, hand fumbling for her pen, unsure if it was time to be the princess or the storyweaver, or both.

Ahead of her, Pickett stopped, realizing that she wasn't behind him. He scowled, but he turned back and grabbed her arm, towing her along. "Now is not the time to space off, Harper!" he shouted as another explosion rocked the palace.

"What about Mama and the others?" she asked, sliding her hand into his. She expected him to shake it off; his fingers went rigid, as if disgusted by her touch. All the same he let her continue to hold onto him. They passed Anrameta's study; the door hung open, projections still running. It was deserted.

"They'll meet us in the hangar." He pulled her into the gallery that overlooked the grand entry hall below. Then he crouched, dragging her down with him. "Stay low."

Harper did but risked a glance through the railing to the entryway. The enormous front doors of the palace had been smashed, and Consortium guardsmen poured in, blasters raised.

Her hand went to the pen in her pocket, remembering Captain Yarrowriver and their squad on Mantalor. She couldn't let that happen again—but did she even have power to expend? Was it better to conserve it? Oh, Silent Star Sea, there were so many things to consider now . . .

"Come on," Pickett hissed. "We're almost there." He reached for a tapestry dangling from the wall—one of many that lined the Cleft's walls. Behind it was a sealable servant's staircase that would lead them downward.

The guardsmen were pounding up from the levels below, shouting at each other. "There!" one of them yelled. Glancing down, Harper realized that a pair of them were on the floor directly across and below theirs. Their armor rattled as they ran for the staircase.

Pickett reached the tapestry as a spray of blaster fire peppered the wall above their heads. He thrust it aside, revealing the stairwell beyond. He and Harper tumbled into it, landing in a tangle of limbs. Pickett leapt up immediately and slammed his hand against the keypad. It ignited at his touch, sliding a thick metal door across the alcove just as the guardsmen reached it. Energy charges whizzed overhead before being cut off abruptly, stymied by the door.

Panting, Pickett slumped beside Harper. "Are you okay?"

"No," she said, clinging to the railing to keep herself upright. "We have to get to the hangar." What if the others weren't there? What if Fayen and Commander Clarkson had been too weak to walk? She gripped her pen, considering her ideas, trying to deduce how much power she had left.

A voice echoed from above. "Ho! Who goes in this desolate shaft?"

"Fayen!" Her cry almost turned into a sob of relief. Peering upward through the dimness, she could see him, Commander Clarkson, Lady Longracer, and Evaly carefully making their way down.

Harper had to do a double-take at the sight of Commander Clarkson. She had been apprised of the woman's relation to Evaly, but seeing her without her mask was jarring. The cunning character Harper had become accustomed to was gone, replaced with a tired girl only a few years older than herself. She gripped the railing as she followed Evaly down, steadying herself. Without the mask, Harper could see the resemblance between the sisters—they had the same facial shape and nearly identical smiles, which the commander displayed as she approached. It was hard to think of her as *the Commander* now, divorced from her ship and mysterious aura.

"Highness," she said, inclining her head. "It's good to see you well."

A snort escaped her. "I don't know that I'm well, Commander, given the circumstances . . . "

"My name is Jael, Highness," the commander replied, pausing as they drew level with them. "I'm in your house now. You can drop the formality."

How could this softer Jael and the fierce commander of the *Star's Ransom* be the same person? Did she shift between her personas as Harper sensed herself to do? "As you wish . . . Jael," Harper replied. The word felt too abrupt without *Commander* attached to it somewhere, but the Outcast smiled. Perhaps it was nice to hear the sound of her own name without an honorific attached to it.

"Are either of you hurt?" Lady Longracer demanded, tightening her grip around Fayen. He was trying to hobble along on his own, gripping a training sword. Despite his attempt to appear strong, his breathing was clearly labored.

"No," Pickett said, reaching towards them in an offer of help.

Fayen scowled and pulled away from him, gripping his sword tighter. Harper frowned at the interaction; were they squabbling? Now was hardly the time!

Pickett dropped his hand, brows lowered. "Mother is below, I presume?"

"Yes," Lady Longracer replied, urging them on. A bang echoed overhead; the guardsmen were trying to force their way through the door. The palace trembled as another bomb struck the shield. How much longer would it hold? "We have to hurry," Lady Longracer urged.

Together, they began their spiraling descent into the darkness.

28

THE CLEFT'S UNDERGROUND hangar had begun its life as a cave, hollowed out by the ocean's waves over the centuries. The natural stone walls had been reinforced with bricks and concrete and set with small lights that illuminated the cavern. It was dazzling after the dim stairwell—and loud; the engines of six dragonfly-shaped transports thrummed like the whine of a thousand cicadas.

Catching sight of them, Anrameta sprinted towards them from where she stood beside one with Lady Kova, and embraced both Harper and Pickett at once, squashing them together in her arms. "When the first bomb hit and I realized that you weren't in the room anymore . . . " She did not finish her thought. "Come, come, we can't delay." She pulled them to one of the waiting ships, leaving Lady Longracer to corral her children and Jael after them.

The ship's interior was simple in its design, with seats that folded out from the wall and harnesses dangling above them. House Evensong's symbol was painted on the ship's exterior flank: the bust of a golden lightfoot surrounded by a wreath of leaves. Its long antlers supported the twin moons hanging just above it. The paint had dribbled from the bottom of the image in streaks, reminding Harper of her fading story threads. Swallowing hard, she scrambled onto the ship after Pickett and turned back to help her mother up.

The queen shook her head. "I'm not going with you."

"What?" Harper leapt back out of the ship to face her. "What do you mean?"

"Your aunt, myself, and Lady Longracer are going to a separate safehouse here in Jana," Anrameta said. "We have to stay central to oversee our resistance efforts."

"Shouldn't I stay too?" Harper demanded, clawing the hair that had escaped her braids away from her face. Several of the nearby ships had started the propellers on their wings, creating wind that tousled their hair and clothes. She could feel the long strands catching in the points of her tiara, coiling tighter and tighter like the knot in her stomach. How did she explain the prognosis of her ability to her mother? Was it even the right time? "I started this. I should finish it."

"And I trust that you will by being who you have been created to be."

And who is that supposed to be? Harper wondered as Anrameta drew her into an embrace. In the motion, she felt something narrow slide into her pocket. Anrameta had tucked something there—but what? She pulled away, reaching for whatever it was, but her mother caught her hands, preventing her from doing so. "No matter what happens," Anrameta said firmly, her face shifting from the soft concern of a mother to the hardness of a queen, "remember that the Creator has placed this world in our hands to care for it."

Harper shut her eyes, trying to push away the rush of anger. Arkron, her mother's extra child, the one that demanded every part of her at the cost of her other children. She felt her head bow under the weight of her crown. What would their stories have been like if they didn't bear the burden of this responsibility?

Anrameta guided her back into the ship, though Harper knelt on the deck, loath to let go of her. The narrow object pressed against her hip—she was beginning to suspect what it was, though she hardly dared to believe it. "I believe that you have an important story within Arkron's tale of healing," Anrameta whispered, resting her head against Harper's for a moment. "But you must remember that you are not the weaver of it. You must simply be faithful to where the Maker leads. You must decide what kind of queen you will be. I cannot make that choice for you. Only you can."

Lady Kova appeared at Anrameta's shoulder. "We have to go," she said, fixing Harper with her familiar hawkish gaze. "Remember who you are, girl. Our world rests upon it." She gripped Anrameta's shoulder and pulled her away.

Heartsick, Harper scooted back across the deck and slipped into a seat beside Jael. The ship's door slid shut, cutting her off from her mother. Harper could see her through the viewports, lifting a hand as the ship lurched and rose into the air with several of its fellows.

"Are all these ships our escort?" Jael asked, craning her neck to peer out of the viewport. "Or a diversion?"

If someone answered her question, Harper didn't hear. The hum of the ship became a roar as it accelerated and blasted out of the cavern. The opening was level with the sea, and for a moment she could hear the hiss of water beneath them. Before them, the shield flickered and then gave out for a half second to allow the ships to blaze through. Once past it, the ships at their flanks peeled away, speeding in different directions while theirs arched towards the northern mountains. The city blazed past beneath them, a tight sprawl of streets and a few landmarks. She spotted the Arena, a great pit sunk in the ground once used for entertainment, and the Sentinels, a quadruplet of enormous statues guarding the bridge that connected north and south Jana. Then the landscape changed to the rolling grassland of central Arkron.

Harper reached into her pocket, wrapping her fingers around the narrow thing there. She pulled it out, letting it roll into her palm. It was a magnificent calligraphy pen. Its black body was inlaid with golden threads twisting around it, and the nib shimmered metallic gold in the low light of the cabin. This was a real storyweaver's pen, like the storyweavers from the tales of Old Arkron had carried. Where had Anrameta gotten it? Weaver Harper was thrilled by the gift. She twirled it through her fingers, feeling the stories within her rise up to meet it. Storyweavers didn't need pens, of course, but they were useful conduits.

Princess Harper was more cautious. If Anrameta was giving her this pen, it meant that she truly believed that Harper could use her storyweaving to free Arkron. And now that she had revealed it and used it to attract the Consortium . . . didn't she have a duty to do?

"It looks like you've got yourself a pretty new tool for your weavings," Jael remarked, gesturing with her head at it.

Harper nodded, pulling the pen close to herself. She wasn't sure if she was ready for the others to see it. Had they heard the commander's remark? Peering over her shoulder, she found Fayen dozing, hand still wrapped around the hilt of his training sword. Evaly sat beside him, lips pressed together as she gazed out at the dark sky beyond. On Jael's other side, Pickett hammered away on his tablet again, probably trying to tell the High General where they were going in case she wanted to reach him.

"It's heavier than I dreamed it would be," she confessed, weighing the pen in her hand again. It was almost as bad as her crown, which was still perched atop her head with her hair tangled in it.

Jael clicked her tongue in understanding. "It's easy to get caught up in our powers and forget that there's a reason the Creator has given them to us—and it's often a reason outside of simply enjoying them for ourselves. But I think that can still be part of it. Being able to communicate with the *Ransom* benefits my crew and the *Ransom* herself—and it brings me double the joy because I'm still doing what

I love—making music—and it benefits those I love." Her eyes flicked towards the ship's viewports as she spoke, scanning the stars above as if looking for her ship.

"I'm sorry you've been separated from them," Harper said, pushing the pen back into her pocket for the time being.

"I'm sure Ziah has things well in hand," Jael replied. "But all the same . . . " She trailed off, her gaze shifting to glance back at Evaly. "It's not so simple anymore." She gave a soft laugh. "I'm living what most Outcasts only dream of—I've found my family again. I'm willing to wager that most of my crew would be sick with envy if they could see me."

"But you've built a thriving community in the Fringe," Harper countered, remembering with a pang the steady song of the *Ransom* and her people. "Surely they're happy."

"Sure. As happy as you can be in the Fringe," Jael replied. "But the Creator didn't design humans to live in the Star Sea permanently. We make do with what supplements we can get our hands on and by staying fit, but we can only do so much. We need fresh air, water, and food. My crew wants houses and gardens and families, not blasters and ships and scars." Her fingers rose to the tangle of twisted skin on the left side of her face as she spoke.

Harper remembered the disagreement over the supply ship while they'd been on the *Ransom*—how desperate the Outcasts had been to claim things that were easy to obtain planetside. With a shiver, she realized just how easily the *Ransom* could become a tomb if they were cut off from their supplies.

"I'm—" she began, but the rest of her sentence was cut off by Pickett's urgent, *"What is that?"*

He was gripping the overhead railing and leaning close to the viewport, staring down at the land below them. Harper scrambled out of her seat, elbowing him aside to see.

A Consortium ship hovered in the air nearby, but it was unlike any ship Harper had ever seen: It had no wings or visible boosters; it was simply a cube hanging in the sky. Blossoming out from its bottom was a bluish cone that grew larger and larger the closer it got to the ground.

"It's a shield," Jael said, peering over her shoulder. "They must be trying to isolate that segment of land."

"It covers at least several miles," Harper noted, pressing her face against the window to eye the lush fields below. "So this is how they're planning to occupy us. They're just . . . cutting us off from our resources."

Their ship dipped, sending Harper crashing into Pickett and Pickett into Jael. Before they could right themselves it banked, twisting into a complicated defense pattern.

"I think we've been spotted," Pickett said, gripping the overhead rail.

"They must have sentries for each of these areas," Jael added, yanking Harper back down into her seat. "Which means, hopefully, they won't chase us for too long . . ."

"If they've got these all over Arkron," Harper began, trying to swallow the bile that rose into her throat, "there's no way our navy could destroy them all." Her hand closed around the new pen, but she stopped herself as she felt the strain of power in her fingertips. There was so little left. How was she supposed to know if this was the right time for it? Perhaps there was another route . . . but what?

"Aren't the independent planets allied?" Jael asked, seizing the overhead rail as they banked again. The ship went through several more dizzying swoops before it leveled out, speeding onward.

"We were on good terms with Bagoon and Inerys," Harper answered, "but they don't have large forces either, and they'll be dealing with the Consortium on their own land." She peered out the viewport on her side.

They were passing over the prairieland that stretched between the Sea of Jewels and the fast northern forests. In the light from the twin moons, the grasses had a silvery sheen to them. It felt as though the world was nothing but a vast, dark sea with waves rolling about below. She could see the scars from the Great War where the land dipped suddenly—trenches that had been carved from the earth and craters where bombs had fallen. They were covered in grass now, life stubbornly overtaking death.

"I could help you," Jael said.

Harper twisted to look at her. "What?"

"The *Ransom*," Jael repeated. "We could help you. We have ships and manpower. Maybe not as much as an army, but we're Deeping good pilots."

"For a price, I assume?" Pickett grumbled, powering on his tablet again. The light bathed his face in a ghoulish glow.

"I don't want orbs," Jael said. "I want land."

Harper exchanged a look with Pickett. He gave a slight shake of his head—they were not authorized to make deals like this. Besides, bringing Outcasts to Arkron? Their people would be distressed enough by the Consortium. What would they think if their princess invited a host of Outcasts to settle on their planet?

I've already mucked things up with my storyweaving. What's another mark against me? House Evensong had land holdings in the north, beyond Solstice. Suppose they released those to the *Ransom*? Besides, Commander Clarkson wasn't violent—she simply wanted a home for her people.

Wouldn't Lady Kova and Anrameta be pleased she was trying to handle something diplomatically?

"I think that could be arranged, Commander," she replied. "If you help us free our home, we'll give you one of your own."

Pickett huffed, scowling, but Jael beamed. "You have yourself a deal, Highness."

29

Fayen woke from dreams splattered with blood, where the knife had cut all the way into Colten's throat. Where had his fellow prisoner gone? Had someone rescued him? Oh, why hadn't he been strong enough to do it himself? He gasped, heart in his throat. Fingers pressed against his neck, and he panicked—someone was trying to strangle him! He jerked backwards, knocking his head into the back of his seat.

Reality came roaring back at the blow. He blinked, fingers going to his neck. He was in the transport shuttle, but the hum of the engines had died. The ache in his core returned, like a bank of coals ready to flare the moment he moved.

Pickett was leaning over the seat in front of him, frowning. His hand hung between them, fingers outstretched from where they had been feeling Fayen's pulse. "You seemed like you were distressed," he said, brisk.

Fayen snorted and slapped his hand away. "Yeah, I'm pretty distressed all right. I suppose you probably told your mistress where we are? We'll be lucky to get an hour's sleep before the Consortium is knocking on our bedroom doors."

Pickett withdrew his hand, face tightening into anger. "Fayen—"

"Yeah, yeah, I've already heard your excuses for her." *I just hope I'm strong enough to face her when she comes for us.* He grabbed the overhead handrail and hoisted himself to his feet, swaying like a drunk. The dim lights swirled in his vision like some sort of insane hologame.

Pickett's hand reached out to support him, but Fayen ignored it. He didn't need help! He could walk on his own!

"Oh good, you're awake!" Evaly climbed back into the ship. Her feline eyes reflected eerily in the low light. "C'mon." She grasped his arm, preparing to help him out the door.

"No," he said, sharper than he meant to. "I'm fine." He hated that she had to see him like this. He should be the one helping *her*. And yet—she was different. Bolder.

She doesn't need me anymore. The thought was blistering. He'd thrown himself into training to be her protector, and now she was trying to be his.

Our worlds have been turned upside down, he thought, stepping off the ship. The simple action made the world tilt. He grabbed the side of the ship, steadying himself, then pitched forward, stubbornly ignoring Evaly's protests behind him.

Harper and Jael stood on the gravel lane beyond, discussing something in hushed voices. Jael tipped her head back, looking up at the stars. Their first introduction had been during their escape from the Cleft. He liked her, he decided. She was strong and no-nonsense. And she was permanently injured but had adapted. Could he be like that someday?

He limped over to them and offered his arms. "M'ladies, it would be a great honor to escort you to your chambers." He infused his voice with all the dramatic bravado he could scrape up.

"It would be a great honor to be escorted by you." Harper didn't match his tone, but she did accept his arm, dropping her hand onto his before jerking it back. "Your skin is hot."

"That would be my passion for serving you, good lady."

She grabbed his face. He yelped at the coldness of her hands; it was like someone had jabbed him with an electro staff. "Fayen, you're not well."

He let his act slip. "You're not either," he said, gesturing to where he knew her odd wounds lay. He pulled away, straightening his shirt pretentiously. "I suppose together, we'll just have to be two halves of a whole person."

"What about me?" Evaly interjected, coming up behind them to stand beside Jael. "I was sick before all of you."

"And I'm missing two limbs, most of my ribs, and rely on a machine to breathe," Jael said.

"We can each be one-fourth of a whole person," Fayen amended. "C'mon, I need some chai."

That got Harper to move. Together they started off down the curving drive towards the house.

The fresh air was pleasant on Fayen's hot skin. He paused for a moment, drinking in the familiar landscape. House Evensong split its time between the Cleft and Solstice; Fayen knew that each of them—perhaps with the exception of Pickett—preferred Solstice to the Cleft. Here it was just them and the wild, almost untouched Arkron. This was where he and Harper had grown up building forts, fishing, swimming, scraping knees, and reenacting their favorite stories.

The lane rounded a tree, and there was the sprawling old house. Its windows were aglow, beckoning them inside. Ivy clung to the stones that made up its walls, giving it the appearance of some eldritch crone. The black paint on the windowsills was peeling, but somehow the roughness made it more appealing. It meant that the house had stood here for generations, welcoming many a weary traveler home. Fayen tried to increase his pace, thinking longingly of the firelit kitchen and whistling kettle that surely awaited them.

Harper grabbed his arm, dragging him to a stop. "There's not supposed to be anyone here."

Jael stopped beside them, frowning. "You mean your mother didn't send people ahead to prepare it?"

"We don't have the resources. Servants are only for the Cleft. Pickett!" she called over her shoulder, shaking something into her hand. A pen, but one unlike any Fayen had seen her use before.

But she shouldn't use more power. Won't it hurt her more? His hand automatically went to his side, where his usual sword should be. Blast. He'd left the training one on the ship—but what good would it do against blasters? "Get back to the ship, Evaly," he ordered.

"No." She had tensed, both hands raised. "You need me."

This isn't how it's supposed to be!

The front door opened. A stream of golden light spilled down the steps. Then it was blotted out by a tall silhouette.

Fayen's snarl was drowned out by Pickett's cry of *"High General!"* He dashed past them and scurried up to the door, bowing.

The sight made Fayen sick. If only Pickett *knew*. If only he believed him! The woman standing before him was a dishonorable traitor to the very codes she forced them to swear to.

Fury gave him strength. He stalked after Pickett, though he refused to bow. "High General," he said, allowing his voice to drip with false pleasantry. "To what do we owe the pleasure?"

She cast a cold eye over him. "You recuperate quickly, Longracer."

"Yeah, having a tyrannical government trying to take over your homeworld really doesn't leave much time for leisure." He crossed his arms. "Why in Silent Star Sea are you here, at our home, without an invitation?"

"Fayen!" Pickett hissed, but the High General waved him off.

"I did have an invitation," she said. "My loyal assistant shared where you were relocating to. Given that this situation has intensified, I thought it practical to visit you myself."

Pickett had *told* her where they were? Fayen swelled with fury, but Pickett pushed him behind him, bowing again. "Please excuse him, High General. He has been unwell and is still recovering his senses. Whatever your reason for being here, you are most welcome."

"I am in perfect control of my senses!" Fayen shouted, catching Pickett's arm and jerking him around. "She is here on behalf of the Consortium, you moron!"

Pickett grabbed him by the neck of his shirt. "Shut. Your. Mouth."

Fayen yanked himself out of his grip. "Are you really this blind, Pickett? You're just going to accept her presence without question?"

"She is my High General."

Fayen slapped a hand against his chest. "And we are your *family!*"

Pickett's lips thinned into a line.

The High General stepped forward. "Perhaps I picked an inopportune time to greet you."

Oh, so she would have hidden in the house, waiting to startle them like a fae leaping out of the wardrobe? Fayen flushed with fresh anger. This was their home, and she was trespassing.

"Of course not," Pickett said. "I'm glad you are here, High General."

"Indeed." Her eyes swept over the girls, who lingered further down the path. Jael stood apart from Harper and Evaly, arms crossed, eyes narrowed. The General's lip curled at the sight of her, and she turned abruptly. "I am here to discuss your place in the Neherum, Pickett, but I insist that you settle yourselves first. After all, I am certain it was a long journey, and you have invalids among you."

"Yes, of course, High General." Pickett hurried inside after her. "Allow me to make you some chai . . . " The front door thudded shut, leaving them in darkness. Before she was hidden from view, she cast a cruel smile over her shoulder at Fayen.

In response, Fayen offered the rudest gesture he knew.

⁎ ★ ⁎

Unease kept Fayen awake into the early watches of the morning. Pickett had instantly offered the High General the guest suite in the main house, fussing about to make sure that she and the Accipiter attendants she had brought were comfortable. Fayen had convinced Harper to return to the Longracer's cottage with him and Evaly, and now she and the girl lay sprawled in a tangle of blankets on the rug, snoring. Jael lay on the sofa, arms crossed, head tipped to the side. He'd insisted that they stay in the same room together for when Vasken attacked them.

For surely she would. Why else would she be here? Seated at the table in the dark kitchen, he pressed his face into his hands. Exhaustion pulled on his limbs, but he refused to give in. Besides, his attic bedroom might have been a million miles away as far as he was concerned.

I can't just sit here. I can't be useless. He uncovered his face, eyeing the tumbler of medicine he'd downed. Even empty, it still reeked of the pungent brew. Before they'd left the Cleft, his mother had forced a bagful of remedies upon him, insisting that he continue taking the cocktail in the hopes that something would work.

What if it never did?

What if he was stuck like this forever? Fragile? Weak?

He pushed back from the table, rising to his unsteady feet. He wouldn't allow it. He began to edge down the hallway, towards the front door. The floor creaked traitorously beneath his foot. He winced; once, he had been well acquainted with the noisy spots in this house. It had been a while since they had been home. Holding his breath, he pushed onward—until a harsh meow made him freeze.

Blocking his path was Catty, his childhood pet. Her green gaze was murderous, and her calico tail twitched back and forth. Clearly she hadn't appreciated being locked up alone, tended only by the groundskeeper while they'd traipsed across the Exlenna.

He knelt, trying to scratch her head in apology, but she hissed and batted his hand away. Before he could catch her, she slunk around him and shot through the kitchen, into the living room.

"If you wake them up," he muttered, twisting about, "I will hang you by the tail out the window . . ."

Catty trotted into the makeshift nest of blankets, stopping beside Evaly's head. Fayen cursed silently, waiting for her to shoot upright. Evaly shifted as the whiskers tickled her face, scrunching up her nose. Her arm came up and swept the cat close against her. Catty began kneading her paws, purring loudly.

He stood there, frozen, until Catty's purring had subsided into sleep. He held himself back from bolting out the door. He selected a staff from the collection of training weapons leaning against the wall beside it and let himself out.

The Longracers lived in a small cottage on Solstice's grounds, affectionately dubbed the Nest. It was connected to the backdoor of the main house via a gravel path, but Fayen strayed off of it, onto the long lawn. The grass was wet with dew; he stepped out of his shoes and sank his toes into it. He sucked in a ragged breath and hefted his training sword.

He began the simplest of *katas*, praying that the medicine would sustain him enough to get through it.

His limbs started shaking instantly. Gritting his teeth, he tightened his stance and moved through the motions. Despite the cool evening, sweat began to gather on his brow. He was reaching the climax of the *kata*, one that involved a spinning kick.

He rose up on one leg, wobbling. He coiled himself to kick. And fell over. He sat up, spluttering, trying to clean the grass from his mouth. In frustration, he tore up a handful of the turf, cursing.

"A valiant effort, Longracer."

He scrambled to his feet as the High General ignited her lantern. She stood on the path, watching him in amusement.

He held his arms out. "Are you here for a rematch? There's no roof for you to try and push me off this time."

"Goodness, no. It would be a waste of my time." She lowered the hood of her cloak. "You barely seem strong enough to duel a mayfly."

Fayen ground his teeth. "I'm getting better."

"Truly? I've seen initiates with better form than you." She laughed, swatting away a moth that flew at her lantern.

"What do you want, then?" he demanded. "Come to kill me so I can't report you to Pickett?"

"You can tell Pickett whatever you like. He will always be mine. No, Longracer, I came to return this." She threw something at his feet.

His sword. He caught its hilt, his fingers finding the familiar groves where his fingers fit perfectly.

It was too heavy for him to lift. He was aware of Vasken's sneer as he dragged it up enough to prop its tip in the dirt. "Why?"

"All retired warriors deserve to have a token of their glory days," she said.

The heat was pounding through him once again, made more vicious by his anger. White spots danced in his vision as he struggled to raise it. "My glory days haven't even begun. I will recover, and I will defeat you, High General. You'll see. You'll all see."

She smiled at him and then walked back to the house, leaving him alone in the darkness.

30

Pickett rose early, despite his late bedtime. It was the grayish-black of first light; he could hear the birds chirping in the forest surrounding the house. He squinted at the timekeeper propped on the nightstand. His eyes struggled to adjust to the darkness; he had implanted contact lenses, but they took time to regulate in the morning.

He yanked open the drawer of his night table and extracted the black-framed glasses he so detested. He settled them on his nose and took another look at the timekeeper. As he had suspected, it was far too early for him to present himself outside of the High General's door.

A mixture of emotions coursed through him. He was glad to see her again. But at the same time, things were . . . complicated. *I have to let go of what happened on the* Void. *She was acting as a Neherum should.*

And yet why do I still feel betrayed that she didn't help us?

And then there was Fayen's maddening insistence that Vasken was working for the Consortium. That couldn't be true. Perhaps she wouldn't have intervened on House Evensong's behalf, but she wouldn't be *assisting* the Consortium, would she?

All through cleansing and dressing, his mind churned. By the time he had finished, his eyes still hadn't adjusted, so he reluctantly left his glasses on and made his way down to the kitchen.

Solstice was a rambling house separated into two segments: The front half boasted a grand room for gatherings, along with several guest suites and a study. The back was where the Evensongs lived in a tight warren of rooms. Separating the front and back sections of the house was a courtyard garden, which was in full bloom. On the main level, Pickett paused in the hallway to open the windows that faced it, welcoming the floral scents as they wafted in.

When he entered the cavernous kitchen, he realized that he was not the only one awake at this hour. Harper and Jael sat at the island, hunched over steaming drinks. A tablet rested on the countertop before them, powered down. Pickett couldn't help but notice the juxtaposition of the dainty porcelain and metal in Jael's grip. It seemed wrong—but also right at the same time. She held the cup with care, somehow both a gentle woman and a hard Outcast Commander.

"I was under the assumption that you were staying at the Nest," he said.

Jael eyed him over the top of her cup. "I'm curious—are you right down to business the moment you open your eyes in the morning? Or is there a warm-up period?"

Harper lowered her cup and dragged her hand across her mouth. "Oh no, he's always like this." She raised her drink again, took another sip, and added, "We got up to comm the *Ransom* about our proposed partnership, but we came here so we didn't wake Fayen and Evaly."

Right. The partnership. Pickett had been so consumed with the High General that he hadn't considered it since the ride home. He lifted the kettle from its trivet and carried it to the sink. Over this rush of water, he called, "You shouldn't have acted without Mother and the Chamber's approval."

Harper's expression creased into a scowl, but it only lasted a moment. She massaged her forehead, grimacing. "I know. But there's just no time, Pickett. We need help *now*, and if Jael's willing to offer it, we should take it." She lowered her head, staring into the recesses of her cup. Though she wasn't wearing her crown, her neck bowed as if its weight were still settled amongst her tangled locks. Pickett found himself struck by the *wrongness* of it. She was sixteen, for star's sake. She shouldn't even have to be making these calls or facing these choices at all.

The kettle started to overflow. Quickly, he shut the water off and carried it to the stove. To her credit, the commander remained quiet during their exchange, cradling her cup close to her chest. She looked normal now that she was healed and without a mask. Well, as normal as *she* could look. She was still peaked but looked much better than someone who had been close to death only a week ago.

She's only partially human, he reminded himself. But no, he couldn't think that anymore, could he? He'd seen her affection for Evaly, her struggle to do what was best for her crew in the face of her own desires. She was more than an Outcast and a cyborg—she was like him, torn between her family and her duties.

But I'm not torn. I've sworn myself to the High General.

But she didn't help us on the Void.

"Something wrong, Highness?" Jael's question shook him from his thoughts. Belatedly he realized that he'd been staring at her while his mind raced.

Yes. No. "I'm just thinking about the High General."

Harper snorted into her cup. "Of course you were."

Jael's attention turned back to her tea. "Fayen is sure upset that you don't believe him."

"He's being unreasonable," Pickett said, turning to pull a cup from the cabinet. "He was tortured by the Consortium. He doesn't know what he saw. The Neherum are scholars. We're neutral."

"Is it ever possible to be truly neutral?" Jael mused. "Isn't neutrality itself a side?"

"I . . . " How did he explain it to her of all people, when everyone was against the Outcasts? They couldn't ever be neutral; they had to be on their own side, and the side of those they held dear. There was nothing else for them.

"Isn't it better to always be on the side of the people you love?" Her brown eyes were sharp. Moons. It was uncanny without her mask.

"It's not that simple," he finally said.

She nodded, as if satisfied with the answer. "It's hard, having your loyalties divided."

"My loyalties aren't divided," he snapped, raising his voice as the kettle began to whistle. He pulled it off, using the moment to let his anger cool. "Forgive me. Would either of you like a refill?"

Wordlessly, Harper held out her cup. Pickett added a new scoop of their chai concentrate, then poured water over it. Jael, however, withheld hers. "No, thanks. Your chai's a bit too rich for me. I prefer a little jolt of caf to wake me up in the mornings."

"You know, caf is bad for your nervous system," he remarked, taking the kettle back to its trivet.

"A good portion of my nervous system is wires. I'm not too worried about the lingering effects of caf." She set her cup down as the tablet chimed. "The crew approved the partnership," she announced. "They'll start scrambling now."

"Excellent." Harper gripped her cup with both hands. "Now I *really* have to draft a formal explanation and apology." She dropped a hand to her stomach. "Maybe not before breakfast, though?" She spun about on the stool, eyeing the kitchen. "What do we have to eat?"

Her concern was a valid one. When it had just been them, the eggs from the henhouse and early-summer vegetables might have sufficed. But now that the High General was here, was chai going to be all they had to offer her? Pickett had dismal cooking skills, and there were no servants here to help. Growing up here, Anrameta had insisted that he learn some basic domestic skills, though few of them had stuck after he'd joined the Neherum. At Anaya, most of his basic needs had been met so he could focus on studying.

Jael looked between the two of them, then smirked. "Ah, the domestic problems of royals." She slid off the stool. "Never fear; assuming you're not planning to tell the High General that an Outcast helped you make her meal, I'll happily offer up my services as chef. Assuming the two of you are willing to humble yourselves to lowly kitchen servants."

"You know how to cook?" Harper asked, following her to the counter.

Jael sniffed, pulling the cupboards open. "Of course I can cook! I was a proper Hylonese girl before I was Outcasted. I'll show you Hylon's specialty: naan." She pulled out a container of flour. "Start mixing this with some oil. What seasonings do you have?"

"Come on, Pickett," Harper called over her shoulder. "She's our commander of the kitchen. We have to do as she says." She was already elbow-deep in the flour; puffs of it settled on her shirt and face, making her look like a half-formed ghost.

Pickett sighed and stepped up beside her. It wouldn't do to have them do all the work. How would that look to the High General?

Under Jael's direction, he and Harper assembled dough and then kneaded it. Harper was overenthusiastic about pounding the mixture over and over, but when Pickett confiscated it from her, he found pleasure in the motion as well. Listening to the girls chatter about something while he knotted and loosened the dough, he realized that he was *enjoying* himself. Even though the kitchen was a mess, he was a mess, there was a quiet peace that hung over the room.

The emotion felt foreign. Wrong. He was the High General's assistant—serious, collected. And yet had his work for her ever kindled such *lightness* within him?

Would it ever? His hands paused wrist-deep in the dough. Or would it always be a game of trying to please her? Of being torn between House Evensong and the Neherum?

Anrameta's voice brushed through his mind: *You always have a place with us here.* His place in the Neherum could be taken away, but no matter how hard he tried to run from it, he would never be able to escape his Arkronen heritage.

Usually such a realization might have come with a rush of despair. In light of their current trials, however, Pickett was surprised to find that he felt comforted.

"You done with that?" Jael appeared beside him, poking at the dough with one of her flesh fingers.

He scrunched up his nose, trying to get his glasses to go higher. They were in danger of slipping off. "I don't know. It's not perfect yet."

"It doesn't have to be." She scooped it up, shooing him back to the island. "I'll get these into the oven. That way we can feed your High General as soon as she rises."

"Thank you. Erm . . . Harper, a bit of help . . . " The glasses had reached a dangerous angle now.

Drying her hands on her shirt, Harper hurried over and pushed them back up his nose. "I like these," she remarked. "They make you look more like you. Like how you were before we went to Mantalor."

Holding his hands out in front of him, he walked to the sink to wash them. "Is who I've become so bad?" The sincerity of the question startled even himself, but he found he was desperate for an answer.

She hopped up to sit on the counter beside him. "No. Of course not. It's just that . . . " She trailed off, looking down at her hands. It was hard not to envision them as they had been on the *Void*, gleaming with molten stories. They were still now. Her fingernails were ragged from being chewed, and there were faint stains on the tops of her hands from the intercessors she had drawn there. "It's just that I can't do this alone," she whispered. "I can't fix this, and I can't tend Arkron alone. I thought I could . . . but if my power is going to be used up, where does that leave me? Who's going to make sure Arkron is cared for in a Creator-honoring way if I'm incapacitated . . . or worse?"

Her hand landed on his arm, gripping it for support. An unconscious chill ran through him, but he forced himself to drop one of his hands over hers, holding her steady. "I need you," she said. "Not as a Neherum, or Prince Evensong, but as you. As my *brother*. Like how you used to be, when we were children here."

That had been a lifetime ago. She knew that. He opened his mouth to point that out but found himself closing it just as quickly. Perhaps they couldn't return to those quiet days, but if this morning had taught him anything, there was still joy to be found together.

"Harper, I—"

Someone cleared their throat from the doorway. Pickett spun about, finding the High General standing there. Her face wore a mask of disapproval. "Pickett," she said. "I see you are . . . prepared for the day."

He released Harper and dusted off his uniform as best he could, embarrassment coursing through him. How could he have let his guard down? He pulled off his glasses, setting them on the counter. His eyes were adjusted enough now. "High General. Forgive me, you weren't awake yet, so I—"

She waved him off. "I was hoping you would join me in the garden for a sparring session?"

Jael pulled open the oven, sending a wave of heat through the room. "If you want to delay a few minutes, then you won't have to practice on an empty belly. These are about done."

Vasken did not conceal her disgust. "No, we will go now. Come, Pickett."

Come, Pickett. The words felt like a jab, as if he were only her dog that she could summon with a word.

What have I become? Is this who I'm meant to be?

But it's who I am. He moved towards her, grasping the hilt of his sword.

"Pickett?" Harper called after him, voice uncertain, pleading.

He lifted one shoulder in a half-hearted apology. "Save me some naan?" And then he followed the High General into the hall.

"I see that House Evensong has become close with the Outcast," the High General said as they stepped out into the garden. The grass was soaked in early-morning dew, Pickett noted; it would make it hard for them to get sure footing for sparring. Not to mention that the bushes and shrubs interspersed throughout the garden would make for unpleasant obstacles. Well, it would make the match more interesting.

"I suppose so, High General." He dragged his boot experimentally through the grass. Hm. Perhaps it would be better to go barefoot. But no, that would be unseemly. "She is Evaly's sister."

The High General grunted, fastening on her gauntlets. "And what was her incentive to remain planetside during this conflict?"

Pickett faltered. "Her incentive? Evaly, I suppose, and as you might recall, she was injured. She has been recuperating." He hesitated and then added, "Her enterprise has struck a deal with Arkron; they will help defend us in exchange for land so that they can leave the Star Sea." He worked his foot across the grass again, mentally flicking through his catalogue of stances to pick one that would be the best for the terrain.

Vasken sighed, and he looked up to see her shaking her head. "High General?"

"Pickett . . . I'm distressed that House Evensong has such faith in her when it is clear that she is only using you for personal gain."

He straightened and pulled his sword from his sheath. Her words caused a spark of indignation to ignite inside of him. He still disapproved of Harper proceeding without Anrameta and the Chamber's consent, but after the quiet morning they'd spent with Jael, could he still say that he was unhappy about the deal? He wasn't certain. An Outcast Commander had helped them make breakfast. Would he have been so humble? Would Vasken have? "I believe you're mistaken, High General. Commander Clarkson is genuine." He tightened his grip on his hilt and assumed a defensive stance.

She freed her own sword and tilted her head in bemusement. "Is that so?" She swung her sword in a tight circle and then expanded it so that it swept towards him. He deflected it, pivoting to keep her in front of him. "She is an Outcast. Do you truly think that she is interested in a *genuine* relationship with House Evensong? She will only use you and your family for gain. Can't you see that she already is through this 'deal'?"

"The *Star's Ransom* will receive their reward only if they uphold their promise to defend us," he replied, deflecting her swipes and pushing forward into an attack of his own. "And I think there's a good chance they will."

Vasken gave a sad little laugh. "Your faith in her is misplaced, Pickett. She will fail you. And I would hate for it to grievously wound you."

Pickett's ears tingled, burning with embarrassment. Stars, did she think he cared for Jael in *that* way? Vasken used his distraction to send him on the defensive again, driving him towards the edge of the decorative pond.

"I had a daughter, you know," Vasken remarked as he backpedaled up a small slope to put himself on more secure footing.

"I didn't know that, High General," he said, trying to keep his eyes on her sword. Was this a diversionary tactic? Was it true? She spoke little of her personal life—he'd known she'd been married once, but her husband was long dead.

"She died in infancy. Too early of a delivery." For a moment, Vasken's hardened face softened into lines of grief. "If she had survived, she would have been about your age. Perhaps she would have been a good match for you, Pickett."

Pickett flushed, remembering how his cover story on the *Ransom* was that he had been booted from the Neherum for making out with the High General's daughter. Perhaps in a different universe, that might have been his reality. "I am sorry to hear that, High General," he panted, swiping the sweat from his forehead.

"Indeed." She followed him up the hill, swinging her blade back and forth while she drew in a few deep breaths. Several flowers lost their heads in the nonchalant assault. "My point is, Pickett, I care for you a great deal. You have been an invaluable aid to me, and your sense of honor is a shining example of what a Neherum should be."

Her words put him more off-balance than the uneven turf. *Then why didn't you help us on the* Void? The question rang through his mind again, accompanied by the uneasy sensation he'd endured since she'd joined them yesterday. "Thank you, High General." He ducked his head. "I owe a great deal of that to you."

"Hm. I would hate to see you squander your future with me and the Neherum because of your family and this Outcast."

He stopped her blade with a calculated strike. Their swords met with a crash that shattered the quiet morning. "Haven't I proven that I have the capacity to maintain my footing with you and Arkron?"

Vasken laughed. "Pragmatism suited you better, Pickett. Look around. You have left me twice: first because of your world and second because of Longracer and the Outcast. It is impossible for a man to serve more than one master. You will always be choosing one or the other." She caught his arm and twisted it behind him.

He yelped, trying to strain away while landing hits with the flat of his blade on her shoulder armor. She released him suddenly, and he tripped down a small hill into a rosebush.

Wincing, he extracted himself and spun to face her again. "High General, did you come here only to ask for my full attention again?"

"Yes, Pickett, I did," she said. "Because your response will decide how the rest of this conflict plays out."

Well, that wasn't ominous at all. He wormed his shoes into the grass, hardening his posture as she came at him again. "You want me to choose," he grunted, "between you and my family."

"You must," she replied, spinning into a furious *kata*. He blocked her as fast as he could, all the while feeling his necklace beat against his chest. His body worked through the motions of the responding *kata*, but his mind drifted away, over the impossible choice before him.

Just as Harper had been conditioned for the role of queen her whole life, he had worked towards a high position in the Neherum. While Arkron had seen him as an extra, the Neherum—and the High General—had found him valuable. They had molded him into the man he was today, and for that, he was grateful.

And yet House Evensong was his blood. Arkron's breath was in his lungs.

"I understand your confusion," Vasken said, slowing her assault. "Perhaps, instead of looking back, look forward. Consider your future, Pickett. With me, or with your doomed world. Here, you are the spare. With me you are something valuable. You could be more than just my assistant. You have the makings of a fine second-in-command and, one day, High General."

Oh, Silent Star Sea. She had all but *endorsed* him. With her nomination, no one would question his ascension into her place when the time came. In the past, it had always been easy for him to imagine who he would be in five, ten, twenty years. He would be at Vasken's side. At last, he would be as important as Harper.

But aren't I important now? The memory of Anrameta's embrace passed through his mind, followed by Harper's plea: *I need you. Not as a Neherum, or Prince Evensong, but as my brother.*

His Neherum necklace thumped against his chest as he tottered for a moment, sword raised. He wanted the life Vasken offered. Wanted the recognition. But if given that, would he always be striving to maintain it?

On Arkron, there didn't have to be any striving. He might not be the heir . . . but he was still valuable to House Evensong as himself.

He wanted more mornings like this one. Free from the pressure of performance. From the push and pull of being split between the Neherum and House Evensong.

He made his choice.

Normally the *kata* he was in the midst of required him to push back harder against Vasken. But instead he ducked into a roll and sprang out behind her.

Vasken spun after him, but her boots slipped on the wet grass, and she landed in the shallows of the pond with an almighty *splash*.

Panting, Pickett sheathed his sword. And then, with a deep breath, lifted his star-tree necklace from his neck. He stepped downward and offered the High General his hand.

She took it and silently hauled herself out of the water. With her other hand, she accepted his necklace. "Are you certain, Pickett?" she asked. "I cannot protect you if you stand with them."

"I'm aware, High General," he said quietly. "But it is where I am supposed to be."

Her jaw clenched, and her hand closed tightly around his pendant. "I had hoped you would choose otherwise."

"I thought I would," he confessed. "But this isn't who I'm supposed to be."

"So I see." She tucked his necklace into her pocket. Pickett took a deep breath as it disappeared from view, realizing that it felt as though more weights than one had been lifted from his neck.

In the next moment, his exhale turned into a gasp as she seized him by the front of his jerkin and shoved him to his knees. Across the garden, a shriek rang out. *Harper.* A squad of Accipiters appeared, dragging her and Jael into view.

Pickett twisted around to look at Vasken, cold horror trickling down his spine. His heart stuttered, unsure if he could believe his eyes. "High General? What is this about?" he spluttered, though he already guessed the answer. *Fayen was right? Oh moons, why didn't I listen to him?*

"You, your sister, and the Outcast are under arrest for insurrection against the Consortium," she replied, cinching binders around his wrists.

"You can't do this," he cried, trying to struggle upward. "The Neherum are neutral! It's how we've survived so long!"

"And it is because of that soft policy that we have been barred from finding our true strength," she replied. "With the Consortium, we will be unstoppable." She beckoned to her Accipiters, ordering them to drag Harper and Jael closer.

Harper was still shouting, trying to twist away from her captors. "You're scholars, not warriors!" she shrieked. "This isn't who you are!"

Vasken silenced her with a savage slap across the face. Pickett leapt to his feet, enraged, but Vasken kicked him back to his knees. Harper crumpled beside him, clutching her cheek. "The Consortium gives us an opportunity to become more than we ever dreamed was possible," the High General said. "The Neherum will help it usher in a new age."

"Neherum study and preserve past ages," Pickett whispered. A knot of horror and despair rose high in his throat, trying to choke him. He hunkered closer to Harper, trying to check on her. Nausea welled inside of him as he risked a glance towards Vasken. If she had been his model, then what was *he* like? The thought sickened him.

Vasken swung her sword in a low arc. "Princess Harper, you have been sentenced to death by the Consortium," she began, "for insurrection and terrorism. To be carried out immediately."

"What? No!" Pickett whipped towards her, trying vainly to pull his hands free. "High General, *please*."

"Groveling does not suit you, Pickett," she snapped, adjusting her grip on the hilt of her sword as she moved to stand in front of Harper.

No, it didn't. But what else could he do? They were cuffed and surrounded by Accipiters, and there were no servants to shout for.

The Accipiters pulled Harper back by her hair, exposing her throat. Her eyes were wide, glancing at him for some sort of guidance. Bound behind her back, her hands started to glow. Another display like the one on the *Void* would only further convince the Consortium that she needed to be crushed. Not to mention that using her power was slowly killing her. And yet—was it their only hope?

"Remember who you are," he finally whispered. It was permission to do what she must and a desperate entreaty to come back to herself when this was over.

Harper dipped her head for a moment. Then her chin came up, and with a toss of her head, she cleared her hair away from her face.

Vasken smiled as she raised her sword. "I respect a person who is willing to look death in the eye."

"Agreed," Harper said. "It takes a lot of gumption to meet fate's starry gaze."

Vasken hesitated, her suspicious eyes skating across Harper's face, like she was trying to find constellations in her freckles.

Harper smiled up at her. With growing trepidation, Pickett saw its maniacal nature. Vasken cursed, catching on, and swung her sword as Harper raised her glowing, magically unfettered hands to meet it.

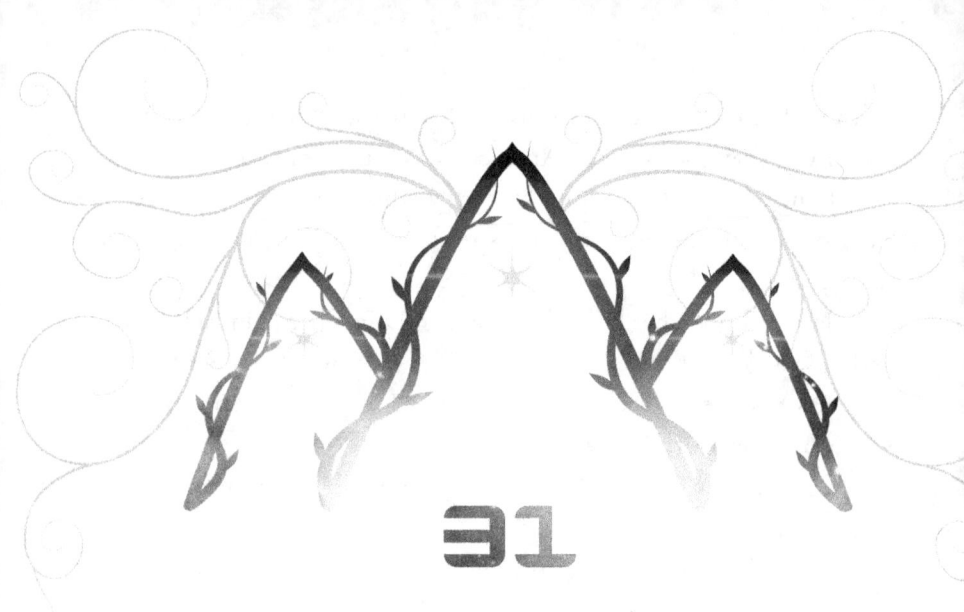

31

EVALY'S HYBRI CIRCLED frantically within her. She rolled her neck, trying to dispel the tightness. She pushed her teacup away, not trusting herself to keep the chai down. *What's the matter?* she asked the creature inside her. *We were doing so well.*

Was it because both Jael and Harper were already gone when she'd risen? Or the knowledge that the High General lurked in the big house? She knew Pickett didn't believe Fayen's story about her, but she was inclined to disagree. The High General had always carried a bitter air about her, with a metallic tang of blood and tears. Despite what he'd endured with the Consortium, Evaly doubted that Fayen would have hallucinated something like the High General attacking him.

Her Hybri knotted tighter inside of her, forcing a gasp. Unconsciously she reached for her jar of oil, only to remember that she wasn't wearing her cloak with the special pouch. She groaned, slouching over the table in frustration.

"Are you all right?" Fayen's feet thumped against the floorboards as he scrambled out of the armchair he'd been sleeping in. "What's the matter?" She heard him stumble, collapsing against the shelves that served as an entryway between the kitchen and common room. *Silent Star Sea.* As much as she wanted him to come to her aid as he'd always done, he couldn't.

She drew in a deep breath. *We have to be strong,* she reminded her Hybri, trying to accept the discomfort. It continued to roil, but she rose from the table and hurried to Fayen. "I'm fine," she said, "but you're not."

He scowled, supporting himself with one hand against the shelf. The other clamped Catty against his side. She was growling, and her tail beat savagely against Fayen's leg. "I'm convinced that this beast is not really a cat," he said, "but a devil come to torment me."

Evaly rescued the calico demon from him, propping her against her shoulder. "What'd she do?"

"She puked a hairball onto my lap!"

Evaly glanced at Catty. The cat replied with a purr, butting her head against Evaly's neck. "Maybe she's worried about you. You look like you've run a gauntlet."

Fayen waved her off, but not before she caught a whiff of sweat and musty frustration. "Did you sneak out last night?"

"And what if I did, *Mom?* I'm not a child!" He limped to the counter and began furiously brewing the medicine his mother had prescribed, clattering the bottles and jars.

Evaly set Catty down and followed him across the kitchen. "No, but you *are* sick!"

He slammed his cup down on the counter so loudly that both Evaly and the cat jumped. "*I am not!* I'm better! I'm just . . . rebuilding my strength, all right? Oh, moons." The cup had shattered against the counter, and shards of it were clattering to the floor, breaking further.

Evaly knelt and picked up one of the shards. Fayen swept the others into the dustbin and started making his brew again. "Fayen," she said, approaching him warily, "it's okay if you don't feel like yourself still."

"I'm fine, Evaly."

She touched his elbow. "It's more important to me that you're alive."

He spun towards her, nearly breaking his new cup. "Listen, I'm getting better. I made a promise to protect you, and I will do just that."

"Fayen—"

He grabbed her shoulder. "Stop questioning my strength. I'll be okay, and you'll be okay." His grip was trembling.

She looked up at him, wide-eyed, unsure if trying to catch his arm would make him more enraged or calm.

And then a faint scream echoed in her ears. She pulled herself from his grip. "Did you hear that?"

He cocked his head towards the window. "Hear what?"

"The scream—that was Harper, I'm pretty sure." She hurried to the kitchen door, but it slammed open before she could reach it.

Catty fled the room in a flurry of scraping claws. Evaly backed into Fayen as a pair of Accipiters charged into the cottage. Her back connected with something stiff, and she looked back to see that he was brandishing his sword. When had he gotten that back? His knuckles were white on the hilt, and his arm trembled. "I knew it," he muttered. "I *knew* this was an ambush. I *told* Pickett. Get behind me."

She started to obey but hesitated. She wasn't made for cowering behind him anymore, and he wasn't going to hold out for long. Though he would never admit it.

She assumed a defensive stance at his side. *We need you,* she thought to her Hybri. *Please. You knew something was wrong before I did. I trust you.*

Heat surged through her limbs as the lead Accipiter stalked towards them, swinging his sword. "Well, Longracer," he drawled, "it seems we get a rematch."

It was the boy Fayen had fought the day they'd left Anaya. The one who'd called her a freak. He must have been promoted to Journeyman in their absence, permitted to go on assignments with full Neherum.

Fayen raised his sword, arms trembling. "Bring it on."

The boy sprang. Evaly moved at the same time. Seizing the end of the table, she hurled it sideways, into his path. With his sword raised, he rammed his stomach into it. His breath escaped him in an audible whoosh.

"Evaly—" Fayen's sword lowered in surprise, but she ignored him as the other Accipiter vaulted over the table. Evaly dragged him around it, into the common room. *Keep moving backwards,* she told herself, recalling her dojo training. *Put as much space between you and them as you can.*

"The High General has sent us to arrest you," the other Accipiter replied, advancing towards them. She was a willowy woman that Evaly didn't recognize, but there was no vengeance in her eyes like there was in the Journeyman's. "I know you're frightened, but if you lay your weapons down, there's no need for anyone to get hurt."

"You obviously don't know Vasken," Fayen said. "She's working with the Consortium. She wants to see our planet overrun and us dead."

"The High General believes that allying with the Consortium will usher us into a new era of peace for us," the woman clarified. Her voice was gentle, almost as if she were trying to explain something to first-year Fledglings.

Evaly's enhanced senses scanned her, trying to deduce where she would strike from. What obstacles could she throw in the woman's way? There was no table in the common room, but there was a rug—perhaps she could pull it out from beneath her, but that would upset herself and Fayen. Her Hybri raged higher and higher, overtaking more of her thoughts. The loss of control frightened her . . . but at the same time, it wasn't the animalistic rage that she expected. It was focused, hungry to *protect*.

"The High General doesn't care about peace," Fayen retorted. His voice was loud and soft in her ears at the same time as her body and the Hybri wrestled for control. "She only wants power, and she's destroying the Neherum to get it. We're scholars, not enforcers—she's trying to strip you of who you are!"

Evaly could sense the uncertainty in the woman, which splashed back and forth like unsteady waves on a sea of convictions, ideals, thoughts, and feelings. Perhaps she could be swayed differently. Not all Neherum were as dedicated to the High General as Pickett.

The Journeyman had recovered by this time and charged past the woman. Behind them, the door that led out to the porch from the common room banged open, admitting two more Accipiters. Fayen cursed, lifting his sword as he looked between their adversaries. Even were he healthy, four would be a challenge. And still he was determined to take them.

Protect. Survive. Evaly drew in a shuddering breath, the twisting in her increasing to a feverish pace. She stood on the precipice of a great chasm. She had stood on its edge before, but this time she let herself fall.

The world spiraled away as the Hybri took over completely. Evaly braced herself for the pain—but it never came. Nor was she lost, swept away in the mind of the beast. When she opened her eyes, she was still her. Evaly, strong and mighty, shrouded in her Hybri shape. She raised her feline head; she wasn't enormous, but she was the size of a fully-grown lightfoot. With sharp claws sheathed in her paws.

The room was frozen, stunned by her transformation. Fear rolled in thick clouds from the Neherum—all save for Fayen. He looked at her with a stricken expression, as though someone had yanked the world out from beneath him.

"Freak," whispered the Journeyman. Then he said it louder, charging at her. "Freak! Monster!"

Evaly swept him aside, careful to keep her claws sheathed. He crashed into the window seat, knocking the several books from the fireplace mantle. "I don't want to hurt you," she said, herding Fayen towards the front room. He stumbled against her, his hand sinking into her ruff, searching for some stability. "You're our brothers and sisters. But you have to start questioning Vasken's orders; otherwise, Fayen's right—you'll lose yourself."

They'd reached the front door. Evaly couldn't detect anyone beyond it, so she backed out of it, urging Fayen along behind her. He kept his hand clenched in her scruff; when they hit the lawn, she started loping towards the house, nearly dragging him along with her. "Get on my back," she said. "It'll be faster."

"I . . . you can't . . . " He gasped, unable to form words. Evaly veered behind an ornamental hedge, trying to shield them for a moment. The Accipiters in the Nest would be after them soon, and there were doubtless more in Solstice itself.

"We have to find the others. Get on my back," she said, leveling her fierce yellow gaze at Fayen. "I can carry you. I know I'm strong enough."

He opened his mouth, ready to argue, then closed it slowly. Painfully he pulled himself over her back, gripping his sword in one hand and her fur in the other. "The Neherum," he wheezed. "Not all of them are loyal to Vasken."

"No," she agreed, leaping over the hedge and bounding towards Solstice. "If they really knew what was going on here—"

"They might be willing to help us," he finished. "But how do we tell them?"

They had reached the house. Evaly tore through the side door and was immediately hit with a wave of sounds and smells: the reek of bloody iron, the smell of something from her years on Hylon, the stench of sweat, and the tang of molten stories. "Later," she grunted, veering into one of the corridors she knew led to the courtyard garden.

As she had expected, the doors to the portico were thrown open. Evaly slipped through them, hunkering against the low wall that separated the garden from the portico. Fayen slipped off her back and peeked over the edge, then cursed, rising. "Vasken's got them, by the pond. They're kneeling—this is an execution."

Execution. No, not when she had just found Jael again. Not when she had such a wonderful family with House Evensong. She wouldn't let Vasken take that from her.

A roar tore from some deep place in her chest, and she cleared the portico wall and part of the garden in a single leap.

But she was too late—Vasken's blade was already sweeping downward. Evaly took another desperate leap, ignoring the Accipiters sprinting towards her.

If she could just knock the blade aside or crash into Vasken—but no, she was too far, the Accipiters were too close—

An outstretched hand, pulsing with molten gold, stopped the blade. And then it shattered into a thousand glittering pieces.

32

VASKEN STUMBLED AS the loss of her sword's weight carried her momentum further than she anticipated. The shards of her blade rained down over the garden in a sharp hail, and the Accipiters threw up their arms in an attempt to shield themselves with their bracers. Weaver Harper shook them from her hair as she rose, palming her new pen.

But no. She couldn't fully be Weaver Harper. She couldn't be the wrathful goddess that she had been on the *Void*. She had caused so much harm ... And her gift—her gift was draining her slowly, her life pouring out.

And yet when she started, she couldn't stop.

"Harper, be careful!" Pickett jumped up, trying to put himself between her and Vasken. "We just need to get out of here, you don't have to fight—"

Harper knocked him into the pond as Vasken, now recovered, hurtled towards them. She dropped her useless hilt and slid a pair of knives from her bracers into her hands, poising them to throw at Harper's throat.

Harper allowed a small smile to twist across her face. She thought that a pair of little knives was going to stop an empowered storyweaver? Hilarious. With a sweep of her arm, the knives were deflected. Moons, stories flowed so dangerously easily from her new pen... Her chest burned, blood running down in small, sticky streams, leaving crimson trails on her shirt. When to stop? Vasken was relentless!

The woman lunged at her again, teeth bared, hands outstretched.

"*Once, there was a wicked general,*" Harper whispered to herself, scrambling out of the woman's way, "*whose servants had loved her. But she had deceived them and set them on a course to fulfill her own evil schemes...*"

The ground caved beneath Vasken, sending her plunging into the earth. She scrambled out of the hole, casting about for a weapon.

Harper ordered the shards of her sword upward and twisted them towards the woman. "*But her schemes would come at a cost; what she sowed, she would reap.*"

Vasken saw the fragments coming and hurled herself into the portico, using its wall to shield herself. Harper's story shards pierced the wall of the house behind her with a dull *thunk*. Cursing, Harper vaulted after Vasken, ignoring Pickett's shouts as he tried to call her back.

Vasken had coiled into a roll and was rising to her feet. Harper was less than graceful; she tripped on the ledge and landed on her face. She rolled over just in time to avoid having a rock collide with her temple. A good warrior didn't lock themselves into one weapon, Harper supposed. However, it was less impressive with Vasken trying to bludgeon her to death with stones from her own house.

Harper reached for her pen and staggered to her feet. The world spun around her, stars exploding in her eyes. Oh, Silent Star Sea, the world was dissolving into fragments of color and sound—did this mean she'd used up her power? Was she dying?

A tight hand closed around her throat, pinning her against the wall. "I see now why your family forced you to suppress this monstrosity," Vasken hissed. "You are too dangerous to be left alive!"

Harper clawed at Vasken's gauntlets as her body convulsed, seeking air. "Maybe the Creator has made me for this moment, to stop the Consortium," she wheezed. "To stop *you*."

Vasken's teeth were bared again, and not in a smile this time. "You are *insane*," she hissed, and tightened her grip on Harper's windpipe.

Harper forced her panicked thoughts towards the pond. The water rose into the air, twisting into daggers of ice. Weaver Harper wanted Vasken run through. But Princess Harper—no, she knew murder wasn't the solution. She commanded the daggers to be blunt and sent them to Vasken.

One socked the general across the jaw. The woman dropped her, reeling.

Harper forced the ice towards her, letting one dagger pierce her shoulder and pin her to the wall of the house. Choking on her breath, Harper peeled herself away from the wall and urged the ice to coil into a threatening arm, hovering inches from the High General's throat.

"Think about this, child," Vasken rasped, eyeing the ice. Wisps of gold rose from it, curling up into misty vapor. "Don't imagine, *think*. I could be valuable to you—"

"I'm not going to kill you," Harper interrupted. To her surprise, she found Weaver Harper and Princess Harper in agreement at the declaration. She couldn't act as she had on the *Void*. But neither could Vasken go free. "But you *will* pay for what you have done."

The corner of Vasken's mouth lifted into a smirk, though lines of pain from her pierced shoulder were pressed into her face. "And you will be the one to dish out my punishment?"

In response, Harper tried to weave the ice tighter around the woman. Pain *exploded* in her chest, jolting all the way to her fingertips and toes. The ground disappeared from beneath her feet. She was falling, falling into an abyss of fragmented words and threads of light.

When she came back to herself, she was sitting in the grass, dimly aware that her pants were damp from the dew. She wiggled her bare toes, knocking the fluffy head off a dandelion. Would Lady Kova have scolded her for getting her clothes wet? Probably.

Then the burn in her chest drew her back to the present moment. She was aware that someone was propping her up—Jael, holding her pen in her free hand. Pickett was kneeling next to her, pressing a sodden handkerchief to her chest. "The markings haven't conjoined yet," he was saying. "I think she's okay."

The unspoken *for now* hung in the air like a vile stench.

"Vasken," Harper mumbled, trying to gather her legs beneath her. Moons, she was as wobbly as a lightfoot fawn.

"Easy," Jael said, pushing her back down. "She's under control."

Pickett glanced over his shoulder. Harper followed his gaze. Vasken was still pinned to the wall, but there was an enormous *something* crouched in front of her. Its striped tail twitched back and forth, a predator watching its prey.

"Did I make that?" Harper asked.

Jael laughed. "No, that's Evaly." There was a note of pride in her voice. "Fully transformed."

"Wow." Harper's gaze slid back to Pickett. His clothing was plastered to him, and his wet hair stuck up in a very undignified manner. "Sorry I pushed you into the pond."

He gave a strained laugh. "Well, unfortunately that's not the worst thing to happen to me today, and it's not even lunchtime yet. Can you stand?"

She nodded, and he and Jael helped her up. "What now?" she asked. "The other Accipiters—"

"They've been dealt with," Jael said, nodding towards a nearby tree. The Neherum were bound there, both apparently unconscious.

Harper winced, suspecting that Jael's metal fist might have had a role to play in their incapacitation.

"And I've got us sealed in here." Fayen limped towards them, eyes on Evaly and Vasken.

"We need a plan," Pickett said. "The Accipiters she sent after you and Evaly will be here any minute, and who knows what reinforcements she has waiting nearby."

"I'm not so sure those reinforcements will be as willing to come as we think," Fayen said, crossing his arms. He was upright, sword strapped to his back—apparently he had robbed one of the Accipiters of their scabbard. "Not all of them agree with Vasken."

"What are you getting at?" Pickett demanded, running a hand through his wet hair.

"The Accipiters that came to arrest Evaly and me—some of them were willing to listen. I think . . . if we could get to them . . . there's a good chance that we could have them on our side."

Pickett rubbed his temples. "But to get to them, we'd have to—"

"Go to Mantalor," Fayen finished. "Back to Anaya. Evaly and I could go."

"You want us to split up?" Harper could feel her voice wobbling. "But you're . . . " She almost said *"not strong enough"*, but stopped herself at the sight of his determined face. She began shaking her head frantically. "No, we need you. *I* need you. You . . . all of you . . . are the only parts of me that aren't shattered, and I need you here."

Jael put an arm around her, trying to calm Harper's tremors with her weight. "Wherever they go, they'll still be with you. They should go, Harper. This is a good idea. I can arrange for someone from the *Ransom* to take them."

"What do you think?" Fayen addressed Pickett, a challenge in his voice.

Pickett met his gaze and gave a single nod. "It could be dangerous. Vasken—the High General—will have loyal Neherum there. But it's a good option. With the Neherum and the *Star's Ransom*, we might really have a fighting chance against the Consortium. If you are well enough, I think you should go."

Fayen straightened his posture. "I'm strong enough." Then he faltered, dropping his arms to his sides. "At least, with Evaly I will be."

"But you're staying?" Harper asked Jael, desperately looking up at her scarred face. If one more member of their band left . . .

"Yes," the Outcast assured her. "We made a deal, remember?" To Pickett, she added, "Do you have a comm? I'll need to reach Ziah."

Harper felt a thousand protests well in her throat, but it ached too much to spit them out. Weaver Harper had exhausted herself, leaving Princess Harper to face this disaster. She looked down at her hands. They felt dry. Empty. She wasn't sure if she should mourn or celebrate that.

Anrameta's voice spoke in her mind. *You will have to decide what kind of queen you will be.* Would she be the kind of queen that allowed her forces to be split like this, even if it was in the best interests of their cause? Or should she order them to stay here and take the burden of defense upon herself?

I don't know. Neither of them seem right.

Fayen caught her hand and squeezed it. "We'll be back quickly. You'll see."

"You don't know that," she whispered.

"No, I don't," he admitted. "But I do know we have to follow this. I don't know where it'll lead for sure, but it's better than sitting here and letting ourselves be pushed along by the Consortium."

He was right. She tried to offer him her bravest smile, but the dishonesty of it rotted her soul. "Just . . . come back. Promise?"

His pale face was creased with worry, but he bowed in a feeble imitation of his theatric performances. "I will, my fair and noble lady. I shall return, with a host of warriors to free you and your world."

"Until then, we'll just have to hold our own," she said, trying to make herself sound valiant. But would they make it that long? An

Outcast, a disgraced Neherum, and a storyweaver whose power was nearly spent? She pressed a hand to her bloody chest, feeling a lurch of foreboding as she realized just how little was left.

PART THREE

33

Hovering high above the planet, Arkron's skylights looked like tongues of green and purple fire, dancing across the atmosphere like bangles rattling on a performer's wrists. They flared brightly for a few moments, then faded to be replaced with a new line of swaying shapes and colors.

Harper had watched them all night from a dim observation deck on the *Ransom's* lowest level. Sitting in the darkness, with the ship singing softly around her, was calming. Here, no one could tell who she was. She was just a small detail in the larger story and, for an inexplicable reason, that loosened the tight knot in her chest.

She settled back against the cold steel wall, hugging a heavy shawl around herself. The proceeding day had been a blur. They had cleared out of Solstice quickly; at Jael's command—with Harper's approval—Captain Ziah had sent a transport planetside to collect them. Once aboard the *Ransom*, Fayen and Evaly had departed immediately for Mantalor, while Jael's crew had helped secure Vasken for interrogation. Exhaustion clung to Harper's body like a bag of impossibly heavy books, but her mind would not let her rest.

The door to the deck hissed open, making her start. She tore her eyes from the show below to squint at the tall silhouette, which was haloed in the light of the corridor beyond.

"You do know that the skylights don't actually offer any sort of guidance, right?" Pickett said, stepping in and closing the door behind him. "They're caused by solar flares clashing with Arkron's magnetic field."

Harper sighed. "Our ancestors used to read them. They would paint intercessors on themselves and then stay awake all night, hoping that the Creator would use the skylights to speak with them."

"Is that why you're here instead of sleeping like I told you to?" Pickett dropped something onto the ground next to her. Harper prodded it with her foot. It was a box of some kind; when he opened it up, the smell of antiseptic wafted out. A medkit, then.

"Have you had any luck with Vasken?" she asked, rubbing her fingers over the new glyphs she had painted there. "Did she spill anything else we didn't know about the Consortium's plans for Arkron?"

"I . . . don't know." She heard him swallow. "I've tried to avoid the brig. I don't think . . . being around her . . . is good for me." He knelt beside her. "Frankly, I don't know that we *can* crack her. She is the High General, after all." He gestured to her chest. "We've left those wounds long enough. Let's get them cleaned."

The chilly air nipped at her exposed skin, but Harper shrugged off the shawl and unbuttoned the top of her shirt. She didn't have Evaly's Hybri enhancements, but she could sense the heaviness rolling off him.

Pickett leaned close, squinting in the weak light of the skylight and the lamps below. He began wiping the dried blood away from her markings to assess them. "There's a new one," he said, swiping an antiseptic-soaked swab over it. "Closer to your heart."

"No surprises there," she whispered, arching her back as the antiseptic stung.

A new skylight flared more brightly below them, illuminating the deck more. Pickett's features became clearer. There were dark circles under his eyes and lines pressed into his forehead that made him look older. He seemed . . . lost, though he was intent on his work. Perhaps it was the only thing he could think of clinging to.

"I'm sorry, Pickett. I'm sorry you had to give it all up . . . *Ouch.*" The antiseptic felt like acid on her chest, eating at her skin.

"Sorry," he said, but only pressed the swab harder against the injury. "If we don't get these cleaned, you could get an infection."

She snorted softly. "Is it even going to matter? I'll probably be dead before it can get infected."

He removed an adhesive bandage from the medkit and placed it over the wound. "Do you expect to die?"

She looked down at her hands. Her palms and the tips of her fingers were slightly discolored, as if they had been stained with russet-colored ink. "I don't know. Maybe. You've seen me. I get started and I *just can't stop.*" She squeezed her hands into fists and lowered them to her sides. "I'm sorry, Pickett. I'm sorry for starting all of this. I'm sorry that you lost your place in the Neherum because of it. I'm sorry for being the princess and the storyweaver, and . . . and . . . " Tears fragmented the world outside the window and Pickett's figure beside her. She furiously dashed them away. The princess was composed and the storyweaver stoic. Who was she, then, in this moment?

Pickett rubbed at his neck where his Neherum necklace used to hang. "This back and forth isn't doing anyone any favors," he finally said, sounding weary. "Not you, not any of us. Either be this deity of chaos and creation or be the princess Lady Kova has been teaching you to be." He sighed, dropping his hand. "But I know it's not that simple. And I know you know that."

She nodded, unable to trust herself to speak.

"Maybe a change of clothes would help?" Pickett offered, beginning to repack the medkit again. "And some sleep?"

She hugged the shawl around herself, shaking her head. If he was going to stay awake to hear the verdict from Vasken's interrogation, and news of Fayen and Evaly, she was too.

Her refusal pitched Pickett from sympathy to exasperation. "Harper, if you think that sitting in your misery is some sort of penitence and is going to fix this, then—"

The door to the observation deck slid aside, revealing Jael. She had already changed back into her Outcast attire: cargo trousers, calf-length boots, a shirt, and a long coat. A holster was strapped to her leg. She was only missing her mask, but a red scarf draped around her head and neck, suggesting that she had been using it to conceal part of her face. Was her faceless character so important that she felt the need to veil herself even in this way? How did she manage to be both the masked Commander, yet genuine and selfless Jael Clarkson?

"I hope I'm not interrupting anything," she said.

"No," Pickett said, turning to her instantly. "Do you have any news? From anyone?"

"I'm afraid not. With your tablet, we thought we'd gotten through to your mother, but there seemed to be a connectivity issue on her end." Jael laced her hands together. "I thought you might appreciate the update, even though it's a dismal one."

"We do," Pickett said, hand going to his neck again, searching for his necklace. Harper mimicked the action, though her fingers found her tarnished book locket. It was stained with blood, just like her shirt. She dropped it back down, tipping her head back against the wall to look at the skylights again.

Jael hesitated in the doorway, as if unsure if she should leave the Evensong siblings alone or continue her intrusion. She stepped closer to them, letting the door shut completely, turning to the large viewport.

"Pickett was just reminding me of my responsibility to dress nicely and sleep," Harper said, hoping that the tightening in her throat wasn't too apparent in her voice.

"Well, I won't make you endure a second reminder, though he's not wrong," Jael replied. She sat down beside Harper, so close that their shoulders pressed together. "I just want to take a moment to enjoy the show." She tipped her head back and laced her hands in her lap. The colors of the skylights cast a dull sheen on her prosthesis. "We don't have skylights in the Fringe. We see the other side of them. The solar storms. Those can cause trouble if you don't have your shields up."

Pickett grunted, then lowered himself on Harper's other side. "I trust the *Ransom* has hers fully engaged?"

Harper sensed an increase in the ship's hum. "She's insulted that you question her ability," Jael said.

"Oh. Sorry." Awkwardly, Pickett patted the deck plate beside him.

"Did you have skylights on Hylon?" Harper asked, tracing the glyphs on her forearms. Dawn would be approaching soon. If the Creator was going to say anything, it would have to be soon.

Jael sighed. "Yes." Harper could feel the deep longing in her voice. "Oh, yes. They were brighter than these, much brighter. Sometimes the night would be as bright as day. The biggest storms happened in the spring and the autumn, and the shepherds would use it to move their herds from the winter to summer pastures and vice versa. I used to sneak out onto the steppes and stay out all night to watch. Sometimes I would bring my flute to play." She laughed. "As if the Creator needed *me* to add on to his story. But I like to think it made him happy, to know I was joining in the chorus." She smiled. In it, Harper could see more memories than most seniors could compete with.

"How did you do it?" she asked.

"Do what?"

"Be so many people. The Jael of Hylon. The Jael of the Fringe. The Jael of Arkron."

Jael's head tipped to the side as her gaze swiveled to Harper. "But all those people are me. Different facets of me, yes. But ultimately still me. Still parts of my story." She draped an arm around Harper's shoulder, pulling her close. For being half metal, she was remarkably warm to rest against. "We like to think that people—ourselves included—can fit under a single label. It makes it easier to identify and categorize us. It helps us know how to interact with each other and the Exlenna. But really, we're as ever-changing as those lights." She pointed at a line of green, dancing over the mountaintops. "We might flare brightly in one aspect of our lives for a while, and then we'll dim and shine bright in another." She pointed to a new splotch of magenta, which glowed more and more vivid while the green faded. "We were made to be infinite." She sighed. "But when the Shattering happened, it trapped us in Time. Even so, the only label we really need for ourselves is *beloved by the Maker*."

"It's a nice thought," Harper whispered, "but Arkron needs me to choose the storyweaver or the princess," she insisted.

Jael's arm tightened around her. "Does it really?"

"Yes. The storyweaver is powerful. Forceful. She causes destruction, but she gets results. The princess is gentler. She seeks to heal, but it takes much more time." The shawl slipped from her shoulders again, and Harper pulled it over her legs like a blanket. Finally the weariness was catching up to her. Anrameta's words echoed through her mind like an incessant gong: *You will have to decide what kind of queen you will be.* "You've seen me. They clash. There can only be one."

"What if there was a third option?"

"There's not," Harper said, and shut her eyes as the skylights burned brightly again. "I will choose who I will be." The motion was all her body needed to doze off. She spiraled into uneasy dreams, curled between Pickett and the Outcast as they continued to watch the sky.

34

"I don't like this."

Evaly sighed, adjusting the bandage wrapped around her head to hide her cat ears. "Well, we're not exactly here on holiday, Fayen. And this was your idea."

Perched on the edge of a stolen hover-stretcher, he crossed his arms. "It wasn't my idea to play the critically injured one. You're younger. I think they'd let us in faster if I showed up carting a critically injured kid."

"You're a kid too," Evaly pointed out. She bit back the urge to point out that he looked the part of a critically injured patient. Their journey from the *Ransom* had taken them to a remote waystation, where they boarded a certified Consortium shuttle to Mantalor. Throughout the journey, his skin had passed from pale to an almost translucent ashen, and his lips were blue.

"Do we even need all of this?" She gestured to the medical equipment littered around the hover-train's compartment. It had been Fayen's idea to pilfer it from their shuttle, even though lugging the large medical bag and collapsible stretcher through the spaceport to the train—in the middle of the night, no less—had earned them suspicious glances.

"Yes," he replied, irritable. "It's not like we can just waltz into Anaya. If Vasken has really joined the Neherum with the Consortium, they'll probably have orders to arrest us. But if we pose as injured Neherum, there's a higher chance of us being taken to see the Passers before they question us." He gripped the edge of the stretcher, trying to balance himself as the train lurched, slowing down.

They were nearing Anaya. The dark landscape outside the window was giving way from the small suburbs that clustered at the edges of Mantalor City to the long acres of Anaya's grounds. Evaly began gathering the stray medical supplies, tucking them back into the bag. "Fine. If you don't want to be the one on the stretcher, I will. But you're going to have to carry the bag *and* push me."

His face hardened. "I can do it."

She didn't reply. All through their trip, he'd been trying to prove himself. Helping her on and off the ships, leading them through the waystation and spaceport—whatever he could to prove his strength. Seeing her in her full Hybri had completely broken something that had been crumbling inside of him, she knew. It made her heart ache to think that she was causing him internal wounds that would take much longer to heal than his physical ones. But she had changed—and he had too, even if he didn't want to admit it.

The train jolted again as it slowed further. Evaly stepped forward, prepared to climb onto the thin stretcher, but Fayen held out a hand, stopping her. "It's fine. I'll do it." He scooted himself all the way onto it and lay down, pulling the thermal blanket over himself. Like her, he had a bandage over his head, concealing half his face.

Evaly made sure his cloak was partially visible. There hadn't been time to gather their Neherum uniforms from the Nest before their evacuation, but they had stolen the Accipiter's cloaks and star-tree necklaces. Hopefully it would be enough to get them past the gates.

The train hummed to a stop. Their compartment door slid open, admitting them out onto the narrow platform. Anaya's sprawling silhouette loomed in the distance, illuminated by the occasional twinkling window. Evaly shunted Fayen onto the platform and then onto the long drive that led to the gates. She jogged towards them—a slow meander wouldn't make much sense given their cover story. All the same, she felt the urge to drag her feet. Anaya would be haunted with the old Evaly, who cowered from bullies. Who had accepted her fate as crippled.

She was different now.

"If we defeat Vasken," she asked Fayen softly, "will you come back here?"

His uncovered eye was fixed on the sky. "I don't know yet." His whisper was faint. "Will you?" She heard the plea in his voice.

"I'm not sure," she said. "Things are so different now. And with Jael, and Arkron..." She trailed off as they approached the gates. The night guards had stepped out of it—a pair of Accipiters, hands resting on the hilts of their swords.

"Who goes?" rumbled one of them.

"Injured," she replied, pitching her voice higher. "My partner and I—Outcasts—" She thrust the stolen ID necklaces at them, praying that they wouldn't scan them before letting them inside.

"You seem awfully young to be a knighted Accipiter," he replied, holding up the necklaces. The green beads twinkled in the light of the guardhouse.

"I'm a Journeyman; please, my partner, he's very ill!" She poked Fayen, trying to remind him to groan or make some signal of being in agonizing pain.

He remained still. Blast. Well, maybe he thought it best to keep still, feigning unconsciousness.

"Check him over," the Accipiter told his partner.

"Please, be careful," Evaly said, catching the thermal blanket as the woman twitched it off. "He's injured . . . " She held her breath, afraid the Accipiter was going to lift the bandages and find nothing there. They hadn't had the supplies to dirty them properly . . .

However, the woman took his vitals, pressing two fingers against his neck to check his pulse and then prying his visible eye open to check his pupil. "His pulse is irregular, pupils dilated," she said briskly. "The girl's right; he needs to go to the Passers. Now."

Wait, what? Evaly gripped Fayen's arm, gently patting his cheek as the Accipiters moved to open the gate. "C'mon," she whispered. "That was just an act, right? It worked."

He didn't reply. At her touch, his head lolled to the side, rumpling his bandage. Oh, Silent Star Sea. He had just spoken to her! What had happened?

When the gate rattled open, she hurried through it with true urgency. She couldn't take him straight to the Passer's clinic—they would be recognized immediately. They had both spent too much time there since her accident.

Take him to Mistress Skene. The old woman oversaw the Fledglings and was a member of the Passer division. She had taken Evaly under her wing after she had arrived on Mantalor. Surely she wouldn't be on Vasken's side, would she?

It was a risk she'd have to take, Evaly decided, steering the stretcher towards the Passer dormitories.

Mercifully, the hallways were quiet thanks to the late hour. Despite that, Evaly sensed an air of unease in the silent corridors. Her Hybri swiveled within her. The Neherum in those dorm rooms weren't resting peacefully. It seemed a dark shadow hung over the campus, and Evaly suspected that its title was High General Rosemary Vasken.

Mistress Skene lived on the top floor of the Passer dormitories, where the faculty were each given a suite of rooms. She opened the door after Evaly banged on it, tying a robe over her sleepwear. "Who . . . Evaly? What is this, child? I thought you were on Arkron . . . "

"Please," Evaly whispered, glancing at the other doors in the hallway, afraid to find someone peeking out at them. "There's a lot to explain, but Fayen needs help. Can we come in?"

In response, Mistress Skene opened her door wider, letting Evaly shunt the stretcher inside. The familiar entryway to her rooms was dim, lit only by a single lamp. Here, though, Evaly detected none of the unease she'd felt in the halls. The many plants the old woman kept seemed to crowd around her, like the arms of friends welcoming her home.

Mistress Skene pushed her round glasses up her nose and leaned over Fayen, taking his vitals and listening to his breathing. She straightened, took hold of the stretcher, and steered it towards a room just off the entryway. It was her workroom, where she conducted her personal research and treated those who came to her with their ailments.

"What happened?" Mistress Skene demanded, moving to lift Fayen from the stretcher.

What happened . . . where to even start? Evaly picked up Fayen's legs, shouldering the brunt of his weight as they moved him onto the room's narrow bed. Mistress Skene stared at her. "You . . . but how?"

"There's a lot to tell," Evaly admitted. "But most importantly, he was poisoned while a prisoner for the Consortium. Mama Longracer has tried lots of things, and he hasn't died . . . but he's not getting better either."

"Poison? Does she know what kind?" Mistress Skene removed a blood test kit from a drawer on one of her desks. She had to sweep away the tendrils of a fern to keep them from getting amputated when she shut it again.

"No. But we're pretty sure the High General gave it to him."

Mistress Skene paused, her expression darkening. Evaly tensed, waiting for a reaction like Pickett's. Since Mistress Skene oversaw the Fledglings, she worked closely with Vasken on the admittance of new initiates.

"That woman," she finally said, voice bitter. "She finally succumbed to the siren song of power. I just didn't know she'd sink to harming *children*." She massaged her forehead. "The Consortium has been trying to get the Neherum to form an official partnership with them since the Great War. We've tried to talk Vasken down for years . . . but I suppose we didn't talk enough." She gestured to a chair near the door. "Have a seat, dear, and let me work while you tell me everything."

Evaly did. She spoke for hours, relating their escape from Mantalor, their time on the *Ransom*, the *Void*, their return to Arkron, and Vasken's betrayal. Mistress Skene asked no questions. She merely listened as she buzzed about, adding mixtures to other mixtures, dropping them beneath a magnifier, and adding droplets of Fayen's blood to it.

"We're here to see if there are Neherum who would be willing to help us," Evaly finally finished, slumping back in her chair. She realized that the first strains of dawn light were beginning to filter through the frosted windows of the workroom. How long had it been since she'd slept? Mantalor had different hours than Arkron, and they'd crossed so much of the Star Sea . . . "Though we know it might be a wild lightfoot chase," she added. "We know we're supposed to be loyal to our High General . . . but . . ."

"You might be surprised," Mistress Skene replied. She secured a port to Fayen's arm and connected its line to a bottle, the contents of which she squeezed into it. "The High General informed us of her partnership with the Consortium just before she left for Arkron. There are . . . mixed feelings."

"That's what we encountered on Arkron," Evaly replied, thinking of the Accipiter who had hesitated. She got to her feet and stepped to Fayen's bedside. He seemed comfortable enough now; his face was relaxed, and he breathed easily. Perhaps he had just been too tired? "We were hoping to find a way to speak with some of them," she said.

Mistress Skene finished the infusion and draped Fayen's arm over his stomach. "Leave that to me."

"You'll help us?" Evaly asked, catching Fayen's fingers and squeezing them.

Mistress Skene put her hands on her hips. "And what do you call what I've been doing half the night?"

Evaly ducked her head, though she smiled. "Sorry, Mistress."

Mistress Skene grunted. "Good—ah, welcome back, Mr. Longracer."

Fayen's eyes had opened, blinking blearily at them. He sighed, raising a hand to rub his eyes—then flew upright, cursing. "Silent Star Sea," he groused, pushing away the blanket and swinging his legs over the side of the cot. The motion started to pull the port from his arm, and Evaly winced as the smell of blood tickled her nose. "I'm fine, I swear I'm fine, I should have seen it coming, but we were in so much of a hurry—"

Mistress Skene grabbed him by the shoulders and dragged him back against the cot. "You are not *fine*, Mr. Longracer," she declared, squinting at him. "You have been poisoned; furthermore, you will be staying *right here* until I've run further tests."

Fayen opened his mouth to protest, but then his eyes landed on Evaly's face. She leveled as much fury into her gaze as she could muster, pinning him in place. He shrank back. "Evaly, I—"

"You're staying," she said.

"But our mission—you can't go alone—"

"If I have to, I will. You can't keep pretending that you're fine. I have better eyesight and hearing than you do. I'm not *stupid*. You have to stop treating me like I'm some little kid that can't understand what's going on!"

Fayen held up his hands as if in surrender. The jerked movement pulled the port fully from under his skin. With a *tsk* that sounded like a hiss, Mistress Skene caught his arm and forced it back down, resecuring it. "Okay, okay," he said. "It's not that I think you're stupid or too young; it's that I didn't want to scare you."

"*Scare* me?" She grabbed her cat ears, pulling on them in exasperation. "It's too late for that. You're not okay, and I wish you didn't feel like you had to hide it from me just because you've taken some self-inflicted oath to protect me." She turned her back to him, hugging herself as she angrily studied the rows of plants settled in the windowsill. "I don't need you to protect me. I need you to be *alive* for me."

"Evaly," Fayen began, and then stopped.

She shut her eyes, feeling a tear slide down her face. But she only clenched her fists and pinned her cat ears against her head. "I will lose you someday, and if it's going to be soon, I *have* to know." Her hands became fists at her sides. "I can't have you just . . . *disappear* like Jael did. Like my first family did."

His face was stricken, eyes wide and welling with tears. "Evaly . . ." he choked. "I'm not dying." He shot a look at Mistress Skene. "Right?"

"Not in the immediate future—unless, of course, you do something foolish, as young men are so prone to do," she huffed.

He looked back at her. "See? I'm going to be okay. I promise *we'll* be okay."

She forced herself to relax and sat down on the edge of his bed. She grasped one of his hands. It was clammy and cold. He looked down at it but did not pull it out of her grasp. "Yes," she said. "We'll be okay. Because from now on, we're in this together." She gave him a sad smile and bumped her head against his. "Promise?"

He hesitated but then rested his chin on her head. "All right. I promise."

35

Moving through a *kata* centered Pickett. The rhythm was calming; his body knew exactly where to go. He held back some strikes and surged forward in others. He brought the routine to an end with a spinning flourish and leveled his blade at his opponent's neck.

Captain Ziah's face split into a grin. "Wow, you are good! You even knew where to find me when I shifted." She stuck her hand out. "Well fought, Journeyman Evensong. Or Highness. Whichever you prefer."

He shook her hand, mopping the sweat from his neck with his other arm. "Just Pickett is fine, Captain. I'm not a Neherum anymore."

"Eh." Ziah planted her staff into the dojo mat and leaned against it. "I bet once the other Neherum hear about what Vasken's been up to, they'll boot her out of her fancy office and you'll get to come back." She gestured to him. "Deeps, with skills like that, they'll probably *beg* you."

"I'm not sure about that." He slid his sword back into its sheath. Working as the High General's assistant had set him apart from the other Neherum; he had no idea what their opinions of him were. Besides, they would probably see him as a threat because of how close he had been to Vasken.

His stomach clenched, and his hand rose once again to his bare neck, searching for his necklace. What if there *was* a chance to go back, when this was all over? What if Vasken's removal from the Neherum would allow him to rejoin their ranks? Could he step back into that life after giving it up? He had made his choice, and there was peace in it. "I don't think so," he replied. "Arkron needs me now."

"Of course." Tipping her staff so that it rested against her shoulder, Ziah popped her knuckles. "I suppose it's best to consider all the paths the Creator might have laid for us. Alright, who wants to take on the champion ex-Neherum and prince next?"

The Outcasts that had been watching from around the *Ransom's* dojo stepped forward excitedly, palming all manner of weapons. It would probably be wise to give them some guidance on how to take on an Accipiter, in the event there were still some on Arkron loyal to Vasken. All the same, the thought made him feel sick.

One Outcast held back from the throng, standing with her arms crossed near the door. Jael. She tipped her chin up when she saw that she had his attention, beckoning him over.

He held up his hands apologetically towards the Outcasts ready to spar. "I'm afraid I'm finished for the day. Perhaps another time."

They protested but parted to let him through. He crossed the room to Jael and awkwardly leaned against the wall beside her. "I hope you found our little demonstration entertaining."

Though she wore the scarf over the lower half of her face, he could tell that she was grinning. "Yeah. I especially liked the part where you tripped over your own feet."

Pickett's face fell as his mind replayed the whole *kata*. He had been sure of his stance; had he missed something? Swordplay wasn't always as graceful as the masters made it seem, but he strived to make himself look like more than just a fool swinging a stick about.

"Pickett." Jael's hand dropped onto his shoulder. "I'm teasing you." She offered him a brimming canteen; he pressed it to his cheek, absorbing the coolness before taking a drink. "Our team at the waystation got word from Evaly. They made it to Anaya and are safe with a . . . Mistress Skene?"

Pickett lowered the canteen, nodding approvingly. Going to Skene had been a good choice. She cared deeply for her Fledglings, and she and Vasken had often bickered about admission and budgeting for family visitation. "I was worried they'd be stopped at the gates."

"Apparently Fayen's injuries sold the show," Jael replied. She waved a hand at the mats. Ziah was sparring with another Outcast now; their staffs made a sharp *crack* every time they collided. "I hope you didn't stop on account of me."

He had. But he couldn't admit that, of course. Not now. Even if he had given up his Neherumship, he hadn't stopped being a prince. And their world was currently being invaded. There was no time for these . . . strange sensations that had started niggling in his chest whenever he talked to her. "Of course not. Any news on Vasken?"

She shook her head. "Harper's watching the interrogations now."

He groaned. "Didn't we just convince her to go to bed?"

Jael gave him a reproachful look. "Aren't you always harping on her to take responsibility? She's making a Deeping good effort for being only sixteen. She's doing better than I was."

"How old were you, when you were . . . you know . . . ?"

"Outcasted? Fifteen."

"Deeps," he murmured. "When I was fifteen, all I was worried about was making the top of my classes."

"No surprises there. I suppose, when this is all over, your idea of recreation will be burying yourself in some history tome?" Jael readjusted the scarf around her shoulders.

He smirked. "You really think so? What are *you* going to do?"

"I'm going to take a nap."

Pickett laughed. "That's it?"

"Yeah. Why, were you expecting something grander? Okay, I'm going to borrow a fancy dress from your sister and run barefoot through the prairie like a maiden from the ballads."

He snorted. He had a hard time imagining Jael in a flouncy dress, but then again, he had never expected her to help them cook breakfast. "No, I completely understand the nap. I think I'm going to read a novel."

"A *novel?*"

"Yes, preferably a children's novel. Something light and funny."

It was Jael's turn to laugh, though it was quickly cut off by the sound of her wrist-comm pinging. "Vasken?" Pickett asked.

"Maybe." She took the comm. "Clarkson here."

"Did you find Pickett?" It was Harper, sounding harried. "She's ready to talk."

Vasken, ready to talk? What had changed? Jael and Pickett exchanged looks and ducked out of the dojo.

The brig was located a short distance from the dojo, within Level Two's labyrinth of pilot dormitories and storage rooms. Harper met them in the viewing room, chewing on her bottom lip and fiddling with her necklace. She had finally changed, exchanging her bloody clothing for an outfit similar to Jael's. Her hair was unbound and mussed from her nap. Suddenly she looked tiny in the borrowed Outcast clothing. Tiny and afraid. His little sister. Barely sixteen, with her tarnished locket swaying back and forth like a pendulum ticking away her life. "This way," she said, leading them towards a large window in the wall.

Pickett braced himself and looked in at his former mistress. Vasken had been installed in a bare room, chained to a seat screwed to the floor. Her armor had been removed, leaving her in nothing but her tunic and trousers. They'd even taken her boots—something he had suggested they do, knowing that she kept blades there. She looked vaguely bored, head tipped back to consider the flickering tube light overhead. There were no signs of injury on her, save for the bruises from her fight with Harper.

"She's . . . erm . . . not hurt," he managed.

Jael eyed him. "What, you thought we'd try to beat the information out of her?"

"Well . . ." *You are Outcasts* was on the tip of his tongue, but he swallowed it back down. They weren't like that. He knew better now. "It might have been the only way to get anything out of her," he said, wincing even as he said the words. Even after all she had done, there was a part of him that was still loath to see her hurt.

It was all fake, he reminded himself. All the same, he asked, "Can she see us?"

"No," Jael said, briefly dropping a hand onto his shoulder. "Don't worry. Highness?"

Harper nodded and pressed a control beneath the window. "All right, Vasken," she said. "We're here. What did you want to tell us?"

Vasken's gaze flicked towards the corner of the room, where Pickett assumed the speaker was located. "Excellent," she said. "But before we proceed, there is one thing I need you to answer first. How long has it been since you captured me?"

Harper glanced at Pickett and Jael, seeking guidance. How long had it been? They'd lost all semblance of day and night after leaving the planet, and the strain of *everything* had disrupted their eating and sleeping.

"A day?" Harper whispered. "It was morning when we left Sol, and we were up last night . . . Is it almost evening now?"

Jael tapped her wrist comm. Pickett saw her working to sync it with Arkronen time below. After a moment, she nodded. "It's been a day and a half," she announced. "Why is it important?"

Vasken smiled. "Because Queen Anrameta will be executed tomorrow morning at the palace in Jana."

A chill started at the top of Pickett's head and spread downward, filling his limbs with ice.

Harper gasped, lunging towards the microphone. "You're lying. This is a trap to get us to go planetside."

"Why would I share such valuable information if it wasn't true?" Vasken countered. "Ask my apprentice. I know he's there."

"I'm not your apprentice anymore," Pickett retorted, stepping up beside Harper. More quietly, he added, "I think she's telling the truth."

"It would explain why we haven't been able to contact your mother," Jael remarked.

"She's been stalling," Pickett said, turning away from the window, unable to stomach the sight of Vasken's smug face. "Making us waste time interrogating her while the Consortium moves below so we're only partially prepared."

"What do we do?" Harper's voice was quiet, almost weak.

Jael switched off the microphone so Vasken couldn't hear her. "We move out. Now."

"But we barely have a plan," Harper protested, trying to comb her hair out of her face. She was wearing her crown, but it was caught in the mess of tresses. "Fayen and Evaly haven't had any breakthroughs yet, and even all your Outcasts won't be enough to free the land from those force fields."

"But we have her." Jael gestured to Vasken. "We have a bargaining chip."

"Maybe so, but I'm not certain that they would trade a *planet* for her," Pickett said.

"They probably won't," Jael agreed. "But if we present her at the execution, at the very least, she could be a distraction while—" Her gaze flicked towards Harper, then down to her hands.

Harper visibly shrank.

Jael closed her eyes, and turned back to Pickett. "I'm going to scramble our forces. Prepare yourselves to leave—we'll plan more in the shuttle." With that, she limped out of the room.

Pickett swallowed hard and stepped up beside Harper. "Maybe you don't have to use *all* your weavings," he said.

She refused to meet his gaze. She didn't seem to see any other way. And frankly, he wasn't sure he did either. If Anrameta had been captured, that meant the royal navy had also been subdued. There was no guarantee that Fayen and Evaly were going to rally any Neherum, and the *Ransom* was only one ship. The Arkronen people were ill-equipped to resist—they were farmers, herders, shopkeepers, traders, and more—it was House Evensong's job to protect them. And they were failing. Only a godlike storyweaving to edit away the Consortium's grasp would be enough to stop all this.

But a storyweaving like that would end with Harper's death. A massive lump rose in Pickett's throat, but he swallowed it back down. Perhaps Harper needed hope right now, not logic. "I'm sure not all storyweavers die when their being is used up," he offered. "There must be records of those who went on to lead long lives without their empowerment."

Her eyes remained dull. "Maybe they didn't banish an invasion. Don't try to make me feel better, Pickett." She turned away from him, wrapping her arms around herself. "I think I'm starting to understand who I am. Who the Creator made me to be. I was made a storyweaver for this time. And . . . it's going to demand all of me." She started to walk out into the hallway, alone.

"It might not," he called after her, preparing a lecture of possible ways she could avoid it. But he stopped himself. A lecture was probably the last thing she needed right now. He jogged after her and caught her arm. Touching her still sent an uneasy jolt through him, but he pushed away the feeling and instead put his arms around her. Harper buried her face in his shoulder. She wasn't crying, but she still trembled.

He had spent years with the High General, building a relationship with her in the hopes that it would fill the void his status in

House Evensong had left. Now he saw how that inattention to Harper and the rest of his family had left them weakened.

That was over now. The weight of his pendant was gone. He was Prince Pickett Evensong, the brother of Princess Harper, heir of the great House Evensong. Harper would save Arkron. And he would do whatever he must to save her.

He kissed her forehead and then walked with her, hand in hand, to their quarters to gather their things. Alarms began to ring throughout the *Ransom*, summoning the Outcasts to their stations. In their quarters, he excused himself to his unused bunkroom. There, he dug through the bags until he found what he wanted: his crown, brought with him from Solstice. The emeralds that made up the triangular plates twinkled, like someone flashing a million smiles because they were pleased to see him.

He hadn't worn the crown since he was thirteen. It had been too big then, too uncomfortable. Slowly, he placed it on his head. It slid onto his brow, resting just above his ears.

It seemed that it finally fit at last.

36

Fayen woke to a face full of Evaly's curly hair. He rolled away from her, trying to clean the loose strands from his mouth. Evaly mumbled sleepily as his flurried movement disturbed her. She was positioned awkwardly in a chair drawn close to the bed; clearly she had intended to sleep in it, but she had slumped forward during the night so she was partially on the bed.

He sighed and scooted close to her once more, smoothing her curls behind her cat-ears. She must have slipped in during the night, seeking refuge from her nightmares. Nightmares that probably involved him dying. She'd had those frequently after her adoption—some dark part of her mind was convinced that she'd lose her entire family again.

But never had those bad dreams come so close to being a reality.

I'm not going to die. I'm going to get better! He pressed a hand against his ribs. See, *they* had healed! He would be strong again soon. He dipped his head forward to rest against hers, imagining himself frightening away the dreams that tormented her so, with only his love as a brilliant sword in his hand.

"Aha. I was wondering where Evaly had gotten off to," Mistress Skene murmured as she pushed the door open. "And how is my patient this morning?"

Carefully pulling away from Evaly, Fayen sat up and swung his legs over the side of the bed. This time, there was no wave of dizziness. No trembling muscles. No weight on his limbs. See! He was recovering. "I feel . . . *amazing*."

Mistress Skene shoved her glasses up her nose and nodded approvingly. She pushed him back onto the bed and began removing the port from his forearm. "I'll comm a copy of the mixture's compounds to you. I would recommend that you forward it to your mother or primary healer so that they can get underway in making a batch for you."

"Oh . . . " he said, accepting a square of gauze to press over the small incision. "Wasn't this infusion enough?"

Mistress Skene removed her glasses, scrubbed them on her shirt, and resettled them on her nose. "No," she said. "You will need some form of this medication—oral or intravenous—every day for the rest of your life."

Horror jolted through him as though he had been speared with some sort of invisible dart. "You mean . . . it's *incurable*?"

She laced her fingers together. "I'm afraid so."

How could she speak so calmly? Couldn't she see him crumbling? Couldn't she see the oceans of panic swelling and throbbing inside of him? "Is it going to kill me?" he asked.

"Without the medicine, it could, but it would take a long time. It seems more interested in keeping you weakened and—"

"—Useless," he finished for her.

She frowned at him. "Fayen."

He turned away from her, searching for something to throw or kick, just to get these feelings *out*. His eyes landed on Evaly, who had awoken and sat up, watching him. He tried to jerk away before she could see his stricken face, but it was too late; she was up and wrapping her arms around him, trying to comfort him.

This is supposed to be my job. But it was her arms that were strong, not his. He let her hold him, hiding his face in her curly hair as he tried to come to terms with this failure.

"It'll be okay," she whispered. "We can be strong together."

"But the accident . . . it's my fault that you . . . you're . . ." He lifted a listless hand, gesturing to her yellow eyes and cat ears. "I was trying to make up for it."

She caught his hand, guiding it back to his side. "You have. A hundredfold. You've protected me ever since, giving me space to heal. But I *am* healing, and I can't live like I'm not. The accident had a purpose, Fayen. I can see how the Creator is using it for good in these times." She sat down beside him. "And maybe that means something good is going to come out of your weakness."

He laughed, a mirthless, bitter noise. How could being weak serve any good? He hadn't been able to save Colten while they were prisoners. He hadn't been able to protect Evaly or any of the others during their evacuation from the Cleft. He had fallen *asleep* on the way to Solstice. "How? Being weak isn't who I am."

She smiled sadly. "But maybe being strong isn't all of who you are meant to be either."

He opened his mouth to retort but then closed it slowly as Colten's words during their imprisonment together floated through his mind. *Did your sister ever ask you to spend your life like this?*

Evaly had never asked him to become strong. He knew she had needed it after the accident . . . but she had changed. And now he had too.

Mistress Skene cleared her throat, turning from her worktable with a tablet clutched in her hands. "I have assembled some Neherum who are interested in listening to you near the library. If you are well enough to make your appeal, it would be wise to do it now, before word gets to those loyal to the High General."

Fayen rose at once, thankful for the mission. Something to pull him away from this awful revelation, this *breaking* of all he was. "I'm ready," he said, reaching for his sword. He might be damaged internally, but at least he could still *look* intimidating. He rolled his shoulders. "Let's get moving."

Evaly stood with him, shoulder to shoulder. His partner rather than his shadow. Moons. That was going to take some getting used to. But what if she was right? What if there was some good that could come from this?

But I'm not going to find it if I keep wallowing here, he thought, following Mistress Skene and Evaly into the corridor beyond.

The sky over Anaya had grown dark, threatening rain, which gave Fayen and Evaly an excuse to bundle themselves tightly in their cloaks as they made their way to the library. As usual, the halls and walkways were filled with Fledgling students, Journeymen like Pickett, and fully sorted Neherum moving to their classes, study halls, and research rooms. Normally a buzz of conversation hung in the air, but today the atmosphere was subdued. People kept their heads down. Fledglings moved in tight groups. Journeymen stuck in pairs. Fayen had a feeling that the tension had nothing to do with the weather. Vasken's choice to align with the Consortium was poisoning them as surely as she had poisoned him.

The library was the crown jewel of Anaya, nestled in the very heart of the castle. It was a rambling three-story structure outfitted with arching stained-glass windows, carvings in the stone walls, and figurines representing the three divisions nestled in the corners. All of them wore wings draped over their shoulders like cloaks.

Surrounding the library was a grove of star-trees like the ones represented on the Neherum's necklaces. Their silvery leaves shivered in the heavy wind, creating a symphony of ominous murmurs.

Mistress Skene led them around the side of the library, where a small, cobbled amphitheater was nestled in the crook between the library and the building nearest to it.

Fayen stopped short, pulling Evaly to a halt beside him. "When you said a *few* Neherum, I pictured . . . you know, a *few*," he said to Mistress Skene. The stone seats of the amphitheater were filled with at least twenty Neherum. He recognized teachers from their classes, Journeymen in pairs or with their mentors, and necklaces from all three divisions. There were even a few interdisciplinary necklaces, bearing the blue, green, and purple of all the divisions. They had taken time away from their busy studies to be here?

"As you can see, there are many qualms among us about the path the High General is taking us on," Mistress Skene said. "To the front, please."

"This is not how I pictured this going," Evaly whispered as they shuffled down the aisle to the amphitheater's stage.

"Me neither," he muttered. He had pictured a table or perhaps a bench with a handful of Neherum. This . . . this felt like a class assignment that they had procrastinated on preparing for.

They reached the stage and turned to face the assembly. Fayen's legs trembled, though he couldn't tell if it was from nerves or from his illness. He pushed back his hood, and Evaly did the same. A part of him had expected some sort of response, to be called traitors and arrested. But the Neherum only settled deeper into their seats, as if waiting for a lecture to begin.

Beside him, Evaly bristled. "They're just . . . complacent," she hissed.

"Fayen and Evaly Longracer." In the front row, a woman stood, clutching her Ibis staff. Her blue star-tree necklace was the same shade as her eyes, and her long braids had silver cuffs adorning their ends. "You have come to us with a serious charge against our High General. One that we are divided over."

"Yes, Mistress," Fayen replied. He cleared his throat, trying to pitch his voice loud enough to be heard. "High General Rosemary Vasken is helping the Consortium take over our homeworld, Arkron. She ambushed us at our home, Solstice, and attempted to execute—without a fair trial—Princess Harper Evensong. We come to you with a plea: Help us drive the Consortium from our world. We need the expertise of the Neherum to guide a functioning resistance."

"We are aware that the High General allied us with the Consortium," the woman answered, leaning on her staff. "To many of us, the news was unsurprising. We utilize Consortium outposts and ships for our missions. The Consortium supplies funding for some of our research. We would not have made such galactic progress were it not for our unofficial partnership. Perhaps it is fair that the High General has made our union official. What is your rebuttal to that?"

Silent Star Sea, this is just like class, Fayen thought, casting about for a response. His strengths lay in physical fighting—his aim had been to go into Accipiter division, to serve as the hands of the Neherum. This verbal sparring was more on par for someone planning to join Ibis.

"It's acting against the codes." Evaly spoke up. "You all know it—that's why everyone is so uneasy around here. Vasken and the Consortium are trying to change you from scholars into a military to enforce the Consortium's will."

"And are you not trying to do the same in asking us to aid your world?" the Ibis woman challenged.

Fayen grimaced. A tremor ran through his body, a warning that Mistress Skene's mixture was beginning to wear off already. "No, Mistress. The Neherum are dedicated to preserving and exploring creation as it is. The Consortium is actively trying to destroy that on Arkron. If you truly believe in our codes and our mission, then help us."

"The codes also direct us towards loyalty." A new Neherum stood—an Accipiter resting his hand on the hilt of his sword. "We are to be loyal to each other and to our High General, whom we elected."

"They're like Pickett, except ten times worse," Evaly murmured.

Fayen nodded, dropping a hand onto her shoulder. It was more to steady himself than reassure her. It had begun to drizzle; the small droplets hitting his face felt like they sizzled on his hot skin. He tried to loosen his cloak to let the breeze in but found that his fingers didn't have the strength to fight the fastenings. "But if we're meant to be loyal to our codes and tenants, and our High General is straying from them, shouldn't our loyalty stay with our ideals?" he asked.

If there was a response, he didn't hear it. The world shrank to a pinpoint, and all he could focus on was keeping himself upright. *Not another episode. Not now . . .*

Evaly's face filled his line of sight, her lips moving. Her voice cut through the whine in his ears: "Fayen? What can I do?"

"I'm . . . I'm . . . " *Fine* was on the tip of his tongue. But it wasn't true. He wasn't fine. He would never be fine again, thanks to Vasken. "A chair," he finally managed. "It hurts to stand."

"A chair," Evaly called. "Please."

Someone brought one. Gratefully, Fayen sank into it and accepted a flask of water someone handed to him. Mistress Skene stooped over him, her glasses sliding precariously down her nose. "Dosage must have been off slightly," she said. "I'll give you another when we get back."

Fayen nodded wordlessly. He was aware of the curious eyes of the assembly.

Evaly shifted to a defensive position beside him, hand on his shoulder. "Forgive us," she said. "He was injured while a prisoner of the Consortium."

"I wasn't just injured." He tipped his head upward, letting more of the cooling rain fall on his face. "The High General participated in my torture. After I nearly escaped, she poisoned me. And"—he swallowed hard but forced the words out—"it's unlikely that I'll ever recover from it."

There. He'd admitted it. It was real now. "I'm weak. But I believe the Neherum are strong—especially when we remember who we are. And that's an Order dedicated to seeing the Creator's story thrive."

"Vasken did this?" The Ibis woman stared at him, brow furrowed. "It has been verified?"

"Yes," Mistress Skene said, returning to her seat in the front row. "I have the evidence, taken straight from his blood. Besides, those of us in Passer were aware that she was exploring herbology in recent months. The choice to use such a debilitating poison on Mr. Longracer was likely premeditated."

"She poisoned one of her own," the Ibis woman gasped. She sank slowly into her seat, still clutching her staff. "And a *child*, no less."

The Accipiter man remained standing, though he had released the hilt of his sword. "The Neherum are loyal to the High General," he stated, "but above all, we are loyal to *life*. These actions on the part of our High General are not the preservation of it."

Murmurs of assent rippled throughout the amphitheater.

Rallying what little strength he had, Fayen appealed as loudly as he could: "Please. Help us. Help Arkron. Don't let the High General lead you away from who we are—"

Whatever he had to say next was drowned out by the collective sound of the gathered Neherum rising to their feet in acquiescence.

"We did it," Evaly said, crouching beside him. "You did it."

"Yeah," he replied. If he weren't ill . . . if Vasken hadn't poisoned him . . . would they have been able to convince the Neherum to help them? "Maybe you're right," he continued, struggling to his feet. Evaly moved to support him, and he let her. "Maybe some good can come of this."

She smiled, trying to comb her hair away from her cat ears. "Now we just need to get home," she said, "and see just how much good can come."

37

THE SIGHT OF the Cleft's soaring spires made Harper straighten her spine as she and Jael walked towards the city, joining the influx of people making their way in for the execution. It had been mandated by the Consortium that the surrounding townships attend the death of their queen. From the murmurs around them, it sounded as though they planned to broadcast it as well for all of Arkron and the Exlenna to see.

Her stomach twisted, and she was suddenly glad that she hadn't eaten the ration roll Pickett had tried to force upon her that morning. The sun was barely peeking over the horizon, bathing the landscape in pure morning rays. She shivered despite the suffocating midsummer heat. Nonetheless, she tried to stand straight and walk lightly as Lady Kova had schooled her to do. She complained that Harper walked like a lumbering farmhand. Harper hadn't noticed that she had slipped back into the habit when they returned home. Today she needed every ounce of regality that she could muster.

Jael elbowed her in the ribs. "Don't walk like that." She had to lean close so Harper could hear her over the bleating of lightfoots and rumble of hovericles around them. "We need to blend in, remember?"

Blending in was hilarious coming from Jael, who had changed back into Arkronen clothing. Her prosthetic arm gleamed from the short sleeve of her shirt. She had combed her hair into a knot atop her head but had left parts down in the front in an attempt to hide her scars. Even so, it was clear to anyone who spared them more than a passing glance that she was not Arkronen. In contrast, Harper wore a wide-brimmed straw hat and a knitted poncho, trying to hide as much of herself as possible. She was fairly certain she was going to cook alive in the costume.

"I don't know that anyone is really paying attention," Harper replied. Most people appeared to be stumbling along, struggling to fully wake up. Babies slept in sacks on their mother's back, while children and seniors dozed in the backs of lightfoot carts and hovericles. "They're all too unsettled. It's not right, forcing them from their homes like this—just to see something the Consortium is going to broadcast." And it made their job so much harder. If it came to a fight, there would be more civilians in the way.

"My guess is that they wanted people in town for a different reason," Jael said, glancing over her shoulder. She stopped short, pulling Harper next to her. "Yep. Look."

Around them, the Arkronens were beginning to also pause, turning back to look at the grasslands behind them. One of the Consortium's shielded areas loomed on the horizon, but it seemed to be moving *upward*. Even from a distance, Harper could hear the snap and groan of the earth as it was carved away.

"What the Deeps," Jael breathed. "They're *literally* stealing your land."

"They're probably going to try and transpose it onto one of their planets," Harper said. "But it won't work. It'll be trying to put someone else's blood into your own—it'll reject it unless it's a perfect match. But it won't be. And yet they'll just keep coming back for *more*."

Around them, the Arkronens cried out. Some started backwards, towards the catastrophe, while others pressed on to the city. Harper stood between them both, utterly torn. Her pen was shoved up her sleeve; she let it drop into her palm, feeling it connect to what little power she had left.

Jael caught her arm. "Not yet," she hissed.

Harper gulped. "But I can't let this continue!"

"I know. And you're not. But we have a plan, and we have to try to stick to it." Jael released her to tap her comm. "I am going to let Pickett know about this."

They had split into several groups after departing the *Ransom*. Pickett and Captain Ziah were entering from the other side of the city with a hovericle containing Vasken, while several other teams of Outcasts infiltrated at other points. They would rendezvous upon the execution site. Jael had pointed out that splitting up would help them avoid attention—with any luck, they would be able to meld with the people streaming into the city.

With difficulty, Harper turned her back on the grim horizon and kept walking towards the city. In the west, the fading twin moons hovered over the world like a pair of eyes somberly watching the scene. They were soon obscured by the Jana's tangle of buildings. With the people pouring in, the narrow streets were more congested than usual. Seeing the business opportunity in the influx of people, vendors pushed carts laden with food or knickknacks through the crowds, hawking their wares. The buzz of anxiety hung in the air, interlaced with the horns of hovericles and bleating lightfoots.

Despite the unhappy cloud hanging over the people, Harper found that being in the midst of this symphony of life inundated her with a burning energy akin to the thrum she felt in the midst of a weaving. She was Arkronen. These people were Arkronen. Finally she milled about them as she had always wished to. She was partaking in their stories. Even if it was in a disguise.

And moons, it was her job to lift this cloud from them. To ensure that they could stay free, allowed to live the stories the Creator had woven for them.

The thought made the prospect of giving up her power not seem so dreadful. What was the loss of one story when faced with the salvation of thousands of others?

She stopped, letting herself stand in the midst of her people for a moment. Drinking in what she could of their stories. It was like when she had been on the *Ransom*, but richer. *Righter.* These were her people.

"*Harper.*" Jael gripped her shoulder suddenly and pushed her into an alleyway.

"Sorry, sorry," she apologized. "I was just—"

"Hush." Jael peered back into the street, hand resting on her concealed sidearm.

"What is it?" Harper stood on tiptoe, trying to see over her shoulder.

"A squad of Consortium guardsmen."

Harper gave up trying to see over her shoulder and instead peered under her arm. Sure enough, a knot of black-suited guardsmen pushed their way down the walkway. Their cloistered ranks and shiny uniforms stood out like a tumor in the midst of the warm Arkronen yellows, greens, blues, and reds. The people gave them a wide berth, eyeing their blasters suspiciously.

"I'm going to see how many more patrols there are," Jael said. "We may need to adjust our route. Stay here."

Harper began to protest, but Jael was gone before a full sentence could leave her mouth. Frowning, she sat down against the wall and pulled her hat over her face, shielding herself from the sun and passersby.

She heard the guardsmen pass. Their uniforms rattled like a tacked-up lightfoot; all she could think about was the sight of them leaching from the penthouse on Mantalor and Captain Yarrowriver falling over again and again before her eyes. She peeked out from behind her hat and saw a few helmets turn towards her. Their veiled gaze slid past her, however, and they continued on.

She sank against the wall, breathing in the musty smell of her hat and the stink of garbage from a nearby dumpster. The sun drifted higher in the sky; how long would Jael be gone? They couldn't be late for Anrameta's execution. Harper fiddled with her locket, pressing her thumbnail into its seam, trying to get it to open. As always, the book-shaped pendant stubbornly refused to budge.

"You look thirsty, Miss."

She twisted to find a small girl standing beside her, arms crossed. Her brown hair was twisted into two braids, and she wore a faded, floral print dress.

"I am," Harper admitted, pressing her back to the wall. Some of Lady Kova's early advice when she had first come to Mantalor had included warnings about tricks like this. Kidnappers employed children to appeal to a victim's kinder sensibilities, and when the child had convinced the unsuspecting fool to follow them, they jumped her.

The girl waved a hand down the alleyway, to the street on the other side. "We've got water in our shop. Or chai, if that's what you prefer."

"I'm fine, thanks," Harper insisted, tugging the brim of her hat down.

The girl put her hands on her hips and tossed her braids over her shoulder. "We won't ask questions if that's what you're worried about."

"I'm waiting for a friend."

"Your friend is going to find a lobster." The girl pointed at Harper's hands, which were beginning to sunburn on the top. She was going to have a few more freckles from this morning, it would seem. "It's not far. She'll be able to find you."

"I'm fine, really." Harper leaned back to peer into the street again. She was met with a sight that made her stomach lurch—another patrol of guardsmen, marching down the street in her direction. With most people streaming towards the palace, she would draw more attention sitting out here alone than if she went with the girl.

Silent Star Sea. "All right, you've convinced me," she conceded, hiking herself to her feet. "You promise you're not leading me somewhere to kill me?"

The girl's nose crinkled. "What?" Her electric blue eyes narrowed. "You must be from outta town."

Harper sighed and pulled her hat off to fan herself with it. "You could say that. Where's this shop of yours?"

The girl swept into a dramatic bow. "This way, Miss."

Wary, Harper followed her down the alley. It let out into the next street over, and here the girl veered to the left, scrambling up a set of low steps to throw open a door. It had once been a scorching yellow, but time had faded the color and left the paint peeling. The rest of the exterior was in a similar state of disrepair. It was clean, yes, but it had seen better days.

The darkness of the interior embraced Harper, and she swept her hat off again, raising her face to a vent piping in cool air. It took a moment for her eyes to adjust, but once they did she saw that the interior was a chai shop. It was mostly empty; a few patrons drowsed over cups in the corner, and a young woman with her hair in a messy knot scrubbed at the countertop. A fussing baby was tied to her back in a sling.

"Nina! I found another customer!" Harper's escort scrambled up onto one of the barstools.

The young woman dropped her rag. "Lune! I told you not to drag people in! The invaders are going to think you're preventing people from going to the execution! Then we'll be in a heap of trouble."

Harper stepped up to the bar. "It's okay. I was thirsty anyway. How much for water?"

"Nothing," Nina sighed. "We don't charge for necessities." She turned to a sink, swaying from side to side in an effort to soothe the baby.

"But Nina . . . " Lune began, glancing at Harper.

Harper dropped several orbs on the counter, cupping them carefully to keep them from rolling away. "For your kindness. It's a hot day. If Lune hadn't found me, I might have cooked to death out there."

Nina set a brimming glass on the counter and swept the orbs into the till. "Thank you, Miss." Her eyes, identical to Lune's, lingered on Harper's face, and her expression hardened. "You in town for the execution?"

Harper eased herself up onto one of the stools, clutching her hands around the cup. "Yes. I'm from one of the far northern villages." She took a drink, feeling Nina's harsh eyes boring into her. *She knows. She knows who I am. At least, she knows my public face.*

Within her, both Weaver Harper and Princess Harper began scheming at once. Weaver Harper advocated for a quick getaway. Princess Harper demanded they keep their head down and pretend they didn't notice.

Neither of those sound helpful. She met Nina's eye and set the cup down. "We like our anonymity there."

She saw Nina swallow and give the slightest nod. Lune had been watching their exchange and scrambled over the stools to crouch on the one next to Harper. Unlike Nina, she had no qualms about pointing out the obvious. "You look a lot like the princess, you know," she said in a dramatic whisper. "Except dirtier. And your hair is messier." She picked up a hank of Harper's hair and let it fall in a slow waterfall of auburn strands.

"Lune," Nina hissed. "Just leave her alone and let her be on her way."

"I'm just saying—"

"Lune!"

The girl glowered at Nina.

"It's all right," Harper sighed, reaching a decision. She pushed her now-empty cup away and added in a low voice, "I am who you think I am, Lune."

The girl's eyes bugged out. "Really?"

Harper angled her body so that her back was to the other customers and twitched the poncho up so that Lune could see her crown, which was bound to her waist. "Really."

"Don't be too impressed, Lune. With the way things are going, she won't be a princess much longer." Nina was back to scrubbing the counter. "Unless, of course, she's planning to use some of that secret power to keep herself on the throne." There was a challenge in her voice. And, perhaps, some bitterness.

"I'm sorry," Harper said. "I'm still learning how to carry all of this." She looked down at her story-stained hands. "I'm not who they try to make me out to be. I'm not a proper princess. And I'm not a powerful storyweaver . . . at least not anymore." A desperation was growing in her heart, a desperation for them to *see* her, not as their princess, or a storyweaver, but one of them. An Arkronen. A fellow shattered story.

"Yeah? Who are you, then?" Nina tossed her rag into a basket under the counter.

"I . . . " Moons. The tangle within her rose dangerously high, and she shut her eyes and swallowed it down. "In stories, the usual response to that question is a complicated title and the character's goal," she replied, opening her eyes to meet Nina's. "But I'm not a grandiose conqueror. I'm Harper. And I want to save my mother and live on a free, healing world." She drew in a deep breath. "And I want to go home and take a nap. And watch the sunset with my friends over a pot of chai." Saying those things felt like telling a story, but a different kind than what she was used to. This one was raw. Honest. Unconsciously she began to rub the faded intercessors on her forearms, pleading with the Creator to let the things she had spoken come to pass.

Lune grabbed her arm with a gasp. "You draw the glyphs?"

"Yes."

"I thought princesses couldn't do that! You gotta keep your skin all smooth and soft!"

Harper smiled at her sadly. "I'm not a very good princess, Lune."

"Hardly anyone draws those anymore," Nina said, repositioning her baby. "It's . . . it's good to know that House Evensong hasn't let their devotion waver. Even with the Consortium about to conquer us."

"The Consortium isn't going to conquer us," Lune insisted, poking a finger at Harper. "She's going to stop them with her magic. Like she did on the Net broadcast."

Harper winced. The wild sorceress that the Consortium had painted her to be was not who she wanted to be. Not who she *should* be. "I hope to," she said. "But I'm not sure I'm strong enough. Not anymore."

Lune's face fell. "Who's going to save us, then?"

"Well, we have some brave people helping us," Harper replied, thinking of Jael's crew. Were they in position already? She should be hurrying to the palace . . . and yet, something kept her here with her people.

Nina grunted and resecured her child against her, in the front this time. "*Some* brave people against the whole Consortium?" She rested her hand on her child's fuzzy head. "It's going to take more than that." She hesitated and then added, "Many of our patrons—myself included—have wondered why House Evensong hasn't called upon us for help."

A dreadful image filled Harper's mind: the guardsmen from Mantalor, moving to gun down Captain Yarrowriver again. But instead of Captain Yarrowriver, it was Nina and Lune.

Lune tapped her arm. "Hey, Miss Princess, are you okay?"

Sucking in ragged breaths, Harper struggled to compose herself. "It's House Evensong's job to protect the people. You shouldn't have to suffer for my mistakes."

"Well, you just said it yourself—you don't think you're strong enough to push away the Consortium. This is our world too. Did you ever think that if the people got to know who you are, they might be willing to help you?"

"I . . . well . . . I'm an Arkronen, just like you," Harper said. "And I want to see this world thrive. How do I help people see that, Nina?"

Nina was quiet for a time, swaying from side to side to soothe the baby. Harper waited in trepidation, fearing that her answer would be a demand for a fountain of power to fix all their problems. "By doing what you're doing now," she answered, taking Harper's glass and setting it in the sink. "By being with us. By telling us your story."

Harper straightened. "That's . . . that's it?"

"Sure. Sharing your story is sharing part of your innermost self. And I think, Highness, that's what the people want the most. If they know you, they'll fight for you."

"What story do you think they need to hear?" Harper asked. Did the people want to know that a storyweaver was coming to help push away the Consortium? Or did they want to know that their princess was among them, working to save Arkron? Which version would be best?

And was there really a difference between the two?

"They need to know the story you've told us," Nina replied. "That you're one of us, with hopes and dreams and people you love. Trying to keep our home free."

"I . . . " Moons. Was Nina right? Perhaps the Arkronens didn't want the princess or the storyweaver . . . but *her*. Harper Evensong. Princess, storyweaver, future queen. Also tired and chai-hungry. *And beloved,* she thought, recalling Jael's words on the *Ransom.* "I understand." Moons, yes, she understood. She slid off the stool. "Where can I find people willing to listen? But I don't have time . . . The execution . . . " She reached into her pocket, curling her hand around the calligraphy pen. What if she created some sort of projection, casting her story about the city? And yet that would be little more than propaganda. Stories had power when they were shared. Not when they were forced.

"Leave that to us," Nina said, tightening the fastenings on her baby's wrap. "We have friends, and our friends have friends. Spreading your story will be our part in this. You had better go resume yours. We'll be there when it's time."

A combination of gratitude and fear rolled through Harper. "Thank you," was all she could muster. It was hard to let go of this. To trust that there was a bigger story at play, one that she couldn't control every aspect of. But if she wanted to give Arkron a chance, she had to. She started towards the door. "Thank you."

"Bye, Your Highness!" Lune called, scrambling down from her seat at the bar to wave.

Harper paused in the doorway, turning back to her. "You don't have to call me that."

"Okay." Lune flashed her a grin. "Bye, Harper."

Harper. Not Princess Harper or Weaver Harper. Just Harper. Inside of Harper, something loosened. Glancing across the room, she saw the other patrons staring at her. Some still clutched their drinks, while others had half-risen, prepared to leave as well. Harper dipped her head to them. Already Lune was scurrying across the room, gesturing wildly at Harper, a tale on the tip of her tongue.

Harper pushed out into the street once more. Something more than her thirst had been quenched in that shop. Harper. Lune hadn't called her Princess Harper or Weaver Harper; just Harper. She rolled her own name over her tongue. *Harper.* Old Arkronen for storyteller, or songkeeper. One who repeated things over and over. Like how a princess repeated the history of her people. Or how a storyweaver repeated stories to bring them to life.

Could Jael have been right last night on the *Ransom's* viewing deck? Could there be something beyond the two selves she held within her? Someone entirely different? Someone wholly loved?

You will have to choose what kind of queen you will be, Anrameta's voice reminded her.

What if neither the storyweaver nor the princess became queen someday? What if this new being that was knitting itself together inside of her was meant to be queen? Queen Harper. What would she be like?

The streets were mostly empty now. It was dangerously close to the time of the execution—there was no time to find Jael. She would have to go straight to the Cleft. She began to run, clamping her hat against her head as she went to prevent it from blowing off. She kept her eyes on the palace's spires, using them as a compass as she navigated the narrow streets. As she ran, some of the heaviness lifted from her heart. Perhaps there was a real chance that Arkron's story wasn't going to end in defeat. Her story was going to weave with that of her people's and the Outcasts and the Neherum, and together they'd reclaim Arkron—

"Halt!"

She tripped over the cobblestones as she pulled up, looking over her shoulder. A squad of guardsmen were amassed behind her, blasters drawn. They must have been lurking in the alleyway, waiting to catch stragglers.

"I'm sorry," she said, turning about and raising her hands. She tried to pitch her voice higher. "My lightfoot went lame. I was tryin' to follow the summons . . . " Moons, if she was being stopped, did that mean that the others had been also? Had none of them made it to the palace?

Two guardsmen pulled her arms behind her back while a third began patting her down. She tucked her chin downward, trying to hide her face, but their squad leader swept the hat from her head and forced her chin up. In the same instant, the guardsman searching her found her crown and pulled it from her belt. "It's her!" they cried at the same time.

The guardsmen holding her pushed her to her knees.

"You're going to regret this," she said, glaring up at their identical black helmets. Their advanced tactical suits looked so out of place against Arkron's weathered background, like ink stains on a white linen dress. What were they like under those masks? Were they like her people, with stories of their own to live out? "It's not too late to turn back," she tried again, pleading.

In response, the squad leader raised his blaster and fired a stunner directly into her face.

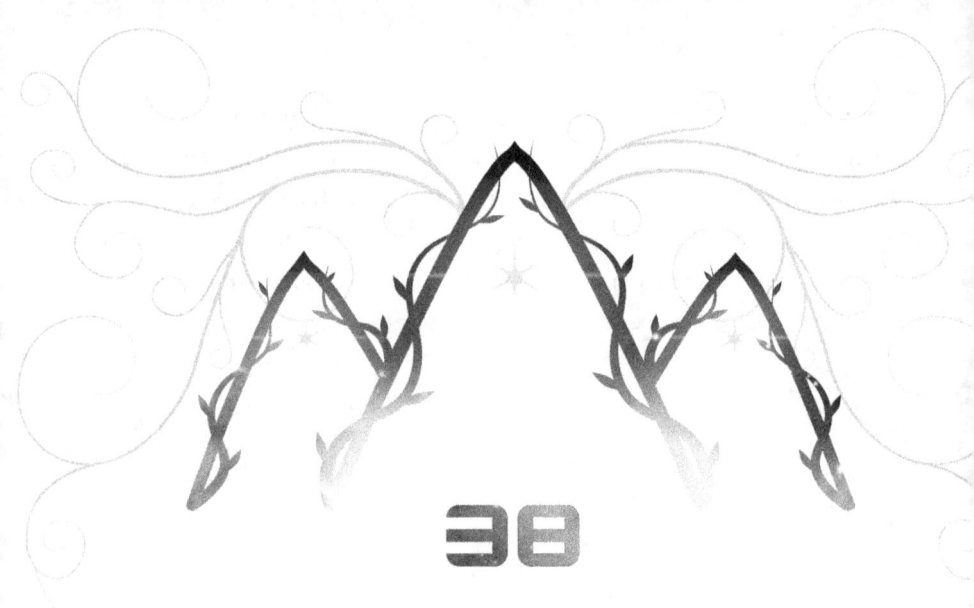

38

Hunkered beside a fountain, Pickett shaded his eyes to see the stage as the noonday sun cast a glare over the square, turning the figures climbing the stage into watery silhouettes. They moved like shadows in a nightmare. Behind the stage, the stone wall of the Cleft's outer courtyard rose up in a brick backdrop, as if this were just all a theater performance.

But it was all too real. Leading the procession onto the stage was Speaker Archer, followed by the rest of the Seven. They were arrayed in flamboyant garments, as if they were attending a sporting event rather than an execution.

Following them, flanked by a squad of guardsmen, was Anrameta. Pickett's throat tightened at the sight of her. Even with her arms bound behind her back, dressed in a plain gown, she still held her head up regally. They had allowed her to wear her crown, and the sun beaming through the sapphire plates cast an iridescent blue halo around her head as the guardsmen thrust her against the wall.

Indignation roared in his chest. How dare they? How dare they stride onto their world like they owned it already, trying to tear down everything House Evensong had worked to build? He grasped the hilt of his sword but restrained himself. *Not yet.*

Around him, the square quieted. It was packed with Arkronens, hemmed in by guardsmen who watched the streets from ground-level and the air, hunkered on the rooftops of the buildings surrounding the square.

Inside the buildings, Outcasts waited for their signal to move. In one group of them was Vasken, gagged, bound, and stunned into unconsciousness. Their bargaining chip—but only if they needed her. Hopefully Harper's power would hold out long enough to rescue Anrameta and get the Consortium away from Arkron—or at least weaken them enough so that Arkron had a fighting chance.

But would it kill her? His stomach lurched, and he pushed the thought away. He couldn't be emotional. Not now.

The Seven arranged themselves on either side of Anrameta, facing each other. Archer stood with his back to her, facing the crowd, hands clasped together in front of him as if he were about to give a celebratory speech. "Arkronens." He must have had an amplifier tucked into the collar of his shirt, for his voice rang across the square without him raising it. "Today, you move into a new era. Today, we free you from the shackles of House Evensong."

The crowd stayed hushed. Pickett heard soft jeers at his words, but with the guardsmen looming around them, they didn't dare raise their voices louder.

Archer smiled. "I hear no voices in her defense."

Here was the trap they had been expecting. Where was Harper? Pickett glanced at the building he had assigned Harper and Jael to. There were so many faces; perhaps they had gotten stuck in its halls because of the crowd?

A hand touched his elbow. He twisted around to find Jael hunched next to him. "I lost her," she hissed.

"What do you mean *you lost her?*" he demanded, cold horror rushing through him.

"I went to scout the patrols, and when I came back to where I had left her, she was gone." Jael mopped her brow with her arm. "The owner of one of the chai houses said that I'd just missed her, that she was headed for the palace, but I couldn't find her. There were so many guardsmen. I'm sorry."

On the stage, the guardsmen forced Anrameta to her knees.

Pickett closed his eyes, cursing, and then sprang onto the fountain. He scrambled to the top of its spire to make himself visible, and pushed his hood back. "I will speak for the queen, Speaker Archer."

The crowd pulled away from him as if he had some sort of disease. He tipped his head back, allowing the sun to catch his simple crown. Where in the Silent Star Sea was Harper? She was supposed to be doing this, not him. She was the heir, and he was . . . the spare.

But he was still House Evensong.

The eyes of the square turned to him. On the rooftops overhead, the guardsmen raised their blasters, though they held their fire.

Anrameta raised her head and met his eye. Pride lit her weary face, sending warmth coursing through him.

Emboldened, he threw a hand towards the building where Vasken had been concealed. "We have come to offer a trade."

At his signal, a group of Outcasts burst from the building, dragging Vasken between them. She lolled in their grasp, still mostly unconscious. Pickett could see her eyes fluttering, but she wasn't lucid enough to hold herself upright. Her hair had begun falling out of its braid, but they had dressed her in her armor once more to ensure she was instantly recognizable. They stopped beside Pickett and Jael, propping Vasken up so that the Seven could clearly see her.

"In exchange for the queen," Pickett said, "we will release your partner and head of the Neherum, High General Rosemary Vasken."

Tactically speaking, he thought it was a fair deal. Arkron was practically damning itself by giving Vasken back. But if it meant that Anrameta would live, it would be worth it. They needed a strong leader. Someone who would know how to guide Harper and Arkron through this.

"That is an intriguing offer, Highness," Archer replied, angling his head back to listen to one of the Seven—a nearly albino woman in a white dress. When she drew back, his attention returned to Pickett. "However, we have a counteroffer." He stretched a hand towards the steps. The stage let out inside of the Cleft, so Pickett couldn't see what it was until the guardsmen were already on the stage.

It was the captain that had overseen their admittance to the *Void*. And slung over his shoulder was Harper, clearly stunned as Vasken was.

"*No*." The word tore out of Pickett before he could stop it. "No, no, no." So much of this had hinged on Harper using her power to stop it . . . And if she couldn't . . . what were they going to do?

The captain dropped Harper onto the stage, where the audible thud of her body hitting the wood echoed across the square. "You surrender," Archer continued, "and we do not execute the princess or harm any of your people gathered in this square."

No . . . Pickett grasped the top of the fountain, trying to keep himself from toppling backwards. With Harper out of commission, they'd lost their one shot at ending this. Below, he could hear the people murmuring, frightened. Some were trying to press towards the exits, but the guardsmen kept them penned in the square. Moons, if they opened fire from above . . . this would be a massacre. Perhaps *that* was what they had planned for.

"Well, Highness?" Archer awaited his response, hands laced in front of him once more. "What is your response?"

"Pickett . . . " Jael's voice echoed from below. "Pickett, Vasken's waking—" Her voice was cut off by a grunt as Vasken collided with her, knocking her into Pickett. His knees crashed into the cobblestones, but he threw himself backwards, bracing himself to keep him and Jael from falling completely. Vasken rebounded, turning to attack her other Outcast guards. She was formidable even with her hands tied behind her back, hurling herself into her Outcast guards, kneeing them in the stomach, and driving her shoulder into their chests and necks.

Stumbling back to his feet, Pickett drew his sword as Archer's voice rang across the square once more. "So you have made your choice, then."

"No, I haven't . . . Oof!"

Vasken plowed into him again. Stars, he should have seen that coming! He brought his blade around towards her back but caught sight of her face. Half of it was still hidden by the muzzle, but her eyes were amused. A flush of anger coursed through him. Did she think that he was too weak to hurt her?

Was he?

A frustrated cry tore out of him, and he brought the blade down—only for her to lunge backwards towards it.

Too late, he realized her ploy: His blade sliced through her electro-bands, freeing her hands.

He backed away, clutching his sword as she pulled the muzzle off of her head. Around them, the square had erupted into chaos. Guardsmen were moving through the crowd, blasters raised. The Arkronens were trying to stampede down the streets to get away, but the guardsmen pushed them back, firing into the crowd. Pickett couldn't tell if they were only stunners or true bullets.

From the stage Anrameta was shouting, and nearby Jael was yelling at her Outcasts. People were screaming, but Pickett's attention was on Vasken. "Thank you," she said, "for making this so easy on us."

Then she lunged.

Pickett brought up his sword, prepared to parry, but he hadn't been her target. With a sweep of her arm, Vasken caught Jael around the neck, wrapping the strap of the muzzle around her throat and twisting. Jael struggled in her grasp, trying to bring her blaster around to shoot Vasken, but the woman kneed it out of her hand.

Pickett ran towards them, raising his sword, but Vasken jerked Jael around so that she was between them, on her knees. "Not another step, Pickett," she said. "Or your Outcast friend leaves you for good." She twisted the noose tighter. Jael continued to struggle, but her movements were weakening.

"Please." Pickett stopped but clutched his sword in front of him. "Don't do this. This isn't what a Neherum is supposed to be."

She tsked. "You're not a Neherum anymore."

He tightened his grip on his sword, stepping towards her. "And I never thought I would be *proud* of that."

"And yet you still refuse to lay a finger on your High General."

"You're not my High General anymore."

"Then do it." She tossed her head backwards. "Strike me down and save your Outcast. I have no sword, and I'm holding her!" She lowered her head, looking at him through narrowed eyes. "It would be easy."

This is a trick. It's a trick. Move, run, do something! His mind screamed. But his limbs were paralyzed. He didn't want to risk hurting Jael—knowing Vasken, she would try using her as a shield. Or she would have some sort of ploy up her sleeve. And . . . and . . . could he bring himself to harm her? Could he be strong enough? What was the best way to attack?

And then it was too late. The guardsmen had closed in around them, blasters raised. Now his only option was to lower his blade. Either that, or die immediately.

"Bind them," Vasken ordered.

"Even the Outcast, General?" one of the guardsmen asked as Pickett was shoved to his knees, wrists cinched behind his back.

"Yes." Vasken released Jael. She slumped forward, gasping and trying to massage her neck before the guardsmen bound her also. "She may be of use later." In two quick strides, Vasken was before Pickett. She knelt and caught his chin in her hand, forcing him to look up at her. "Well, you tried, Pickett. I'm impressed with you for that. But I thought that one of the best lessons I ever taught you was to know when it was time to stop fighting."

"No," he growled. "You taught me to *never* stop."

She cocked an eyebrow. "Well. My apologies for leaving out that crucial lesson." She rose. "Take them up."

The guardsmen hauled him towards the stage. The crowd parted before them, cowering away from the guardsmen and their guns. How many dead littered the streets leading to the square? He couldn't bring himself to look at the faces of his people. After so many years of trying, House Evensong had failed to protect them from the Consortium.

The guardsmen tossed him and Jael down beside Harper. He tried to crouch closer to her, to see if she had further injuries, but the guardsmen forced him upright. Instead, he looked back to Anrameta as Archer began speaking again.

Her weary gaze softened. "My son," she whispered. He strained to hear her over the propaganda spewing from the Consortium's speaker. "You're alive. And Jael." She smiled sadly at the Outcast. "How I wish we could have spoken more."

"I'm sorry, Mama," Pickett said. "We had plans . . . and then Harper . . . "

Anrameta dipped her head. "She will find her way."

Pickett resisted the urge to roll his eyes. "Right. Why can she never find it when we need her to?"

Anrameta laughed softly. "That is how these things tend to go, Pickett. You didn't until it really mattered."

He glanced backwards to where Vasken stood at the edge of the stage, accepting a new sword from the guardsman captain. It was because of his negligence that she was still standing there. Why couldn't he have acted? Brought his sword down on her?

Archer had finished speaking and stepped aside, letting a trio of guardsmen take his place. Their blasters admitted a high-pitched hum as they charged up.

This was happening.

They were out of time.

Suddenly there were so many things he needed to say, things that he'd kept buried for the last six years as he tried to separate himself from House Evensong. But how to condense all that into the space of a few moments?

"Mama. I'm sorry," he burst out. "I'm sorry I'm *me*."

"No." Her voice was sharp, eyes blazing. "Never . . . apologize for that." The blasters clicked as the guardsmen switched off the safety. "You," she continued, "*both* of you, are exactly who you need to be."

"Arkron needs you," he said. Though he knew it sounded childish, he added, "*We* need you."

The halo of blue from her crown shifted as she raised her chin to pin him with a fierce look. "No, Pickett. Arkron needs *you*."

The guardsmen fired. Pickett squeezed his eyes shut, snapping his head away. He could feel his own pulse raging in his veins, his stomach clenching and unclenching. He expected panic, sorrow, some other high emotion. But all he felt was cold. There was a high-pitched whine in his ears as the square erupted into shouts and wails, which were immediately silenced by a succession of gunshots.

Arkron needs you.

Yes, but would Arkron even want them now that they'd failed so badly? Hands clamped around his arms, pulling him to his feet. He sensed a dark presence looming over him, and he cracked open his eyes. Vasken. He should have guessed. "All this could have been avoided, Pickett." Her tone was almost motherly.

"No." He curled his hands into fists. "You wouldn't have helped me even if I was still your apprentice. You never loved me. I was just a tool to you."

"Ah, but at least you had a purpose with me." She brushed past, elbowing Jael in the stomach as she passed her. "Here, you are only the spare."

He shut his eyes again. "No. No, I'm not. I'm the prince. I'm House Evensong. And I'm the son of a queen I will make sure is avenged." He opened his eyes, breathing raggedly. The cold that had wrapped around him felt as though it were shattering, leaving in its place blistering, white-hot agony.

Vasken turned about, a bemused expression on her face. "Was that a challenge?"

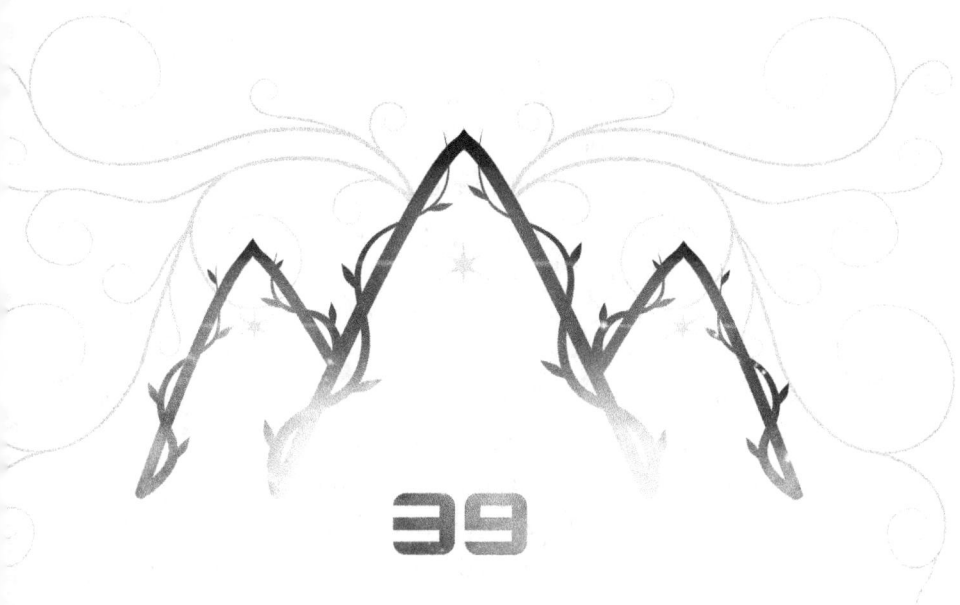

39

HARPER AWOKE TO the tolling of bells. At first her disoriented mind identified it as the breakfast bell Lady Longracer kept in the kitchen at Solstice. She would give it a sound ringing to summon the stragglers to the breakfast table in the mornings. But as the ache in her head subsided, Harper recognized the somber tone. Ten bells, in slow succession. A pause. And then ten bells again.

This would be repeated ten times for one hundred tolls, to mark the death of a royal. If it was the reigning queen, the bells would be rung one more time.

She tried to stir but found that she was chained to a wall, arms over her head. Her hands tingled from lack of blood flow. Her power surged beneath her palms, but she was too disoriented to force it out.

"Welcome back, Highness." A familiar voice made her head snap up. On the other side of a translucent barrier, Speaker Archer stood, watching her. Vasken reclined against the wall beside him, arms crossed.

Was she in a cell somewhere? But where? They must still be on Arkron; otherwise, she wouldn't be able to hear the bells.

"How long have the bells been tolling?" Harper demanded, jerking fruitlessly on her bonds again. The chimes echoed through her mind, harkening back to the overcast day when her father had died. She had been barely old enough to understand what was happening then. But the bells still sang their dirge in her mind.

"Only a few moments." Archer cocked his head, listening to them along with her.

Good. So she would be able to count, to see how many dead there were. *Please no more than one,* she begged. *Please . . .*

The bells continued to ring. Holding her breath, Harper counted each one. The seconds dragged between each *gong,* and with each interlude Harper's stomach clenched in dread. She imagined that this was what a condemned prisoner must feel as they were led to the gallows, each footfall on the scaffold an echo of the despair to come.

The hundredth peal came, and the bells fell silent. Heart thudding in her chest, Harper listened to the quiet. Who was it? Lady Kova? Pickett? Her mother? No, there hadn't been a final ring, not yet . . . The world was growing fuzzy. She had to take a breath or her lungs were going to explode. But she couldn't, not until she knew, not until she could at least narrow it down—

A final peal shattered the silence.

Harper's breath escaped her in a sob. Her throat, so constricted with cries, nearly suffocated her.

Anrameta was dead. Her mother was dead. She hadn't been able to save her.

Vasken straightened, deactivating the cell door. She invited Archer in with a sweep of her arm. "All hail the new Queen Evensong, Speaker."

Harper turned her face away from them, squeezing her eyes shut. Her face was sopping wet from her eyes and her nose. A good queen would save her tears for private and raise her chin to demand to be released. But she was not that kind of queen. She was a shattered storyweaver, trying to keep the fraying strands of her world together under her own feeble strength.

Archer stopped in front of her. "For what it's worth, Your Majesty, I am sorry."

A hysterical laugh tore out of her. "Sorry? You're *sorry*? You caused this!"

"Some might argue that you only fanned the flame."

She slumped against the wall, letting the chains take some of her weight. "I was just trying to protect my world... What do you want?"

"The High General and I are here to fetch you for another audience with the Seven," he replied. "Hopefully a more *civil* audience than our last one."

"Was it very civil when you tortured my friend?" Harper retorted, squeezing her hands into fists. She could feel her power thrumming there, slowly pulsing its way up from her heart. Surely now was the time to expend it! "Was it civil when you invaded my home and started *literally* stealing our land? And . . . " Her voice broke. "Was it civil to murder my mother, the best queen we've had since the Library Age?" She could feel a rush of threads shooting up her arms, towards her palms—

—And then an electric charge shot through her arms and into her core. It felt like her power was going *backwards*. She shrieked, trying to summon more threads, but was met with another shock. Was her power used up? Was this what happened when it was gone?

Vasken leaned forward and tapped the thick cuffs around her wrist. "You won't be spawning any portals this time, Highness. See, we figured that your power makes your hands warm up when it comes—and these cuffs will electrocute you if they sense too much heat. You'll be in a world of pain if you try to use your powers."

What? But there was no way out of this without her powers!

Vasken smiled, a wicked, delighted smile. "You're powerless. And now I would like some recompense for the way you humiliated me at

Solstice." Grabbing Harper by the shoulder, she threw her around to face the wall.

"Vasken, what is this?" Archer demanded, stepping closer. "The Seven are waiting; we must be on our way."

"Not just yet."

Something cold slipped down the back of Harper's shirt. The blade of a knife. With a savage jerk, Vasken tore the fabric away, baring her skin. With growing dread, Harper tried to twist back around, but Vasken snarled and shoved her back against the wall, where the rough stone scraped Harper's cheek.

Something crackled to life behind her. Archer protested, but there was a snap, and white fire exploded across Harper's back.

She screamed, collapsing against the wall.

"One for the princess," Vasken cried, "and one for the storyweaver." The electro whip cracked again, and another searing wound opened on her back, curling around her side this time. "And, perhaps, one for the new queen—"

"*Enough!*" Archer thundered. There was a scuffle, the sound of bodies bumping into the wall and the scrape of fingers against leather. Vasken cursed, and something clattered to the ground.

Painfully, through streaming eyes, Harper looked over her shoulder to see Archer stooping to pick up the now-deactivated whip and pass it to a guardsman. "I am sorry this child has so bruised your ego, but we must have her alive and well enough to stand before us! Leave us, now. Don't you have another plaything waiting for you?"

Vasken scowled, clearly angered at being ordered away—but her lips turned upward in a grim smile. "Indeed. A duel with the prince will be invigorating."

A duel? With Pickett? At least he was alive. For now.

Harper squeezed her eyes shut and pressed her face against the stone wall. Her back throbbed, a hot, pulsing ache that she felt in every part of her body.

When she opened her eyes again, Vasken was gone.

"Fetch a medic," Archer ordered the guardsmen, "and a new garment for her. And one of you, let her down."

They scurried to obey. A guardsman left the cell while another came forward and loosened the chains holding her up. Harper slumped to the floor, aching arms cradled in her lap.

Archer stooped over her, holding a flask. "A drink, Highness?"

She glared at it, remembering what had happened to Fayen during his time with the Consortium. "Is it poisoned?"

A humorless smile flickered across his face. "Of course not." Uncapping it, he took a small drink himself before proffering it again.

Harper wanted to refuse, but she was thirsty. The last time she'd had anything was with Lune and Nina. What had become of them? Had any Arkronens tried to help? Were they dead now? With her bound, shaking hands, she accepted the flask and brought it to her lips. The water was stale and tasted metallic. It dribbled over her chin, but she didn't care. "Why are you doing this?" she asked, lowering the now-empty cup.

Archer straightened, pushing his glasses up his nose. "To achieve peace and progress, all planets must be under the Consortium—"

"I meant this." She lifted the cup. "Helping me."

"Well. You are about to stand before us once more. You must look like a queen, no?"

She arched her back, feeling rivers of blood trickle down it. "So it's all about appearances again. Making it look like this is a nice takeover, that no one got hurt . . . "

A medic stepped into the room. He wore the same armor as the guardsmen, though there was a crimson circle on his shoulder plate, and he carried a heavy satchel of supplies over one shoulder. Archer held up a hand to make him pause. "You don't wish to look like the queen that you are?"

She refused to look at him, fresh tears slipping down her cheeks. "What's the point? I'm going to be about as good a queen as I was a princess."

Archer was silent for a moment, and then to the medic said, "See to her. We are overdue for our audience."

The medic obeyed, crossing to Harper and dropping his satchel down beside her. She bit her lip as he began cleaning the lashes and applying an antiseptic solution. Archer turned away, offering some semblance of modesty. As the medic wound a bandage around her torso to cover the wounds, he called, "Do you want me to administer an antibiotic, sir?"

In other words, should I avoid wasting the resource on her if you're going to have her killed anyway? Harper mused.

"Yes," Archer replied, back still to them.

Yes? Why was he allowing her care? Did the Consortium truly care that much about appearances for this meeting? She bit her lip as the medic injected a canister of the medication into her arm. Afterward, he and another guardsman finagled her in a new shirt. "She's ready, sir," the medic announced, rising.

"Good." Archer turned to them—in his hands was Harper's crown. He handed it to her.

She stared at it, dangling in her bound hands. The plates seemed dull in the cell's weak light. Then, awkwardly, she lifted it onto her head.

The guardsmen closed in around her once again, gripping her arms. They steered her out of the cell and into a courtyard, where fresh morning light cast their shadows on the cobblestones. So they *were* still at the Cleft; Harper had known that the palace contained holding rooms, but had never had cause to be in one of them.

Overhead, the *Void's* hull shimmered like some sort of glittering eyeball scanning the city. A transport shuttle waited for them in the center of the courtyard. The guardsmen hustled her into it, with Archer following. It figured that the Seven wouldn't want to dirty themselves by staying on Arkron.

As the shuttle lifted off, Archer spoke, "I am aware that you do not believe me when I say it, but I am sorry that you are in such a position. I . . . " He trailed off, resettling his glasses on his nose once again. "I have a son, about your age . . . the thought of him . . . fighting, and ruling . . . I can't imagine it."

A son? He was a father? Something beyond the Speaker of the Consortium and invader of her world? She tried to cling to that definition of him. He had executed her mother, he was stealing her world . . . and he was a father. To a son her age, whom he loved. His story didn't only involve these vile politics.

Just like hers didn't only involve being the princess or the storyweaver or the queen. Her story was a mix of those things, tied together by Jael's words that night on the *Ransom*: *The only label we really need for ourselves is "Beloved by the Maker."*

Oh, moons, she thought as the shuttle carried them higher and higher toward the *Void*. *This confrontation with the Seven is going to have to look so much different than the last.* She was Queen Harper Evensong now. This was a new chapter in her story—and it was going to have to involve listening to their stories as well, rather than forcing her own upon them.

40

THE MORNING AIR was hot and heavy. Even before the sun rose, Pickett felt suffocated. He would have given anything to be able to tear off his armor; its weight was almost unbearable. Beneath it, his clothes stuck to him.

But Vasken wanted to torment him as much as possible. And so he was garbed in a full Neherum uniform, complete with leather shoulder armor, thick gauntlets, and calf-length boots. Inside it, he felt hollow.

The sun peered over the lip of the Arena, illuminating its sandy floor. In ages past, the octagonal pit had been used for gladiator fights and other gory spectacles. In recent years, it had become merely a landmark that people occasionally tossed their trash into.

Now Vasken and the Seven were reviving its bloody history. People clustered at its lip far overhead, leaning against the chains that made up its ceiling. Across the Arena, Vasken stood with her few Accipiter attendants, whom she'd reclaimed sometime during the long night. They were buckling her into her armor while she tested the weight of a new sword in her hand. Pickett was only attended by Jael, who stood silently beside him, and several guardsmen. He had struggled into his outfit, his limbs weighing like lead. He had wept more tears last night than he had known he was capable of producing. Who would have thought that crying took more energy than a duel?

He glanced at Jael. Her face was haggard, her hair limply hanging around her face. She worried over her crew, wondering who had been lost in the skirmish. Last night, their tears had mingled as they'd sat close in their cell.

She noticed him looking and tried to muster a smile. "You're going to kick her rump. Like you did at Solstice."

"I didn't win that fight. Harper did." He tightened his gauntlets. "Besides, the field's level this time, and she's mad. She'll win."

"Don't sell yourself short," she said. "You're a great swordsman."

He poked a finger towards Vasken. "And *she's* the one who taught me."

Jael sighed, reaching up with her bound hands to push her hair out of her face before the guardsmen grasped her arms and secured her to a post. "But you're not *hers* anymore."

She was right. He'd made his choice. When the guardsmen brought his sword to him, he accepted it with all the confidence he could muster. He turned to face Vasken, who approached, holding hers. She wouldn't be used to it yet, which gave him a slight advantage.

"I propose a game, Pickett," she began. "Instead of a duel, you keep me from killing your Outcast. It will be like Capture the Castle. I'm told it's a popular children's game on Arkron."

It was. Although the castle was usually a rock, and the only weapons were your fists. Or sticks, if you could get away with hitting each other before the adults noticed.

"Her name," he said, "is Jael. And she's Arkronen now."

Vasken comically rolled her eyes. "Of course. You keep me from killing *Jael*."

A long, lonely note sounded from somewhere overhead. Vasken sprang before it had finished.

With no time to dodge—and really, dodging would only deflect her to Jael—Pickett lowered himself into a defensive *kata*. Vasken slammed into him, the force of her blow driving him backwards. "I thought you wanted to avenge your mother," she hissed into his face, "and protect your Outcast. You promised me a fight, boy."

He grunted, throwing his shoulder into her chest plate, trapping her blade flat between them. They tussled back and forth, Vasken trying to twist her blade so that the edge would cut into him, Pickett trying to do likewise.

Finally she hooked her foot around his ankle and jerked him off balance. He landed with a grunt in the sand but rolled out of the way before her blade could slice his head off.

She was leering, her teeth bared in a manic grin. To her, this was entertainment. An invigorating morning warm-up. She strode towards Jael, tossing her sword from hand to hand in anticipation.

Pickett scrambled to his feet, throwing himself into her path. Their blades met with a resounding crash that echoed through his skull. They were pressed close together once again, wrestling for dominance.

"I gave you three chances to come back to me. And three times, you turned your back," she snarled. "This is discipline. This is *justice*."

He tightened his stance, pushing her back. "I chose to be where I was needed. I did not break the codes. I am still the Neherum I swore to be. Can you say the same, High General? Or have you let your thirst for power lead you astray?"

Her eyes flashed, and she drove into him, shifting into a furious *kata*.

He shifted his to match, blocking each of her strikes in quick succession. She had trained him, after all. He was familiar with her favored techniques and guessed which ones she would replace them with to throw him off.

She didn't gain an inch of ground towards Jael.

Overhead, the crowd was silent as they watched the duel. The crashes of steel on steel echoed like thunderclaps. Pickett and Vasken were both panting; this was more a contest of strength than agility. She spun away from him and planted her feet. Her hair was falling out of its braid in bunches, clinging to her sweaty face.

Pickett allowed himself a small smile. He was making her look bad in front of the crowd, which would irk her. She was supposed to be the unstoppable head of the Neherum. And to reach a stalemate with her own ex-apprentice . . . well, it didn't exactly inspire confidence.

"Yield," Vasken finally snapped, spinning away from him. "And I will permit both you and the Outcast to live."

"No," Pickett said, raising his sword again. His muscles screamed in protest, but this was more important than how he felt right now. This had to end. Today.

Vasken huffed. And then charged at him.

He raised his sword, expecting an onslaught, but she wasn't fighting with her sword. She bowled into him, knocking him backwards. They grappled with each other, fists flying.

"This," he grunted as she socked him across the jaw, "is not proper form."

She paused to grin down into his face. "It is a lesson I took from you, my boy."

Then she drove her knife into his shoulder. He hadn't even seen her palm it, but now it was stuck fast in him. And in his dominant arm, no less. He roared and kicked her off and struggled to his feet, the blade still embedded in his flesh.

They were dangerously close to Jael now; she was straining against her chains, trying to scoot around the post so that it offered her a weak form of protection.

Gritting his teeth against the pain, Pickett passed his sword to his other hand and swung at Vasken.

She batted it away and landed a strike in his side. His armor mostly protected him, but he still felt the bite of her blade. Not to mention the impact. He staggered to the side, gasping.

Vasken kicked his leg out from beneath him. He fell to one knee, practically against Jael's post. He raised his sword to block her overhead strikes. But she didn't rain them down, as he expected. Instead, she poked her sword near the hilt of his and flipped it from his grasp.

It landed in the sand with a dull *thunk*.

Beaming, Vasken stepped back and raised her weapon towards Jael. "You have fought, Pickett, and you have lost."

"Not just yet," he growled, lurching to his feet once more. He gripped the knife and yanked it out of his shoulder, raising it before him. Immediately blood welled from the wound, soaking his shirt. He gritted his teeth against the burn that danced down his arm, but continued to advance.

Vasken laughed. "Not quite finished, are we? If you insist—*argh!*" Her voice cut to a cry of surprise, and then curses as she dug at her ear, pulling out a small device. It was her in-ear comm; even from a short distance away, Pickett could hear the shrill stream of feedback. Around the edges of the Arena, the guardsmen were likewise yanking off their helmets or banging on the sides of them as their comms shrieked.

Pickett allowed himself to slowly lower the knife, exchanging a look with Jael. Was Harper doing this, wherever she was? Trying to distract Vasken and the guardsmen by hijacking their comms? Or . . . could it be . . .

A dark silhouette covered the Arena, blotting out the sunlight. Explosions rocked the air. Pickett threw his hands over his ears and staggered towards Jael. He could hear dull thuds as the ceiling chains hit the sand around them. The rush of engines stirred the sand on the floor into clouds; it stung his eyes and caught in his throat as he found the Outcast, gripping her with his good arm.

"Behind you!" Jael shouted, jerking him to the side. He collided with the post as Vasken sprang past, sword poised for his heart. Her momentum carried her past them, but she pivoted, streaking back towards them.

Pickett raised the knife, pushing himself into a defensive posture and trying to blink the sand from his eyes. The silhouette overhead was lifting once more as the ship took off, letting blinding light cascade into the Arena. He cursed, squinting. This wasn't good. He didn't have a clear visual—

There was the sound of a collision, the thud of flesh meeting flesh. But Pickett found himself still standing. Prying his eyes open, he found Vasken on the ground, pinned by an enormous paw on her chest. The lightfoot-sized cat leaned down and snarled directly into her face.

Perched atop her back was Fayen, dressed in a full Neherum uniform. His sword was strapped to his back, and from the expression on his face, it was clear that he was prepared to fight. For now, though, he let the Hybri lead.

"Evaly!" Jael's voice was exuberant. "You're *marvelous!*"

One of Evaly's ears flicked towards her, but her gaze remained on Vasken. Fayen slid off her back and limped up to them, fishing a lockpick from his belt to free Jael.

"The Neherum—" Pickett began, but Fayen silenced him with a smile.

He gestured around the Arena. "See for yourself."

Scrubbing the sand out of his eyes with his good hand, he scanned the Arena. Everywhere he saw the familiar, dark blue uniforms subduing the guardsmen. Helping to conserve Arkron. Upholding the codes.

His throat grew tight as he pressed a hand against his shoulder, trying to stop the blood there. "You did it."

Fayen finished unlocking Jael's chains and gestured to Evaly. "*We* did it." He straightened, tucking the lockpick away, and produced a roll of emergency gauze from his pocket, which he offered for Pickett's shoulder. "Some Passers came with us. They can see to your wound." He frowned, leaning to the side to see the rest of Pickett. "And your side. Moons, she tried to tear you to pieces, didn't she? C'mon, let's go find them before you pass out or something."

"But she didn't tear me apart," Pickett replied. "She *didn't*." He limped over to Vasken, who was still prone beneath Evaly. Her hands were wrapped around the cat's paw, but Pickett saw why she hadn't tried to throw Evaly off. Evaly's claws were out, dug slightly into Vasken's armor. If she tried to struggle, they would sink deeper.

"It's over, Vasken," he said, at last tasting the bittersweet finality of the words. A squad of Accipiters was jogging up to them, prepared to take her. Pickett let them, returning to Fayen and Jael. After a moment, Evaly joined the trio, shaking off her Hybri form to embrace Jael tightly.

As they made their way streetside, to the Passers who would tend Pickett's shoulder, Fayen produced a holo-projector and switched it on, displaying an image of the city. He poked a finger at the south-central side where the Arena was located. "Between the Neherum and Jael's Outcasts, we have a perimeter established. The Ibis were also able to scramble the Consortium's comms for now, so the guardsmen are somewhat blinded. But we haven't been able to do anything about this—" He widened the scope of the hologram, revealing the areas where the Consortium was tearing up the ground. "The Ibis are trying to find a way to hack those ships, but they're afraid if they just have the ships drop it, it'll be more catastrophic."

Pickett winced, pressing the wad of gauze harder against his shoulder. "They're not wrong. Maybe we should just focus on taking the city back. How are our numbers?"

Fayen and Evaly exchanged a grim look. "Enough to control this," Fayen replied, gesturing to the Arena walls around them. "And some of the surrounding blocks. But not enough to launch an assault." He powered off the projector, leaving the stairwell in darkness. "Where is Harper?"

"We don't know," Pickett confessed, his stomach tightening. The thrill of their victory was giving way to the realization that they weren't finished yet. "She was captured at the same time as us but placed elsewhere. My best guess is that they still have her at the palace or they've taken her to the *Void*."

"Then getting her back will be our next priority," Fayen said. He shoved open a door that admitted them into the street.

There was an assemblage of shuttles from the *Ransom* waiting there. Jael hurried off to reunite with Ziah, Evaly on her heels. Fayen went to confer with several Neherum. Pickett let him, feeling no desire to intervene. Fayen clearly had things in hand, and frankly, if he had listened to him before, they might have been spared much trouble.

A Passer beckoned him over to the ramp of one of the ships and helped him strip off his armor. She began tending his wounds, *tsking* along with him when he hissed at the burn of the antiseptic. He looked away as she began to clean his shoulder.

The motion caused his eyes to land on the face of a child, who was peeking out from around the ship. When she realized she'd seen him, she stepped fully out and pointed to his crown. "You're the prince," she said.

"Yes, I am," he replied, reaching up to touch the emerald plates. He was glad for the distraction from the pain in his shoulder and side.

The girl crept closer. "I met the princess yesterday. She told us her story."

"Did she?" he asked. Was that where Harper had disappeared to when Jael couldn't find her? "What's your name?"

"Lune," she replied, clambering onto the ramp. "My sister and I, we told her story to other people, and then they told more people."

Leave it to Harper to spark something like that. "What's the story about?" he asked, grimacing as the Passer began stitching his shoulder.

"A princess who wants to save her world," Lune said. "But she needs help. So we got help to finish the story."

"You got help?" he repeated.

Lune bobbed her head, pointing down the street. "We got help."

Pickett rose and stepped down the ramp, ignoring the Passer's protests. There was something coming. A mass of people bearing blasters, swords, staffs—even pots and pans. They wore no uniforms, but somehow the sight of them was more beautiful than a battalion of organized troops.

The Arkronens had risen to defend their world because of the story of their princess.

41

The *Void's* stateroom bore no traces of Harper's previous assault. The doors had been rehung, and the walls and floor were smooth once again, clear of any evidence of her verdant attack on the Seven. The room felt eerily bright as the ship hovered in the upper atmosphere; clouds drifted past the tall windows, and sunlight danced off the glass chandelier. If it weren't for the rumble of the engines beneath her, Harper would have thought that they were simply high in a skyscraper.

The room had been rearranged to fit a large holographic node in the center of the floor, which projected an enormous image of Arkron. Blinking around it were triangular red markers: the places where they were tearing up the land. There were so many of them, clinging to the face of the world like spots on a diseased person. The rest of the Seven milled around it, discussing their progress. Some of them clutched teacups or glasses of brandy as if it were nothing more than a gathering at their private club. Rage licked at Harper's insides, and her powers surged like rising flames. The cuffs around her wrists hummed in warning, and she forced the power back down. *Not yet. Maybe not this time.*

"Fellow leaders," Archer proclaimed, directing the guardsmen to lead her towards them, "Queen Evensong."

Queen Evensong. Not Princess Evensong or storyweaver. *Queen.*

And over all of that, *beloved by the Maker.*

She forced her hands to relax from their fists. "Highnesses," she said, lowering her head. "Thank you for a second chance at an audience."

From around the hologram, someone snorted. Harper bristled but kept her expression schooled. Empress Lara—dressed in her typical white—set her drink on a floating service tray. "An audience? We have summoned you here to offer you the same choice we offered your mother." She lifted a tablet from the floating tray and carried it over to Harper, turning it towards her. She refused to come within arm's reach, so Harper had to squint towards the tablet's screen. It appeared to be a treaty.

"Simply agree to a partnership with the Consortium, and all this can be over." Her voice was almost singsong, as if she were trying to explain the situation to a small child. "Your mother didn't need to die, and you don't either." She waggled the tablet towards Harper. "No more of your people will be harmed. We may even let you hold your throne—under us, of course."

"In exchange for the world we were entrusted with," Harper replied. The knot of heat rose in her chest, threatening to pulse down her arms to her hands. "In exchange for who we are." The bands around her wrists began to hum in warning again. They were all in the room with her. It would be so easy to end this, once and for all with her last bit of power . . .

Enough. She cut off the line of thinking as Anrameta's words rang through her head. *You will have to choose what kind of queen you will be.* She wouldn't be a queen of bloodshed, using her stories to harm. Storyweavers were meant to create, not destroy.

She forced herself to look at each member of the Seven, seeing them as more than the cause of all this sorrow. On Mantalor, Lady Kova had forced her to memorize each of their names and faces: Empress Lara of Catena, who held the tablet towards her. Prime Minister Teaka of Hylon and Queen Petina of Evony stood close together, as if they were prepared to shield each other should Harper erupt with power once more. President Watt of Zeanna scowled at the hologram while King Beta of Weylan and Chairman Killian of Mantalor stood with hands resting on the blasters tucked into their belts. And Archer, standing near her, fiddling with his glasses again.

They had names. They had stories that she didn't know. Did they have children, like Archer? Families waiting for them at home? Motivations for being a part of the Consortium, engaging in the takeover of her world? The weight of their stories pressed down upon her.

"I offer a counter deal," she said. "I'll consider your treaty. If you listen to a story."

Empress Lara lowered the tablet, bemused. "A story?" She fluttered a hand towards Harper's bound hands. "But you cannot."

"Not that kind of story. It wouldn't really change you, not if I tried to force it upon you. I could bewitch you, of course, but then it wouldn't touch your heart." She dipped her head, her crown slipping more securely behind her ears. "Besides. That's not the kind of queen I will be."

"We should let her speak." Queen Petina stepped forward. Her voice was heavily accented; it was clear that Common Tone was not her primary language, and yet she pushed on. "If she is truly willing to consider signing, let her tell this tale."

"What story do you so desperately want to convey?" Chairman Killian's hand continued to rest on his blaster.

"A story from my childhood," Harper replied. She had planned to use the one she had told Arkron's Council, but she wasn't certain that she had the strength to orate it with as much fervor as she had only days ago. Moons, it seemed like a lifetime had passed since then.

"It was the last one my father ever told me." The memory of the moment was bathed in golden lamplight; she could recall the delicate floral pattern on the wallpaper but not her father's face. "It's an old Arkronen story: *The Girl Who Tried to Catch the Sun*."

Empress Lara's lips curled, mocking. "Charming."

"It is." Harper ignored the barb and shut her eyes, imagining the story as best she could. Barred from weaving, her words alone would have to suffice. "It takes place soon after the Creator wove the worlds and set them dancing. But it was also right after the Shattering." She imagined the silhouette of a girl running down a grassy slope.

"For the first time, Arkron knew fear. The people had risen against each other, and there was a great darkness over the land. There was a girl who despised the dark, and so she wanted to catch the sun so that it would always be light. She would wait for it to come up in the morning, and when it peeked over the mountains, she would climb onto the roof of her house and try to scoop it into a jar. It never worked, of course.

"Finally she decided that if she was going to catch it, she would have to chase it across the world and snatch it while it was at rest, wherever it sank to. She packed her things and set off across the world. Neither ocean nor forest nor mountain could stop her—but the darkness did. It wasn't an ordinary nighttime darkness, mind you—it was a living darkness, a monster that swept up from the Deeps and prowled the land, searching for souls to fuel it.

"After another day of failing to catch up with the sun, she took shelter at an inn and asked for a cup of chai. The innkeeper asked her, 'Where are you going, child?'

"To which she replied, 'To capture the sun.'

"'For what purpose?'

"She hunched over her drink, for she was tired. 'So that there will be no more darkness, because the light will always be here.'

"The innkeeper laughed. 'Look around you, child. The darkness is not here.'

"She looked around the inn and saw that it was full of firelight and candles, and people talking and laughing and singing. 'Where there are people gathered together for a common purpose, there will always be light,' the innkeep promised.

"'Perhaps,' the girl agreed reluctantly. 'But what about when there aren't any people around?'

"'Even then there will still be light. Every heart is a burning flame. Even when we are apart, we glow like stars in the Star Sea. It is impossible for the darkness to squelch us entirely. It can lie to us and fan our flame to make it burn us from the inside out. In the end, though, that flame is kept alive only by the Maker's good pleasure.'

"The girl nodded her thanks for his wisdom and went back to her drink. The next morning, she was up and off chasing the sun again. She walked farther than she had ever walked before and crested a giant mountain as the sun began to set. She stretched her jar out, trying to catch the sun's dying light, but as it always did, it shone in the glass for a moment and then vanished.

"She stood alone on the mountaintop, without any light. It didn't take long for the darkness to find her. It rose up in a swirling cloud and plunged through her like a sword. It was harsh and cold, and the girl was certain that she was going to die. But she remembered the innkeeper's words. She didn't need the sunlight to drive away the darkness. The Creator had given her a flame. He had given all of them a flame to drive back the darkness. As the darkness plunged deeper and deeper into her, she sought the flame that her Maker had given her. She was his creation, and that was all she needed.

"The girl erupted with light, and the darkness was driven away. Those who saw her also yielded to the light, and Arkron became a constellation of little fires until the darkness fled back to the Deeps.

"And so the people learned that if they remembered who they were, remembered who had imprinted his very self on their souls, they could drive away the darkness. And so the world was free for a time. The darkness would return—because of the Shattering, its reach was great. But in times of great need, one would only need to remember whose they were, and it would be beaten back."

Harper opened her eyes, finding the Seven still watching her. Someone had powered down the hologram to allow all of them to see her clearly. Moons, this was even better attention than what she had gotten before the Chamber.

Archer adjusted his glasses, breaking the spell of stillness. "Well, Highness, what is the moral?"

"Indeed," President Watt rumbled. "What maxim were you hoping to impress upon us, Queen Harper?"

Harper licked her dry lips, trying to soften them. "A reminder to remember who you are. To remember that this galaxy belongs to the Creator. And also a warning: If you keep disrupting his story for it, he will cause others to flare in remembrance and others will flare with them. And you will not be able to keep your grip on the Exlenna."

Empress Lara dropped the tablet back onto the tray, making a disgusted noise in her throat. "I presume this means that you will not be signing our treaty?"

"I . . . " Moons, the crown was so heavy on her head. The treaty would stop the impending bloodshed for the moment. But it would come at the cost of ruining the world they had worked so hard to heal. Harper arched her neck, forcing her head back. "I cannot."

A chime echoed through the room. Empress Lara's displeased expression shifted into one of victory as she exchanged looks with the rest of the Seven. Prime Minister Teaka tapped a foot on the floor, summoning the hologram once more. The red markers surrounding Arkron were turning green. "First excavation complete," Archer intoned. "Prepare to initiate a second."

Harper's hands balled into fists once more. Treaty or no treaty, story or no story, they weren't going to stop. Not now, not ever. She had tried to resolve this gently—she didn't want to hurt the Seven. She couldn't, not now. But she couldn't let them continue to ravage Arkron.

Her heart raged in her chest, mingling with the pulsing of her story threads. It was time. She knew it, with painful, burning certainty.

Turning from the hologram, Archer caught her eye and saw the flare within it. "Remember, Highness, your stories will electrify you."

"Arkron is worth it," Harper replied, and raised her bound hands.

The pain was instantaneous and blinding. Her flesh screamed as shocks danced up it from the bracelets, and heat ran down it from the story threads pulsing from her core. Light exploded from her hands, threads weaving themselves upward, crashing through the glass dome of the ship.

Vaguely, she heard the Seven's cries of alarm and the sound of the guardsmen's blasters going off as they tried to stun her. She was so ensnared in story threads that they simply rebounded from her. She was aware that her whole being was aglow, every vein alight with gold. Her chest was pulsing with pain, blood seeping into the fabric of her new shirt. And still she pressed onward, stretching her story to the bits of Arkron the Consortium was trying to steal.

"The enemy would not have them," she whispered, *"for the queen had claimed them as hers to tend."*

On the hologram, the green markers turned red once more and then, one by one, winked out of existence as Harper brought the land back to where it belonged. It grew harder with each one; the threads were thinning, splitting, and dissolving.

But she made it, bringing the last piece of Arkron back to its proper place as the molten threads spreading out from her heart began to dim. Gasping, Harper choked out, *"And the enemy would not be able to steal more, for she broke their instruments of thievery."* The drones used to gather the land erupted; the nearest echoed throughout the room, cracking the tall windows that lined the walls.

There.

Panting, Harper raised her eyes to look at the Seven. They had gathered together on the other side of the hologram, which flickered lazily. The floor was littered with debris from the ceiling and the windows, but they appeared unscathed.

"Arkron belongs to the Maker," she rasped, "and House Evensong is its caretakers. You will not have a further chapter in its story, not now, not ever." Blackness crept across her vision, but she ground her teeth and held on to the weaving, wrapping the weakening threads around herself until the *Void*'s stateroom disappeared from view and she disappeared into her own weaving as the very last story embers drained from her fingertips.

Her last sensation was blood dripping from the neck of her shirt, the ink with which this new chapter in Arkron's story would be written.

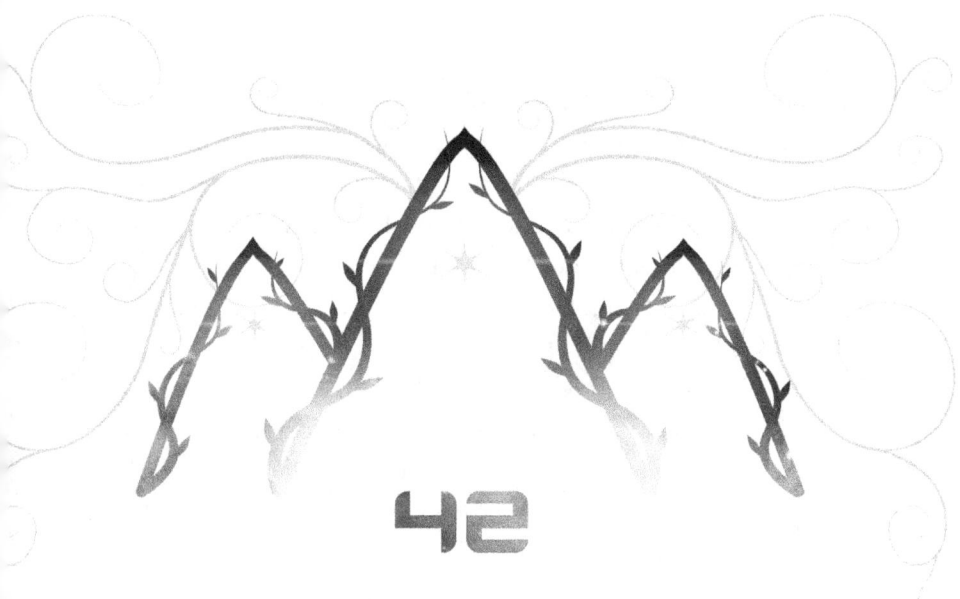

42

Even though it was late morning, the sky felt eerily dark after the threads of golden power vanished. Standing on the Cleft's front steps, Pickett stared at the hologram in Fayen's hand, swiping sweat from his brow. It showed a clear image of Arkron rotating slowly in its orbit. "The excavation ships. They're really gone."

"She did it," Fayen rasped.

"But where is she?" Fear gnawed at Pickett's stomach; stepping back, he looked up at the *Void*'s shimmering underside far overhead. With the people's help, they'd quickly retaken the palace, cornering the guardsmen garrisoned there. But neither the Seven nor Harper were there, which meant that they were in the looming ship overhead. "We need to find a shuttle," Pickett urged, starting down the steps. "We can't leave her up there with them."

He stopped when he realized Fayen wasn't following. "Come on!" he implored irritably, turning back to him.

Fayen was slipping the holoprojector back into his belt, unable to meet Pickett's eye. "Pickett," he began, voice broken, "do you really think . . . after that . . . that she's still . . . " He slowly lowered himself onto the step, resting his arms atop his knees.

"Yes," Pickett snapped, stalking the rest of the way down the steps, casting about for an Outcast he could ask to bring them a shuttle. "Yes, she's still up there. We have to rescue her—"

"It might be a recovery, not a rescue." Tears glimmered in Fayen's eyes.

"*No.*" Harper was too blasted stubborn to die. If they could just get up to the ship, he knew that she'd meet them in one of the hangars, probably bloodied and exhausted but still alive.

And yet when he closed his eyes, he could see the bloody brand carved into her chest, the scars almost conjoined. All of his research suggested that a storyweaver died when their power was expended. But they couldn't lose Harper now, not after Anrameta—

"Someone find me a ship!" he bellowed in frustration.

The Outcasts, Neherum, and Arkronens gathered in the courtyard glanced at him, though none of them left their posts. They were assembling the guardsmen there in rows on their knees. Several Arkronens sorted through a growing pile of discarded armor and weapons.

"Pickett?"

Jael's voice made him turn back around. She and Evaly had exited the palace—with them were Lady Kova and Lady Longracer. Their clothing was rumpled and their faces haggard, but otherwise they appeared unharmed from their imprisonment in the palace.

Lady Longracer knelt beside Fayen at once, enfolding him in a tight embrace.

"Is it true about Anrameta?" Lady Kova demanded, stepping towards him.

The sound of blasterfire echoed through Pickett's head again. He sucked in a ragged breath, avoiding her gaze. He had to stay composed. If he and Lady Kova were the last members of House Evensong, he couldn't afford to lose his head. "Yes."

"I see." Lady Kova's piercing gaze dropped. "And where is Harper?"

"On the *Void*. We think," Pickett added.

"She's used up the rest of her powers," Fayen interjected.

"We don't *know* that," Pickett retorted. Too late, he realized how desperate he sounded.

Lady Longracer rose and put her arms around him instead, cradling his head to her shoulder. The embrace made him want to crawl out of his skin. While comforting, it reminded him too much of Anrameta and the embraces he would never have again. Besides, he didn't need comfort. He needed action.

"We need to get up to the *Void* and find her." He looked at Jael. "Can you get us a ship?"

"I can try . . . but most of the shuttles are occupied taking the wounded to the *Ransom*," she replied, pulling out her wrist-comm.

Lady Kova held up a hand to stop her. "You do not seem confident that Harper is alive," she said somberly. "Thus, I think it in our best interests to start making plans for succession. According to the *Accords of Arkron*, a regent must be named until a suitable . . . "

Pickett felt as though he was listening to her speak underwater. How could Lady Kova be thinking like this *now*? When there was the slimmest chance that Harper might still be alive?

But still, he understood. They had to make plans. Arkron would need to be guided through the cleanup. Why couldn't he think about this clearly?

A collective chime rang from all of the nearby devices. An Ibis approached them, clutching a tablet. "It appears to be a message from the Consortium, Highness. Shall I let it through?"

"Yes," Pickett said, stepping closer to the device. A hologram blossomed over its screen—the bust of Speaker Archer. "Due to internal discussions about our actions on Arkron and the destruction of our equipment, the Consortium has decided to momentarily withdraw from this world amid ongoing talks about how to best handle the situation," he said. "Guardsmen will be recalled, and we ask that any held captive by Arkronen forces be released.

"In the future, we hope that Arkron reconsiders the partnership opportunity they have with the Consortium."

With that, his image faded. A moment later, the *Void*'s silvery shape disappeared from overhead, zipping away beyond the blue. Pickett found himself reaching after it, as if he could, by some force of will, pull it back long enough for him to find Harper.

"She did it," Jael exclaimed, tipping her head back to look at the clear sky. "She got them to go. Arkron is free again!"

Cheers erupted in the courtyard. Pickett could hear them ringing from the palace and the streets beyond. *She should be here to hear this. The Creator gave her storyweaving for a reason. But why couldn't he have spared her too?*

He brushed past Lady Kova and the others, ignoring their hands as they reached for him. He needed to be alone. To hide from the fact that once again, he was the spare. The leftover. He ducked into the palace, wondering if his bedchambers were untouched.

"Prince Pickett?"

The urgent hail made him stop partway up the staircase. He turned back around to see a young woman leaning out of one of the throne room doors. He knew her, didn't he? Wasn't she related to Captain Yarrowriver? "You'd better see this," she said, thrusting the door open wider.

He hurried back down to her and stepped into the room, only to stop short.

Lying sprawled on the throne was Harper, her head propped on one arm of the seat, feet on the other. Her crown was askew over her brow, and her shirt was drenched in blood. Her arms draped over her stomach; it looked as though someone had planted seeds in her fingertips and now russet-colored vines twisted up her elbows.

He approached her slowly, afraid of knowing the verdict. She was so still, the light from the stained-glass windows behind the throne bathing her face in a rainbow of colors. Had her final weaving deposited her here as it fled? Or at the Creator's own story carried her here as a kindness, letting her rest on the planet she had given herself to save?

Then she sighed, head tipping further to the side. Her crown fell down atop her eyes, as if she were still a small child and it didn't fit quite right just yet. A cry of relief tore from Pickett, and he covered the remaining steps to the throne in a single bound, pulling her into his arms. He pressed his face into her tangled hair, weeping. He didn't care how undignified it made him look. Her story hadn't ended with the pouring out of her weaving.

Arkron's healing had begun, and she would live to oversee it.

And he would be right beside her.

43

Harper woke to silence. Both within herself and without. She lay still, letting her other sensations return slowly. She was lying in a bed with blankets tucked around her. Someone was holding her left hand, and the grip was cold. Jael. Another person held her right and was half on, half off the bed, almost crowding her. Based on the snores, she figured that it was Pickett. And the hands resting near her knees? That had to be Fayen and Evaly.

She sighed, keeping her eyes shut. If this was the Arkron she had used up her power for, it was well worth it.

Jael's metal fingers suddenly tightened, and Harper heard a ragged sigh. She opened her eyes to meet the Outcast's. "Good morning."

Jael rubbed her eyes with her other hand. "Is it morning?"

"I'm making an educated guess," Harper rasped. "Where are we?"

"The palace."

Harper inhaled, the motion tightening the wounds on her chest. "Is it over? Did I . . . did I weave my last story?"

"Yes," Jael said. "It's over. Although I'm not entirely sure you're *not* a storyweaver anymore," she remarked, squeezing her hand again.

"No," Harper replied. "It's gone. I can feel it. The Creator gave it to me to use for this, and now that part of my story is over." She breathed in deeply, ignoring the pain from her wounds. "And I'm okay with that."

"Maybe your empowerment is gone," Jael answered, brushing her fingers over Harper's. "But I still think there may be many weavings inside of you still."

On her other side, Pickett grunted and then yawned. "Are you having a moment without me?" He sat up, rolling his shoulders with a soft groan.

"To be fair," Harper said, "you've never been a big fan of *moments*, Pickett. They're too emotional for you."

He poked her in the side. "What if I'm changing?"

"He was bawling over your unconscious body when we found him," Jael said.

Harper craned her neck to look up at him. Moons, he looked dreadful. He could use a shave. And maybe a cup of chai. *I doubt I look much better.* "You cried for *me?*"

"Yes, and if I get teased about it, I never will again." He smoothed some of her hair away from her face. "How do you feel?"

Harper stuck her nose in the air, trying to scrape up some bravado. "Like I was just resurrected, and all of you are my patrons, come to worship me at my bedside."

From somewhere by her feet, Fayen mumbled, "She's fine."

Pickett and Jael laughed. Harper tried to join in, but the motion caused electrocuting pain to shoot through her chest. "Take it easy," Pickett said, scooping her up to prop her on her pillows. "You could tear your wounds open if you're not careful."

"Mm." Her eyes found his. In a more serious tone, she added, "Really, Pickett, I think . . . I think I'm okay." Her hand went to her neck, feeling for her locket. The pendant had slid around her neck and rested against her back. She pulled it around to study the tarnished face of the book. Her name was engraved on the cover, barely visible after years of corrosion.

As the others began to rise and move about, calling for chai and breakfast, she pushed her frizzy mane out of her eyes to study the pendant she had worn around her neck for years. She pressed her thumbnail along the seam where it should open. As always, it was stuck fast.

After receiving it, she had often pestered Anrameta about the secret to unlocking it. Anrameta had always staved her off, hinting that it was Harper's task to understand how it worked. And then she'd gone to Mantalor, and the locket had become more of an object to fidget with than a puzzle to solve.

She turned it over in her fingers and ran her fingernail over her name, trying to scrape away some of the corrosion. It came away in little aquamarine slivers, dusting her shirt. There was a stubborn layer in the very bottom of the engraving. Grimacing, she pressed her thumbnail as deeply as she could into her name, slowly tracing the cursive swoops that spelled H-A-R-P-E-R. She had to twist the pendant back and forth in her fingers to keep her thumbnail on the track. When she reached the end of the *R*, there was a soft *click*. She gasped as the locket swung open, attracting the attention of the others.

Evaly scrambled up onto the bed. "Did you get it open?"

"I—I did." Harper cupped it in her palm, stunned.

Pickett returned to her bedside and sat down. "Is there a picture in it?"

"Yes. A holographic one." She activated it. And, for the first time in ten years, looked into her father's face. He had blue eyes and *so many* freckles. Anrameta stood beside him, looking much younger. Pickett was hanging over their father's shoulder, while Anrameta held a much younger Harper in her arms. She didn't even recognize herself; in the picture, she was nothing but bright smiles and fuzzy auburn hair.

"There's a note." On her other side, Fayen picked up a scrap of yellowed paper. Harper took it and unfolded it. She was met with familiar, untidy handwriting—Anrameta's. The sight of it made her throat tighten.

"What's it say?" Evaly demanded.

"It's short," Harper said, smoothing it out. She cleared her throat, choking back a rising sob. "*My love, never forget that you are first and foremost beloved.*"

Beloved. Not princess, storyweaver, queen, or even Harper. *Beloved.* With that simple phrase, galaxies could spin and sing. Shattered stories could heal. War-torn lands could mend. A tired girl could be both a princess and a storyweaver, and a queen and daughter and friend, because they were all important, but not as important as the fact that she was *beloved* by her Maker, her mother, and the rest of House Evensong.

Harper admired the picture for a few moments longer, then closed the locket and tucked it under her nightshirt. It felt warm against her chest, a soothing weight against her wounds.

"Can someone order me some eggs?" she asked. "There's a lot of work to be done, and I'd rather not do it on an empty stomach."

44

THE NEXT WEEK passed in a blur. Harper felt like a captain trying to survive a storm when her ship was little more than a bundle of crushed timbers tethered together with twine. She and the others gave speeches without preparation, helped with the wounded, arranged memorials for the dead; they oversaw cleanup and the transport of disgraced High General Vasken and the captured Consortium guardsmen back to Mantalor. And, in the midst of her duties as a queen and friend, Harper told stories. Short, funny tales at first to the people she served food to and then more to those she helped bandage.

And the longest ones she told her mother as she sat at her bedside, watching as she was prepared for burial. The stories remained within her, yet they had morphed somehow. No longer did they pulse against her palms like birds fluttering against the bars of a cage trying to escape but sat like a fountain within her, pouring out cupfuls for those most thirsty. Their very presence brought her comfort; perhaps, if she could find her storyweaving book, she could put it to use once more, though in a less desperate way.

"There is more peace within you," Lady Kova remarked as she and Harper made their rounds about the Arena, where the dead had been laid.

"Some," Harper agreed. "There is still much that is unresolved, though." She brushed some of her loose hair out of her face. Lady Kova had encouraged her to dress regally as they had on Mantalor, but Harper had refused. She was Arkronen and would dress as such. "But I'm learning to accept that its resolution may come later in my story."

Lady Kova dipped her head, looking pleased. "It takes maturity to realize that we are always a work in progress."

Few people lingered in the Arena. The sun was beginning to set, signaling that time was continuing onward even though, in the moment of grief, it felt as though it should have stopped. There were still meals to be made and living people to attend to. Whenever Harper came upon one of the remaining mourners, turned to stone by their own sorrow, she would squeeze their shoulder—assuming it wasn't bandaged—trying to impart what weak comfort she could through the gesture.

At the far end of the Arena, she stopped beside a mourner who sat on her knees, clutching the hand of the covered corpse before her. Lady Longracer's lips moved quietly as she said a soft blessing over the fallen. Harper knelt beside her, helping to finish it, before rising with her.

"Thank you, lass," Lady Longracer sighed, dabbing at her eyes. "I know we can't save them all, but at least I can make sure they don't go to the Most High unblessed." Intercessor glyphs were drawn on her forearms, reminding her to turn the despair upward.

"That's good of you," Harper said, touching the glyphs marked on her own arms. "I think Mama would have been pleased."

"Speaking of Anrameta . . . " From her pocket, Lady Longracer produced the storyweaver's pen Anrameta had given Harper. "I found it in the throne room after we'd gotten you tidied up."

The sight of it made Harper's heart ache. "You can keep it," she said.

Lady Longracer lifted it up and studied the tip for a moment, then held it out to her. "It would be better for it to stay with a storyweaver."

Harper shook her head. "I'm afraid I'm not able to use it anymore. I've used up my empowerment."

She caught her hand and pressed the pen into it. "Please, lass. That may be so for now, but there's no telling what Arkron's future might hold. Your mother gave it to you for a reason. It belongs with you."

Harper's fingers closed around it of their own accord, as if they sensed something she couldn't yet. "Thank you," she said, drawing it close to herself. If anything, it would be a comforting token from her mother. A reminder that she had loved all of Harper even when Harper had been incapable of doing so herself.

Lady Longracer smiled, then gestured to Lady Kova. "I'm glad I caught you. I heard from some of the Chamber. We've received some offers of communication with the Consortium, whenever you're ready to address them."

Lady Kova perked up at the prospect of a negotiation. She had been out of her element as of late; Harper knew the nitty-gritty of tidying up did not agree with her. "I am. Perhaps this evening, when I have finished my rounds with Her Majesty . . . "

Harper waved her off, fingering the tablet in her pocket. "Go now, Aunt Kova. I've got one more stop to make anyway."

The *Ransom* hovered against the backdrop of the sunset as if she were a creature from the Deeps come to float on the surface of the ocean. Many of her people were ranged along the rocky beach, trying to accustom themselves to walking on solid ground. A large bonfire burned near the water, a tiny mimic of the great orb of light that was sinking into the ocean. Outcasts from the *Ransom* gathered around it, finishing their memorial rites for those that had fallen during the conflict. Someone played a flute in a slow dirge, and a few people swayed to it slowly.

Pickett sat on one of the large rocks a little ways up the beach to watch. Jael had come to sit beside him and was stretched out on the warm stone, her hands laced behind her head. Her eyes were shut, but even so dark circles were apparent beneath them. "Would you like to go back to the Cleft?" he asked, thinking longingly of a hot cup of chai and an armchair.

"No," Jael replied. "I'm afraid that I'm going back to the *Ransom* tonight."

Pickett looked down, running his fingers on the stone of the boulder. "Ah. I suppose it's right for your people to want you close again. Will you be back in the morning?"

She was silent; for a moment, Pickett wondered if she'd dozed off, but then she opened her eyes and sat up. "I don't know, Pickett. Harper's doing her best to mend things. I'm afraid that our presence will start to aggravate your people."

"Wait—you're leaving? But she made a deal with you. Your people *died* for us."

"I know. And I believe Harper will make good on her promise. But her reign is still young. It's going to take her some time to get it sorted." She tipped her face towards the sky and the Star Sea that was just beginning to become visible. "Besides, I'll never be too far away. Just up there."

A tangle of emotions swept through Pickett, startling him. He was grateful for Jael's help, of course—but why did he feel such a loss at the prospect of her leaving? "I think I speak for all of us when I say that we don't want to have to search the stars for you," he said, feeling his ears tingle in embarrassment. "I would rather you be within arm's reach, with us."

She smiled, dropping her metal hand onto his arm. "I appreciate that. More than you know. But Arkron is yours to tend, and you shouldn't let my crew and me distract you from that."

"But Arkron is supposed to be yours too."

Jael dropped his hand suddenly as Evaly and Fayen wandered towards them from the bonfire. Evaly scrambled onto the rock and settled down beside Jael, resting her head on her shoulder.

"What's the matter?" Jael asked, dropping her hand to rub Evaly's back.

"This feels wrong," the girl replied. Her cat eyes reflected the firelight, looking like a pair of glowing moons in her face.

"What does?"

Fayen plopped next to Pickett, draping his arm around his shoulder. "The fact that we're down here enjoying music and a fire while there are a whole bunch of people up in the Arena who won't have that chance ever again."

"They will," Pickett said. "They died nobly, and the Creator will raise them when the Healing comes." He glanced at the high walls of the Arena. "They wouldn't want us to hold back on their account, even if that sounds cliché."

"I love clichés." Jael kissed the top of Evaly's head. "Sometimes they have the most truth—that's why they endure. Survivor's guilt is normal, Evaly. Grief is not something to be ashamed of."

Fayen dropped his arm from Pickett's shoulder as he twisted about to look behind them. "Harper's here!"

"What? You're supposed to be with Lady Kova!" Pickett protested as Harper clambered up beside Fayen.

"I was," she said. "She's gone back to the Cleft with *Amitan*."

Jael raised her eyebrows and frowned. "If I had known Lady Kova was planning to attend our celebration, I would have made better accommodations for her."

Harper shrugged. "It's all right. She wasn't coming to make a fuss. I just needed to give you this." She passed a tablet to Jael.

Jael powered it on and began to skim the surface. Her hand flew to her mouth, suppressing a cry—whether in delight or horror, Pickett couldn't tell as he and Fayen crowded closer, trying to read it.

Evaly beat them to it; craning her neck over Jael's arms, she read, "'Permanent planetside pass for the *Star's Ransom*, effective as of the

Second Month of Summer, Seventhday, Fifth Age, signed by Her Majesty Queen Harper of House Evensong'."

Pickett looked back to Harper, who sat with her legs folded beneath her, smiling serenely. "The Chamber was a bit hesitant, but I convinced them to ratify in the end. We're thankful for your sacrifices in protecting our world, Commander Clarkson. Welcome home."

Jael only rocked in place, tears streaming down her scarred face. Her smile was so bright that Pickett was certain it could be seen from the Star Sea. "May I escort you to share the news with your crew?" he asked as Evaly pulled Fayen to his feet and made him jump with her in a jubilant circle, chanting, "Welcome home, welcome home!"

She nodded, letting him help her to her feet. Before they scrambled off the rock, she stopped beside Harper. "Thank you."

Harper smiled, dipping her head. "You don't have to thank us for doing what's right."

"Maybe not," Jael answered, swiping some of the tears from her face. "But even so, I have a gift for you."

"Just as long as it's not one of your metal toes."

Jael bent over double with a laugh. But when she straightened, she produced Harper's storyweaving book from somewhere on her person. "No. But now it's a gift from one Arkronen to another."

Harper's face went slack, and she accepted the book, pressing it close against her chest. "It's the best one you could give."

"All right," Pickett said, tugging on Jael's elbow hopefully. "We have good news to deliver."

She laughed, and together they ran towards the bonfire. As they approached, Jael thrust the tablet over her head for her Outcasts to see, and shouted at her crew, "We're home!"

Pickett felt his heart soar at the words. *Home.* Yes. Home was here on Arkron; he was more sure of it than ever. The whoops and cries of delight shook the beach, and the musicians took up a triumphant theme. Pickett offered Jael his hand and, laughing, she accepted it. Together they joined her crew in their jubilant dance around the fire. They belonged here. And so did he.

⁎

Harper's storyweaving book bore evidence of slight damage; she had carried it with her up until her capture by the guardsmen before the execution, but after that she had lost track of it. How Jael had recovered it, she didn't know. All the same, she was delighted to have it back in one piece, and lovingly thumbed through the pages. She hadn't realized how full it was; there were only about ten pages left towards the back of the book, deliciously tempting with their unmarred crispness.

Fayen settled down beside her and dangled his legs over the side of the rock. "Looks like you're going to need another one of those soon." He flexed his fingers. The motion was still weak. "Maybe I'll try to bind one myself. I should have more time to fool around with artistic pursuits since I'm taking a break from training."

"Yes," she agreed. "It would be lovely if you would. There are so many more stories I want to weave."

"Will you have time?"

"I'll make time," she said, smoothing down a blank page. "Just because I'm the queen doesn't mean I won't be able to do this too. There are only so many hours you can sit on a throne before your butt goes numb."

Fayen leaned back on his hands. "What are you going to write about?"

Harper propped her chin in her hand and watched the dancers down on the beach. Evaly had joined hands with some of the other Outcasts, and together they had formed a ring around the bonfire and were dancing around it. Arkron's twin moons had risen and cast a silver sheen on the Sea of Jewels, as if the ghost of the beautiful land she had once been was trying to visit her new children. "This. All of this. Storyweavers don't just come up with *new* stories, you know. They're also recorders and interpreters of existing ones."

She smiled as her eyes found Jael and Pickett, who moved in a slower dance away from the circle. Oh, Pickett would *murder* her if she wrote about him and Jael, but she intended to do it anyway. She wanted to capture all of it, every last detail: the firelight on Evaly's face, Fayen's warm presence beside her, and the way her own shattered soul was beginning to mend.

"Do you have a pen?" she asked Fayen.

He put on a mockingly shocked expression. "What's this? Storyweaver Evensong doesn't have a pen on her? Who are you and what have you done with Harper Evensong?"

She snorted and showed him the storyweaver's pen. "I do have a pen, but it's out of ink."

"Ah." Fayen fished around in his pocket for a moment before coming up with a stubby pencil. "Sorry, this is all I've got."

"It'll do," she said, and flipped to the end of the book.

"Erm . . . if you're going to tell a story, aren't you supposed to start earlier in the book?"

"Yep," she said, rolling the pencil between her fingers.

"Then why are you on the back cover?"

"Because I know how this story ends, so I'm writing the end inscription," she replied, pressing the lead to the page.

"Why not just write 'the end'?"

"Because it's never really *the end*, Fayen," she said, blowing a lock of hair out of her eyes. "Endings are promises that there are more stories to be told. They're just a backwards beginning." She leaned back, accessing her work. Then she nodded to herself and closed it for the time being. Against the weight of the pages, a single phrase sat scratched into the final leaf:

An end is only a beginning for another story.

AUTHOR'S NOTE

It would be impossible for me to pinpoint the exact place where this story came from. Much of it was drawn from the influences of my childhood: the books, movies, and shows that fell into the great stewpot of my mind and mingled with the questions of *Who am I? What defines me? What has God placed me here to do?* In many ways, this story grew up alongside me. I was thirteen when I wrote the first draft, and by the time that it's out into the world, I'll be nearly twenty-two. Like Harper, I spent most of my preteen and teen years believing that my identity was defined by *one* thing. For some, it was sports; for others, it was academics; others, the arts. Whenever I looked at a person, I wanted to know: What was their *thing*? What made them who they are? And what happened if they ever lost that "thing"?

As Harper (and I) came to terms with this, through the drafting of *Weave the Worlds*, we learned our true identity is not found in the things of this world. Roles come and go. Interests change. If you're looking for stability, you're not going to find it in this world.

Unlike us, God is unchanging, and He is infinite, not bound by one thing. Ephesians 2:10 reminds us that "We are his workmanship, created in Christ Jesus for good works, which God prepared beforehand, that we should walk in them" (ESV). Notice how it says *works*, plural? We are created for many things but must ultimately be rooted in the truth that we are His workmanship. His creation, His Sons and Daughters. His Beloved.

There's so much freedom to be found in this truth. My prayer for you, dear reader, is that Harper's story reminds you to look beyond the things of this world that you think give you meaning, and realize just how beloved you are. The Maker of the stars knows *your* name. And He loves you so much that He traded His life for yours, rose again, and is now preparing a place for us in His Father's house.

There truly is no story more beautiful than that.

ACKNOWLEDGMENTS

I fantasized about writing the acknowledgements for this story for *years*. To finally get to sit down and do it brings tears to my eyes. Writing is often viewed as a solitary pursuit, but truthfully it's the furthest thing from that. There are so many people that I'm eternally grateful to for helping this story reach readers, especially after my publisher unexpectedly closed midway through the publication process. It's been a long road, but I'm so grateful to be walking it, and thankful to the people who were willing to walk it beside me.

The Story-Weaver Team: Even though *Weave the Worlds* ultimately didn't release under you, I'm still so grateful that you took a chance on it. Stephen, thank you for teaching me about all the behind-the-scenes of publishing a book. Emily, thank you for your insight on the developmental edits—*Weave the Worlds* is so much stronger for it. Brianna, thank you for your guidance as project manager and your critical eye as proofreader. Cheyenne, thank you for your careful copyedits, and Benita, thank you for the BEAUTIFUL cover and formatting! Thank you, all of you, for coming around us authors with support, guidance, love, and shared tears in the wake of Story-Weaver's closing. There was never a moment during the transition where I felt abandoned in any way, and this book is still out because of your tireless effort to see it through.

Isabel: I decided years ago that this story would be dedicated to you. It was the least I could do after all those emails and four-inch-long texts desperately asking, *Does Archer's arc made sense? Does Jael's character feel flat? Should I even stick with this story?* Your steadfast encouragement throughout the countless drafts makes this book feel as though it's your victory as much as it's mine.

Mom and Dad: Thank you for homeschooling me, giving me good books to read, buying me my first laptop, letting me transfer universities to pursue Creative Writing, and all the hundreds of thousands of things you do that have made it possible for me to become an author. I'm so blessed to say that my family has my back no matter what.

Emery and Ruby: Thank you for putting up with me all the times I begged you to turn the piano down or put the kettle on so that I could keep writing. I'm blessed to have such cool siblings.

Abbey and the Guild: You were my first sounding board and critique group for this story. Without our weekly meetings, lessons, and shared dreams, I don't know if I would have learned how to persevere with a story, share it with others, and take feedback. Thank you for everything. You were the best part of my high school years.

Anna: Thank you for asking if you could be the first in my fandom all those years ago. And also for being brutally honest and telling me that my first chapter was boring. Without your feedback, I never would have finally found the right note to start this story on!

Amelie: The Lord sent you into my life at just the right time! I'm so thankful for your encouragement and feedback when *Weave the Worlds* needed it the most. Here's to many more years of being bookish besties!

My June 2024 Beta Readers: Thank you all so much for your insightful feedback on *Weave the Worlds* (then Project Shattered Stories). You were the first "official" group to read through the whole story, and your excitement and feedback gave me the confidence to finish strong.

King Jesus: Thank you for saving me and patiently teaching me, day by day, to cling to You. You know how many times I begged to be allowed to stay with this story and share it with the world. Thank you for using every aspect of this long road to pull me closer to You. May my stories only ever glorify You.

Thank you so much to everyone who helped this project come to life via Kickstarter!

Outcast Explorer

Nicole Aisling, Sergey Kochergan, Максим Стоялов

Crewmate on the *Star's Ransom*

Jewel, Ellie, V. Wieben, Joseph Procopio, Grace Neufeld, dtill359, Jesse Hereda, Donovan Bergin, Emily Vest, DF-17, Rachel Simpson, Sara Shepherd, Morgan

Hybri

Kelly and Lee Havemeier, Claire W., Deanna, Lacey Shannon Cornwell, Elaina, Anna and Nathan Royer, Abrianna Johnson, MCM, Cheyenne, Abby, Kathy Stone, Amelie, Jacque Johnson, Gabby Utrie, Alayna, Daniel, Bekah and Corey Huet, Giselle Trejo, Joy Sugden, Margaret Willinsky, Kristin Hendrick, Brian and Melissa Netherton, Megan Powers, Samantha Roth, Jayson, Jessi Hafeman, Lisa Ellsbury, Abigail, Lynne Henson, Michelle, Mark and Lisa Knapp, Joe and Beth Gittins

Neherum

Brandon and Nichole Case, Laci Clapper, Anna Lindsey, Galadriel and Monte Miller, Isabel Simpson, Lynsi Pasutti, Beth and Travis Wilkins, Kara Wishman

Passer Division

Dan and Teena Case

Commander of the *Star's Ransom*

Mary Rose Nichols, Jesse and Jennifer Morrill, M. Simpson, Madison

Princess of Arkron

Lisa Logan

Storyweaver

Megan Cline, Anthony and Lynn Royer

House Evensong

Drew and Jordan Miller

Backer

Nicole and Travis Connick, Benita J. Thompson, A. Hays, Dennis DiNoia, Doug Poganski, Jennele Swalla, Austin and Melissa Grapp, Addie, Barbara Burket, Samantha Davis, Michael Evans, Howard

DISCUSSION QUESTIONS

1. Harper likes to hear about people and places to inspire her weavings. In your life, whose story haven't you heard yet? How can you show that person you care about hearing it?

2. For most of *Weave the Worlds*, Pickett feels like his loyalties are torn between the High General and House Evensong. When have you felt torn between two people or places? What did you do?

3. Fayen struggles to admit that he is weakened and needs Evaly's care. When have you found it hard to admit that you need help?

4. Evaly often feels like her Hybri is a curse, but it ends up helping her in many ways. Have you ever experienced something painful that seemed unnecessary at first but later equipped you to handle something else?

5. When she first meets them, Harper tries to scare the Seven away from Arkron so her planet is left alone. However, her plan backfires. When was a time you set out to do something with good intentions, but it had unintended negative consequences? How did you react?

6. Some of the characters in *Weave the Worlds* own things that show parts of who they are. Harper's crown represents her role as a princess, while her pen and storyweaving notebook represents her role as a storyweaver. Pickett's star-tree necklace symbolizes

his commitment to the Neherum. What are some symbols from your life and homeworld? What do they say about who you are?

7. Harper often views her world as a story, with the people as characters and places as settings. If you could write your own life story, what days would you want to erase? Why do you think they were kept in instead?

8. In *Weave the Worlds*, everyone wrestles with their identities. Evaly thinks her Hybri is all wrong. Arkron wants Harper to act one way, but she feels a different way inside. Pickett struggles to find his place in the Evensong family. Fayen doesn't know who he is without being Evaly's caretaker. When is there a difference between "being ourselves" and living rightly? How can the way you live define the person you are instead?

Norah Case has been a student of storytelling since her early teens. Her goal is to write stories that encourage readers to remember who they are: sons and daughters of the King. Her short stories have been featured in the *Illuminate the Dark* and *Of Storm and Sea* anthologies. When she's not writing, Norah can be found reading, sampling chai lattes, playing Minecraft, and watching Star Wars. She lives in a river valley in central Iowa with her family and a posse of cats. Find her on Instagram **@storyweavers_jargon**.

www.ingramcontent.com/pod-product-compliance
Lightning Source LLC
LaVergne TN
LVHW010307070526
838199LV00065B/5473